Shadow of Hyperion

Turn Four of the Hybrid Helix

JCM Berne

The Gnost House

ISBN-13: 978-1-961805-01-9

Cover image by Chris McGrath

Cover graphics by Jake Caleb

Acknowledgments:

I have more people to thank than I can easily count, starting with my wife, Moneeka, without whose support none of the rest of this would have happened.

My alpha reading group: John (aka Kevin), Karl, Andrew (Zombie), Richard, Allison, Kay, Brian, Kassan, and Jonathan, who contributed immeasurably to early drafts.

My editor, Lauren Donovan of The Book Foundry, who (gently) pushed me to make changes that really needed to be made. Chris McGrath, cover artist extraordinaire, whose work inspired me, along with Jake Caleb who did some wonderful graphic design on some very short notice. Special shout-out to Jeff Brown for some badly needed advice on typography.

Jordan, Andrew (The Wizard), Craig, Boe, A.R., Kayla, Usman, Chris, Lezlie, HC, Esmay, and Raina, who brought me the thing I couldn't bring myself: more readers.

My sensitivity reader, acquired much too late in the process (entirely my fault, not his), Sridhar. Mistakes in early editions of previous books are not his fault.

My web and marketing guru, Marc Greenwald.

My online teachers: Brandon Sanderson, the cast of Writing Excuses, and Mur Lafferty, all of whom were there for me and asked for nothing in return (at least in part because they have no idea who I am).

The rest of my Twitter and Discord communities, who brought me so much encouragement and support.

Contents

1

Not a Prologue

Rohan floated outside Wistful's southern arm, eyes closed and arms stretched out to catch as much of Toth's warming rays as possible.

"What should I do for lunch? Back to the Kratic soup place? Or try the new Drexian barbecue spot Ben wanted to check out? Maybe the lines have died down; it's been open for a week."

The music playing in his helmet, one of seven mixes of "Dhoom Machale" in his collection, lowered to near-inaudible levels as a voice piped through. "I do not understand the question, Rohan. Please restate."

"Lunch. I'm trying to decide where to go for lunch."

"Your lunch break begins in forty-seven minutes. Your next assignment is to bring *Love Boat* in to North A-3."

"Thank you, Wistful. On my way." It was most likely his personal AI talking to him, not the station herself, but it never hurt to be polite.

The music resumed as lines projected onto the inside of his facemask directing him to *Love Boat*'s location, right outside the buoy perimeter that demarcated Wistful's protected space. The il'Drach Hybrid sang along to the song's repetitive chorus as he turned away from Toth and *pushed* himself through space toward the waiting ship.

Love Boat came into view. Tall and very narrow, she had graceful curves accentuated by her white, gold, and platinum trim.

"Hail, *Love Boat*."

"Oh, hello, Tow Chief Second Class Rohan. It's a pleasure, as always!" Toth was a regular stop on *Love Boat*'s itinerary.

"As always, *Love Boat*. Ready for your tow?"

The ship hesitated before responding.

"Sugar, would you be a darling and permit a little tightbeam communication? Just between the two of us?"

That's odd.

"Of course, *Love Boat*. Holding position." Tightbeam communications were linear, not broadcast. Nothing could intercept the transmission without being physically between them.

A few seconds later, he heard *Love Boat*'s voice over his comm again, with a subtle change in audio quality as if the ship were sharing a room with him.

"Thank you, sugar. For the tightbeam. I do understand it's a breach of protocol."

Rohan scratched at his beard, right behind the seal his mask made to his face. "Of course. Is everything okay?"

She hesitated again. "I certainly do hope so, Tow Chief. My captain wanted to make sure I took the time to inform you of an . . . oddity we noticed out near the edge of the system."

Rohan sighed. "Tell me."

"Tow Chief, I'm sure you know as well as I do that a part of our tour of this lovely system includes a swing past each of the five wormholes. It is, in fact, a highlight of our package, right up there with the culinary marvels available on Wistful herself. We get passengers from half the galaxy with this tour."

She's dragging this out. Probably nervous. "I'm aware."

"Well, since the wormholes are far out in the system, I fly through paths most ships just wouldn't take. No reason for them to, really. Too out of the way."

"I get it, *Love Boat*. Can you tell me what you saw? Please?"

"I couldn't believe it at first, you know. So strange, what with Wistful and the Empire being on, let's just say, tense terms with one another. Not that I'm judging."

"Of course not."

"But I checked again, and surely enough, out at the edge of the system, there is an Imperial ship. Just sort of . . . lounging."

"A ship?"

"No, I am sorry, sugar, I suppose I misspoke. Not a real ship, just a cargo transport. One of those big ones. Military shuttles. But it must have been brought here by a ship. Surely it didn't fly all this way at sublight speeds, and I am unaware of any way a shuttle could open its own wormhole!"

There's a way, but it's better I don't bring it up.

"Okay, *Love Boat*, thank you very much for that information. The shuttle is nothing to worry about. I can bring you to dock now."

"But are you sure? An Imperial ship in the system! Surely that's a violation of some treaty or another. Is there bound to be violence? I hope not. My passengers prefer their danger at a distance and confronted by people paid to do that job."

"No danger, at least not from that shuttle. Wistful gave them permission to stay there for a time. It's part of a . . . negotiation."

"Ah!" *Love Boat*'s voice sang with harmonies of relief. "That is so very good to hear, Tow Chief. Thank you! And yes, I'd be pleased to be towed to dock right now. Engines are offline."

"Great. I'm closing the tightbeam connect, *Love Boat*. Approaching your anchor point now."

Rohan flew across the ship, skimming her gleaming hull, and approached the cutaway in her center that exposed a handhold meant for towing. He positioned himself next to it, grabbed the metal sphere, and *pushed*.

Love Boat began to move.

Three songs later, she was docked into her berth at Wistful.

It took Rohan five songs to get the next ship out past the buoy perimeter, and four more to bring in the final ship in his morning queue, a cargo vessel that happened to include in its manifest a shipment of Andervarian bourbon coming from a distillery that he owned.

Looking forward to trying some of that!

He was checking his queue again, tapping at the side of his mask to scroll through the docking requests and verify that nothing was urgent enough to postpone his lunch break, when his song died and a sharp beeping rang in his ears.

"What is that?"

"You set this alarm to monitor onboard news feeds and sound under certain conditions."

"I did? Are you sure? Never mind, that was rhetorical. Of course you're sure. What conditions?"

"This alarm corresponds to 'situations which directly endanger Ben'"—Rohan began accelerating toward the station—"or Marion Stone.' It seems there is an occurrence on the station which fulfills both sides of that conditional."

There was no sound, no crack of wind, as Rohan sped through space toward Wistful. "Show me. And give me a location."

"It is inadvisable to travel at these velocities while—"

"Don't make me call up the real Wistful. I'll have this subroutine erased and replaced before you can say 'safety hazard.' Give me a location, then show me that video feed."

"Yes, Rohan. The situation is developing on West Block 25. Pushing video to your mask."

He grunted and turned a tight arc toward Wistful's western arm. A feed took over the bottom half of his mask.

The view was familiar: the fifty-meter-wide promenade that centered each of Wistful's four spindly arms, flanked by two solid walls of living space, ten stories tall and another fifty meters deep. The promenade itself was grassy and rolling, dotted with parks, benches, and the occasional gazebo.

A featureless, opaque shell covered ten meters of lawn and three stories of building It was round, smooth, and matte-black. A dozen uniformed security officers walked near the edge of the black, weapons in hand, warily observing the light-absorbing surface.

A female amateur reporter Rohan had seen before, filming similar videos of less-dire circumstances, was facing the camera and providing a voiceover.

"We are still live in front of the Makhara Bistro, and I'm still Jou'nell Jou'nhar, bringing you all the news that's worth bringing from the western arm of our home, Wistful."

Rohan decelerated hard as he approached a western-arm airlock. It cycled open and admitted him to the station.

"Today's news is a far cry from our usual hard-hitting exposés on the newest eateries and finest shopping to be found here. Today, Makhara Bistro, home of the finest pressed meat sandwiches for ten blocks, is inside an impenetrable black ball. There it is, right there, over my shoulder. Rough calculations put the center of the sphere deep inside the bistro. Security forces are surrounding it but seem to be unwilling to make contact with the surface."

He flew down the promenade, skimming close to the single-facet diamond plates that protected the avenue from the harsh vacuum above, superheated air warming his cheeks and forcing his hair to stream behind him in a deep-brown cascade.

"What is this field of darkness? Is it a hazard or just an optical effect? What has happened to the people inside? Keep watching as I work to uncover—"

He cut the feed.

The barrier was just as opaque to his Third Eye as it had been to light. *I can't sense any spiritual energy in there.*

Rohan flew in a wide arc around it, studying the array of station personnel on the ground who were milling about and keeping civilians clear of the sphere.

A voice rang out from inside the field, loud enough to echo off the far wall of the promenade. "Stay back! We have weapons and we're not afraid to use them! Nobody has to get hurt!"

A ping sounded, metal striking metal. The security officers looked around, surprised, until one shouted, "Shots fired! Shots fired!" They scrambled for cover.

Rohan exhaled slowly as his Power surged at the base of his consciousness. *Ben and Marion are inside that thing, next to someone dumb enough to start shooting inside a space station.*

"That was a warning shot! Stay back!"

Security Chief Wei Li darted out into the open area in front of the field and waved her people back. She was reptilian, with lines of red and green scales streaking her yellow skin. Once she saw that everyone was maintaining distance, she ducked behind a portable shield.

Rohan landed next to her in the ankle-high grass.

She turned to him. "Ah, Tow Chief Rohan. I'm glad you arrived. Your levelheadedness and cool demeanor are exactly what we need to help defuse a precarious hostage situation."

He nodded. "Glad to help." He paused. "Hold on. You're being sarcastic, aren't you? You're not happy to see me."

"Here I thought I was the empath and you the living war machine. How confusing to find that you've decided to somehow switch roles with me."

He turned to look at the black bubble. "Well, like it or not, I'm here now. I'd like to help. I heard the Stones are inside."

"That is accurate. The Drs. Stone are currently being held hostage inside that field. I would very much like to see them freed without loss of life. Especially not theirs."

"Do you know who's inside that thing? And what do they want? Any demands so far? If it's money, I can scrounge some cash together. I just brought in a shipment of Andervarian bourbon. I'd trade a case or two for the Stones if it would help."

"They have yet to place demands on us, though I will let you know the moment they request a liquor delivery. I believe they want something from the Stones, and all they have asked from station security is to be left alone."

"Which you're not going to do."

"Not unless the Stones are in agreement with that arrangement. Which they are not, as it was Marion Stone who summoned security to this location initially."

Rohan studied his friend's face. Her forehead was tight with concern, but he'd seen her express greater tension in other situations. "Why aren't you more worried about those guns?"

She waved a hand in dismissal. "They fired a warning shot. They hit a sign, a target of very low risk and equally low value. Had they wanted to injure or kill somebody, it is likely they could have done so."

"And you're not surprised they have a gun on the station."

"There are two million people on board, Rohan. As well as substantial manufacturing facilities. There have always been guns on the station."

He nodded. "I can't see inside that thing. Can you? Maybe with infrared?"

One of her officers ran up and spoke rapidly to his chief. Wei Li listened, then nodded and waved him away.

"Sonar is set up, which is telling us that the people involved are inside the building and not much more. We are still trying different imaging technologies. I suspect they won't work."

"Why not?"

"This reminds me of something I've seen before. A Power to nullify electromagnetic radiation. In that previous case, the Power blocked all wavelengths inside a particular space."

"You've run into these guys before? Or just someone with similar Powers?"

She shrugged. "It's hard to say."

"Can't you *feel* anything from inside? You're a, what is it, a Class Three Empath. Right?"

She smiled at him, baring very sharp incisors. "Class Four. If I didn't know you were teasing me, I might have been irritated by that."

He smiled back. "Still. What's inside?"

"Something is blocking my Third Eye as well."

Another uniformed officer ran over to Wei Li. "We received a response from Fago City, ma'am. An answer to your query about those two prisoners. Authorities released them six months ago. Current whereabouts unknown."

She pinched the skin above her nose, right between ridges of scale that would have been eyebrows on a mammal. "That answers your question, Rohan. Andervarian Powers."

His mouth dropped open. "Andervarians? Does this have something to do with me? I do a lot of business with Andervar."

She shrugged. "I believe this is another case where your very male tendency to believe yourself the center of every narrative is a threat to your sensibility. They want something from the Stones, and it is most likely information about one or more of the wormholes. If they wanted you, there are many more direct ways for someone to reach you."

"Okay, I get it. What are we going to do about this, though? That field is impenetrable to light, but it lets sound through. Can you blast them with a loud sound? Disorient them?"

She sighed. "Of course I could. Yet I haven't. Perhaps you can think for yourself of a reason why I have not."

"Oh. Maybe because the Stones are inside with them. And they might not want to admit it, but they're not getting any younger, and setting off a flash-bang near them might give one or both of them heart attacks."

"You see? When you apply yourself, you are capable of rational thought. I had full confidence in you." Her smile took the sting out of her words. Mostly.

"Very funny. What do you want me to do?"

"You? I want you to do your job. Go tow some ships. This is a security issue."

"Come on, I can't just walk away. Those are my friends. Maybe my best friends. What if something happens to them while I'm off . . . doing my job? What will I tell Hyperion when I meet him again in the afterlife? 'Sorry I let your sidekicks die? It wasn't my job to save them?'"

"Hyperion was your homeworld's greatest hero, was he not? I'm sure he chose assistants he trusted to care for themselves. In addition, they are no longer sidekicks to anybody. And it is not, in fact, your job to save them. But if you want to stay here, I don't have the energy to try to drive you off."

He nodded and stared at the sphere of darkness. "What does Wistful want, Wei Li?"

"You mean in regards to your involvement?"

"Yeah. That."

"Did she ask you to come here?"

"Nope."

"I believe that answers your question."

He waited next to Wei Li for the next seventeen excruciating minutes while nothing at all happened.

2

Cloak and Shadow

A pair of bangs broke the relative quiet of the cleared-out promenade.

Rohan and Wei Li locked eyes.

He looked down at his hands, clenched into fists, then back at his friend. "Those were gunshots."

She nodded, green lips pressed tightly together.

"No more waiting. I'm going in."

She started to shake her head; stopped. "You can't see."

"Show me that sonic image. I can go in blind. What's the worst that will happen? I'll bump into something? I'm pretty tough, remember? Nigh invulnerable."

"I do not think this is a good idea."

"It's a terrible idea, but it's fantastic compared to just standing here and hoping my friends aren't bleeding out inside that bubble of darkness."

Wei Li waved over one of her techs. "Show him the scan."

Two minutes passed while Rohan memorized the black-and-white image of the area. The space in front of the building was clear except for three tables and assorted chairs.

Rohan pointed at distortions around the edges of the scan. "What are those?"

The tech shrugged. "Not sure. Probably an effect of background noise. We're not really used to working with this tech."

"I guess that's good enough, then. Thanks."

Wei Li patted his back. "Shout if you need backup. We can still hear you."

"Is this where I say something inspiring? Like, that they're going to be the ones shouting for backup?"

"If it makes you feel better, you can."

"I'll save it for another day."

"As you wish."

He stepped out from behind the portable shield; let out a long breath; approached the bubble.

Have to assume they can sense me somehow. They wouldn't stay inside that field if it blinded them as much as us. So stealth is out. That's fine; stealth was never my strong suit.

Rohan patted the back of his neck, where his mask waited inside the jumpsuit's hood. He tilted his head from side to side, cracking his neck, then lifted his hands to his jawline and squeezed them into fists.

His lips parted in a grin as he called out to the darkness.

"You guys picked the wrong people to mess with. Those are my friends you're holding hostage. Drop this field and let them go, and things will end up a lot better for you."

Another step; the world disappeared as he entered the orb. He blinked against the complete and utter absence of light. He paused, hearing a soft click, but nothing came of it.

A fresh voice spoke back to him. "We're not going to hurt them. We just want the key to opening the wormholes. We can't stand by and let the Empire have it." Female, by the sound of it. Older. Andervarian accent. Another click.

Rohan strode forward, pausing as he knocked aside one of the chairs he'd seen in the image. "What she does with the wormhole key is up to Marion Stone. You can't just force her to do what you want. She's stubborn that way."

A small cough. "So we noticed. You shouldn't be fighting us on this, Hybrid. You know the evil of the Empire. You should be helping us convince her. Talk to her. It's better than us having to rough up her husband." A click.

Rohan laughed, his hands high, near his face, his body tense, anticipating an attack. He walked closer to where he thought the entrance was. "What are you, separatists? You know how that story goes. How it ends. It isn't worth it. This won't help anybody."

A laugh. "What do you suggest? Should we follow your lead? Open a distillery? Provide good, solid jobs for our young, our poor?" The voice sneered. A click sounded, from closer this time. "As if jobs will return our pride. Our freedom."

Something struck Rohan in the solar plexus, just below the lower tip of the sternum. That impact would have left a human convulsing and breathless on the ground; it knocked the Hybrid back two steps.

He swung a pair of punches that hit nothing but air.

Another click. Something thudded hard into Rohan's left calf with enough force to knock a rhinoceros off its feet. Rohan stumbled but caught himself, hands up. He lashed out: jab, right straight, hook; all missed.

He grunted. "You can't possibly believe you can win this fight."

"I believe many things, some even more outrageous than that." Punches bounced off Rohan's arms hard enough to leave them numb and achy; something more substantial, possibly a knee, struck his lower abdomen, too close by far to some sensitive portions of his anatomy. Another click.

He hopped back, one hand dropping to cover his groin. "Hey, be careful with that."

"This is a fight, Hybrid."

"Still, no reason we can't be civilized about it. You don't want to make me angry. You wouldn't like the aftermath. Neither of us would."

"I've been hearing the Empire hang the threat of Hybrid rage over us for decades. Repetition has blunted the effect." A loud step, clothes rustling through air, and a foot struck Rohan's belly with enough force to knock him back.

"Oof. Good one. Which one are you? Cloak? Shadow?"

A chuckle. "My disciples. It's nice to see their fame has spread."

He hopped forward and swung a wild punch in the direction of the voice, hoping to catch something, but missed.

"So, you are . . .?"

"I am an old warrior, Tow Chief. Too old to think I can beat you in a fistfight, even with you blinded by my disciples."

"You're giving up, then?"

"No. I said I can't beat you with my fists. Let's see if my odds improve in a swordfight." A snick, metal rubbing against wood. Another click.

Sharp pain blossomed across Rohan's cheek.

"Son of a—what was that?"

"I told you, I brought a sword."

Rohan hopped back, shifting from left to right as rapidly as he could, working to keep vital areas away from the woman's blade.

Not too many weapons in the galaxy that can cut me like that. This woman is no joke.

"You sure we can't talk about this? Sit down, discuss things like reasonable people? Maybe over coffee. Tell you what, I'll buy. I know a place."

A whistle of metal cutting air. Rohan reached behind and grabbed the chair he'd bumped into earlier, then threw it in the direction of the sound.

Another snick, from a few meters farther away. He'd driven her back.

"There's nothing to talk about. The Empire must be stopped. The only weapons that scare them are on the other end of those wormholes. For better or worse, only the Professors know how to open the wormholes."

"Talk it over with them. Make your case. They'll be reasonable."

"They work for the Empire, Tow Chief. Have you forgotten?"

Wei Li called out to him. "Rohan, she's using echolocation. We've recorded the sound and are ready to broadcast it from multiple sources. That should nullify its usefulness."

He grunted. "I knew that. I was just waiting for you guys to figure it out. Didn't want to steal your thunder."

He heard another whistle and ducked, then slid to the side. A moment later, dozens of clicks began to echo through the clearing, coming from all sides.

Now we're both blind.

"This fight is over. We've taken away whatever advantage you thought you had. Give up now or I'm going to get mean." Rohan set his feet and prepared to attack.

The woman laughed. "So typical for a Hybrid. You think that by taking things away from us, we'll become weak and capitulate. I'll teach you a valuable lesson: it is when we've lost everything that we become the most dangerous."

A rush of air and the blade dug into the Hybrid's chest.

He grimaced as his psychic energy sparked and flared through his body, meeting the sword as it split skin and entered his pectoral muscle, the tip grating harshly against one of his ribs. He reached up with his left hand and grabbed the blade, pinching it tightly, and lashed out with his right in a slap at where the swordswoman's head should have been.

His fingertips grazed something, and the woman grunted as she let go of the sword and retreated.

She exhaled loudly. "That should have killed you. Nothing can withstand the Blade of Tisch'ahl."

"You haven't stabbed many Hybrids, have you? There's a reason the il'Drach run the sector, and it isn't because they grow the finest tea. If it makes you feel any better, that really hurts."

"In the end it seems *I* have underestimated *you*."

Rohan pulled the sword out of his chest and held it in the air. "What do I do with this thing? I can't just toss it; with my luck it will hit somebody and take their head off. Hand me the sheath so I can put it away. And have your friends turn off this stupid field. I can't see anything." The chorus of randomized clicks continued.

The woman laughed. "You're very confident."

"Look, I believe that you don't want to hurt the Stones. I just need to check on them. I don't take kindly to my friends being around gunshots. So, drop the field and we'll talk."

As he spoke, bright light blossomed through the plaza. He blinked, eyes watering slightly, and took in his opponent.

She was definitely Andervarian, purple skin wrinkled enough for a grandmother, white hair cut short to her scalp. Geometric yellow tattoos covered her exposed skin. She was turning to face the storefront. "What?"

As the light returned, so did Rohan's ability to *feel* the subtle energy of the woman. Her spiritual Power was strong, but not strong enough to account for how hard she'd struck him. It was also fading quickly. Unnaturally so.

She must have taken a big shot of Boost. That stuff makes my life so much more difficult.

Rohan tilted the sword down and drove it into the grass so deep that the pommel rested flush with the ground. Wei Li and her officers were approaching, spread out in a wide line and carrying clear single-facet-diamond riot shields to protect against gunfire.

Rohan looked at Wei Li, pointed at the sword in the ground, and yelled. "Take care of that thing! It's dangerous. And get her medical attention; she's coming down off an overdose of Boost and she's about to collapse." He spun and flew at, then through, the front windows of the cafe where his friends were being held hostage.

He landed amid a clutter of overturned tables, accompanied by a shower of glass.

"Rohan! You look terrible. Marion, forget these ropes, look at Rohan. His face is a mess." Benjamin Stone smiled, accentuating the crow's feet in the corners of his eyes. Tall and rangy, he sat in a bar chair as Marion Stone leaned over him and worked at the knots in the ropes that secured him in place.

She looked up and straightened, her blonde-going-to-gray hair falling back from cheekbones sharp enough to cut glass. "Rohan! Good, you undo these knots. My arthritis is acting up."

Among the chairs and tables littering the cafe floor were a half dozen prone and apparently unconscious Andervarians, two of whom wore heavy black leather with aggressive zippers. The others wore casual business clothes. Another twenty or so bodies of various species lay strewn around the cafe, including a few in what looked like staff uniforms.

Several twitched at the sounds of his entrance, and at a glance, all seemed to be breathing.

"Never mind my face, are you two okay?" Rohan stepped forward, got a grip on the ropes, and pulled them apart with a snap.

Ben hopped off his chair and rubbed his arms where the ropes had cut into his skin. "For the most part. They weren't trying to hurt us. To be honest, I don't think they really planned for things to go this far."

Marion snorted. "If I'd known they were revolutionaries, I would have expected less of them. Hotheaded morons." She faced the street, where the swordswoman was being cuffed by station security officers.

"Now, Marion, don't beat yourself up. You didn't know."

Rohan looked up at his two friends. "Do you mind filling me in on a few more details about what's going on here?"

Ben nodded. "Of course, of course." He rubbed his wrists. "These gentlemen"—he nodded toward the leather-clad Andervarians—"asked to meet with us to discuss some research. They claimed to have information about the wormholes that the Empire didn't want them to have."

Marion shook her head. "I should have investigated more. But I thought, what harm could come of meeting in an open place on the station like this?"

Rohan wiped his hand across his face, the palm coming away smeared with blood. "Yeah, what harm?"

Ben shushed him. "Don't be like that. We didn't realize how desperate they might be. The woman was asking for our help, and those two started getting worked up. Then one drew a gun, and, well, things got out of hand."

Rohan looked around. "I assume we should be calling for medical help and not coroners?"

Ben smiled. "It's just somnabutol."

Marion pointed to her shoe. "I never leave home without it. Saved our lives a half dozen times in the old days. You'd be amazed at how often we were kidnapped by Hyperion's enemies. One click of the heel and this starts to disperse. Twenty minutes later . . ."

"I should have remembered. It was in all your comics." Rohan's eyes widened as he covered his mouth with his hand. "Is that going to knock me out, too? Do I need my helmet?"

Marion shook her head. "It's dissipating already, and it's slow acting, so it's not likely to affect a Hybrid. Maybe the security people coming in should use some protection."

Ben nodded. "I'll talk to Wei Li about it." He walked over to the security chief, waving his arms to indicate the area of concern.

Rohan stepped closer to Marion. "Are you sure you're okay?"

"You're the one bleeding from two fairly serious-looking cuts."

"I'm not the one who was held captive for half an hour."

She sighed. "As I mentioned, it's far from the first time. I've been getting held captive, and getting free, since before you were born."

He examined her expression for signs of trauma and didn't find any. *Wei Li will make sure they're really okay.* "Fair enough." His comm beeped at him; he silenced it with a gesture.

"Do you need me to look at those cuts?"

He dragged his palm across his cheek. "Are you missing the old days? Patching up Hyperion after all his battles?"

She smiled, her face lighting up and reminding him of why her poster had once been on the bedroom wall of half the teenagers in North America. "You know, I *am* one of the foremost experts in the sector in administering first aid to a Hybrid without access to Imperial technology. I always forget to put that on my resume."

He looked at the smear of blood on his hand. "I'm going to grab a towel. Did you guys get to eat before the shooting and the tying up started? I've been meaning to try this place." He stepped behind the counter and ducked to find a clean towel.

"Sadly, no." She raised her voice and pointed to the leather-clad Andervarians. "You'd better cuff these two before they wake up. They're Powers."

Rohan stood and wiped the blood off his chest as best he could, then held the other end to his face.

Marion looked at him. "What did that to you? We couldn't see."

"She had some kind of artifact. A sword. Something with Power."

"Not common."

"No. It's an Andervarian specialty. Part of why the Empire is so harsh with them."

She nodded. "They're getting brazen, these separatists. When the Hybrids rebelled, it made sense; they were the military power of the il'Drach. With people like this . . . I don't understand their confidence. Acting out in the open this way."

Rohan shrugged. "It's been getting worse these last six months. They think Wistful is safe, ever since she faced down that Imperial blockade." His comm beeped again; he ignored it. *Hold your horses. I'll get back to work soon.*

Marion stared off into space for a moment, then shook herself and looked at Rohan. "Your cuts are closing already. You want me to pour some disinfectant over that?"

He was about to say no, but changed his mind. "Yeah. What do we have?"

Ben walked over to them. "They're getting masks on now; they'll have these jokers restrained in a minute."

Marion joined Rohan behind the bar and found a bottle of something clear and obviously meant to end a very bad day. "This will work."

Rohan winced as she poured the strong liquor over his chest, then face. "How come you guys don't also get knocked out? Somnabutol is powerful stuff."

Marion patted the excess alcohol off his uniform. "Ben developed a symbiote that metabolizes it, back in the Hyperion days. He inoculated both of us forty years ago. To be honest, I wasn't sure they were still functional. But my husband does good work."

Ben smiled. "We appreciate your concern, Rohan. But we can still take care of ourselves. Not so far over the hill. Yet."

Rohan's comm beeped again. He sighed and pulled the helmet out of his uniform hood, turning it so he could read the screen inside. "What is the hurry? Oh. This message isn't from Wistful."

Ben stepped closer, his bushy eyebrows gathering in concern. "What is it?"

"Tamaralinth wants to talk."

3

Haunted by the Past

B en stepped back into a spot between two tables as a pair of security officers carried an unconscious revolutionary, slung between them like a trussed pig, out of the cafe.

"Tamaralinth? That name is familiar. Isn't she the woman you dated . . . two years ago?"

Tamaralinth Lastex of Lukhor. Daughter of the First Citizen of Lukhor. Mother of Amarinthicus Lastex.

"Eighteen months, six days, seven hours, and fifty-two minutes. Since we broke up."

Ben's face lost some color. "Really? You . . . I'm not sure what to say."

Rohan laughed. "I'm kidding. I have no idea. Well, it was about a year and a half, so I have *some* idea. Not that I'd forgotten her."

"No. I recall you were rather smitten."

"She's quite the smiter." His mask beeped; he ignored it, picked up one of the fallen chairs, turned it upright, and sat down. "My mind is whirling. I'm thinking of all the possible reasons she might want to talk to me."

Ben righted one of the chairs nearby and settled into it. "Do you need me to tell you not to let your imagination get the better of you?"

"Yes, please."

The older man put a hand on Rohan's shoulder. "Don't let your imagination get the better of you."

"Thanks. I needed that. Not sure my imagination is listening."

"When is the last time you spoke to her?"

"I think the day we broke up. I've hung out with Rinth a few times, tossed the Frisbee around, taught him some meditation. But she was never there. I would just run into the kid on the promenade."

"It's probably nothing. Didn't she get back together with her husband?"

"Ex-husband. Rinth's father. And yes, that was basically the issue. I mean, other than her being in a monogamous relationship with another man, she and I were great together."

"Do you even *want* to talk to her?"

Rohan stared into his helmet, eyes going over the message displayed there over and over again. "Not really. But I doubt I'll be able to say no."

"Then, get it over with as soon as you can. Rip the bandage off. So to speak."

Marion pulled over her own chair and sat across from them. "We're probably going to have to leave soon. This probably qualifies as a crime scene."

Rohan's helmet beeped. "That's Wistful telling me to get back to work. Which I should probably do. If you guys are really okay."

Wei Li stepped over to the trio. "Professor Stone is correct; I'd like this area cleared for forensics. Do either of you require medical attention?"

The Stones shook their heads. Wei Li looked at Rohan. "You are in just as much distress now as you were when you first approached. Then it was an active hostage situation involving unknown Powers. What's wrong now?"

He pointed to his mask. "Beautiful woman problems."

She nodded. "I should have guessed. Do *you* require medical assistance?"

He laughed. "No, my heart isn't in that bad a shape."

"I was referring to the cuts on your face and chest."

"Right! I knew that. Totally. Those are closing, I'm fine." He looked at the blood-soaked towel still clutched in his hand and dabbed it at his face and chest. "Well, maybe I'm not fine, but I will be. Probably."

Wei Li tilted her head and examined him through vertically slit eyes. "If you like, I can inform Wistful that you require an afternoon of leave."

Rohan shook his head. "Let me sit for a few minutes, then I'll go back to work." *What does Tamara want? Should I ask Rinth about it? Maybe ask him how his dad is. No, that's too heavy-handed.*

Ben looked at his wife and raised his bushy eyebrows, holding out a hand. She passed him the bottle of liquor she'd used to disinfect Rohan's wounds. Ben offered it to Rohan.

"I prescribe one good swallow out of that bottle. It won't cure anything, but it won't hurt."

Rohan smiled. "Nobody wants me drinking and towing. I'll be fine, really." His comm beeped. "I guess somebody doesn't want me getting any rest right now."

He looked down into the mask and tapped the side of the frame. "I got caught up in a situation here, got stabbed a couple of times. Wei Li can give you details. I need a few minutes for these holes to close up, then I'll fly out to finish my shift."

Wistful's voice was resonant, carrying some subtle quality that wasn't present in the subroutine that acted as his personal assistant.

"Tow Chief Second Class Rohan. I am not calling to discuss the remainder of your shift. I've already dispatched shuttles to handle your afternoon work queue."

"Oh. Really? Are you firing me? I mean, yes, I did abandon my job without any warning. But it was kind of an emergency. Maybe cut me a break? I don't think I've taken a day off in six months."

"Your position is not being terminated. Currently. But you have a visitor, and I suspect you will need some time to address whatever it is she wants to discuss with you."

Tamara? A visitor? What does that mean? She lives on the station. Why would she go through Wistful to talk to me? Or is she—

"What visitor, Wistful? Maybe it's the blood loss, but I'm confused."

"A woman has appeared in one of the fish tanks." Wistful had massive fish tanks for food production at the tip of her southern arm. "An Earth human."

"Oh. In the tank? She fell in?"

"No. I said she appeared there. And she has asked to speak with you. After she dries off."

Rohan led the Stones to a small cafeteria close to the staff locker room where the Earth visitor was cleaning up. Located in Wistful's bulbous center section, it served security personnel and other crew during breaks and between shifts.

Ben smiled and patted the chair next to his. "Rohan, sit. I'm sure she'll be here soon. You'll start leaking blood on the floor."

Rohan turned sharply and faced the older man. "You're right. Just feeling a bit wired. Lots of things happening at once."

Marion sipped carefully from a mug, wisps of steam caressing her cheeks. "Rebels congregating on Wistful isn't new. It's been going on for months. You just haven't been paying attention to it."

He started to respond, stopped, then continued. "I've been trying to ignore them. And in my defense, they haven't actually been *doing* much. If I start hanging out with them, even if it's just to try to get them to see reason, it will only make their lives harder."

Ben nodded. "The Empire will start to see them as a threat."

"Them, or me. Either way, it's not good for anyone. And, like I said, they haven't been doing anything other than, you know, existing. Which isn't a crime anywhere I can think of."

Marion sipped again, then pointed down the hall. "Here she comes."

The woman approaching them appeared in her twenties, with pale skin contrasting her black-with-gray-accents jumpsuit. A pair of trench knives were strapped to her hips, and she blew a frizzy strand of hair out of her face as she entered the cafeteria.

"Amber!" Rohan stepped forward, then stopped. *Do we hug? We used to hug, but she was a kid. We hugged last time, but she was traumatized.*

Amber stepped closer to him, smiling, and wrapped muscular arms around him. Her body felt hard against his, like a professional fighter's, thicker than the last time he'd seen her.

"It's good to see you, Griffin! I mean Rohan, sorry. And Dr. and Dr. Stone! I didn't know you'd be here."

Ben smiled and drew closer, hand outstretched. "Amber! You're making a habit out of teleporting into the fish tanks here."

Amber smiled. "Lyst's magic. It's faster than walking."

Marion took her turn hugging Amber, and the four took seats.

Rohan pointed to Amber, then to the food counter. "Do you want anything? They have drinks, snacks. Some pastries with savory fillings that make for a pretty decent meal when it's the middle of the night and you're hungry and realize you don't know how to cook. Uh, so I hear. From friends."

Amber laughed. "I'll take a pastry."

Marion pointed to Amber's unkempt hair. "Nobody told you to ease through the hydrophobic field, did they?"

"Somehow that instruction was skipped over. This is still better than smelling like fish."

Ben chuckled. "It's nice to see someone from the homeworld. Before we get too comfortable, are you here to tell us about another apocalypse?"

Amber shook her head while Rohan gathered up some snacks to bring over. "Nothing quite so dramatic."

Rohan distributed the pastries and drinks. "As long as it's not giant sharks again."

Ben smiled. "Would you prefer giant squids? Or nautili?"

"I'd really prefer the Earth not be endangered by any mega-sized sea creatures. Or land creatures. Really, not to be endangered at all. But I'm not sure why else Amber would have come the way she did."

Marion lifted her chin. "Lyst sent you. So it's not a social call."

Amber sipped her drink, something very similar to mint tea with a sour undercurrent. "I can't tell you."

The other three exchanged glances. Marion swallowed. "Are you under some sort of magical geas? Or a threat? A brain implant?"

Ben nodded. "Psychological conditioning? I hate those. A vision from the future telling you that if you explain things to us, disaster will occur?"

Amber smiled. "Those are not the things normal people would jump to first. No, none of that. The thing is, I promised I wouldn't say."

Rohan held up a hand. "Let's step back. You must be able to tell us *something*, right?"

A frown bent her pale lips. "Masamune sent me."

Ben's eyes widened. "Immortal swordsmith Masamune? Who lives in a mystical mountain on another plane of reality?"

Amber nodded. "Do you know another one?"

"No, but if both Masamune and Lyst are involved in this, it sounds a lot like an apocalypse."

"No, it's strange, but not that. Look, Masamune said something very specific. He wanted me to find ar'Tahul, and to ask him to come to Earth. I told him I have no idea who that is, and he said I should talk to you, Rohan. And to remind you that you owe him a favor. Which he's calling in."

Rohan scratched at his jaw under his beard. "He used those words exactly?"

"Does this sound like something I'd make up? Do you know who that is?"

"It's me. Masamune is a member of a very old species. They're very hierarchical, maybe fanatically so. And, long story, I killed a fifty-thousand-year-old insane vampire who happens to have been the head of their warrior caste. Which means that now I'm the head of their warrior caste. ar'Tahul is a title. My title. I guess. Congratulations to me."

Amber nodded slowly and bit into one of the pastries. "You're not teasing me, are you? Getting back at me for the giant-walking-sharks thing?"

Rohan shrugged. "I kind of wish I were. My simple life as a tow chief here on Wistful is not quite as simple as I was aiming for."

"Okay, okay. Crazy as that all sounds, we live crazy lives. Fair enough. So, it's really you I'm looking for. Masamune has a job for you, and as I said, he wants you to come to Earth with me to do it."

"What's the job?"

"That's part of what I promised not to tell you."

Ben leaned forward in his chair. "But you're also telling us the Earth is *not* in danger? This isn't an all-hands-on-deck, last-ditch-attempt-to-save-humanity kind of thing?"

She chewed and swallowed. "Not as far as I can tell. It's just . . . weird. And Masamune thinks Rohan can help."

Rohan ran his fingers through his hair. "He's not wrong, I do owe him a favor."

"He said you should bring the cape, too."

Rohan sighed. "Hyperion's cape? Sure. I'm just not really comfortable leaving Wistful right now."

Ben shook his head. "You go on, son. We can take care of ourselves. As I believe my wife demonstrated just a half hour ago. And Wistful will be fine. She survived tens of thousands of years without you; she can manage a few days or weeks."

"You're making me feel both comforted and discarded in the same breath."

"That's my gift." Ben smiled and bit into one of the sweet pastries, an orange gel squeezing out onto his cheeks.

Marion handed him a napkin. "If Lyst sent Amber here, she must agree that your presence would be a good idea."

Rohan rubbed his forehead. "Amber, you brought the message. Does that mean you think I should go? Or something else?" *If I go, I can't talk to Tamara. Which gives me extra days of childish hope. And dread.*

She nodded. "I can't tell you exactly what's happening, but I can tell you that it's strange, people are in danger, and I think you can help us get to the root of it. So, yes, I'd like you to come. And I happen to think this is something you'll want to see for yourself. But it's not like we won't survive without you."

"I think that's good enough. I mean, bottom line, I owe Masamune, and he's calling in his marker. So off we go. What do we do, jump back into the fish tanks? Will Lyst whip up a fresh portal?"

Amber choked softly on her food. "I think we assumed your ship could bring us back. I don't have a way to contact Lyst and ask her to make a portal. I'm not even sure she's available."

"Ah! *Void's Shadow.* I'll ask her."

Wei Li entered the cafeteria and sat next to Rohan. "Hello, Amber of Earth. Welcome to Wistful." A nearby speaker piped up, translating her words into English.

"Wei Li, right? Sorry for just gating in like that. We don't have any ships." The speaker translated Amber's words into Drachna.

Wei Li waved her hand. "Lyst has permission to connect with Wistful anytime. They are old friends. I assume you are taking our tow chief? Are you taking our scientists as well?"

Amber chuckled. "Not right now. This is a Rohan thing. At least, that's whom I was sent for."

Ben held up his hand. "Wait, wait. There is a very important question to be answered!"

Amber shook her head. "I told you, I can't—"

"Not you. Rohan. Are you going to try to see Tamaralinth before you go? Or dash off into the unknown with nary a word for your former love?"

Rohan swallowed. "I wouldn't say 'love,' exactly. We dated for less than two weeks."

"The question remains." Ben grinned.

"You're killing me, Ben."

"Perhaps, but that doesn't answer the question."

Rohan hunched forward in an exaggerated slump. "I would absolutely talk to her first, clear up whatever it is that she wants to discuss, but this thing with Amber sounds really important. Maybe even urgent. I'm going to have to go to Earth immediately, no procrastinating. Yup. Right away. If Tamara wants to talk, she's just going to have to wait."

Ben nodded. "While you're on Earth, maybe say hello to Bright Angel. Give her my regards."

Marion elbowed her husband, whose grin stubbornly persisted.

Rohan slumped further. *He had to mention my first love. A love who very definitively told me she wasn't interested in a relationship the last time I saw her.* "How is it that you're such a nice man, yet you delight so much in sticking knives into my heart?"

Amber's face had tightened, her brows lowered and her lips pressed together.

Wei Li smiled. "You are an unnaturally tempting target for such torment, Rohan. It is a result of your endearing incompetence." Wistful's voice followed hers, translating.

"I'm going to add that to my dating profile. 'Endearingly incompetent.' I'm sure that will bring the women storming my door."

Marion looked at Amber. "What is it? You look tense."

"I'm not sure I'm supposed to tell you this, but I didn't promise not to. Bright Angel's hurt."

4

Road Trip

Thirty minutes later, Rohan and Amber were settling into the reclining crew couches in the center of *Void's Shadow*'s cabin. He rubbed his chest, wincing at the pain in his healing stab wound.

The ship's voice broke over the comms. "Captain, are you upset? Did I do something wrong?" She was speaking English, a show of politeness for her guest.

Rohan let out a long, slow breath. "Yes and no."

Amber narrowed her eyes at him. "*Void's Shadow*, what Captain Ambiguous is trying to say is yes, he's upset, but no, you didn't do anything wrong. I gave him some bad news, and he's . . . trying to process it."

A pause while the ship considered. "I didn't realize Captain Rohan had gained a new title. Is *Ambiguous* the name of another ship?"

Amber sighed. "That's not what I—"

The ship interrupted her. "I am teasing you. It's a joke! Was it funny? I'm trying to learn how to tell jokes. Captain Rohan has been teaching me. It's very hard to be funny, though I seem to be much better at it when it's by accident."

Amber watched a smile creep its way up Rohan's cheeks. "I'm not sure it was funny, but it was very clever. I bet you'll get better at joke-telling with practice."

Rohan rubbed at the fresh scab on his cheek. "I'm sorry, *Void's Shadow*. I wasn't trying to be mean. I'm glad you're helping us get to Earth."

"It's my pleasure, Captain. Are you two ready to go? I have the course plotted. I know I'm not supposed to, but I kept the directions in memory from the last time." Earth was under embargo; it was technically against Imperial law to travel there by starship.

"That's good thinking, *Void's Shadow*. Start the trip whenever you're ready."

They watched on the ship's main display, a screen that took up the entire front wall of the cabin, as she pivoted away from Wistful's buoy perimeter and accelerated smoothly toward deep space.

Ten minutes later, she opened a temporary wormhole that would take them part of the way to Earth.

Amber looked over at him. "Should I not have told you?"

He let out a sound somewhere between a cough and a laugh. "Maybe not. No, I take that back. I'm an adult. It's just a very helpless feeling, you know? She's hurt, and I'm halfway across the galaxy. Tell me again what happened."

"Nice try. I can't tell you, not exactly. I'll say that she was poisoned."

"No poison on Earth could overcome the healing powers of the Angelium."

Amber bit her lip and didn't respond.

Rohan turned his head to look at her face. "So, it was something from off-planet. An alien."

"I didn't say that."

"What species?"

Amber shrugged. "I don't know what they're called. Red skin, black horns. Yellow eyes. They look like devils. At least, like the version of a devil you'd see in a comic book."

"Drexians. Why on Earth would Drexians be on . . . Earth. That came out wrong. You know what I meant."

"I don't know. And I'm not giving you any more clues."

"Is she okay, though? Or am I coming home for her funeral?"

"She was recovering when I left. Out of action, but also out of danger."

"Okay, that's good. It also partly explains why you were sent for me, right? I mean, she's a heavy hitter. Not much I can do that she couldn't. But once she got hurt . . ."

"You also have knowledge and abilities that she doesn't have. For example, you know these aliens are Drexians. I'm not sure anybody else other than Lyst and maybe Masamune knows anything about them."

Rohan studied the screen as a rift opened in space before them. The entire visible starscape changed instantly as *Void's Shadow* took careful aim and passed through its center.

Amber followed his gaze to the screen. "It's not like wormholes on television shows back home. They always enter one side, then fly through some weird cloudy tube."

Rohan laughed. "I forgot about those. No, there's no 'inside' a wormhole. It's just a hole in space. One side is in one place; the other side is someplace else. Could be a kilometer away, could be a hundred thousand light years. The trick is making it so the other side is close to where you're going."

"Why doesn't she just open a wormhole directly to Earth?"

"It's a whole complicated thing having to do with potential energy. Lots of math. Really complex math. I'd be happy to explain it, but you wouldn't understand. Otherwise, I totally would."

"You have absolutely no idea, do you?"

"Not a clue. But she does." He reached down, outside his cradle, and patted the floor of the ship.

Amber nodded. "With your own ship like this, I'm surprised you don't travel more. See the galaxy."

"You make me feel old sometimes, Amber. I've seen a lot of the sector already. Usually in the form of fighting in some war or other. I'm happy to stay mostly in one place for a while."

Amber climbed out of her couch and picked her way to the kitchenette. "Don't mind me, I'm going to do some stress eating."

Rohan sank back into the cushioning. "I kind of wish I'd stashed tequila on board. But I should probably stay sober for whatever I'm getting myself into. *Void's Shadow*, how long until we reach Earth?"

"About eleven more hours, Rohan."

"Okay. Thanks. Can you play us a show or something? I need to be distracted."

"You know I have a number of shows stored, Rohan. Do you want to show Amber *Swords of Lukhor*?"

Rohan turned to look at the woman, who shrugged.

"I'll watch anything. As long as I have snacks."

"There are snacks. But nothing from Lukhor, please." *Nothing that's going to remind me of Tamaralinth. I wonder what she's doing now? Is it her shift? No, too early. She's probably still in bed. Stop thinking about her. Especially her in bed.*

"Amber, what's been happening on Earth? I mean, generally. Since we sent back the sharks. Anything dramatic?"

Amber paused. "I remember you asking me this last time. Hold on, let me sit. I made a list of things you might want to know. We can start with the World Series winners."

"I'm Canadian. How about we start with the Stanley Cup?"

"I have those, too!"

⬥ ⸱•⸱ ⬥

An hour later, Rohan had sufficiently caught up on Earth trivia. Amber rummaged through the kitchenette. Again.

"What are you looking for?"

"I'm hungry. And how often to I get a chance to eat space food?"

"Everything on Wistful was space food, too. I mean, she's a space station."

"But on a ship. That's traveling. It's exotic." She unscrewed the top of a cylindrical container and peered inside. "Why do you have a two-gallon container of chocolate pudding? Is this a fetish thing? Wait, do I want to know?"

"It's not a fetish thing, but no, you probably don't want to know."

"Now I really want to know. What is this stuff? Should I try it?"

"You won't like the answer."

"Tell me anyway. You know I'll keep bothering you until you answer."

"Okay, but you've been warned. It's the output of the long-term food recycling system."

Amber frowned at him. "Explain that as if I didn't already understand what you mean."

"This ship has to accommodate longer missions. Too long for her to just store the food we'd need. So, it recycles all our waste with a kind of bioengineered algae. Shine some light on it, add water and carbon dioxide, and it spits out that stuff. We call it sludge."

"Oh. Would I sound very provincial if I said that's kind of gross?"

"It's the same thing that happens on a farm, just on a more intimate scale."

"What does the sludge taste like?"

"Weirdly enough, pretty much chocolate pudding."

She eyed the brown gel skeptically. "I'm trying some."

"Be my guest."

Void's Shadow chimed in. "Opening another gate, Captain. Nine and a half hours to reach Earth."

"Thank you. Amber, what do you think?"

"It's actually tasty. I'm a little grossed out by how good it is."

"The il'Drach didn't really believe in providing gourmet food for Hybrids, or soldiers in general, so we lived off that stuff year-round. You get pretty sick of it after a while."

She closed the sludge container and sat.

Rohan watched the younger woman. "You filled me in on Earth politics and stuff, but how are you, Amber? Everything okay? Generally?"

She swallowed. "You know how it goes. There's a lot of suffering. People are still rebuilding, especially around the Pacific. So, I don't want to overlook all of that."

"I get all that. But how are you, specifically?"

She shrugged. "I'm actually pretty good. I like my life."

"What have you been doing? This past year?"

"Same things. Training, mostly with Spiral. Fighting some, also alongside Spiral. Outmaneuvering the Sons of Atlantis and the Children of Mu as they try to pull off ever more ridiculous schemes and plots in their quest for world domination."

"Do you get tired of it? The fighting? You ever want to settle down, live a normal life?" *Maybe shack up with a green-skinned shuttle tech—I've got to stop doing this.*

"Do what? Get my engineering degree and work out of a cubicle for the next thirty years? Get married, buy a house in the Jersey suburbs, drive a coupe style Mercedes SUV around town?"

"That's oddly specific, but sure. I was thinking more, open a coffee shop. Same idea."

She stuffed a forkful of leaves into her mouth, chewed, and swallowed. "Nope."

"That's it? Nope."

"Look, I have these Powers, right? I can distort time. I can use them to help people in a pretty unique way. Not to put down engineers, but very few of them can have an impact the way you or I can."

"I don't know. Engineers invented the internet. That's impact."

"I meant positive impact."

He laughed. "Ouch. You're saying your Power makes you feel responsible."

She nodded. "Someone has to fight the bad guys. I don't see a big line of volunteers who can actually do the job."

———◆·••·◆———

Void's Shadow's voice penetrated a very nebulous dream. "Captain, you should wake up. We are approaching Earth atmosphere."

Rohan sat upright, rubbing his eyes. "I was having a great dream. I think." He yawned. "Where are we going, Amber?"

"Masamune said we should go to Sahara City. He knocked out the Imperial surveillance satellites so nobody's going to notice us landing." Hyperion had created a company to manage the alien technology Earth had been granted by the il'Drach and named it after himself. Its headquarters, and the central location for all Earth's Vanguard teams, were in Sahara City. "Bamf can teleport us from there to where you're needed."

"We can't just fly there?"

She shrugged. "Not directly, and I can't tell you why, Rohan."

"We're near Earth. Call me Griffin. Please."

"Right, sorry."

Graphics popped up on the front screen, displaying transcripts of the ship communicating with Sahara City authorities as she sought permission to enter their airspace.

Rohan rubbed his stomach, annoyed by the hollow feeling inside. "Are we in a rush?"

"Take all the time you need."

"Great."

"But you're going to be the one explaining any delays to Masamune."

"Less great. Let's go directly there. I can visit people afterward. I guess. Am I going to die on this mission?"

Amber shrugged. "I doubt it, but you never know."

"Very comforting."

"It's a gift."

"Entering atmosphere now."

Rohan adjusted his seat so he could watch the screen, Earth's familiar blue-and-white image dominating the picture.

"Home sweet home."

"You could visit more often, you know."

"I know."

Africa's shape came into focus, then the yellow and brown of the northeast quarter of the continent. The ship continued to close on the part of the Sahara where Egypt, Libya, Sudan, and Chad almost met. The place where Rohan's mother had built an entire city, pulling carbon directly out of the air, powered by sunshine and alien technology.

Sahara city took up one quarter of a broad circle nestled among the dunes and plains. The other three quarters were shiny solar panels providing power for the city's industry.

Void's Shadow closed on a flat patch, landing strips demarcated by colorful lines. The surrounding buildings were black and glass, an overwhelmingly complex network of walkways and elevated roads soaring and swooping between them, dots of color swarming over it, the clothes and vehicles of the city's citizens.

"I don't see protesters this time."

"Things are quiet. Everybody's a bit less tense. Or busier."

Rohan and Amber stood as the ship slowed to a halt a few meters above the ground.

Rohan patted the ceiling. "Just like last time, *Void's Shadow*. Don't let anybody but us inside."

"Yes, Captain. Can I go play in the asteroid belt?"

He looked at Amber. "Am I going to need a quick escape route? Or is this not that kind of thing?"

She pursed her lips. "Not that kind of thing."

"All right." He looked at the front screen. "Go play. Try to stay where you can read my comm signal if I need you."

"Yes, Captain. Have fun!"

He opened his brown messenger bag and pulled out his old mask: a gaiter with an eagle's beak printed on the front. He slipped it over his head, adjusting the front seam so it covered his nose.

He flipped open the hatch, waited for Amber to climb out, then slipped the messenger bag over his shoulder and followed her. As they dropped to the ground, uniformed police jogged over to their position. They waited while the ship pivoted and accelerated up and away from the city.

"Griffin, sir. Amber, ma'am. Welcome to Sahara City. Where would you like to go?"

Rohan looked at Amber, who nodded. "Take us to Bamf."

"Yes, ma'am."

5

Found Family Reunion

The puff of air that blew through the gate smelled of salt and seaweed. Rohan shuddered. *I do not like that smell. Reminds me of something. But what?*

Amber met Rohan's eyes, nodded, and stepped through. Rohan shrugged at Bamf, who giggled in response, his head loose on his shoulders, eyes unfocused. Rohan took a sniff of the air, then followed Amber.

The space on the other side of the gate was dimly lit, with a ceiling far away and hidden by shadow.

Rohan sniffed again. "We are in a cave. Underwater. Or is it a cavern?"

Amber pointed to a group of people standing in a cluster about twenty meters away. "I think a cavern is just a type of cave. And before you ask, no, I don't know which type this is. Go talk to Masamune before you ask me any more questions that might make me break my promise."

Rohan walked toward the shadowy bunch.

Masamune stood at the head. Short for a human, outside his sharply pointed ears and a few odd facial marks, he could have passed for an actor playing a warlord on the set of a Japanese period drama.

Behind the smith stood a statue that Rohan had met before, the soul of a long-dead warrior trapped in stone. Facing them were three people in jumpsuits of matching cut. One, a woman with startlingly blue eyes and gray-streaked corn-yellow hair, wore a solid yellow outfit. On the other side, a boy on the edge of adulthood wore blue to match his deep-blue hair.

Between them was a person of indefinite gender, slender with bright-green hair and outfit.

Rohan looked at Amber. "Rainbow Stars?"

She nodded as they approached the group.

Masamune stepped toward Rohan; his eyes widened in an expression the Hybrid couldn't interpret. As they drew close, the smith bent forward at the waist, his right hand pressed to the left side of his chest, and spoke.

"ar'Tahul. Thank you for coming." He stayed bent, eyes directed toward Rohan's feet.

"Um . . . at ease? I guess. And please don't call me that. I'm not super comfortable with the, uh, selection method for that title." He faced the statue. "Hey, Hiroshi."

The statue rumbled a barely audible greeting, like a small pile of stones falling.

Masamune straightened. "Titles are given, not chosen. You are what you are."

"I guess I can't argue with that." He took in the other heroes. "I don't think we've met. I'm The Griffin."

The older woman nodded. "I'm Yellow, and these are Green and Blue." They had died fighting the sharks.

"Yeah. Sorry to hear about Indigo and Violet."

She smiled warmly. "Thank you. It was very sad, but The Light has provided; we have a new Indigo and Violet now."

Rohan looked at Amber, who shrugged, then back to Masamune. "Will you please tell me what's going on?"

The smith nodded. "Look at the far end of this cave. Use your Third Eye."

Rohan let out a long breath and opened his spiritual eye. His sensitivity to spiritual energies was greater than a normal person's, though it paled in comparison to an empath like Wei Li.

"All I see is a great big wall of energy blocking that end of the cave."

"That is correct."

"And . . . you want me to break it down for you?" He focused. "That's going to be tough. It's a pretty solid field. Can't we go around? What's on the other side?"

"I do not think you *can* break it down. We have a different plan."

Yellow nodded, her hair bouncing with the motion. "We are gathering the Stars. Once the others join us, we can create a gate that penetrates the energy field."

"I didn't think that was possible."

"It's a difficult technique. A specialty of the Rainbow Star Power. Reserved for emergencies."

Rohan opened his mouth. He felt an army of questions fighting one another to get out into the open first.

"Is this about saving Bright Angel? What's really going on here?"

Masamune shook his head. "Bright Angel was injured, yes, but she is recovering. There's nothing you can do for her right now. Someone else is being held captive inside that field, and I want you to go in and save them."

"Who?"

Yellow opened her mouth, but Masamune held up a hand to silence her. "It doesn't matter. ar'Tahul, on your word you owe me a favor. This is the favor. I want you to rescue, then protect, the person held captive inside that field."

"But you won't tell me who it is."

Masamune exhaled. "Does it matter? It would only raise more questions. Answering them would either be impossible or take time we don't have. I believe that person is in some danger."

Rohan exhaled, blowing air across taut lips. *Do I trust Masamune? I do. I have good reason to. And I suppose I can bail if I don't like the look of things inside that field.*

"This whole situation is really weird, but I made a promise, and I try to keep those. But why me?"

Yellow answered. "The Rainbow Bridge can only carry a single person across the barrier. Bright Angel might have been strong enough to send in, if she were healthy, but . . ."

"Rainbow Bridge? Did you check with the Norse gods for copyright on that?"

Masamune snorted. "The Norse gods died a long time ago."

"I was . . . never mind. Look, I get it. You need a big gun. I take it Lyst isn't interested?"

Masamune shook his head. "As usual, Lyst is monitoring a great many situations. And while she was willing to send Amber to you, she is not convinced that this situation merits her involvement."

"Kid Lightning?"

Amber shook her head. "Retired. He's running a diner in Staten Island. Trying to learn how to speak again." Overuse of his electrical powers had badly injured the hero while fighting the sharks.

"Poseidon?"

Yellow smiled. "Poseidon is leading a battle against this field from the ocean side. That's why our presence here has gone unnoticed. It is taking all of his great strength to distract the occupants. Spiral is similarly leading our brothers and sisters in combat aboveground." She pointed up, toward the surface.

"Okay. The Green, I mean the other one, would be too hard to manage here. He'd probably get mad and bring the whole cave down, drown us all. There aren't, or shouldn't be, any other Hybrids on the planet." He tapped fingertips against his forehead. "Man, we lost a lot of heroes fighting those sharks. I can't think of anyone else. Which leaves . . . me. How much time do I have?"

Yellow looked at Green, who stepped aside and put a device shaped like a cell phone to their mouth.

Yellow nodded. "The others are coming now. Prepare yourself."

Rohan held his bag up to Masamune. "You want me to put this cape on?"

"No, the cape is for me. Here, put this comm on." He handed Rohan something that looked like a Band-Aid or a nicotine patch. "Behind your ear."

"I'm familiar." Rohan pulled back his shoulder-length hair and affixed the comm to his skin. "Are you going to tell me anything else? What am I facing in there? Vampires? Cephalopods? Nazis? Sentient robots?"

"Just punch them until they fall down. You killed the former ar'Tahul, you can certainly handle what's inside that field."

Rohan sighed. "I'm not sure you got the full story about that fight. I wasn't the only one involved."

"Tollan says you're the new senior warrior, that's good enough for me."

They turned as sounds came from a tunnel entering the cave from the right of the energy field.

Four people flew in.

Red was a petite woman, barely a hundred fifty centimeters tall, with flaming red hair and proportions that would make a Barbie doll envious.

Orange was taller, only a bit less voluptuous, and chewed gum loudly as they flew toward Masamune's group.

The men were bigger. Indigo had the physique of a diver, lean and ripped with a square jaw and chiseled features. Violet stood close to two meters and was thick all over, like a professional wrestler or strongman. His face was obscured by a shock of colorful hair and a purple beard that hung halfway down his chest; it was so thick Rohan thought if he poked inside he'd find an animal den or a bird hiding there.

Amber stepped forward. "Where's Spiral? I thought he was fighting with you?"

Orange turned and pointed up the cave. "He's holding the tunnel against the last of the minions. Don't worry, he's fine. I don't know when he powered up like that, but he's quite the bruiser now."

Indigo nodded, his cheekbones catching the dim light. "He's amazing."

Rohan looked them over. "I'll let someone fill me in on what that means later. Along with the identity of the person I'm rescuing, who I'm fighting, the fate of Bright Angel, and . . . did I forget anything? Is there another piece of information that needs to be kept from me right now?"

Grim faces were his only answer.

Masamune pointed to the Rainbow Stars. "Send him through. We don't have time to waste. I'm worried about . . . the prisoner. Griffin, you'll understand the secrecy when you're done. For now, please trust me."

Rohan sighed and shrugged.

The Stars formed a circle, Yellow and Orange showing Violet and Indigo where to stand. Yellow smiled at Rohan. "As I said, they're new. It's their first time. But they'll do wonderfully, I'm sure. The Light provides."

"Sure." Rohan looked at Amber.

She walked up to him and patted his shoulder. "Go save the prisoner. It's what you do."

"Okay. I got it. I guess. Man, I do not like the smell of this place. What is it reminding me of?"

"I don't know. Quick, they're getting ready."

The Stars held hands, forming most of a circle, Violet's and Red's palms close but not touching. Rohan slipped between them and stood in the center.

Streams of colored light began to emanate from the Stars: first Red, then Orange, then Yellow. The streams warped and twisted, surrounding Rohan. The colors wove together in a swirl, a tornado of light, Green's blast twisting in with the others, then Blue's, then Indigo's, and finally Violet's.

Each band was thicker and brighter than the last. Red's light danced and frolicked in between the others; Indigo's surged: dense, almost opaque, bands of energy that barely managed to turn and twist back into the cylinder.

The circle opened, Indigo and Red stepping away from each other. Green spoke, their voice soft and confident.

"Walk to the field. The Bridge we've formed will pass you through. Good luck on the other side."

Rohan walked to the end of the cavern as the light pulsed and twisted around him. As the bands touched, they combined colors; when those combinations met, lines of pure white streaked the storm.

He set his shoulders as he approached the field, let out a breath, and stepped into it.

The colored bands touched the field first, mixing and dodging together, biting into the wall of energy. Each color seemed alive, seeking out some morsel, some nuanced expression of energy, making distinctions Rohan couldn't follow. Each band nullified a piece of the field.

"Hurry!" Green's voice called.

Rohan lowered his chin and pushed his forehead into the force field.

It gave way.

He pressed, his head passing through, then his shoulders, followed by his body. The field closed around him, pushing his legs through from behind, shoving him stumbling into the cave beyond.

The Hybrid patted his arms and legs and took in the cave. It matched the area on the other side: dozens of meters high, scores of meters across; lit by slicks of fluorescent moss and streaks of glowing liquids dripping across the rock walls.

"I'm in. I seem to be intact." He spoke softly, shuddering as his voice echoed off the distant walls. "I really hate this smell." *I could have been having tea with Tamaralinth right now. I wonder what she'd be wearing? Her uniform? Something less formal?*

A tunnel extended out of the back of the cave with a pool of liquid alongside. The water lapped gently at the lip of the mostly flat tunnel floor.

Rohan walked, trying to look in all directions at once as he crossed the cave. A splash brought him up short.

Something emerged from the pond, water dripping off its sides. Then another; and a third.

The creatures continued to rise as they stepped forward onto the rocky floor, not stopping until their heads were two and a half meters above the ground. The first one coughed, then again, spitting liters of water out onto the floor, then drawing a ragged, raspy breath. The others followed suit.

They were roughly human-shaped, with disproportionately large eyes shining white in the darkness. Each had a pair of tentacles extending from their backs, four meters long and as thick around as a powerlifter's thighs, rubbery and twitching.

"These guys look familiar, but I don't remember them being so big."

Amber spoke over his comm. "What is it, Rohan?"

"You remember the tentacled vampires that were attacking the refugee camps last year?"

"Yeah."

"Like those, only fishier. And bigger."

Spiral answered. "Hey, Rohan. Sorry I missed your big entrance. They're tough but not very bright. Not much smarter than a dog. But less cuddly. Don't let them eat you."

"You took your time, Spiral. I'm glad, I might not have thought of that on my own. 'Don't let them eat you.' I have no idea how I survived this long without your wisdom and guidance."

"You want details? I don't want to ruin all your fun. Figure that part out yourself."

The lead vampire's mouth split open, the top half of its head tilting all the way back, displaying a wide, loose-lipped mouth full of sharp, jagged teeth.

Rohan nodded to the creature. "Hey, man. Are we going to talk this out?"

With a cough, a burble, and a growl, the creature began to run. It took two steps with its feet, then looped its tentacles over its shoulders and planted them in the floor, lifting and swinging the creature forward and into Rohan.

"I guess not."

The Hybrid ducked low, then launched himself directly at the vampire. It reached for him with burly arms and gaping jaws.

As he charged, Rohan *pulled* energy from a spot he pictured down below his tailbone, the root of his Hybrid curse. It surged and frothed, eager to be tapped, and leapt upward in twin arcs that spiraled around his spine, crossing with a flash of sparks every few vertebrae, rising higher with each turn.

The creature grabbed; Rohan ducked lower, the front of his jumpsuit skimming the ground, and drove his forearms through the vampire's shins. It upended and rolled behind him.

The channels of energy inside Rohan met for one final time at the base of his skull, completing a metaphysical circuit that instantly burst, sending streams of raw Power to every corner of his body. The dim corners of the room brightened; he could smell the human blood and deep ocean salt on the breath and skin of the vampires, feel every crack and pebble on the rough ground underfoot. Lines of energy pulled at the stab wound in his chest, knitting the tissues together.

He planted his right foot and drove off it, propelling his body into the surprised vampire on the left side of the second rank.

Rohan struck its face with his extended fist, the momentum of his entire body crunching into the center of its maw.

Teeth shattered, sharp bits of bone flying as Rohan's fist destroyed the creature's mouth. His knuckles impacted the monster's soft palate, sending shockwaves into its brain.

It stumbled backward, freeing Rohan's arm, and collapsed to the ground. He turned to face the next vampire just as a tentacle swung into his face like a baseball bat.

The Hybrid flew back, his momentum cut short by impact with the rock wall behind. He was in the mouth of the tunnel.

Amber's voice rang in his ear. "Rohan! Are you okay?"

Spiral shushed her over the channel. "He can handle these guys. As long as they only come one or two at a time, it won't be a problem."

Rohan grumbled, "Busy!" and pushed off the wall.

A tentacle swung at his face again. He braced and caught it with both hands, fingers digging deep into moist flesh. Rohan pulsed energy into his feet, rooting them to the floor, and pulled down savagely on the tentacle.

His motion whipped the vampire into the ground.

Rohan stood straight, yanking the tentacle up and over his head. The vampire hurtled up into the air.

The Hybrid stepped to his left, then forward, guiding the vampire's flight. As it reached the apex of its path, it looked down, eyes widening as it saw the tip of a stalactite emerging from its chest.

Arms wrapped around Rohan's chest from the side; the first vampire had rejoined the fray. It opened its mouth, its head extending for Rohan's. He bent his neck, hunched his shoulders, and jammed the top of his head into its open mouth.

Teeth splintered, gouging ruts in Rohan's forehead.

The creature reeled back, stunned. Rohan followed it, kicking its weakened shins, hearing bone give way before each impact. Blood trickled down his face.

The Hybrid stalked the third vampire.

He stepped to his left and watched it flinch back. The vampire collected itself, growling, and rushed him.

He bent into a squat, let out a breath, and jumped, lifting his right knee into the vampire's head.

Its face caved inward, and the vampire fell to its back, twitching and spasming. Rohan looked down the hall. "I finished the first three. Any idea how many more I'm going to have to deal with?"

Spiral answered through the comms. "Don't worry, there are plenty. Enough to give even a Hybrid a decent workout."

That wasn't really the spirit of my question.

"Roger that."

6

Is There a Doctor in the Cave?

G rowls and the sounds of gnashing teeth echoed through the tunnel from the depths of the cave system. Rohan wiped his forehead with the back of his hand, grimacing at the blood staining his uniform sleeve, and peered into the dark.

"What do I do? Just follow this tunnel?"

"Spiral again. Head toward the growls. They'll be between you and . . . the prisoner."

"Got it." *Still not telling me who it is.*

The tunnel widened, and a second pond opened up on the other side of the stone path. A loud screech sounded from up ahead, followed by a second, then a chorus of screams like tearing metal, ripped from very inhuman throats.

The sound was enough to disguise the disturbance in the water as a pair of tentacles slipped out and lanced toward the Hybrid's head like striking rattlesnakes.

Rohan twisted to the side, bent at the waist, and raised his arm, deflecting the tentacles above his body, while a second pair swept his feet out from under him.

As his back hit the stone, Rohan spun like a break-dancer on cardboard, lashing both feet into the face of the creature slithering out of the water.

Slippery weight settled on his body as three of the creatures landed on the Hybrid.

Rohan's heart pounded in his chest as he twisted to one side, then the other, knocking one vampire away while the other two settled more firmly, their tentacles spread wide for added stability.

Starting to feel panicky. Why do I feel panicky? I've been in trickier situations.

He panted and grabbed at flesh, fingers tearing at anything he could reach. An eye the size of a tea saucer popped under his thumb; his fingers gripped and tore through another vampire's cheek.

Heh. That's a fishhook! I fishhooked a fish-vampire. Why isn't anybody laughing?

He slammed the head of one vampire into the face of another, scrambling to get his feet under him as their bodies went limp. Rohan gripped the second vampire by the neck and clapped their heads together again, then a third time, stopping only when he noticed the squelching sounds.

He panted and tossed the bodies into the water, then turned and continued up the path. He noticed a tremor in his hand. *I don't like this. I really don't want to be here.*

"Hey, guys."

Amber answered. "What is it?"

"How far down are we?"

"Not sure exactly, but I can find out. Why?"

"Can I break through the roof? Let in some sunlight? Should fry these guys." Shrieks built up in the cave ahead of him.

Masamune interrupted. "Don't do that. We're underwater. All you'd do is flood the cave, which would be bad for everyone but the things you're fighting."

Rohan sighed as he willed his hand to stillness. "It was worth a try."

The tunnel widened into a cave twenty meters across. Its floor was smoother, tool-finished. The mossy walls met the ground at nearly right angles. Lines were etched into those surfaces, shallow marks that swirled and swooped like the output of a drunken Spirograph. Only the ceiling had kept the look of a natural cave, studded with stalactites and deep crevices whose depths were lost to shadow. Long white objects like slender stones or fungi littered the far corners.

Or bones.

This must be the pantry.

Five more of the creatures rushed him.

He took to the air, skimming the craggy cave roof, then dropped down on the group.

A quick stomp tore apart one thick, slimy leg.

An overhand right to a throat left another creature on its knees, retching and choking.

He panted as he leaned back, out of the way of a wild punch, then forward again, driving his left elbow into a forehead with a crunch of bone.

Tentacles wrapped around his body from the back. He hopped up and kicked with both legs, launching a creature across the room, sliding into the pile of bones in the corner with a crunch. Then Rohan flipped up and over, coming down behind the vampire that had grabbed him, slipping free of its tentacles as he twisted them past their normal articulation.

The creature spun to meet him, finding instead the top of his foot as he drove a kick through its face.

Rohan stood over the body. He wiped blood off his forehead; the flow was diminishing as the cut closed. The markings on the floor drew his gaze.

I recognize that. It's writing. But not human writing.

"Did I mention where else I saw these guys? The half-vampire, half-octopus guys?"

Spiral responded. "Where, Griffin?"

Rohan swallowed. His chest was tight. He pulled at his uniform collar as he wondered about the air supply in the underwater cave.

"Anybody else having trouble breathing?"

A throat cleared over the comms before Masamune spoke. "I'm monitoring your oxygen levels, Griffin. They're well within your tolerance, but dropping. I suggest you get to the prisoner quickly."

A humorless chuckle bubbled out of his mouth. "To be fair, I never got a great look at them. I mean, it was dark. I was being tortured relentlessly.

Introductions weren't made, you know? But I could swear that there were guys who looked just like these guys working for Dr. Kraken."

Spiral's voice was steady. "Focus, Padawan. Just fight the monsters. Everything else is a distraction."

Rohan kicked one vampire to the side and crossed the cave. Three tunnels led out: the one he'd come through and two others.

"Eenie, meenie, minie, moe. Catch a Kraken by its . . . I never looked at old Doc Kraken's feet. Does he have toes? Flippers? Stumps?"

He took the left tunnel. Fifteen meters of claustrophobia opened up into a circular chamber. Three vampires charged.

Rohan *reached* up with his energy and pulled at the ceiling.

Dislodged stalactites fell like rain, accelerated unnaturally by Rohan's Power.

The vampires dropped, each pierced by half a dozen shards of rock. Rohan shook his head as he picked a path between the shattered bodies.

"I must be losing my mind."

"What do you mean, Griffin? I'm sure you're fine." Spiral's voice was full of confidence.

"I'm worried about the air in here, but I have a fully functional air supply in my hood. I'm just going to slip it on. I'm sure I'll be breathing easy in a second."

His mask sealed onto his face with a comforting hiss of compressed air.

Five vampires stood in the next chamber. Closer to three meters tall, each was half again as thick as the ones he'd already fought. They spread into a semicircle and gazed at him with flat, dead eyes.

"I am highly disappointed that the standardized atmosphere provided by this mask has not helped my breathing at all. Hey, you know what would be really cool? Telling me that I'm wrong, that Dr. Kraken is not somewhere in this cave complex. That the resemblance is just a coincidence."

The two center creatures rushed at Rohan. Dozens of palm-sized suckers, each sporting a ring of inward-pointing jagged teeth, dotted their tentacles.

Rohan lifted his arms.

A pair of massive stalactites dropped into his hands. The Hybrid caught them without taking his gaze off the vampires. He swung them back behind himself, then down close enough to scrape the ground, completing the circle with an upward arc that met the charging vampires right at their chins.

Blood and ichor sprayed as the stone clubs took off the front of the vampires' faces.

Amber's voice. "Is he okay? Can you sense anything?"

Spiral's. "The field blocks everything. He'll be fine. I think."

Rohan cleared his throat. "That's so strange. I could swear I just asked you guys to tell me something, and yet I must be mistaken, because that's absolutely not what you're saying. Have I mentioned that every week or so I wake up in a cold sweat? Guess whose tentacle-sporting face I see? Every time?"

He flicked his wrist, sending one club across the room. One vampire swatted it to the ground with a casual tentacle swipe.

A stone structure squatted in the very center of the room: a platform one meter high with smooth sides and a hole in the center big enough for a bowling ball. Power pulsed through the structure, a deep reservoir of energy that thrummed through the living rock. *Must be the source of the force field.*

Rohan walked to it, thinking of hopping onto the top so the vampires wouldn't be looking down at him. Up close, he could make out the writing etched into the platform.

I definitely recognize that script. Very definitely familiar.

His heart pounded in his chest. Two of the vampires spread out to flank him. On no observable signal, all three rushed in.

He tried to let out a long, slow breath, but it caught in his chest and he gasped for air instead. The three were *powerful*; their auras more intense than those of the other vampires by an order of magnitude, filling the air with a fog of hunger lined by moist, sticky overtones. He warily eyed the toothy suckers as six tentacles stretched out into the air.

Rohan turned to the vampire coming behind his left shoulder, right fist raised for a punch.

The creature halted in place, forearms held high near its head for protection, while the other two lashed out at the Hybrid's back.

"Damnit." Rohan ducked and rolled to his right, absorbing three stinging slaps across his back but remaining free. He quickly got to his feet.

The three vampires hurried to enfold him in a fresh circle.

"You guys are going to ruin your reputation as mindless animals, using tactics like this. Then again, this is how animals hunt, too, right? I probably shouldn't be disparaging them. Some animal rights group is going to come after me. Throw paint on my leather jacket or something. Except I don't actually own a leather jacket. You know, I used to have a nice one. I wonder what happened to it."

Tentacles struck out at his calves, one set of suckers landing and coming away with a strip of cloth from his uniform.

Rohan reached down to grab it, but its retreat was too quick. Another pair lashed out at him, forcing him back.

Amber's voice. "Griffin, who are you talking to?"

"You know how you sent me in here because I'm the big gun? Well, it turns out these guys have some sizable guns of their own. And I'm talking to them. They're not really answering me, though. It's highly unsatisfying."

Spiral. "Stop playing with them, Griffin. Oxygen levels are still dropping."

"Not exactly playing. They're cheating; they're fighting smart."

"What would Musashi say?"

"What?"

"*Book of Five Rings.* What would Musashi say? When your opponents fight smart, what should *you* do?"

"I don't know. Fight dumb? Or is that more *Art of War*?"

"Exactly. Now you're thinking. About not thinking."

Amber spoke. "Spiral, you're not helping him."

"Trust me. I'm helping him help himself."

Rohan turned to the right, saw the vampire there cover up, then spun to his back and launched a kick.

The creature behind him reacted just in time to take the brunt of the attack on its forearms. The vampire to Rohan's left drew its tentacle across his calf, tearing off a layer of skin.

It opened its mouth wide and screeched.

The Hybrid huffed inside his helmet, fog building near his mouth, then dissipating as the mechanicals compensated.

He turned in place, slowly, and watched the vampires react.

Screw this. Spiral's right; it's not a time for finesse.

Rohan growled and *pulled* more Power up into his body, flooding it through his limbs, feeling little pops in his toes and fingertips as the energy of his curse reached the ends of his corporeal form.

He looked directly at the vampire that stood between him and the exit tunnel. Pointed at it with one now-steady finger.

"You."

He dug the ball of his right foot into the stone just behind himself, the ground shattering with the impact, shards of living rock flying up like a Jet Ski's wake. With violent acceleration, the Hybrid launched himself at the vampire.

It stepped back, wide eyes unblinking and unafraid, as he crashed into it.

Rohan heard two bones break as his forehead cracked into the vampire's raised forearms. He continued driving it backward, unrelenting, his fists tearing brutal hooks into its ribs with each lightning-quick step.

Left foot move; right hook. Right foot move up; left hook.

Suckers lashed across his back, tearing away uniform and skin. He ignored it.

On the third punch, ribs gave way. He hit higher, his face in the beast's chest, reaching around its back for its spine. More bones broke, and the vampire's tentacles flailed wildly.

Teeth dug into the meat of his deltoid. He willed more energy into his skin, armoring himself, and continued pounding.

The little group halted as the wounded vampire stopped short, its back embedded five centimeters deep in the suddenly shattered rock of the cave's back wall. Rohan leaned back, giving the creature some space, then immediately snapped his head forward again, disintegrating its lower jaw.

Suckers tore through his side, drawing blood. A knife struck the back of his leg, penetrating a surface layer of skin and digging for the muscle underneath.

The Hybrid raised his right fist, folded it close to his shoulder, and twisted his body, bringing the bony tip of his elbow directly into the vampire's sternum.

The heavy strip of bone cracked.

Another elbow strike as teeth bit into the base of his neck on the left.

The creature's sternum parted; Rohan pushed through, his elbow penetrating into soft, pulsing tissues inside the vampire's torso.

He spun and jabbed, bouncing off a head as the damaged vampire collapsed to the ground.

Energy crackled along his meridians and chakra lines, pressing together the edges of broken wounds and electrifying il'Drach muscle fibers.

"You guys underestimated how dumb I could fight. Or overestimated. Whichever."

He pointed at first one, then the other. "Eenie, meenie . . ."

Another kick at the wall behind and Rohan was on top of a vampire, too fast for their eyes to follow. It lifted its arms reflexively, tentacles waving in the air before it.

He grabbed a rubbery appendage.

Dug a finger deep into one of the suckers, twisting until it was buried up to the knuckle. Dug a second finger into another sucker, farther up, closer to the root.

The vampire screeched. The other vampire lashed at his back, its tentacles acting like a whip, flailing away strips of uniform and skin.

Rohan tore the tentacle apart.

The vampire sagged; he threw a left hook; it slid forward so his fist went behind its head.

He grabbed the back of the creature's neck and put his entire body behind a strike, bringing his right elbow in toward the grabbing hand.

The vampire's head flattened.

Rohan turned to face the last of them.

The creature stood, its face eerily free of expression. Hybrid blood dripped onto the floor.

He tried to slow his breathing; failed. Willed his lungs to be still, to hold; a moment later gasped for more air as the burning in his lungs intensified.

The vampire charged first.

Rohan met its rush with stiffened fingertips, destroyed both its eyes, then crushed its throat.

He dug thirsty fingers into its gills and yanked. Skin, muscle, bone, and balls of pink spongey flesh came free.

"That will teach you guys to count on a Hybrid being smart."

A voice came from the exit tunnel.

"The Griffin, returned. You mammals consistently surprise me, even after thousands of years of observation."

A shudder began at Rohan's lacerated calves, shaking his knees, then his thighs, finally twisting his back so badly his shoulders listed from side to side.

"Dr. Kraken."

7

By Any Other Name

R ohan's left foot dropped back, kicking into the ground, ready to launch him at the cephalopod that had spent days torturing him a year before.

"Stop, human. No, not that. My mistake. Stop, *Hybrid*."

The last word wasn't English, or Cephalopod, or any other spoken tongue. It wasn't even Fire Speech, the language that lay at the undiscovered core of all other communication.

The word was layered, complex. It was spoken and felt; projected mental energy, shaped into a key, alongside the sound. A spiritual hologram that didn't simply denote a Hybrid; it spoke of all qualities essential to that breed, all their characteristics, in their full complexity.

It referred to a Hybrid's alienation; half il'Drach, destined for service in the Empire, never truly part of its mother's world or her people's destiny. It spoke of the Hybrid's desperate longing for its father's love, for acknowledgment, for valuation. It spoke of the curse; of the rage; of the immense Power and the equal cost that sang through a Hybrid's soul.

Dr. Kraken spoke the name of Hybrids. It was something Rohan had never heard before, hadn't even been sure existed.

And when it was spoken, Rohan *listened*.

Dr. Kraken moved forward out of the shadows, approaching the man who dripped blood and vampire ichor in equal measure. His own tentacles, far more slender and dexterous than those of the vampires, quickly grazed some of Rohan's blood and brought it to his fleshy mouth.

"Ah. Still delicious. I do appreciate your visit, though the amount of destruction you have caused is quite inconvenient."

Rohan swallowed and tried to answer, but no words would form.

Spiral spoke through the comm behind Rohan's ear. "Griffin, hold on. You know what he's doing. Think. He's a wizard. An old one, a strong one, but just a wizard. He knows the name of Hybrids. It's a spell. You know how this works, right? It's like a lever. A machine. It just gives his Power extra purchase. Extra effect."

Rohan panted softly, eyes darting from side to side, taking in the thin layer of fog that swelled and shrank on the inside of his mask with each breath.

Dr. Kraken came closer. A few centimeters taller than Rohan, his humanoid body was topped by a blob of cephalopod flesh, four long tentacles descending from the curtain of meat that ran around his neck. Two black rectangular eyes twisted to bear on the Hybrid, each embedded in its own prehensile extrusion of flesh on the man's head.

"I won't tell you not to struggle. I know you will, regardless. You Hybrids are nothing if not predictable. But it won't help. I can hold you here by my will and magic, at least until we can administer something to make you more . . . pliable. You remember the drugs, don't you?"

Rohan shuddered softly. He couldn't answer.

Spiral continued. "He's not stronger than you, Griffin. He just has that leverage. But so do you. Don't forget that!"

I really wish he'd just tell me what he wants to tell me instead of doing the whole wise martial arts master speak-in-riddles thing he loves to do.

Dr. Kraken lifted his arm. A pair of vampires scuttled forward from behind him. He turned to them and gave brief instructions in a cephalopod language: leave, get restraints and certain chemicals, return.

Sweat soaked through Rohan's hair as he recalled the last time he'd been in that situation.

He had not been able to free himself, that time. Others came to rescue him. Something told him not to expect a repeat.

"You may speak, Griffin."

Rohan swallowed. "Are you the one who hurt Bright Angel? Revenge for last time?"

Dr. Kraken stepped back, eyes drifting apart on their short stalks to look at the far corners of the room. "While I would have been happy to injure or kill that pesky mammal, I had nothing to do with it. Didn't they—ah, I see. You weren't told. You were sent in, how do your people say it, blind."

Spiral continued. "He's trying to distract you, Griffin. Look, you can free yourself. You're stronger than him." *But he has leverage.* "He might know your name, or part of it, the part of you that's Hybrid. But you know everything else about yourself."

One shivering tentacle took a dab of Rohan's blood and curled up on itself, dipping its tip into his mouth. He sucked at it loudly. "Bright Angel hurt. Lyst away, doing whatever it is that she does. That traitorous Tolone'an off on the other side of the galaxy. Nobody is going to save you this time, Griffin. You're alone in here, with me. A stroke of fortune."

Rohan coughed gently. "Actually, you're the one who's trapped with *me*. Exactly as I planned it." He focused intensely on his right hand, willing the fingers to curl into a fist. *Come on. Come on. Just a little.*

The humanoid cephalopod paused. "Is that a joke? I'm not following you."

A finger twitched.

Dr. Kraken looked down at Rohan's hands and exhaled, moist flesh flapping with the flow of air, small bubbles forming at the bottom of the curtain of flesh cascading down from his head.

The miasma of Power surrounding Rohan intensified. Its aura was cold, the chill of waters so deep they never felt the touch of sunlight, pulling at Rohan's soul like a violent undertow, a whirlpool that spun around and around, suctioning at Rohan's will in tiny, undeniable increments.

The finger stilled.

"I see. You were trying to distract me. It's a good knack you have, this banter and teasing. It disorients people. I've seen it. They become angry and careless. Lose sight of the fact that you're actually fairly clever. In a limited way."

Amber spoke. "He knows you're a Hybrid, but he doesn't really know all that you are. Don't forget, he still thinks you're The Griffin. You're more than that now. You've become more than that. Listen to me. *You know your own name.*"

Rohan grunted and redoubled his focus.

I'm a tow chief. Second class. I own a bourbon distillery on Andervar. I'm not a soldier anymore.

He tried to picture himself as others might see him. A couple of centimeters shorter than the average human male. Scarred knuckles. Built like an amateur kickboxer. Shoulder-length black hair. Thick beard, trimmed short.

Is that who I am? No, that's just what I look like. What AM I?

A man who was kind to people. Tried to maintain good humor. Tried to stay positive. Tried to be nice. Also a man who had destroyed entire civilizations.

Spiral cleared his throat. "You're not alone, Griffin. You're defined by your friends as well. Remember the people who care about you! That you care for!"

Ben Stone. Rinth. Wei Li. Wistful. *Void's Shadow.* The people who cared about him.

He willed his finger to move.

Dr. Kraken's head bobbed up and down. "You are stronger than your reputation indicates. I see the time you've spent off-world has been good for you. But it won't be enough, surely you see that? Ah, my minions are coming with the anesthetics. Almost over."

A distant voice carried over the comms. "What's happening? Is he trapped?"

Masamune responded. "I thought he could handle this. Maybe I was wrong."

Spiral grunted. "He can do it. He just has to remember who he is, that's all."

Amber sighed. "You spent an entire year meditating under a waterfall to figure that out, didn't you? He's supposed to reach that level of self-knowledge in the middle of a fight with an octopus?"

Not just a fighter. Not just a soldier. What else, then? A lover? Is that how the saying goes?

Tamara's smile flashed across his mind. Pale-green skin. Twin antennae bouncing high on her forehead. Thick hair fanned across a pillow.

"You are stubborn, little Hybrid. Others have suggested I tame you, enslave you. Use you. That won't work, will it? I'll never bend you to my will. No, I think you'll never be more than food for me."

Rohan's grip on himself dimmed. His will was a pillar of energy propping up his essence, his soul, and it narrowed and faded with every second.

What am I to her, after all? Nothing. Not now. To Rinth? Barely a friend. To the Stones? Not a replacement for Hyperion, that's for sure. An annoyance to Marion; casual drinking buddy for Ben. To Wistful? An employee. My closest friend is Wei Li, and she doesn't even really like me.

"Ah, good." Dr. Kraken slurped up another trace of blood. "Now, what shall I do about the others outside? You've depleted my resources. It might be time to arrange an exit."

Rohan choked out half a growl. *Trying to come up with a snappy comeback, but I'm all out at the moment.*

The vampires appeared at the end of the tunnel, carrying a pair of cube-shaped steel containers.

Rohan grunted again.

I'm doing this wrong.

I'm not a wizard. I don't study things, analyze their characteristics, encapsulate their essence into names. That's not what I'm good at.

I'm a Hybrid.

Time to cut loose and show Dr. Kraken what that really means.

Let the temper out.

All the way out.

He stopped thinking about himself. Stopped examining his life, his connections, his past, his feelings. Let go of any thoughts of self-knowledge, of self-examination. Any thoughts of connection, of relationships, of friendship, of more-than-friendship.

Parted his lips and drew in a sharp, deep breath.

Focused his eyes on Dr. Kraken.

Forced his mind back to the last time he was captured by the cephalopod. The whine of a motorized sawblade. The gurgling of the blade biting into his flesh.

Trapped arms. Unresponsive limbs, nervous system dulled by powerful narcotics. Chained to a metal frame for days.

Power began to bubble and churn, just below Rohan's consciousness.

He tortured me.

Shamed me. Tormented me. Fed on my blood. My flesh.

Intended my death.

Me.

Survivor of two years on the Ringgate.

Scourge of Zahad. Conqueror of Tolone'a.

Me.

The Griffin.

My name is a curse on a thousand worlds.

Amber's wrong. That's still who I am. What I am.

Power surged and frothed.

Rohan chuckled as he imagined his Power lapping at the edges of his restraint like waves nibbling at a shoreline.

"It's like the sea. It's funny, because you're a sea creature." The words were slurred and incoherent; the laughter less than sane.

"What?"

Rohan bared his teeth as the Power answered his rage with its own.

I was born to conquer worlds. A weapon of mass destruction. The unfair side of asymmetric warfare. I'm a gun brought to a knife fight.

I'm the one the Fathers turned to when even Hyperion couldn't handle their problems.

Ended the Hybrid Rebellion by squeezing its throat in my hot, sore fingers.

Killed the strongest of them with my bloody fists.

Energy climbed up his body, pouring through his tailbone, then his spine, pushing aside everything else like an icebreaker ship clearing a frozen lake. It was slow; not because it couldn't have been faster, but because it was taking its time. Relishing the fight.

Pushing aside Dr. Kraken's control, one metaphysical centimeter at a time.

My father raised me to be the il'Drach Emperor. To sit on the throne of Drach, Matrons kneeling at my feet, my word law for every living being in the sector.

This creature would sacrifice me to his pathetic gods? Asleep for millions of years, too fat and soft to even stay awake to watch over their subjects?

This sad little thing would threaten my life?

This nobody? This second-rate villain? This cartoon character? This ridiculous caricature of a man?

The rage continued to climb.

His breathing eased as it passed his diaphragm; he sucked in air, blowing it out through loosened lips.

How dare he?

Rohan's focus narrowed.

"How dare you!"

"What? I can't . . . hurry, you two. Bring the drugs. He's fighting me again."

The Hybrid's mouth opened, and a growl came out.

His Power rose up past his mouth, then his palate, finally surging through his skull.

Fingers curled into a fist.

His weight settled to the floor, freed of the Power that had been lifting him. His knees bent as his feet rooted into the stone.

Rohan screamed as he pulled his right fist up into an arc directed at Dr. Kraken's gray-fleshed face.

"Damnit." The cephalopod spoke his own language.

Dr. Kraken leaned back; Rohan's fist sailed past his face.

The Hybrid stepped forward, lips split in a humorless smile.

The vampires dropped their medical cases and charged forward.

Rohan's leg flicked up, into the first vampire's chin.

Its head exploded in a cloud of brain, shards of bone, and a puff of cerebrospinal fluid.

Dr. Kraken's eyes remained impassive.

The second vampire hesitated; Rohan skipped to his left and slapped the creature, his palm catching it across its slimy cheek.

The vampire's neck elongated, stretching and turning, cervical vertebrae popping loudly as the head continued all the way to the rear. The creature dropped.

Dr. Kraken took a half step backward, and Rohan pounced.

He pushed the villain to the ground, an artless two-handed shove to the chest. His Power welled and surged, filling the space between them with raw, untamed hatred.

"Do you even know who I am?" Rohan's words were distorted, incoherent.

Amber spoke over his comm. "What's going on? We don't understand what we're hearing."

Spiral broke in. "Griffin, I'm feeling a lot of anger. Are you okay?"

Rohan jumped onto the doctor's prone figure, his left hand posted on a slimy chest, his Power adding weight to his body, pinning Dr. Kraken to the stone.

He slapped the creature, his right hand snapping across its rubbery face with a sound that split the air.

Gray liquid began to ooze from Dr. Kraken's face.

"Do you?"

Rohan backhanded the cephalopod, whose head snapped back, his cheek bouncing off the stone.

"You want to sacrifice me to your gods? *I* should be your god!"

He punched into its chest. Ribs bent and cracked; the cephalopod coughed, blue fluid spraying out onto Rohan's chest.

"Not those *things* you worship! This is my world! My destiny!"

Another slap.

Wet flesh bounced off the ground.

Rohan growled and punched again, the doctor's humanoid shoulder crunching and disintegrating before the force of his blow.

"Threaten me? Torture me? You should be bowing at my feet!"

He slapped again. Another spray of fluids.

Dr. Kraken's eyes stared at Rohan, black, unblinking, showing no sign of focus or consciousness.

Alien.

With another growl, Rohan grabbed one of the tentacles, anchored to the flesh below Dr. Kraken's maw, and began to pull and twist.

"You unhinged, demented, waste of carbon. Waste of space. Waste of a soul." He twisted again, watching with gleaming eyes as the flesh at the base of the tentacle began to split.

"Threatening my people. My woman. Thinking you *know my name*."

He yanked; a spurt of blood. Yanked again, and the tentacle came loose.

"My name!" His shout echoed off the rocky walls of the chamber. "You don't know one-tenth of what I am! But I'm going to show you!"

He swung; slapped the cephalopod with the severed end of the tentacle. "I'll show you!"

Amber spoke over his comm. "Griffin, what's happening? You're not making any sense. Do you need help? We're trying to bring down the force field. We'll be there soon!"

Another slap; another.

Fluids leaked from Dr. Kraken's head. His body was limp and flat on the ground, his arms splayed to the sides, twitching with each strike.

"Show you!"

Rohan dropped the tentacle and balled his right hand into a fist. He reached up, behind his ear; took a deep breath and prepared to drive his fist down into the cephalopod's face.

A hand caught his wrist.

A man spoke.

A voice that brought back old, painful memories.

"That's enough, chum. He's down. You can stop now. This isn't what heroes do."

Rohan paused, panting, eyes focused on Dr. Kraken's motionless form.

Very slowly, he turned.

A hand held his wrist.

A hand connected to an arm. Attached to a shoulder. Belonging to a man.

A few centimeters shy of two meters tall. Well over a hundred kilograms of lean muscle, sculpted like a boxer's.

Dark hair, graying at the temples; pale skin. A perfect rectangular mustache over his softly smiling lips.

Dressed in a white-and-blue jumpsuit, torn and bloody but oh, so familiar.

Rohan coughed.

"Hyperion?"

8

God or Zombie?

The man pulled on Rohan's wrist, bringing the Hybrid to his feet.

"You all right there, chum? You're leaking quite a bit there. Blood, I mean." He smiled wide, exposing perfect square teeth.

Rohan panted a bit, then slipped his helmet off and into his hood. "Hyperion." His rage popped and dissipated, blown away by a wind of confusion.

The bigger man spread his legs a bit, straightened his back, and pushed both fists into his hips, elbows flared wide. He lifted his chin. "I see you've heard of me. Yes, I am . . . Hyperion." A moment later, he relaxed and held out a hand. "And you are?"

Rohan shook it absentmindedly, his legs weak. "I'm . . . you don't remember?"

Hyperion ran his hand through wavy hair. "Oh, have we met? I'm sorry, my memory isn't quite what it should be. I thought you'd simply heard of me. I'm quite famous."

"Yeah, I know . . . Hyperion."

Hyperion nodded. "Yes! And you are?"

"Oh. Uh . . . The Griffin. Sure."

"Well, I'm pleased to meet you, The Griffin. It looks like you've lent me a solid supporting hand in this particular predicament. Put quite a beating on Professor Octopus here, didn't you? That rubbery flesh is tougher than it looks."

"It's Dr. Kraken."

Hyperion smiled. "Excuse me?"

"His name. It's not . . . Never mind. Just call me Griffin."

"Whatever you say, chum. Now, how about the two of us find a way out of this sea cave and go rescue our friends?"

Rohan's comm chirped. "Griffin! What's going on?" It was Amber.

He coughed. "Dr. Kraken is down. I guess the force field is still up, though."

A pause. "Did you find . . . the prisoner?"

"You mean my old friend Hyperion? He's right here. It's quite a surprise."

Hyperion looked at him. "You weren't expecting me? I thought for sure the other heroes knew I was down here."

"They sent me down in kind of a hurry. I didn't get a full briefing."

Hyperion nodded. "Of course. Only the need-to-knows. Makes total sense."

Rohan's chest felt tight. "There's also the fact that you're dead."

Hyperion tilted his head back and released a loud laugh. "I think it's pretty clear that I'm not, isn't it? Unless you think I'm a zombie. I don't think I am. I'm hungry, but I'm not in the mood to eat brains at all."

"I was there, you know. When you died. Hyperion died. He's dead."

Hyperion nodded and clapped a hand over Rohan's shoulder. "I think you're suffering from some trauma here. You really lost your temper with tentacle-face over there. Just relax and catch your breath. We'll find our way out in no time, and you'll feel better. And don't feel bad, lots of people have been telling me I'm dead. I won't hold it against you."

Hyperion stepped over to Dr. Kraken's body and nudged it with his foot. The cephalopod rolled a bit, then settled back in place, arms twitching. "Still alive."

He repeated the process with the vampires in the room, none of whom proved to be as resilient. Then he knelt by the cylindrical hump in the center of the room.

Masamune spoke to Rohan through the comms. "The force field is still active. There will be a sizable device generating it somewhere in the caverns. Probably close to where you are now."

Rohan tapped the comm to answer. "We're looking right at it."

Hyperion pointed at the hump. "I'm pretty sure this is the source of that force field. If only we can figure out how to disable it. I sure do miss Marion Marley right about now. She was always so good at doing the thinking parts! Oh well, you can't have everything."

Rohan sat heavily, his breathing shallow. "Stone. Marion Stone."

Hyperion turned to him, then slowly tapped the side of his head. "No, I'm pretty sure it's Marion Marley. My memory isn't *that* bad."

"She got married. Took her husband's name."

"What? Really? Gee whiz, I guess I *have* been gone for a while. Well, good for the old gal. Married. To whom?"

"I told you. She's Marion Stone now."

Hyperion laughed. "No way! You mean she married Benjamin! Little Benny? That's fantastic. You know, between you and me, I always thought she kind of fancied me. But I can't blame her for moving on, not with me gone for so long. A girl's got to do." He turned back to the cylinder and ran his hands over the surface, feeling for controls or aberrations. "Do you have any idea how to turn this off?"

Rohan shook his head.

Spiral spoke to him. "Griffin, are you okay?"

"I really don't think I am. I seem to be hallucinating. Was I drugged? I don't remember being drugged."

"What do you mean?"

"I see Hyperion. He's standing right here. Well, not standing. Now he's kneeling and he has his arm stuck down this thing that looks a little bit like a toilet and he's fishing around in there like a man who dropped his wedding ring."

"Okay. Okay, look, Griffin . . . you're not hallucinating. That's Hyperion. He's really down there."

"See, that's where I get confused. That's not possible."

"I know. I know, really. It's been strange for all of us."

"Strange. That's the word you're going to use."

Hyperion looked at Rohan. "Are you talking to me, The Griffin? Sorry, had my ear pressed against this thing."

Rohan tapped the side of his head. "Radio. Talking to the guys outside. Spiral, Amber, Masamune. The Rainbow Stars."

Hyperion nodded. "Great. Carry on. See if they can tell you how to shut this off. Oh wait, I have an idea!" He popped up and walked over to Dr. Kraken.

"Oh look, my hallucination has an idea. Great. I bet he'll get us out of here in no time. I should lose my mind more often."

Spiral coughed. "Look, Griffin, I get it. I can imagine what you're feeling."

"Can you? Really? Because you've been in similar situations yourself? Oh, no, wait, you haven't."

"I knew him, too, Griffin."

"I fought side by side with him on the Ringgate for two years, Spiral. And I was there when he died. It's not quite the same thing."

"Look, okay, I take it back, all right? I don't know how you feel. And I'll be honest, I—we—don't really know what's going on."

"Now you tell me. You didn't think this was information I needed before coming in here?"

"How long would it have taken to explain? To try to explain? Because we don't have any answers. And we couldn't afford to take a few hours or days to hash it out."

Hyperion picked up Dr. Kraken's severed tentacle and walked over to the field generator. He reached over it and lowered the tentacle into the hole in the hump's center.

Rohan called out. "What are you doing?"

Hyperion shrugged. "I thought it might be like a cell phone. You know, you swipe your fingerprint over it, unlock the phone. Except with tentacles."

"That's . . ." *That might actually work.* "Carry on, then."

Hyperion nodded and wiggled the tentacle, dragging it around the inside of the hole, then over the top surface of the generator.

Spiral continued. "If it's any consolation, I'm sorry. I wanted you to know Dr. Kraken was in there, but I was outvoted."

"As long as my trauma was the result of a fair and even electoral process, I suppose I can't complain."

"Ha ha. I'll tell you what we know. This guy appeared a few weeks ago. He's real, flesh and blood."

"Not a shapeshifter? A clone?"

"He's not a shapeshifter. Lyst tested him. And I don't think he can be a clone. He looks exactly like Hyperion, for one thing. And it's supposed to be impossible to clone a Hybrid."

"It's *supposed* to be impossible to come back from the dead."

"I know. It's weird. We had empaths test him. He really believes he's Hyperion."

"He believes. What do you believe?"

"I . . . I honestly don't know, okay? It seems impossible. But we've seen some strange shit in our lives, Griffin. You really want to tell me that you're positive that anything is impossible? You've traveled across the galaxy."

"Right. I've been across the galaxy, and every place I've gone, everybody agrees that people don't come back from the dead." Rohan slouched forward, wrapping his arms around his knees, the cold of the stone floor slowly chilling his rear end.

Hyperion stood and tossed the tentacle to the side. "Nope. Not working. You think it needs his face? Maybe that's it! I'll try that."

"Don't take his head off, Hyperion."

"You're too funny! I'll just drag him over. No face-removal happening here. Ha! Take his head off. Funny. We should be friends."

We were *friends.*

Amber took over the channel. "Griffin, you need to hurry. Oxygen levels are falling. I know you guys aren't exactly human, but you need air. If you fall unconscious, we have no easy way to get you out."

Rohan sighed and hung his head. "I need a minute."

"You don't have a minute. If you're feeling crappy, it could be the beginning of hypoxia. Start working on an escape."

I'm wearing a helmet, but maybe Hyperion is weird because of the oxygen levels.

The Hybrid grunted and watched as Hyperion shoved Dr. Kraken's limp head into the generator's hole over and over, like a bully giving swirlies to a child in elementary school.

I need to stand up and do something. This isn't like me. All that anger drained out when I saw him. Hyperion. Or whoever he is.

Rohan set both hands on the floor and pushed himself up into a bridge, then stood wearily.

"Hey, Hyperion."

The other man turned. "What's up, chum? Did you have an idea?"

"Yeah. Stop messing around and just tear that generator apart."

"What?"

"You heard me. You're Hyperion, aren't you? Strongest person on Earth. Maybe the strongest person in the entire sector. Just tear it apart. Rip it to pieces."

The man's jaw dropped slightly. He swallowed. "We don't really know what this is, or how it works. What if it explodes? People could get hurt."

"Yes. People could get hurt. But if we don't get out of here soon, people will definitely get hurt. Us. When we suffocate. So, stop messing around; you're getting nowhere. Just tear that apart."

"Look, chum, violence doesn't solve any problems. It just creates more problems."

"Are you kidding me? Violence solves all kinds of problems. You're famous because of violence. You're really, really good at it." He began to feel energy stirring inside again, his Power responding to his irritation.

"No, that's not right. Yes, I'm very strong, but I help people find peaceful solutions to difficult situations. That's why I'm famous."

Rohan blew through his lips. "Bull. What do you think you are, a chess player? A diplomat? Your face is known across the planet because you can pound your fist through a ten-centimeter-thick plate of titanium without batting an eye. So do it."

Hyperion shook his head slowly. "I negotiated a treaty. With aliens. Got all sorts of great technology for this planet."

"Why do you think they gave us that technology? Because you offered to take me and every other Hybrid on Earth off to the Ringgate and kill Wedge. Thousands of them. Millions. You—no, we—earned that treaty by being weapons of mass destruction."

Hyperion held his hands up. "I'm sure it seemed that way to you at the time, but—"

Rohan growled, stepped forward, and brought a fist down in a hammer-strike on top of the generator.

Runes flashed and sparked across the surface of the meter-high stone structure. The cave echoed with the sound of the impact.

"Like that." He hopped up, reaching his other hand toward the ceiling, then dropped it down onto the same spot.

More sparks flared. Hyperion winced away from the collisions. Rohan's Power surged again, pushing up against the lowest levels of his consciousness.

"This is what you are. Right, Hyperion?" He said the name with a sneer. "What we are."

He punched the generator again, Power pulsing through his lower belly, up across his body into his shoulder, through his upper arm, crossing the elbow, and finally erupting through his clenched fist.

Runes flared and died.

Stone chips flew. Hyperion stepped back.

Rohan growled. "This is how we stop things." He began alternating fists, each hand stretching toward the ceiling, then slamming onto the generator, his hips dipping into a deep squat with each strike.

Stalactites loosened and fell around them. Pieces of stone dropped like a scree monsoon.

"This is what we do. What you taught me. Remember, Hyperion? This is what *you* taught *me*. At the end of the day, when the talking's done, when the negotiations have failed, everything will be fine if you can just keep hitting hard enough."

More runes burst into short-lived flames. Chunks fell out of the side of the generator.

Amber spoke over the comms. "It's working. The field is flickering now. Keep doing whatever you're doing."

Hyperion shook his head. "Maybe that's what you are, but it's not what I am."

Rohan pounded away. A stone chip struck his facemask, pinging off the diamond plate.

"You don't know what you are! Where were you six months ago? Where were you a year ago when giant sharks almost ended the human race and I had to stop them? What happened when you died? Where did you go after Rhyllax Four?"

Amber's voice, conducted directly through his cheekbone. "Don't push him so hard, Rohan. We don't really know what he is. Or what will happen. He's as confused as the rest of us."

Rohan growled as he spotted a crack in the generator. He jammed his fingers into the fissure and yanked at the stone, widening the space, splitting the hump almost in half.

He fell back, landing on the ground as the generator fell apart.

Hyperion looked up at the ceiling. "That doesn't look so stable, chum. We should get out of here."

Rohan panted and nodded, slowly standing.

Hyperion smiled. "That's the spirit. Let's go rescue our friends."

"Rescue who?"

"The others, of course! The Fluorescent Moons. Muramasa. That Helix fellow."

"Rainbow Stars. They don't need rescuing, Hyperion. We came here to rescue you. From Dr. Kraken."

"Yes, Professor Octopus. I had him right where I wanted him. Lulled into a false sense of confidence. Torturing me for a day got him to really let his guard down."

Rohan exhaled. Inhaled again; too fast. He couldn't slow his breathing. "That's . . . quite a plan. You really showed him."

"I know! I'm quite clever. Sometimes I even surprise myself. Now, are you certain the others don't require rescuing?"

"They're safe." Rohan flinched as a large chunk of stone fell from the ceiling and crashed to the floor. "Let's go see them."

"You got it, chum." He turned around, surveying the exit tunnels. "Which way is out?"

9

Pizza and Beer

An hour later, two nurses were chatting about their romantic misadventures in one of the Sudanese languages while putting the finishing touches on Rohan's bandages. He sat on a neatly made hospital bed, his fresh jumpsuit, identical to the one he'd been wearing before entering Dr. Kraken's cave, open and hanging off his waist, leaving his upper body exposed. The sheets were stamped with the logo of Vanguard Medical Center, the hospital in Sahara City that was dedicated to keeping the Powers of Earth in fighting shape.

He bit the end off a triangular wedge of pizza, fresh from the Vanguard kitchen, sighing at the perfect chewiness of the crust.

"Gluten just might be the greatest contribution of Earth to galactic cuisine."

One of the nurses smiled and answered in English. "Yes, sir. Almost finished."

He answered in Fire Speech. "You should give the short one a second chance. There are plenty of tall men in the world, but someone who will take you to the hospital and sit next to you all night is somebody special."

The nurses exchanged a glance, then continued in English.

"See, that's just what I was telling you, too. He's a good man. Your standards are too high."

"I know that, I do. And he's cute, too, in his own way."

A knock at the door drew their attention.

The Director of Hyperion Industries, the most powerful person on Earth, stood in the room's entrance. Slender, with dark eyes and cheekbones that had been almost enough for a film career, she wore a blue, green, and gold sari. Her expression was composed.

Rohan swallowed.

The first nurse looked up. "Almost done here, ma'am."

The Director nodded. "Just make sure he's taken care of. The way things have been going . . ."

The second nurse nodded. "Of course, ma'am. One minute." She finished adjusting the bandage on Rohan's shoulder and deftly scooped wrappers and instruments into a stainless-steel tray for removal.

The nurses' eyes met, and they hurried out.

The Director watched them go, motioning to two black-suit clad security men behind her to step back as she closed the door. A quick tap at a keypad near the door, then she turned to her son.

She crossed the room in three quick steps and bent to hug him, then leaned back and held his face.

"Are you okay?"

"Yeah, Mom. Most of it was superficial stuff. I'll heal up in no time."

She nodded and examined him, patting his belly. "You're getting skinny. I thought there was good food on that space station of yours?"

He smiled. "It's fine. Just been training a lot."

She raised an eyebrow. "Oh? Why?"

He shrugged. "You know, I try to live a peaceful life, but stuff keeps happening. And since I don't know how to make it stop, and I can't just ignore things when people are dying, I end up getting involved. Which means fighting."

"And if you're going to fight, you'd better be prepared to fight. As your father used to say."

"I mean, Dad might be a jerk, but he wasn't wrong."

She smiled and eyed the full pie perched on a table next to him. "May I?"

"Of course. I can't eat all that. How's Carla?"

She took a slice and bit into it. "She's good. We're good. Busy rebuilding the Pacific Rim. You don't want to hear about all of that."

He swallowed another bite. "Good. I'm glad."

"How are you, Rohan? Really? You look tense."

He grimaced. "I kind of lost my temper in there. Something I've been trying to avoid. Dr. Kraken had me trapped, and the only way I could get free was to just work myself into a rage. I would have killed him, if not for Hyperion."

She rubbed the back of his hand. "I know I've been telling you to control your temper for years, Rohan, but that doesn't sound like the worst thing. And he *did* stop you."

"I know. Sometimes punching things is the best solution. But I always feel crappy afterward, wondering if there was another way. And I know that if I stop doing that, stop questioning and regretting it, it's just going to keep getting easier. Then I'll be back to where I was three years ago."

She smiled. "Sounds like my son has done some growing up."

"Not too much. Maybe a little. Anyway, right now I just want to see Bright Angel, make sure she's okay, then get out of here."

Her eyes widened. "You're in a rush?"

"I need to get back to Wistful."

She smiled. "Is this about a girl?"

"Yes. Maybe. I'm not sure. But, yes. You're a good guesser."

"I know my son. But what about . . . our other guest?"

"You mean Hyperion?"

She nodded. "Is he Hyperion? What do you think?"

"You tell me."

"I have, literally, my best people working on that. We've run every medical diagnostic we can think of."

"And?"

"All inconclusive. It's not like we had his DNA on file. You know how the il'Drach are about Hybrid biological samples. But every test result is consistent with that man being Hyperion."

"Except that people don't come back from the dead."

"The only proof we have that Hyperion ever died is your word, son. Maybe you were mistaken? Maybe it was a ploy? A way for him to get free of the il'Drach?"

Rohan shook his head. "I can't say I haven't been thinking the same thing, Mom. But it doesn't add up. If it was part of some scheme, what happened to him? His memory? Where was he when the sharks attacked Earth? If he had to go into hiding, why is he just walking around now, telling everyone who he is?"

She nodded. "Does he . . . feel like Hyperion? I knew the man, but you spent more time with him than anybody still on the planet. What do you think?"

Rohan paused. "A little bit. Parts of him. But really, he acts like the Hyperion from the kids' cartoon they made. Or from the comics. I'd almost think he was a cosplayer or a robot, except . . . he's not."

"We thought the same thing. We checked."

There was a knock on the door.

The Director stood and tapped it. The door slid open, and a portly orderly came in with a tray. He put it down, then smiled and left.

A half dozen cans of beer were on the tray, their sides moist with condensation.

Rohan shrugged, took a beer, and popped the top. "He's not my Hyperion. My Hyperion is dead. I just want to see Bright Angel and get back to my job."

"I think Masamune will want to talk to you about that."

"What do you mean?"

"Didn't you owe him a favor?"

"Yeah. Rescue what-do-we-call-him. Maybe-Hyperion."

She shook her head. "That's not what you agreed to. He said rescue, then protect. It was an open comm."

Rohan pinched the skin between his eyebrows, massaging away the beginnings of a headache. "Oh crap. You're right. I did. I forgot. There's too much going on. But wait, we took care of Dr. Kraken. He's not going to be bothering anybody else for a while."

"Dr. Kraken isn't the only danger to Hyperion."

"Of course it's not that easy. What else?"

"There were attacks before Dr. Kraken captured him."

Rohan groaned. "The Drexians. That's how Bright Angel got hurt. She was protecting Hyperion."

The Director nodded as she put down a half-eaten slice of pizza. She picked up a can of beer, popped the top, and sipped. "This is awful."

Rohan shrugged. "You don't drink beer, Mom."

"Then why is this here?"

"I asked for it. To go with the pizza. Stay on track, Mom. Why are the Drexians attacking Hyperion?"

She narrowed her eyes at him. "I thought you could tell me. Not many people around even recognize the species."

Rohan drank. "I can guess. Actually, I can make a lot of guesses. If people off-world think that Hyperion is alive, a whole lot of them are going to be very interested in that fact. I wasn't really thinking it through." He put the beer down and ran his fingers through his long hair. "This isn't great. Especially not with that guy as useless as he is."

"Is he useless? He has Powers. I'm not sure he's Hyperion level, but they're considerable."

"He does, but he's not a fighter like Hyperion was. The Empire is going to want to talk to him. Everyone who hates the Empire will want to talk to him even more. I can't decide if he's going to have more people out to kill him or recruit him. And none of them are going to take no for an answer or be pleasant about it."

"So, he's not safe here."

Rohan drained his beer. "He's not safe anywhere, and neither is anybody around him."

"Then, we should move him. Right now, everyone in this city is collateral damage waiting to happen."

Rohan cracked open another beer. *I was never much of a beer drinker, but apparently I missed it.* "Did you have anyplace in mind?"

She sipped her drink, grimacing again as the hops hit her tongue. "I was hoping Masamune would take him, but he thinks that could be worse. Something about 'consequences' if the il'Drach find a deserter staying with him."

"Ouch. Yeah, I guess technically, if this guy is Hyperion, he deserted from Fleet."

She pursed her lips. "Someplace underground? Find a secret location and hope he's not found? Or build a fortress somewhere and put everyone we have in it?"

"Are you still studying him? Do we need a bunch of lab stuff and techs along?"

She put the beer down and took another bite of pizza, a strand of cheese hanging down her cheek. Rohan reached up and pushed it over so she could eat it.

A smile flashed over her lips, then passed. "The science people aren't giving me any answers, and to be honest, they're not suggesting any further avenues of research. You can ditch them."

Rohan scratched his beard. "Okay. Let's get him away from populated areas. Spiral and Amber have a few safehouses scattered around. Cost of doing business when you spend your life fighting secret societies. Let me ask if they'll let us crash in one of them."

The Director nodded. "That seems sound. What then? Do you have any longer-term plan?"

"No. One thing at a time. Right now, I just want to check in on Bright Angel."

"I'm sure you do." Her tone was suggestive.

"Mom, it's not like that."

"Of course it isn't. Of course."

"Who taught you to be sarcastic, Mom?"

She patted his hand. "I must have picked it up from my son. I'll find out if she's awake."

The Director stepped to the door and composed herself, her features cooling as she readied to face the outside world. A world that didn't know Rohan was her son. Then she opened the door and spoke softly to the people waiting outside. Rohan finished his slice, lined beers in the emptied-out side of the pizza box, and closed it.

His mother turned from the doorway. "I have a meeting, Griffin. As always. I'll leave Albert right here. Whenever you're ready, he'll take you to Bright Angel."

Rohan nodded. "Thank you." Then quickly added, "Director."

One of the security personnel held a hand to his ear, nodding, then spoke. "Director, ma'am, there's a disturbance at Hyperion Headquarters. One of the Vanguard ready rooms."

She opened her mouth to answer just as a gust of wind blew by, drawing the breath out of her.

Amber materialized in front of Rohan. "Hey." The Director's security guards paused, hands halfway to their guns.

Rohan blinked. "Emergency?"

Amber shook her head as she gathered her hair into a ponytail and slipped a tie over it. "Not yet, not exactly. Poseidon came back. He's in a mood; he's kind of wrecking the break room. Which is fine, I guess, but I'm worried he'll escalate to doing structural damage."

Vanguard Headquarters were part of a massive building housing Hyperion Industries offices. If it were damaged, or came down in a way that damaged adjacent buildings, the losses would be tremendous.

"You think I can calm him down?"

"Not sure. Right now, Spiral is getting ready to fight him."

"Can Spiral stop Poseidon?"

Amber shrugged. "The real question is, can Spiral stop Poseidon without bringing the building down? And the answer is, I'm not sure. I think Bright Angel could restrain him if she were healthy, but . . ."

He pulled his mask over his face. "Okay. Speed me over there."

She nodded and waved him over. He set down the pizza and stepped close.

Rohan felt the world shimmer as Amber bent time, accelerating its flow for the two of them relative to the rest of the world. She grabbed his hand and hurried through the door and down the hall.

He smiled as they passed his mother and her security team, their expressions frozen, arms locked into fixed positions, sealed in a single moment.

Amber led him through the cavernous building, down a dozen flights of stairs, through an underground tunnel, and into the Vanguard Headquarters area.

She released her Power as they neared the break room. Splashes and shattering glass greeted them.

Spiral turned to face them from his spot by the open doorway. He had a similar height and build to Rohan, but with features more common to Eastern, not Southern, Asia. He wore a loose red cotton jacket and black pants tightened close to his ankles. His hair, as always, was cut close to his scalp, the same length as his beard. He pointed through the door. "He's in there. You want to try talking to him?"

"What happened?"

Spiral shrugged. "He fought Dr. Kraken's minions for two whole days. I think he overextended. It's like he doesn't have enough left to hold himself together. Hyperion's return already freaked him out. And he's always volatile. God of storms, remember?"

"He got back from the fight with Dr. Kraken and ran up to see Hyperion in Medical. Went to give the big guy a hug and lost it. Started yelling, said he wanted to beat the truth out of him. I got in his way, he threw a punch, I stopped it."

Rohan scratched under the gaiter covering his face. "You. Stopped a punch from a god."

Spiral shrugged. "It's my new technique. I'll show you later. Now . . ."

Another crash.

Half a dozen Hyperion Industries security personnel stood around, armed and dressed in light armor, chattering into phones as they eyed the break room. None seemed eager to face off with an angry god.

Rohan sighed and walked through the open door.

The screens that covered the room's walls were shattered, two of them dislodged from their mounts and sagging against the floor. The furniture had been overturned and wrecked, rendered into a sea of unrecognizable, jagged wooden ends and strips of upholstery.

Poseidon stood in the middle of the room next to a stack of three crates. The top crate was open, polished wood torn away, revealing a diminishing forest of wine bottles. As Rohan watched, he tipped his head back and inverted an open bottle over his face, wine streaming into his mouth and over his cheeks in equal measure.

The god was tall and muscular, with long white hair and a full beard that covered his chest. He stood stripped to the waist, his bare feet pressing carelessly into the shards of green glass that littered the floor.

When the flow of wine stopped, he shook the bottle, then tossed it against the far wall.

Rohan cleared his throat. "Hey there, buddy. What's going on?" He tried to keep his voice calm.

Poseidon turned bloodshot eyes toward the Hybrid. "Griffin! You sorry excuse for a hero. I heard they called you in. Is that really you? Or another of those damned hallucinations?"

Rohan moved a few steps closer, hands open, palms up in what he hoped was the universal posture meaning 'I am harmless.'

"Hallucinations? What's going on? Have you been having some problems? Maybe we can help with that."

Poseidon laughed and turned to his crate. He rummaged through the bottles, then settled on one and plucked it out. He held it out to Rohan. "Drink?"

Rohan shook his head. "I've already had a couple of beers."

Poseidon nodded and held up the wine. He took careful aim with the edge of one hand, then violently struck the tip off the bottle. Rohan sighed as the god upended it over his mouth.

"Poseidon, you want to tell me why you're causing such a ruckus?"

The god didn't answer. He let the rest of the bottle's contents pour over his face, then smashed it against the far wall with the others. "What difference does it make, Griffin? What difference does any of it make? He got away again, you know. As always."

"Who got away?" A sour feeling in Rohan's gut told him he already knew.

"Your nemesis, and mine. Dr. Kraken. I searched his caves after they collapsed. Sent fish through the rubble. I can see through their eyes. Did you know that? Not many people know that."

"I think everybody knows that, Poseidon. It's kind of your thing. God of the sea."

"People think they know. But do they really know? Do they know that they know? What do any of us know, or know that we know?"

"You lost me, man."

Poseidon picked up another bottle. "I thought I knew things. Mortals die, they don't come back. I've seen it so many times. So many. All those years, learning to live with those losses. And yet . . ."

"Ah. That. I'm not sure what's going on with Hyperion."

Poseidon swung toward Rohan, wine-stained beard flipping up as he spun. "Don't you call him that! Do not! I knew Hyperion, more than knew, and that . . . thing is not him!"

Rohan backed up a step, arms up again. "Okay, okay. Got it."

"Gods have died. Ares is gone. My friends are gone, most of them. They have died and not come back. That's not supposed to be the way, Griffin. We are meant to be immortal. Yet we die. And that . . . thing has the audacity to claim to be a mortal, returned?"

"I can see how that upsets you. I can. But smashing wine bottles isn't going to make anything any better."

"Who is to say, Griffin? Who is to say what is, or what will be, or what better even means? The world has grown beyond my understanding, Griffin. It has betrayed me and I. Will. Not. Have it." He looked around the floor and spotted an intact table leg. He lifted it, along with an attached piece of marble, and hurled it into the monitor to his left.

The screen shattered completely; the walls of the room shook. Rohan turned to the doorway where Amber and Spiral stood. They shrugged in unison.

Poseidon raged. "I will not have it! I will not have this world of lies!"

Rohan cracked his neck. "I really need you to be more careful, Poseidon. You can drink all you want, and smash up this room if you think it will help, but you're going to take down the building and hurt a lot of people if you don't scale this back."

Poseidon turned to him and smiled. "What will you do, little Hybrid? Will you fight me? Do you think yourself enough to stop me without, as you say, taking down this building?"

A new voice called in from the doorway. "Poseidon. That's enough."

Bright Angel stepped inside. Skin a few shades darker than Rohan's; hair braided tight to her scalp; wearing her costume, white with silver and blue accents. She stood on a pair of wooden crutches, her right leg immobilized in heavy bandages.

Rohan swallowed.

Poseidon held up his bottle. "Are you threatening me, Bright Angel? What will you do?"

She grunted. "I know you're hurting, Poseidon. I know seeing Hyperion is hard."

Rohan cleared his throat. "You maybe shouldn't—"

Poseidon shouted. "Don't call him that!" The third monitor fell off its brackets and crashed to the floor.

Bright Angel nodded. "Fine. Whatever he is. It's hard for all of us, Poseidon." She part-walked and part-hopped forward on her crutches, halving the distance between them.

"You don't understand, woman. Thousands of years on this world. Everything I've learned is being stripped away. A human, without Powers, stopped a blow from my fist. I am diminished beyond reason."

She shrugged. "We all have different burdens to bear, Poseidon. I know what will help. Come on, come here." She propped one crutch with her armpit and reached an arm out.

"What?"

"I said come here. You need a hug."

The god's face was damp. "You think I need . . ."

"Come here. Come on. Mortals live with uncertainty and confusion all the time. We've had to figure out ways to live with it. This is one of them. Come on. Give your old friend a hug."

Poseidon dropped his bottle and stumbled toward her, glass crunching under his feet.

She nodded. "That's it. Come here. Everything will be better."

"Will it?"

"It might not get perfect, and we might not fix everything, but yes, it will be better. Have a hug. Then we'll get you some food. Maybe pizza."

He leaned in and wrapped heavy arms around her body. She hugged him back, squeezing him close.

He leaned his head on her shoulder and wept silently. "Pizza sounds good."

10

True Mythology

B right Angel hobbled along beside Poseidon, directing him to an undamaged cafeteria down the hall. Security guards followed at a distance, their faces relaxing with every step, and someone called for a team to clean and repair the break room.

Amber looked at Rohan, shrugged, and followed.

Rohan turned to Spiral. "You think I should have hugged him? I think so. Didn't occur to me."

Spiral smiled. "You just wish you'd thought of throwing a temper tantrum of your own. Then she might have given you a hug, too."

Rohan sighed. "Am I that transparent?" He began walking after the others, Spiral alongside.

"Nah, you're fine. Are you still pining after her?"

"Only when I think about it. I mean, she's pretty great. And hot. As you can see. But everything she told me about why we wouldn't work a year ago still holds true."

Spiral patted his shoulder. "Just keep remembering that and you'll be fine. And hey, thanks for showing up. Masamune seemed to think you were the best chance at that rescue."

Rohan shrugged. "I didn't have much choice. And it's not like I made an informed decision, is it? Nobody told me what was going on."

"No. It's not how I would have handled things, but I'm not in charge." Spiral stopped walking and pulled at Rohan's shoulder. "Listen, let me talk to you for a minute. Separately."

Rohan turned as Spiral ducked into a darkened office, following his friend. "What's up?"

Spiral palmed on the lights and faced him. "I have something to give you."

"A present? Is it tequila?"

"Not exactly. Maybe I should say, something to pass on."

"Huh." Rohan scratched his beard. "Are you dying?"

Spiral laughed. "Not that I know of. No, this is Orphan Clan business."

Rohan frowned. "This is about martial arts?"

"Yes. Spiral branch of Orphan Clan martial arts. I'm naming you my disciple."

"Me? You're asking me to be your disciple?"

"Not asking, naming. You don't have a choice. You're my disciple now, remember? You have to do what I say."

"I'm not . . . shouldn't it be Amber? She trains with you, like, all the time."

Spiral shook his head. "She doesn't really study my style. I mean, yes, I train her, but I train her to use techniques that work with her time-controlling abilities. And, sure, some basics from Orphan Clan Style, but it's not the full art."

"I didn't learn the full art either, did I? I always mixed in flying and stuff."

"I know. What you have isn't exactly . . . Look, let me start again. I developed the final form for my art. The ultimate technique."

"Well, that's cool. Awesome. Is that how you stopped Poseidon's punch? And fought on a level with the Rainbow Stars? Because neither of those seem like possible things."

"Yes. Look, I've been working on something for a while now. You know what my goal has always been: to develop a martial art that enables regular people to stand up to Powers."

Rohan ran his fingers through his hair. He leaned back against the edge of a solid wooden desk. "I remember."

"I figured it out. It's sort of a way to cancel out a Power differential."

"That's . . . I don't know what to say. You used that to stop Poseidon's punch?"

"I did. It's not easy, though."

"If it were easy, other people would have worked it out. And they'd be using it."

"Right. So, here, take this." He reached over to Rohan, a slender chain in his hand.

The Hybrid took the chain. From the middle dangled a pendant, a simple fixture with a clear gemstone the size of the last joint of his pinky.

"Is this . . . what is this? Is this a soulgem?"

Spiral nodded. "Lyst helped me make it. She thought it worthwhile. In case something happens to me. If you *push* some ki through the gem and open your Third Eye wide, you can see the shape of the energy that makes the technique work. If you figure that out, you'll understand how to use it."

Rohan's heartbeat quickened. Soulgems were rare. And precious.

"This doesn't *do* anything, does it?"

"No, no. It's just enough for you to see what the technique looks like. Like a picture. It's how wizards pass on spells. Same idea. I trapped the spiritual image of the technique in the crystal."

"Why are you giving this to me now?"

"Because you're here. I would have given it to you months ago, but . . . space."

"I mean, why me? Why not Amber?"

Spiral sighed. "She has the wrong sort of ki. It has to be firm, but flexible. Hers is too rigid. Too sharp. She can make her ki into a sword. Bend time. But she can't do this."

"And mine is the right kind?"

"Yours is the right kind. The question is, can you shape it the right way? I'm not sure. Once your anger flares up, you can't really do the subtle work anymore. So you'd have to stay calm to use it."

Rohan turned the necklace over and over in his hand. The chain looked like gold but probably wasn't gold. The soulgem looked like, if anything, a huge diamond.

"I don't know what to say."

"Take it. Study it. If you really can't figure it out, pass it on to someone else. It's important."

"I think I know what you mean, but why don't you pretend I don't and explain it?"

Spiral nodded. "It's a leveler. A way for the weak to face the strong. It's probably the most important thing I've ever done."

"You saved Amber's life. And lots of others."

"Yeah. I know what I've done, and I know what I said."

Rohan slipped the necklace over his head. "Okay, man. I'll look at it. Right now, I want to talk to Bright Angel and find Hyperion. I haven't seen him since the caves."

Spiral pointed to the hallway outside, where Hyperion was walking toward the cafeteria, whistling softly. His face brightened, handlebar mustache twitching with his smile when he saw the two.

"Hey, The Griffin! Single! Did you guys see the break room? It's a mess! Someone must have really not liked the pizza." Rohan rubbed his forehead. *Stay here and guard this guy or go back to Wistful and meet up with Tamaralinth. Keeping my promises is becoming less and less appealing.*

Spiral walked over to the big man. "It's Spiral."

"That's what I said! Spiral. Maybe they put pineapple on it! Some people get really touchy about that. So I hear. Anyway, good news, they let me out of the medical wing. Said I'm okey-dokey to walk around."

Spiral nodded. "That's great, that's great. Let's get some of that pizza, shall we?"

"As long as it doesn't make us do what that last guy did. Am I right?"

Spiral put his hand on Hyperion's back and gently nudged him down the hall. "You're right. Come on, Bright Angel is in there. I'm sure you want to thank her for saving you from those assassins."

"Save me? I had them right where I wanted them. I sure am sorry that she got in the way and got hurt, though. I should probably tell her that."

"Yes. Or no. Maybe don't say too much; she's still weak. Just thank her for being there for you, maybe?"

Hyperion nodded. "Thanks, Specific. You're a pal."

Spiral turned to lock eyes with Rohan, who shrugged. "Just go inside."

Amber's voice was audible in the hall. "Does anybody have a better idea? If not, we should take him to our safehouse as soon as possible."

Hyperion stepped through the door. "Oh, pizza!" He crossed the room and grabbed a slice off the long table that dominated one wall. Poseidon grunted and moved to the other side of the room.

Spiral entered the room. "Which safehouse?"

Amber turned. "I was thinking the place in Canada."

"Not bad. Mountains. Remote. We have a lot of tech there. Monitoring, cameras."

Bright Angel, on a chair with her bad leg propped up straight in front of her and crutches propped up against her back, looked up at Amber. "Who knows about it?"

Amber shrugged. "Bamf has sent us there. I don't think the house has ever been connected to us, and we did all the security work ourselves. It's the best we're going to find, I think."

Bright Angel nodded. "That's probably good, then. How are you for supplies?"

Spiral grabbed a slice for himself. "There are military style rations for months in the basement. It's off the grid but well stocked. We can have Bamf send through some fresh food and snacks."

Hyperion swallowed. "A trip! That sounds like fun. Who's going?"

Bright Angel looked at him. "You are, Hyperion. It's not safe here." She pointed to her leg. "Too many people around who are going to get hurt."

Hyperion frowned. "Well, I can't just run away to the mountains in Canada. Or anywhere. I'm Hyperion."

Bright Angel's eyebrows came together in a frown. "What do you mean?"

"I'm a hero of Earth. What would people think if I just ran away and hid? That's not good. I need to be out there, fighting. For justice."

Poseidon cleared his throat. "You're not Hyperion."

Hyperion scratched behind his ear. "I know that you don't believe me, but I am. I'll show you. But I can't do that by hiding up in the mountains."

Bright Angel shook her head. "We can't protect you anywhere else, and we can't protect the innocent people around you."

"I'm not asking you to protect me. I'm Hyperion; I'll be doing the protecting."

Amber looked at him. "If you don't want to go to the mountains, where do you want to go? The Director said it isn't safe here."

He took a bite of pizza large enough to feed an entire person and spoke while chewing. "You know, I've been thinking about that. I was just in the hospital, getting checked out, and they put on the television. To keep me occupied. And I saw the most wonderful show about a place I'd like to see. I'm sure I've been to other cities but I only remember Chicago."

Rohan cleared his throat. "Where, Hyperion?"

"Las Vegas."

Poseidon shook his head. "He'll level the place. Shame, too. I liked Vegas."

Amber rubbed her forehead. "Vegas? Really? Why?"

Hyperion shrugged. "It's pretty. Lots of lights. And they seem to have a lot of fun there."

She turned to Rohan. "Vegas? You're the one who's supposed to keep him safe, say something!"

Rohan sighed. "Hyperion, are you sure we shouldn't go to the mountains for a while? There are a lot of people after you. The Empire could get really annoyed by the fact that you're walking around. It's dangerous."

Hyperion laughed. "Danger? I scoff at danger. See, I'm scoffing! Oh wait, is that a cough? Or was it a laugh. Never mind. If the Empire wants a piece of me, let them come."

Bright Angel shook her head. "This is a terrible idea. Hyperion, you can't just walk around Las Vegas while there are teams of alien assassins roaming around trying to kill you."

"Of course I can. I'm a hero. That's what we do: when danger is near, we continue the fight for justice."

She turned to Rohan. "You can either talk some sense into him or beat it in. Your choice."

Hyperion straightened, sticking his chest out. "You won't find it so easy to beat sense into me! I'm Hyperion."

Rohan shook his head. "Relax, buddy." He turned to Bright Angel. "I . . . we can't. Not really. What are we going to do, stick him in a cell? Because people are after him? That's not right. Let me take him to Vegas. Maybe we can flush out whoever's after him. First sign of trouble, I'll hightail us both out of there."

Bright Angel shrugged, the silver accents in her uniform catching the light. "I almost lost the leg. I need a couple more days to heal. I can't come, but I'm not going to try to stop you either. Even though I think it's a bad idea."

Rohan looked at Amber, then Spiral. "What do you guys think?"

Amber nodded. "I agree with both of you. It *is* a terrible idea, but we shouldn't force him to stay here. We can go with you."

Hyperion stuffed the remaining half slice of pizza in his mouth, freeing his hands, and clapped. "Yay! I'm really excited! Chicago was not as much fun as you'd think."

Amber shook her head. "You were homeless, with no money, walking around Chicago in winter dressed in nothing other than that uniform and telling everybody you were a long-dead superhero. I promise, visiting Chicago as an actual tourist would be a lot better."

Rohan nodded. "This might be good. I'm rich, let me go to Vegas and spend some money. Have a little fun." *Keep me from thinking about where I really want to be.*

Spiral shrugged. "I'll pack our stuff."

Amber looked around the room. "Someone should tell the Director."

All heads pivoted toward Rohan.

"I see how this is going. I'll tell her."

⬤ ⋯ ⬤

An hour later, Rohan ducked his head through the door of the ruined break room, a freshly issued credit card with a limit high enough to purchase a small country in his pocket.

"Poseidon?"

The god had returned to the scene of his crime and was methodically, though less destructively, working his way through the crate of wine he had been smashing.

Poseidon looked up, his long white hair falling in a tangled curtain over his face.

"Ah, Griffin, my friend. I hope you are holding up better than I." The god tilted back an open bottle of wine and took a sip.

Rohan walked over to the crate and picked up a bottle that looked good. He held it at arm's length, stiffened his hand, and sliced the tip off with a chop.

"Like that?"

Poseidon laughed. "Well done! Not bad at all for a Hybrid. Though Hyp—" His voice cut off.

Rohan sat on the floor next to him. Someone had come through and swept up the broken glass, leaving wine stains across the floor and walls for later.

"I know. Hyperion could do it better."

Poseidon raised the bottle in his hand, as if preparing to throw it against the wall, then lowered it. "Bah. You must hate seeing that thing as much as I do."

Rohan shrugged. "I don't know what to think. I'm kind of numb."

Poseidon took another swallow of wine. "Then, you have achieved the goal for which I am striving, young Hybrid. I envy you your numbness."

"I have a bad feeling it just means everything is going to hit me harder in a little while."

"Hyperion was your mentor, was he not?"

Rohan drank some wine and scratched his beard. "He saved my life a hundred times. Taught me to fight. Taught me how to survive. My father was . . . never mind. I didn't have a father I could look up to. Hyperion gave me that."

Poseidon nodded. "I never had a true father."

"I thought Zeus was your father? No, Cronus? I'm sorry. I should know those stories better."

"Aye, Cronus was my father. But I never knew him. I first existed as you see me now, Griffin. I never knew a childhood, or mother or father. Or family. Not truly."

"Huh. You just . . . appeared?"

"Verily. Already, by appearance, a grown man, with the powers of a god."

"Where did you come from?"

Poseidon laughed. "That is a most excellent question, young Hybrid. And one for which I have no adequate answer. Do you remember your own birth, sliding squalling and damp into a cold, bright world?"

"I guess not." Rohan drank more wine. "So why do you care so much about Hyperion?"

The god sighed heavily. "I loved him. A rare kind of love, the sort that I find perhaps every hundred years."

"Oh. Um, loved? As in . . ."

Poseidon chuckled. "Why so surprised, little Hybrid? Are you one of those who frown upon men loving one another?"

"Not frown. I'm not frowning. Just surprised. Sorry, I guess I shouldn't be. Didn't realize you leaned in that direction."

"I see you paid little attention during your school days when mythology was taught."

"I don't remember studying that very much."

"I predate your strange notions about same-sex love by a thousand years, Griffin. Compared to the gap between mortal and god, the difference between the sexes is all but insignificant. Hyperion and I were together for several years. He was magnificent. Sex with mortals is always so tenuous, so careful. They are so fragile. But with Hyperion I was able to truly let go."

"Ah. I get it."

"We could mate as men are meant to mate, with all our passion and vigor on display. You cannot imagine the glory of it, young Hybrid. The powerful thrusting, the force of our coupling. It was seismic."

"Yeah, I got it."

"You should try to picture it, young Hybrid. But don't; perhaps your mind is not ready for such vivid imagery."

"It's cool, I hear you. We can just move on to another topic."

The god shook his head. "When he left, I felt his loss acutely. More so when I learned of his death. But I have learned how to survive loss."

"Yeah? Want to fill me in on the secret?"

"One must focus on the treasured memories in place of dwelling on what is missing from the present. That is all. But when the source of those memories returns, or when something else returns wearing its face . . ."

"I get it. Messes you up."

"I expended too much of myself fighting Dr. Kraken's forces. Hoping to rescue Hyperion. Then you saved him, and I went to see him. What I found instead . . ." Poseidon laughed heartily.

Rohan waited while the laughter continued. The god leaned back, pounding the ground as he roared, his voice echoing loudly in the contained space of the break room.

"I smelled him, you see. He looks like Hyperion. Sounds like him. But I wanted a better test. Who better than I would know his odor?"

"And?"

"Little Hybrid, let me tell you. He smells divine. And that is how I knew it wasn't my Hyperion."

He leaned his head back against the wooden crate and began to snore.

11

What Stays in Vegas

Rohan tugged his mask into place as he, Amber, and Hyperion waited outside Bamf's chamber. Hyperion vibrated with excitement, rubbing his hands together, a wide smile underpinning his heavy mustache.

"Oh boy, I am excited! Las Vegas! The City That Never Sleeps!"

Amber sighed. "That's New York, buddy. Try again."

Rohan looked around. "No Spiral? We're leaving in a couple of minutes."

She shook her head. "Lyst called for him. You know how that goes. He does whatever she tells him to do."

Rohan pointed to Hyperion. "She's not worried about this guy?"

Amber shrugged. "You don't see her here, do you? It's always hard to say with Lyst. Either she's not worried because she knows he's safe with us or she just doesn't care. Or there's something going on somewhere else that's a much bigger deal. There's no way to tell."

"Right, right."

Hyperion clapped his hands. "I remember! City of Brotherly Love!"

Rohan patted his shoulder. "That's Philly. Try again."

"I was so sure. City of Angels?"

Amber checked her phone. "Two minutes. And no, that's literally what Los Angeles means."

"Darn it. Wait! Charm City, definitely! What could be more charming than the famous Vegas Strip?"

Rohan shook his head. "Baltimore. Come on, you can figure this out."

The door slid open, and Amber led them through.

Bamf's room was circular, ten meters across with a two-story ceiling. An attendant in medical scrubs stood close to the Power's wheelchair, ready to attend to his needs.

Amber approached the chair. Bamf's head hung at an odd angle, his eyes pointed up and unfocused as always. If he could speak, he never showed it, but he understood what was asked of him well enough.

Amber smiled. "Hey, Bamf. Can you send us to Las Vegas, please?"

Bamf's head shook from side to side, the extent of his communicative ability, and Rohan ushered Hyperion over to Amber's side.

A moment later, a hole tore open in the space behind them, and a shadowed alley appeared on the other side.

Amber looked back. "Thanks, Bamf. I'll call you if we need a pickup!" The attendant watched with stony eyes as they walked through the portal to the other side of the world.

"City of Love!"

"Paris. Keep going."

Hyperion shook his head as they paused to orient themselves. They stood a few meters away from a busy, brightly lit sidewalk.

Rohan looked the tall man over. "What do you want to do first, big guy?"

Hyperion paused. "I'm not sure. What should we do? I've never been here before. It just looked so pretty onscreen. All the lights. And the cool attractions. Can we look at a fountain?"

"You bet we can. Amber, you know your way around?"

"No, but I have a phone. Give me a sec. Is that our plan? Wander around, looking at fountains? I think there's a pirate ship to see."

Hyperion yelped. "Pirates! Awesome!"

Rohan shrugged. "We should visit a bordello. Big guy here's been dead for two years; I bet he'd like to get laid."

Hyperion turned to him. "Bordello? What's that? Is it a place where you play board games?"

Amber scowled at her friend. "You're going to drag me to a bordello with you? Really?"

"I mean, it's legal. And no, Hyperion, not a place where you play board games. Though I bet if you paid enough you could get a round of Settlers of Catan going."

Amber grunted. "Hyperion, it's a house of prostitution. We can go there if you'd like; I'll survive."

Hyperion's eyes widened alarmingly. "Prostitution? You mean, um . . ." He swallowed. "I really don't think that's anything a hero should be engaging in. Can we find some crime to stop? Or see the pirates? That sounds like fun."

Rohan smiled. "I'm sure there are guys. I mean, I think. If you'd prefer. Right, Amber? There are men available in Vegas."

Hyperion stammered, his cheeks blossoming red. "No, really. Let's just go see pirates. I think there's a pyramid, too. I'd love to see a pyramid."

Amber looked at Rohan with arched eyebrows.

He shrugged. "What do I know? Pirates it is. Pyramid, too. We can wander the Strip, then get rooms somewhere. I wouldn't mind a meal. I'll pay; I've got the fancy credit card." They turned onto the sidewalk.

A small commotion started a few meters away as a pale, skinny boy wearing a tank top and shorts with Miami Heat logos on them tugged on an older man's arm and pointed to Hyperion.

"Look, Dad, check it out! That guy's dressed just like Hyperion! They must be making a show or something."

The man, wearing a T-shirt and cargo shorts that matched his wife's, sighed. "He looks great, son."

"Can I ask him for a picture?"

The adults exchanged looks as another kid began begging for a picture. Within five minutes, a queue of children were lined up for photos.

Hyperion smiled. "Costume? Why, that's so funny! This isn't makeup. No, we're not filming a show. I'm Hyperion! Yes, I'd be happy to lift you up for the photo. Hold still!"

Amber and Rohan stepped back as Hyperion negotiated his line of admirers. The brunette scanned the crowd. "This is the plan?"

Rohan stepped back, barely avoiding a collision with a small running child. A pair of women whose dresses showed far more skin than they covered stood with Hyperion, holding phones up to the sky for selfies.

"My plan was to be on Wistful right now enjoying a candlelit dinner with Tamara. This is the not-plan, and so far it seems to be working."

"How do you figure?"

"Nobody's dead yet, so the plan is working."

"We're not exactly keeping a low profile, though, are we? Anybody after Hyperion will know we're here soon enough. It's all over social media."

"That's also the plan."

She tapped her phone. "Are you trying to draw in an attack? Flush out whoever's after our boy here?"

"I guess. I mean, it would be nice if he would hide. Or if we could get some reinforcements. What happened to the Rainbow Stars?"

"That bridge thing they did put them out of commission for a few days. Violet actually passed out right as you went through the force field; they had to carry him off."

"Masamune? And Hiroshi?"

"Hiroshi? Oh, Masamune's golem? They left. Masamune wanted to do some research, try to figure out where Hyperion came from. Said you'd keep our boy safe while he did his thing."

Rohan nodded and scanned the crowd. A preteen girl walked up to him. "Aren't you The Griffin?" She twirled a braid that hung over her shoulder while she spoke. "You saved the world last year."

He shook his head. "Just an actor, kid. We're shooting a commercial. I'm nobody."

She looked around. "I don't see any cameras. Or a crew."

"Well, we're shooting on the other side. We're on break."

"Then why are you still wearing your mask? Isn't it hot?"

Amber smirked. "You caught us, kid. He's The Griffin. But he's under-cover, don't tell anyone."

The girl nodded solemnly. "I won't tell anyone. But could you do something for me?"

Rohan nodded. "Sure. What do you want?"

"I heard you know Bright Angel. My brother says you used to be boyfriend and girlfriend, but obviously that's not true, because she's way too pretty for you. But could you tell her that Ashley from Oakland said thanks for saving the world?"

"Ashley from Oakland. Got it."

"Thanks. I won't tell anyone who you are."

"They probably wouldn't care anyway."

Ashley bounced away and joined the line for a picture with Hyperion.

Amber jabbed Rohan with her elbow. "You don't get any respect, do you?"

"I'm used to it."

"What was that whole thing about Hyperion and prostitutes? I mean, if he wants to, sure, but why bring it up? Doesn't seem like your style."

Rohan checked to see that their charge wasn't within earshot. "Hyperion was, let's say, very promiscuous. Very. And enjoyed the company of both men and women a great deal."

Amber swallowed. "That's not part of his Wikipedia page."

"I know. It wasn't in the comic books either."

"Still, sleeping around and visiting sex workers isn't the same thing."

"It's not, but I've never met anyone who slept around a lot who would blush and stammer over the very idea of visiting a sex worker."

"No, that seems odd. What do you think it means?"

"It's like this guy was programmed to act like Hyperion's public image. Or something."

"You think he's a robot?"

Rohan noticed the crowd dissipating. "No, I meant programmed in a very not-literal sense. Oh, look who's coming back."

Amber sighed. "I have to pee. I'm going to run and find a place, maybe scope out the pirates. You'll babysit our very large child?"

"I've got it."

Hyperion reached them. "Hey, guys. That was fun! Always good to meet fans."

Amber walked past him. "Be right back."

Hyperion's smile broadened. "We'll be waiting!" He turned to Rohan. "Hey, buddy. That was fun!"

"I'm glad you enjoyed. What were you telling them?"

"Oh, I don't know. The usual. Smile, which one has the camera, is this my good side. What one says."

"No, I mean, were you telling them who you were?"

"Of course! I don't hide my identity. See, no mask!" He touched his own face, fingers poking at his cheeks and nose.

"Everyone on Earth thinks you're dead. Were they asking who you *really* are?"

Hyperion shrugged his bowling-ball-sized shoulders. "I guess some of the adults didn't believe me. A few asked what agency I was with or what project we were working on." He paused, his eyebrows crunching together. "That reminds me, I've been wondering. Why do people think I'm dead? I keep hearing that."

Rohan sighed. "I guess you can blame me for that. I'm the one who told them."

"I see, I see. But, why?"

"I was with Hyperion when he died. On Rhyllax Four." Rohan studied Hyperion's face, searching for clues in his expression.

"But that can't be, can it? I mean, here I am. Very alive. So I couldn't have died on Rhyllax Four."

"I guess not. If you didn't die on Rhyllax Four, what actually happened? Why didn't you leave the planet with me? Why didn't you come back and help fight the sharks?"

Hyperion looked from side to side rapidly, his eyes scanning the street. "I don't know. I don't really remember."

"What *do* you remember, then? Do you remember the Ringgate? Making a deal with the il'Drach? Leaving Earth for the first time?"

Hyperion ran his fingers over his head. "I don't know. It's all so muddled. So confusing. I remember fighting for justice. With Ben and Marion."

"What about before that? Do you remember being a kid? Or after? Leaving the planet?"

"Not so much. I get flashes sometimes. Like just now! It's like I just remembered you. You're wearing that mask, with the pigeon beak on it—"

"It's an eagle. An eagle beak."

"—but you take it off and you're clean-shaven. No beard. There's blood on your hands. No, all up your arms. But I don't think it's your blood."

Rohan's heartbeat quickened. "What am I wearing?"

Hyperion closed his eyes. "Details are hard. It's all fuzzy. It's stiff, like leather. Not shiny. Black. No, not black exactly. It's red, but so dark that it looks black except where bright light hits it. And those cool boots where each of your toes is separated from the others. Oh, I like those. Can I get boots like that?"

Rohan swallowed, his mouth as dry as the desert air. He looked around wildly, searching for Amber. She wasn't back. His hands were shaking.

That's what we wore on the Ringgate. While fighting for the il'Drach. How could he know that? Nobody on this planet should know that.

Hyperion continued. "The Griffin? Are you okay? You don't look so great."

"In this memory of yours. Where's the sun?"

"The what? I don't know. Why?"

"It matters. Concentrate. Where's the sun?"

"I don't see it, The Griffin. I wasn't looking up. I was looking down, a little. You are quite short, you know. For a hero."

"Yeah, sure. You were looking down. Think about the shadows. Do you see any shadows?"

"I . . . think I do. Maybe? But the shadows are right below you. Like it's high noon. Like the sun is directly overhead."

Rohan panted, his breaths high in his chest. His upper back felt tight, as if his shoulders were too close together.

"Overhead."

Hyperion shrugged. "I told you, it's fuzzy. Distant. Almost like a dream. Hey, are you okay? You look a little pale. Not as pale as me, but paler than usual."

"I'm fine. Let's go find Amber." Rohan's voice cracked as he spoke.

"Yes! She should be back by now. She's very fast, isn't she?"

"Yeah. She can bend time. It's her Power."

"Maybe she can take me back. We can go to that planet, Rhinebeck Five, and see why I didn't die. Maybe I got hit on the head."

"Rhyllax Four. She can't go back in time; that's not how it works. What do you remember about being on Earth? I mean this time. What's the first thing you remember?"

Hyperion sighed. "Chicago. I was walking around Chicago. It was cold."

"That's where you started your hero career. Where you spent the most time. Chicago."

Hyperion shrugged. "That's what I remember, from before. Fighting crime in the city. The Windy City! Did I get that right?"

"Yeah. You did. Where is Amber?"

Tires screeched up the block. A white panel van going too fast for the corner lifted up onto its two outside tires before settling back onto four wheels with a thud and more rubbery squealing.

Rohan tried to exhale fully, but his chest was too tight. "Want to bet that has something to do with us?"

Hyperion's eyes widened. "Why would you think that, chum? Did my impressive physique distract the driver? Should we see if they need help? I can lift a van that size with my hands; I've done it before."

A second van rounded the corner, in just as much of a hurry. The first van skidded to a stop near the two heroes. The side doors slid open.

"I think you should get ready to fight, Hyperion."

Figures piled out of the open van.

At first Rohan squinted, thinking he had misjudged the height of the van, but in fact the figures were not quite adult-sized. Barely a meter and a half tall, each wore a floor-length gray trench coat and a matching top hat pulled over their faces.

Hyperion looked at them. "Those guys are definitely dressed for rain, The Griffin. It doesn't feel like it's going to rain, does it? I don't have an umbrella. Should I find an umbrella?"

"They're in disguise, Hyperion. Look at the ones in front. Running toward us. You see their skin?"

"Oh! Red scales. Yellow eyes. Look, that one lost his hat. He has horns! Black horns just like a goat. What fun!"

"I don't think it's fun, Hyperion. Those are Drexians. I'm pretty sure they're not here for autographs or selfies."

12

Demon Show

Eight identically dressed creatures rushed out of the first van toward the two heroes.

Hyperion raised his fists, palm side toward his face, and made small circles in the air. Rohan stepped back with his right foot, lifting his right fist to his cheek, covering his belly with his left.

Hyperion called out. "Are you lads sure you want to start a fight with me, Hyperion? Save yourselves some pain and surrender now!"

They swarmed the heroes in a rush, trench coats flapping, red scaly hands and the occasional tail emerging from their disguises.

Rohan parried a punch, then a second; took a kick to the ribs; knocked one creature back hard enough to send it into the side of the van.

They're fast.

A glimpse of fangs.

A punch came up short; an obsidian spike extruded from the creature's fist, between the first and second knuckles, thirty centimeters of glistening razor. The spike dug into Rohan's flesh, barely breaking the skin.

Hyperion's back was exposed, his shirt ripped from neck to waist, a welt oozing blood along that full length.

Hyperion grunted. "These little fellows are quick! And strong! Hey, they're not kids, are they? I would feel weird fighting kids."

Rohan dodged two more spikes. He kicked one of the assassins across the road.

"They're not kids, they're Drexians. Aliens." *Though I'm not really sure why these are so short.*

"Great news!" Hyperion hit one of the Drexians with a solid uppercut, sending it sailing into the air, while two others wrapped scaly arms around his legs. Two others tangled in his arms.

Rohan spotted an assassin running at full speed, arms outstretched, toward Hyperion's exposed chest. Rohan leapt forward and knocked him aside with a knee. "Watch it, these things can break skin. And they're probably poisoned."

A sharp pain sprouted at the back of his ankle. He whirled and saw a Drexian retreat. Another stabbed him in the back.

The eight from the second van had joined the fray.

"There are too many, and they're too fast!"

He slapped a Drexian to the ground and absorbed two kicks to his legs. He grunted, his Power rising in anger.

Hyperion brought his thick arms together with a tremendous clap, dislodging the two who had trapped him, then shook his right leg to try to free it. "What do you suggest there, chum? I seem to be at a loss for how to handle these little fellows."

Rohan grunted as a Drexian leapt onto his back and hooked arms and legs around his torso. "Get into the air! Fly!" He followed his own advice, *pulling* himself off the ground.

Hyperion shouted. "That's a great idea! I forgot I can fly!" He jumped, fell back down for a moment, then asserted his own Power and carved a path following Rohan's.

The Drexian on Rohan's back struggled to wrap a forearm around his neck. He spun savagely, throwing the creature off with a soft yell.

"Follow me!" He turned, looking for the shortest route to an area with low population density.

"I still have two on my legs, The Griffin! It's rather uncomfortable. They're—ouch—stabbing me with those little horns on their fists."

"Coming." Rohan turned and flew straight at the larger man, skimming him and knocking one of the Drexians off. He looked down at the street where they'd been attacked.

Two, then four, then eight of the assassins were shrugging free of their trench coats. They hunched forward, wriggling their shoulders as bat wings a full four meters across unfurled.

The first two launched themselves off the ground, wings beating madly at the air. A crack and a horrific buzzing accompanied them off the ground.

"I was not expecting that. Hyperion, they can fly."

"I see that, chum. We should lead them away from the citizens of this great city!"

"Yes. Yes, we should." Four Drexians bore down on their position. Rohan pointed. "Head that way."

"On my way, chum."

Rohan and Hyperion began to fly. Rohan led the way, twisting and spiraling through the air, taking sudden sharp turns, hoping to throw the Drexians off their tail.

The assassins closed, apparently able to fly faster in a straight line while also being more agile.

Hyperion shouted. "Are all male Draxes this fast? And strong? Must be quite a planet!"

Rohan grunted as he exchanged punches with two of the creatures. "No. They definitely aren't. And they don't have wings."

"Well, these fellows definitely have wings. What does that mean? Are they mutants? A different kind of alien?"

Rohan grabbed a Drexian by the neck and switched to Drachna. "Where are you from?"

The creature opened its mouth, baring an impressive array of sharp teeth, and spat at him. He tossed the creature aside.

Another Drexian yelled at him from behind. "You've been marked by the Cult of Karnuhl! We will not rest until the tall one is dead!"

Hyperion shouted as he punched another of the assassins. "Well, I hope you like coffee, because I am not going down easily!"

Rohan looked at the big man. "Coffee? What are you talking about?"

"Yes. Because they won't rest. And I'm not going to die. So they'll be tired, and, you know . . ."

"Right. Coffee." He coughed as an assassin caught him in the belly with a kick.

The Drexians were flying in formations, driving the two men back into the city center and away from any open routes to the desert. *They think we'll fight more cautiously around people. They're probably right.*

More gashes had appeared on Hyperion's body. Blood stained his white uniform. Rohan looked down and saw cuts up and down his own body to match.

Hyperion dodged a spike and pointed down. "Hey, I found the pirate ship."

"Not now . . . wait a minute. Amber should be near the pirates, right?"

"I suppose. Why?"

"She can help us with these guys."

"Can she? I thought we were drawing them away from her." Hyperion sounded doubtful.

"No, we were drawing them away from the regular people. Amber's not regular."

"Oh, right. What do we do?"

"Head for that open plaza by the ship. Go first; I'll cover you."

Rohan barrel-rolled into two Drexians, knocking them off Hyperion's tail, and slowed to stay behind the bigger man.

Hyperion flew toward the plaza, then fell a few meters, then caught himself and continued.

"Chum?"

Two Drexians grabbed Rohan's feet. He spun like a screwdriver and flung them off.

"What is it?"

"Not . . . feeling . . . so great."

Rohan watched as Hyperion began to tumble, his flight path changing to free fall.

"Oh crap."

Rohan dove and caught the bigger man close to the ground. Hyperion's eyes were fluttering, his body clammy and sweaty even in the dry air.

The Hybrid landed and set Hyperion on the ground.

His Power bubbled and churned against him, urging him to lash out against the Drexians. He eyed a nearby coach bus.

Faster than me? So are flies. I just need a big enough flyswatter.

The bus door opened, and a uniformed driver stuck her head out. Her eyes widened as she spotted the swarm of assassins streaming down. She ducked back into the bus, slamming the door shut behind her.

Maybe find an empty bus first.

A gust of wind blew dust into his eyes; Rohan blinked.

Amber stood in front of him, knives drawn.

"I can't leave you boys alone for five minutes to pee in peace. What's the problem here? These look like the guys that poisoned Bright Angel."

He panted, his wounds stinging, anger surging.

"Drexians. One of the cults." His Power surged again, red spikes thrusting against his self-control as he thought of Bright Angel.

"Powers?"

"Yes. Tough. Faster than they have any right to be. And the wings are new."

"What happened to the big guy?"

"Poison. A half dozen doses at least. We can't keep up with their attacks. I know a way to stop them, but it involves knocking buildings over. Which would kill a whole lot of other people."

"Let's look for an alternative. You're saying it's a speed problem?"

Rohan grunted. "Basically."

"I can cover speed. You want me to run Hyperion to safety?"

His breath ran hot in his throat. "Not really."

"Then what's the plan?"

He exhaled, the anger continuing to rise. "There is no safety with these guys around. We stop them here."

"But not by pulling hotels down on their heads. Shall I piggyback?"

He bared his teeth in an expression he thought might resemble a smile. "Yeah. Let's play teacher. Give these guys a little lesson."

"Just remember I can't keep up the field for very long if you're fighting, moving erratically. A few seconds at most."

"I won't need longer than that."

Rohan *reached* down inside his soul, into the dark corners where his sins and curse reigned unfettered. His astral hands grabbed a pair of red-hot cylinders of rage as they snaked and surged, eager to be pulled up into the light.

The streams of Power rose and curled around his spine in opposite directions, meeting every few vertebrae with a bang and a release of metaphysical sparks only visible to his Third Eye.

As they rose, rivulets of energy trailed off and invigorated his body, waking up tired muscle fibers, winding around and reinforcing strands of collagen in his skin, weaving dense, dark resistance through his bones and cartilage.

When the currents met at the base of his skull, they joined, suffusing his higher mental functions with a pop of releasing air, and Power exploded through his body.

He lifted one hand and beckoned Amber to him. She nodded, stepped around to his back, and hopped on.

"This is embarrassing. I feel like a baby chimp latching onto its mother."

"Think of it as an MMA fighter going for a rear naked choke."

"Thanks. I'll try not to cut off the blood supply to your head. Ready?"

He tapped her thigh where it hugged his waist.

The world shifted.

The air stilled. A falling scrap of paper halted midair, suspended. Silence settled over the street.

The Drexians slowed down; four were on the ground, running at an angle to Hyperion's position, obviously trying to circle around and come at the group from their rear.

Eleven others were in the sky, diving for the heroes like eagles stalking a rabbit.

Rohan met the lead Drexian with an elbow to the face.

Fangs shattered with the impact, the creature's vertical nostrils erupting in blood.

White bone fragments hung in the air, creeping on separate paths away from the assassin's nose. The fountain of blood froze in place, like a painting of an ocean wave.

Amber grunted, her arms trembling as she clutched at Rohan's back.

He flew past and into the second assassin. With quick twists, he fractured its forearms, pausing just long enough to see its eyes widen with shock.

Rohan moved from one flying demonic creature to the next, taking just enough time to incapacitate each before moving on.

A crushed larynx.

A kick to the forehead that would likely cause permanent brain damage.

Two obsidian spikes torn from Drexian arms by the roots and jammed deep into its shoulders.

Knees and elbows dislocated with savage twists.

A knee driven hard into a leathery sternum, cracking a ribcage.

Two dislocated shoulders.

Two creatures blinded by fingertips dragged along their blank yellow corneas.

Amber was panting in his ear, her legs shaking with strain. Rohan could *see* her spirit flagging as her energy depleted.

He approached the last flyer and grabbed at the bone connecting its wings, just over the creature's shoulders.

A sharp pull. The wings came away, revealing a wide, shallow face with its own circular mouth and an array of inward-facing fangs.

He tore the wings away and tossed them to the side, noticing that the Drexian was still twenty meters off the ground. He released it.

They landed.

Rohan paused as Amber's arm slipped on his shoulder. She adjusted, gripping her other wrist with her hand, and he continued.

Swept the legs out from a Drexian, breaking its shins.

Punched one in the side of the head, red scales splitting with the impact.

The last two were almost on top of Hyperion.

Rohan ran up to them, ducked, and grabbed one by the ankles.

He stood, lifting, and spun, turning the child-sized assassin in a wide arc, accelerating it into and through its companion.

Amber slid off his back; time restarted.

Drexians dropped in a rainfall of chaos, blood, and high-pitched screams.

Blood spurted; teeth fell and clattered, bouncing off the asphalt; thuds as assassins tried to put weight on freshly destroyed limbs and hit the ground.

Rohan growled in Drachna. "You come to my planet? Poison my friends? Attack me? Do you even know who you're dealing with?" *I should kill them. Make sure they don't come back.*

Amber croaked something unintelligible from where she lay on the ground.

"Earth is off-limits. Slink back to whatever hole you crawled out of.

"You know what people here used to do? We'd take the heads of our fallen enemies and put them on pikes. Long, pointy sticks. Set them all around our cities so anybody who comes by knows that these people are not to be messed with.

"I think your heads would look great on pikes. What do you think?"

Yellow eyes glared at him with anger.

Amber croaked again. Hyperion rolled over and looked at Rohan.

He spoke through wheezy breath, his words barely audible. "Not what heroes do."

Rohan grunted and straightened. He exhaled slowly, emptying his lungs, holding them free of air as he counted.

. . . eight.

Several of the Drexians were rising to their feet. Rohan pointed to one and spoke in Drachna.

"You. Earth is off-limits. What are you doing here?"

The Drexian spat greenish phlegm onto the Vegas street. "He has to die. If not today, then tomorrow."

"He's not going to die. Rudra save me, he's Hyperion! Look at him, he's already shrugging off your poisons. Bright Angel took one stab, and she was down for days. What can you do to *him*?"

The Drexian shook its head. Other standing assassins dragged their fellows back, away from Rohan and the scene of the battle. Engine sounds grew as the vans approached the area around the fake pirate ship.

Rohan bent to Amber, who was on all fours, dry heaving.

"You okay?"

She nodded. "Just . . . overdid it."

A different assassin spoke to them in English, its voice surprisingly deep for such a small body. "The Fathers themselves will his death, Griffin. Thus you know he will die. No other Earthlings have to die at his side. You can preserve your people and your planet. Leave him to us. We'll finish him."

Rohan exhaled. "You have to know that's never going to happen. Right? I mean, I know I talk a lot, and we all realize I'm not really going to put anybody's head on a pike. Where would I even find a pike? Is there a pike store? Pikes"R"Us? And where would I put it? On the moon? Who would even see it there? But that isn't the same as me going back on my promise to keep this guy alive."

"Then, we shall come back. We, or others like us. Until he is done." He switched to Drachna. "As the Fathers command."

The conscious Drexians murmured in his echo, "As the Fathers command."

Two of the fallen Drexians erupted into flames, a momentary bonfire that ignited the asphalt underneath them. Amber looked away as Rohan shielded his eyes.

When he looked back, the remaining assassins had escaped.

Amber coughed, wiping her mouth on her sleeve. "Should I go after them?"

"I think you've had enough. Don't you?"

"I can still fight. Put me in, coach." She smiled as she said it, then coughed weakly.

"It's fine. Let them go back. Let their friends know that we're not going to make this easy."

"Yes, boss."

Rohan turned to where Hyperion lay on the ground. The big man was breathing harshly. *At least he's breathing.*

"How are you doing? Gave me a bit of a scare there, falling out of the sky like that."

"Had a rough few minutes there, chum. Then you reminded me, I'm Hyperion. I'm too tough for poison to take out. Started feeling better straightaway."

Rohan looked him over.

The uniform was a loss, but the cuts were healing quickly.

Almost as quickly as Rohan's.

"Yeah, you'll be fine in no time. So will Amber. What do you want to do now?"

"I still want to see the pirates."

Amber chuckled. "Let's get you some clothes first."

Hyperion nodded. "Do you think they sell clothes here? The people in the ads aren't wearing very many."

Rohan nodded. "I'm sure we can find you something."

The big man rolled onto his stomach, then pushed up into a crawling position. He planted first one foot, then the other, and stood.

"Sin City! Right, Griffin? That's the nickname. Because . . . I don't know why."

Rohan slapped his back. "Exactly right. Let's go find out."

13

Steak and Whiskey

Two hours later, Rohan was taking a first tentative sip of a whiskey that cost more than a month's rent for his first apartment.

He looked at Amber. "This whiskey cost more than a month's rent for my first apartment."

She raised a single eyebrow and sipped her own. "It costs more than a month's rent for any of our seventeen safehouses."

He shrugged. "I love the complexity. The oak tones. You can really tell it was aged in . . . barrels. That's what they do, right? Barrels?"

Hyperion eyed his own glass warily. "Whiskey? I'm not sure I should be indulging in alcohol. I am a hero, after all."

The fourth person seated at their table looked at him with wide eyes. "It's okay, sweetie, you can drop the act; we're behind a two-way mirror. Nobody's watching."

He cleared his throat. "It's not about who's watching, Stacey. It's about being a hero. Right, Griffin?"

Rohan reached over the thick white tablecloth and patted Hyperion's hand. "It's fine, man. Have the drink. You'll burn it off in no time anyway. It's not like you're going to get drunk."

Stacey's face twisted with confusion as Hyperion shrugged and sipped the amber liquid.

They sat at a heavy wooden table on the second floor of a steakhouse that Stacey had assured them was the best and most exclusive establishment in Las Vegas. They could see down onto the main floor, crowded with tables and the bustle of waitstaff meeting customer needs, but their booth was almost eerily quiet.

Stacey quickly rearranged her expression into a genuine-looking smile. "Shall I order for you? I can get a selection of the best cuts. Wagyu, mostly."

Amber swallowed abruptly and coughed. "Ooh that burns. But in a good way. Wagyu? Is that the super fatty stuff?"

Stacey nodded. "Did you want a salad, sweetie? Something lighter? Maybe fish?"

"Heck no. Get me a rib eye. One of the big ones. Tomahawk? With the bone and everything."

Rohan held up his glass. "I want a salad. Caesar. And get more of this stuff, it's excellent. See if they have any really good tequila. I haven't been back in a long time."

Stacey's smile remained frozen on her face. "Back to where? You mean Las Vegas?"

Rohan shook his head. "Earth."

Amber spoke over him as she stuck her elbow in his arm. "The US. He's kidding. He's so funny. Right, Rohan?"

Stacey nodded. "I'll go place the orders. You guys sit here and enjoy, I'll be right back."

Rohan waved as she left the booth. Amber glared at him. "I thought we were trying to keep your identity a secret."

"What? I mean, yeah, sure. But Stacey's cool."

Hyperion took a larger sip, spots of red growing on his cheeks. "How do you know this Stacey person, Griffin? She is quite lovely."

Rohan chuckled. "I don't. But we showed up at the Waldorf Astoria, and I started waving this credit card around. You were . . . I don't know where you were. What were you doing?"

Amber laughed. "He was checking out the lobby."

Hyperion nodded. "It's amazing! So much . . . stuff. It's just like how I imagined all of Las Vegas would be! But most of the rest of the city isn't."

"That's the perfect description! Anyway, they saw the credit card and next thing, the hotel basically offered us a concierge for as long as we want her. Who was I to say no?"

"Because they recognized you as a hero, right?" Hyperion adjusted the collar of his white button-down. Stacey had taken them shopping on their way to dinner; each had selected an outfit that would blend into their surroundings better than hero uniforms.

Rohan laughed. "More likely they recognized the complete lack of a limit on my credit card."

A server slid into the room and placed two baskets of bread and rolls on the table; a second followed on his heels, cradling a pair of butter dishes.

Amber's eyes widened, and she grabbed a slice of white, crusty bread as soon as the basket hit the table. "You're both rich, aren't you?"

Rohan swallowed as Hyperion looked at her, eyebrows raised in surprise. "Am I? I sure wish I had known that in Chicago. I was sleeping in a cardboard box."

Rohan looked between them. "Nobody knew that was you, man. You've been gone for years. And they're still not sure you're really Hyperion. Give it some time."

Hyperion nodded and drained a second glass of whiskey. "I'm not worried about money or riches. Like I said, I'm a hero. But it would be nice to sleep in an actual bed. And use a real bathtub."

"I promise, your suite at the Waldorf will be a lot nicer than a Chicago sidewalk."

Hyperion stood. "I need to use the little boys' room. I'll be right back."

Rohan looked at Amber, who shook her head subtly. They watched as Hyperion left.

She leaned close to her friend. "You're talking as if you believe him now. What happened?"

Rohan sighed. "I'm not sure he's Hyperion. It doesn't make sense. People don't come back. But he has memories that are hard to explain."

"What kind?" She buttered her bread, leaning back in her overstuffed leather chair.

"Memories of me. Off-planet. Little details about what we wore while on the Ringgate. Me being clean-shaven."

She bit into the bread. "Is he the only person who would know that? Were you two alone?"

"No. Not really. But the people who were there, who would know, aren't anywhere near Earth. They're all Imperial Fleet personnel. Or other Hybrids."

"Occam's razor, Rohan. Is him being Hyperion the simplest explanation of what we can observe?"

"Occam's razor only works if we have at least one theory that's somewhere close to being simple. I don't know of any. Do you? Have you been holding out?"

She chewed, nodding. "No. I just want you to keep your skepticism. I know you liked Hyperion. Admired him. I don't want your desire to have him back clouding your judgment."

"It's not." *Maybe it is, a little.* "Why are you so skeptical?"

She put the bread down, reached up, and pulled the tie off her ponytail, shaking loose her brunette hair. "It's my job. Spiral is great, don't get me wrong, but his head is always in the clouds. Thinking about some fighting technique or new training method. It's up to me to figure out all the layers of crap being spun by the Children of Mu. Or whoever is behind our conspiracy of the week."

Rohan pulled his necklace out from under his forest green shirt. He rubbed the gemstone.

Amber pointed. "See, like that thing. He's been obsessive about getting that made. Couldn't talk about anything else. Before that, it was about perfecting that technique."

"The technique that let him stop a punch from a god."

"Right. I get it, absolutely. It's an amazing thing. And no, before you ask, I'm not upset that he's not teaching it to me. I saw what he went through to master it."

"I wasn't—okay. Good."

"It's really something."

"I'll have to check this out. Haven't had a chance yet."

"No, of course not. Stacey's coming back."

The door opened, and the concierge entered. She wore a black suit with a white shirt and black tie, her long blonde hair tied back in a severe ponytail.

Her nails were painted in a subtle shade of red that was barely noticeable yet screamed out how expensive it was at the same time.

"The food will be ready soon. They'll bring two bottles of their best añejo for you to sample, Griffin." She took her seat. "Why are you guys using codenames instead of your real ones?"

Rohan smiled. "That guy's a method actor. He's going to play Hyperion in a film. So for a month, we have to all use our movie codenames."

Her hair bobbed as she nodded. "I should have realized it was something like that! He looks great. Just like the real Hyperion! That must be why you guys were in costume. So interesting!"

Amber finished her slice of bread and motioned for Rohan to take one. "It really is. We're constantly rehearsing, so you'll hear us talking about a lot of stuff that's not real. All having to do with the film. Method acting."

"Got it! Just tell me if there's anything I can do to help!"

Rohan smiled. "You've been great. Getting us this table on short notice."

"Nothing is too good for our guests. Especially guests taking the executive suite."

Rohan opened the brown leather messenger bag Stacey had picked out for him and took out his helmet, tapping on its communicator function.

No messages.

Of course there are no messages. Who would be sending you a tachyon transmission here?

The door slid open, and Hyperion entered. "These pants are great! Did you see how many pockets I have? On the sides, on the back, and these big ones on my thighs! Why don't all pants have this many pockets? Just think about how much stuff I'll be able to put in here! Hey, can we buy some more stuff after we eat? I don't have anything to put in my pockets."

Stacey nodded. "Of course. There's plenty of shopping. Just tell me what you'd like to buy."

Rohan smiled. "We'll fill those pockets right up. Maybe get you a cell phone in case you get lost and need to call up a ride."

"That sounds great! You'll have to show me how to pay the bill, though. I don't have a credit card. Or bank account. Or any money."

Stacey cast a confused glance at Amber, then relaxed her features. "Whatever you like. The appetizers are coming now. I ordered one of everything so you can sample. Just say the word if you want seconds of anything."

More waitstaff streamed in, covering the table with bowls of hot meats, cold seafood, crispy vegetables, and tangy salads.

Hyperion took a cold shrimp and popped it into his mouth, tail and all. He smiled as he crunched through it. "This is great!"

Rohan placed a forkful of salad into his mouth, shivering at the delicate bite of anchovy in the dressing. A server entered with a tequila bottle cradled in one arm, clean glasses in the other. The Hybrid waved him over and pointed to a clear spot on the table.

The server obliged.

Hyperion picked up a strip of thick-cut bacon, folded it in half, and stuffed the entire thing into his mouth. "Mmm!" He watched the tequila-serving server and pointed to a spot next to him.

The server obliged.

Rohan sipped his drink, an exquisite cascade of balanced vegetal notes and caramel undertones so smooth that the fire erupting in his chest came as a warm surprise.

"That's the stuff."

Hyperion looked and tipped back his own glass, draining it in a single swallow.

Rohan laughed. "You can't even taste it that way! Try sipping it!"

Amber sighed. "It's like taking an overgrown kid to a fancy restaurant."

"You can leave out the word 'like.' He's exactly a big kid. He doesn't remember most of his adulthood."

Hyperion chewed the bacon as he motioned for a tequila refill. "So good."

Stacey stared. "Is he going to be all right? That's a lot of liquor he just drank."

Rohan waved her off. "He'll be fine. He's a big guy."

Amber shook her head. "We don't actually know that for sure, do we? Hey, Hyperion. What else do you want to see? We did the pirate ships. Pyramids?"

He answered with a vigorous nod. "Pyramids!"

Rohan sighed. "You do realize we were a short flight away from actual, real pyramids just this morning, don't you? It's not called Sahara City because it's named after a stripper."

Amber elbowed him. "Shush. If he wants to see Vegas pyramids, we can take him to Vegas pyramids. Don't be that guy."

"Fine. But we're going to run out of tourist spots soon. I mean, it's Vegas, so it might take another day or two. What else? Are we going to gamble?"

Amber sighed. "You two are rich enough to buy out the entire city. Why would we gamble?"

"I don't know. In the movies, it's always really rich people who gamble. But I don't care."

Hyperion shook his head. "Not what heroes do. What would people think, seeing Hyperion sitting at a slot machine somewhere? Or playing cards? No. Let's see the rest of the sights first. Then . . . let's see. Stacey, what do you think?"

"Oh, me? About what?"

"What should we see after Vegas?"

"Well, that depends. Is there anything you've always wanted to see?"

The big man's voice dipped into somber ranges. "I can't remember."

"Where have you been? The Grand Canyon? Niagara Falls? Hollywood? Gosh, I don't even know where I'd start. Times Square?"

He settled lower in his seat, lifted his tequila, and took a sip. "I should know that, shouldn't I? I should remember those places. Those things. Why don't I?"

Amber reached over the table and squeezed the back of his hand. "Hey, it's okay. We'll figure things out. You just have to be patient."

"I know. I'm trying. Those red guys sure were angry at me, weren't they? I don't even know what I did to them."

Rohan shook his head. "Nothing. But they work for the il'Drach. And you promised them that Earth's Hybrids would fight for them, not come back to Earth and take selfies on the sidewalk in Vegas."

"Is that what I did? Fight for the il'Drach?"

"Yeah. For a long time."

"But then I died."

"Well, yeah. Except, you're sitting here, drinking tequila and eating three shrimp at the same time. Here, pull the tails off, they're tastier that way."

Hyperion swallowed and sipped his drink. "What about you? Aren't you a Hybrid? Shouldn't you be fighting for them?"

"I retired. It's a long story. But they agreed to it. I've been on my own for two full years. But you're supposed to still be with them, so . . ."

"I don't think I want to fight for the Empire. Do I? Do I . . . like it?"

Rohan leaned back and smoothed his hair with his fingers. "I don't know, buddy. I don't think you did. Not really."

Hyperion nodded. "I don't want to go back. I want to see Earth. See my old friends. I have friends, don't I? I know! Let's visit Marion! And Ben! You said they're married, right? I bet they have a ton of kids. I can be their Uncle Hyperion. That sounds like fun."

Amber cut off a half piece of the bacon and took a handful of oysters. "That's going to be harder than it sounds."

Stacey scrunched her face. "Ben and Marion? Hyperion's sidekicks? They've been gone for ages, haven't they?"

Rohan nodded. "They're not on the planet, Hyperion. Maybe you can visit them someday."

"Yes! I should visit them." He drank more tequila, his eyes widening as the door slid open and a team of waitstaff brought in plates adorned with steaks still bubbling in butter. "Those smell amazing!"

Amber slurped back an oyster, washing it down with her whiskey. "We're always too busy to sit and eat like this. I should bring Spiral."

Rohan smiled. "Bring him and I'll pick up the bill. Maybe I can leave you my credit card. Just don't go on some kind of crazy shopping spree."

"Please. Have you seen what I wear? This is the second dress I own, and I bought it today. It's all uniforms and generic hair care products for me. Side effect of growing up inside a crystal prison."

Hyperion turned to her. "You grew up in jail?"

"Sort of. My father . . . he wasn't a good person."

Rohan nodded. "That's understating things, but yeah."

Hyperion grunted. "Was my father? I don't remember him."

Rohan cut into his steak. "We're il'Drach Hybrids. None of our fathers are good people. We could form a support group. 'Powers with Manipulative Fathers.' Maybe Stacey's dad is a good guy. She can tell us stories."

Stacey looked up. "Don't look at me. My dad abandoned us when I was two."

"Well, there you go."

A knock echoed through the room. Stacey stood. "I'll see what that is." She slid the door open and slipped out.

The heroes chewed on mouthwatering slices of seared meat as the voices on the other side of the door grew louder.

Two minutes later, the door opened again.

Stacey entered first, holding her hands up apologetically and pointing at an aging man walking right on her heels.

Rohan looked up. "General Ryan." He was a few centimeters above average, with the rigid posture of a lifelong military man, dressed in sharply creased fatigues.

Ryan's gray eyebrows rose as he took in the scene, his gaze settling on Rohan. "Griffin? No mask?"

"I'm just an actor. Nice to see that I look the part, though! Thanks!" He winked one eye, slowly, and popped another bit of steak into his mouth.

Ryan shook his head. "If that's how you want to do things. This is the man calling himself Hyperion?" His gaze settled.

Hyperion grunted. "I'm Hyperion. Who are you?"

"General Hugh Ryan. Which you would know if you were really Hyperion. Because I've met Hyperion. Many times."

Hyperion looked up from his seat, squinting. "Ryan. Seems familiar. How do we know each other again?"

The general sighed. "I've been the primary liaison to Powers from the US military for the past twenty-five years. Not my choice, but five different presidents have each decided I'm the right person for that job. So yes, I've worked with Hyperion plenty."

"You smoke cigars. You have a daughter named Bridgette. Cute little girl. Pigtails."

Ryan took a short step back and looked at Rohan, who shrugged. "It's complicated. Why don't you sit? Have a drink? I'm sure Stacey would be happy to order you a steak. My treat."

"Bridgette isn't a cute little girl. She's doing her first year of residency at Cornell. And I'm not here for steak."

Rohan glanced at Hyperion, who downed a full glass of tequila, muscles in his cheeks bunching along his jaw. "Which is what makes this conversation so weird, seeing as we're in a steakhouse."

Ryan sighed, looking over Hyperion. "My God, you really are his spitting image."

Hyperion shook his head. "I am Hyperion. I would really like people to stop talking about me as if I'm not. At least to my face." His jaw muscles bunched as he spoke.

He looks like he's getting angry. He didn't get angry before. Not even after Dr. Kraken tortured him.

"Look, General Ryan, let's try this one more time. Why are you here?"

The general looked over the table. Amber raised her eyebrows at him.

He sighed. "I brought a message."

Rohan took a piece of bread and dipped it into the butter and steak juice puddle that had formed on his plate, then bit into the bread. "We're listening."

"This—Hyperion—this man is a problem." He paused. Stacey looked at the door as if she wanted nothing more than to leave the awkward scene.

Rohan nodded, putting his hand over Amber's forearm as if to stop her from standing and doing something dramatic.

"That's a statement, not a message. You're going to have to clarify. Explain it to us like we're children, General. Give an order. A demand. Something concrete."

Ryan paused, gathering his thoughts, then continued. "Whoever this person is, he's presenting as Hyperion. God, I can't believe I'm saying that. It's like he's choosing a gender or something. Never mind."

"The point is, he's claiming to be Hyperion, and there's enough corroborating evidence to cause issues. He's been attacked by aliens, right here on American soil. We can't have that."

"Is this an immigration thing?"

Ryan shook his head. "It's a treaty-with-the-il'Drach thing. If Hyperion is dead, the treaty is intact. If he's alive, and hanging out on US soil, then he has broken the treaty. A treaty, I'll remind you, that provides us protection against interference from an overwhelming interstellar power which has a history of violence and capriciousness."

Hyperion pointed to his glass, and a server with visible sweat on his forehead filled it with tequila. The big man drained it in one swig.

Rohan sighed. "Please sip the very expensive tequila, Hyperion. That stuff is precious. You don't just guzzle it."

Hyperion shook his head. "He's being mean to me. I don't like it. That's not how heroes should be treated."

Ryan turned to the big man. "Your presence here puts this country at risk. This entire planet. The il'Drach are well-known for sterilizing planets that engage in behavior they don't like. You—Hyperion fighting for them bought us our independence. Yet here you are."

Rohan nodded. "I get it. You're afraid. Look, I'll take care of the il'Drach, okay? They're not going to nuke the planet over this guy here."

"How can you guarantee that?"

"Because if they were going to do that, they'd have done it already. Instead, they sent a team of pint-sized demon-looking assassins after him, and we kicked their tiny butts this morning. So the Earth, and by extension the US, is safe, okay?"

Hyperion shook his head. "This isn't how heroes should be treated. Not at all. We fight and sweat and bleed to save people, to protect people, and you come here and interrupt my dinner and you're mean to me? That's so very much not okay."

Ryan waved his hand at Hyperion and faced Rohan. "We need him to leave. It's one thing if he's in Africa somewhere and the il'Drach come after him, but we can't have him here. He's a danger."

Rohan swallowed. "We'll take care of the Drexians, General. I'm telling you, it's not as bad as it looks."

"Maybe it isn't, but we can't afford the risk. My job is protecting this country, and to do that I need you out of it ASAP."

Hyperion stood, sending his chair crashing to the floor. He held his plate in trembling hands until it shattered under the pressure of his fingertips.

"I keep telling you. You shouldn't treat heroes this way. It's not right."

Rohan *felt* the big man's anger. He stood and slid around the table. "It's okay, Hyperion. He can't make us do anything. He's just a bureaucrat."

Ryan huffed. "You don't want to push me on this, Griffin. Don't test me."

Hyperion turned to the general. "You're telling me to leave? Me, Hyperion? I've saved this country a dozen times. Two dozen. No, the entire planet. And you're telling me I can't sit here and finish my steak because of some treaty? Because of a piece of paper?" His face reddened, his mustache twitching with every syllable.

Ryan took a step back. "It's your treaty. Hyperion's treaty. Promises were made. We're just saying that those promises have to be kept."

Hyperion's voice rose in volume; the window overlooking the main floor of the steakhouse shook. "No! You don't tell me what to do! Not me! I'm Hyperion! You'd all be squid food if not for me. Or something. I don't even know. If I want to sit here and eat, I will! And if I want to go to Niagara Falls tomorrow, I will! What are you going to do? Send tanks and planes after me? You want to see what I can do against your pathetic little army? You want to see me tear your planes apart? Shred your tanks with my fists? Because I can. Maybe I should start right now. With you." His breath was heavy and loud in the enclosed space.

Rohan stood and edged around the table. "Hey, Hyperion. Calm down, buddy. These guys think you're dangerous. Sending their general back in a shoebox isn't a great way to prove them wrong."

"It doesn't matter, Griffin. I can stop them. Stop them all. They can't fight me. I'm Hyperion."

"Of course they can't fight you. But take a breath. Think. How annoying would that be? You kill a bunch of soldiers, start a ruckus . . . nobody would want to give you steak anymore."

Ryan shook his head. "You'll find we're more capable than you think. You don't want to mess with the United States military, son."

"I'm not your son. I'm Hyperion. I'm going to show you who should worry about who, starting right now." He lifted his left fist and started to bring it back, preparing to throw a punch.

Rohan's eyes widened; he poured energy into his arm, darted forward and reached for Hyperion's hand in one smooth motion, catching it along its backward path.

Two centimeters away from Stacey's fearstruck eyes.

Amber stood and leaned over the table. "Do heroes scare people, Hyperion? Look at Stacey. She looks scared, doesn't she? Is that what heroes do?"

Hyperion turned to the concierge.

Her face was paper pale, her eyes so wide he could see whites all around her pupils. His fist had almost decapitated her, and she knew it.

Hyperion looked at Rohan. "What? What's happening?" His arm relaxed, his fist going limp in Rohan's grasp.

Rohan leaned forward and, with great care, put his palms on Hyperion's upper chest, pushing the big man away from the humans. "It's okay, big guy. Just lost your temper a bit. Everything's going to be okay."

14

Spiral's Spiral Spiral

Morning sunlight streamed in through the window of the suite Rohan had secured. He poked at a plate of steaming eggs and lightly browned toast with his right hand, his left holding his new diamond pendant up for examination.

The suite was enormous: three bedrooms separated from a central entertainment area, every corner and surface decorated with some amenity, surfaced with something rare, or containing a piece of expensive artwork. The big table held several trays of food, a silver pot of coffee, another one of tea, and a slender glass bottle of amber liquid by Rohan's elbow.

Amber exited her room wearing a thick white terry cloth bathrobe, monogrammed with the hotel's initials, patting her hair dry with another towel as she crossed the room.

"Our boy is still asleep?"

A loud snore from the closed door behind Rohan answered her question. He pointed his fork at the table. "There's breakfast. Order more if it's cold. The eggs are great. I haven't tried the coffee."

"It's not even seven and you're starting on the tequila? I know it's Vegas, but still."

Rohan waved. "Time zones. I'm from space. It's late afternoon on Wistful."

"Really?"

He paused. "I have no idea. I could look it up, but my mask is in the other room. To be honest, I just felt like drinking tequila. I don't think I'm coping very well with the last couple of days."

She sighed and poured herself a cup of coffee, then took a sip. "You want me to nag you into taking better care of yourself or leave you to wallow in your misery for a while?"

He scratched his beard. "Let me wallow a bit. If I'm still dawn-drinking the day after tomorrow, you can schedule an intervention. Or a stern talking-to. Whatever you think is appropriate."

"Will do." She uncovered a plate of eggs and sat in front of it. "Hey, I've been wondering. What's the story with the cape?"

"What cape? You mean the cape Masamune asked me to bring?"

"Yeah. The one we used to fight that shark." Amber had wrapped herself around Rohan inside that cape and turned them into a time-traveling air-to-surface missile with a payload of caustic insect venom.

"It's not my cape, it's Hyperion's."

"But he didn't give it to Hyperion."

Rohan thought. "Masamune's people are kind of sticklers for rules, propriety, that sort of thing. I imagine he feels that since he made it for Hyperion, and Hyperion is alive, I shouldn't have it anymore. But he's not convinced that's really Hyperion."

She nodded and sipped her coffee. "This stuff is amazing. It's like coffee for the gods. Ambrosia. No, that's not coffee. You know."

"Nectar. I always thought of that as more wine-like. The gods I know are always trying to get drunk, not wake up."

"How many gods do you know?"

He laughed softly. "Not that many, really. I knew Ares a little. We weren't friends. And I've spent some more time with Poseidon. That's about it."

"Wistful isn't full of gods? Walking around, taking in the sights?"

"No. Earth is really unusual that way. Very few planets have gods walking around. Pretty much none of those are allowed interstellar travel."

She swallowed a mouthful of eggs. "Why do you think that is?"

"Not sure. il'Drach not liking competition? Some gods are nearly as strong as Hybrids. But I don't really know." Rohan took a big sip of tequila, enjoying the warmth as it spread through his chest. He straightened in his seat and bit into a piece of toast.

"Okay. Next question."

"You're very talkative. Are you that much of a morning person?"

"Griffin, I control time, not the other way. I'm a whatever-time-of-day-I-want-to-be kind of person. I don't have a circadian rhythm, my circadian rhythm has me."

His mouth dropped open. "That last part made no sense at all."

"It didn't, did it? But I made you smile. I think that's a smile."

"All right, go ahead. Ask."

"Are you making any progress with the soulgem?"

He held the diamond pendant up to the window and watched the sparkling as sunlight cut through it. "Not yet. I know the idea of how to work one of these, but I've never done it before."

"I don't think you're supposed to hold it like that, Griffin."

"What do you mean?"

"Isn't it supposed to be, you know . . . inside you?"

"What? You mean, like, put it in my mouth?"

Her smile broadened, tears forming at the corners of her eyes. "Not your mouth." A giggle burst out, escaping as if it had been trapped in her throat.

He grinned. "You're messing with me. Again. Don't do that. I was about to lube this thing up and have a try."

"I wouldn't. Unless you're into that for its own sake. But seriously, I know a little. I helped him make it."

"Okay." He took another sizable sip of his drink. Another rumbling snore sounded from the other room. "No time like the present."

He exhaled slowly, emptying his lungs, and *reached* inside for a line of Power. It answered, eager as always, leaping for his ethereal grasp like a fish jumping for bait. He held the energy, turning it back and forth, gauging its heft, its tempo, its solidity.

He *pushed* the stream into the diamond.

At first the energy split around the soulgem, arcing around the back and rejoining itself. Rohan focused on it, squeezing, redirecting it into the tip of the pendant.

The stream of energy entered and lit up an eldritch pattern, etched into the crystalline structure of the soulgem, with metaphysical light only visible to his Third Eye.

A band: not straight but curved, arcing gently to one side. He couldn't say if was to the right or left; directions and physical space only corresponded loosely to spiritual objects. But turn it did, enough to reverse completely, rising ever so subtly as it did.

He followed the path, his eyes darting back and forth even though their physical presence had nothing to do with what he was *looking* at.

"Son of a gun. Is this another joke? Is he kidding me?"

Amber tilted her head. "Why? What do you see?"

"It's a spiral. Is this, just, his signature? His emblem? Is this like the Bat-Signal? Am I supposed to shine this in the sky and he'll know to come running and save me? How is this a technique?"

She sipped her coffee. "Griffin, in all seriousness, it's not a joke or a prank. I promise."

"Then what the hell is it? How am I supposed to make a technique out of a spiral?"

Amber leaned forward and forked some eggs onto a piece of toast, then slid the corner into her mouth. "I'm not supposed to tell you. He said you have to figure it out."

"Seriously? I think he's watched too many bad kung fu movies. He's convinced that he's some kind of sage up on the mountain."

"Hey, don't get mad at me. And maybe lower your voice or you'll wake sleeping beauty in the next room."

Rohan lowered the pendant and rubbed between his eyes. "Sorry. Sorry. Not coping well. I'm worried about things on Wistful. Now this . . . I don't even know what to call this thing with Hyperion. I looked up to him, so much. And this guy, he's exactly like him sometimes, you know? Then the next second, he's so completely . . . not. And everyone is counting on me to figure out the political ramifications of him being here, and who should be told what, and how to keep things from escalating, and all I can think about is Tamara."

She nodded and bit into her toast. "I sympathize. I really do. More than most people might."

He sipped the tequila again. "What do you mean?"

"You did not just seriously ask me that. Me? Miss sealed-in-a-block-of-amber-for-five-years-because-of-her-Power?"

He sighed. "Sorry. No, you're right. You haven't had it easy."

"We're not competing. But nobody can afford for you to keep walking around in a daze whining about a woman who dumped you a year and a half ago. It's a little pathetic, honestly."

"Ouch."

"I call it like I see it."

"Fine. Maybe I'm being a little self-indulgent."

Amber pointed to the bottle of tequila. "A little?"

"I'm starting to dislike you, Amber."

"No you're not. I'm delightful." She smiled and gently rubbed her hair again with a towel. "Seriously, look at the soulgem again. Or look at it later. But he's one hundred percent serious."

"His ultimate technique just happens to match his hero name?"

She shrugged. "Is it coincidence? Is it destiny? Maybe somehow he knew that shape would wind up being important. Intuition. Or thinking about that shape daily for year after year led him to the technique. You don't need a weird mystical explanation for it to make sense."

"I guess not." Rohan ran his fingers through his hair. "I'll look again. Not sure more power is what I really need, though, to be honest. I'm a Hybrid. My goal in life is avoiding situations I have to punch my way out of, not, like, getting better at punching."

Amber smiled. "He didn't punch Poseidon. He stopped Poseidon's punch. Not the same thing."

"Are you going to explain what that means?"

"Not yet. Spiral doesn't want me giving you too many hints. Study the soulgem again. You'll figure it out. I have confidence in you."

"I wish *I* had confidence in me."

"Do you need a hug? I'm not Bright Angel, and you're not Poseidon, but you sound like you need a hug."

Rohan shook his head. "I don't think I'm in that kind of headspace. Thanks for the offer."

"Good, it would have been awkward. But don't say I didn't offer."

The bedroom door swung open, and Hyperion walked out wearing white cotton pajama bottoms and no shirt.

Amber smiled up at him. "Good morning. How'd you sleep?"

His face was drawn, his lips turned down in a grimace. "My head hurts. Why does my head hurt?"

Rohan shrugged as he snatched the bottle on the table and slid it onto the floor, out of sight. "Take your pick. You drank a liter of tequila yesterday, and that's after taking a beating from some Drexians and suffering a near-fatal dose of alien poison."

Hyperion nodded and sat down. He poured a mug of coffee and drained it quickly. "That's bitter. I don't like it." He refilled the mug and drank it down.

Amber pointed to the sugar bowl. "You can try adding some of that, to sweeten it." He was already drinking his third cup.

Rohan pushed a tray over. "Eat something. It will help. And drink some water."

Hyperion nodded. "I did *not* sleep well. My mind was under something."

Rohan looked at Amber, mouthing Hyperion's words voicelessly. Amber snapped her fingers. "You had something on your mind?"

"No, that's not it. It was hanging over me. Weighing me down. I was under it."

Amber sighed. "Okay, prepositions aren't the important part here. What was bothering you?"

"I realized sometime yesterday. I'm not proud of it, but I don't think I can ignore it. That's not what heroes do."

Rohan took a deep breath. "What did you realize? Maybe we can help you figure out what to do about it. We're your friends, after all."

Hyperion nodded, folded a piece of toast in half, and put the entire thing into his mouth. As he spoke, crumbs fell onto the table. "I realized I don't know who I am."

Rohan's eyebrows shot up. "What do you mean? You're saying you're . . . not Hyperion?" Amber leaned forward in her chair, gazing intently at the big man.

Hyperion was shaking his head. He swallowed. "No, that's not it. Of course I'm Hyperion. Who else would I be? But I don't know what that means. I don't know what it means to be Hyperion."

Rohan looked at Amber, who shrugged again. He turned to the big man. "I'm not sure I understand. Can you try to explain what you're saying a little bit?"

"I'll try. It's confusing. Maybe you guys aren't able to understand. See, I'm confused about what being me actually means. It's a sort of . . . I don't know the word."

Amber nodded. "Existential crisis?"

"No, that's not it. I'm sure I exist."

"That's not—"

He interrupted her. "I thought I knew what being Hyperion *was*. It meant I was strong. That I did the right thing. That I was a hero. But yesterday I didn't feel strong. I felt sort of weak, especially after the poison got into me. I didn't even realize I could *be* poisoned."

Rohan cleared his throat. "Weren't you captured by Dr. Kraken the other day? Didn't that bring up any of these thoughts?"

Hyperion's dark hair waved with the motion of his shaking head. "It didn't matter then. It wasn't the same. My head was so foggy it was like nothing mattered. But in the restaurant, I got so angry. I wanted to kill that general. Tear him apart. Why did I feel that way? I'm not supposed to feel that way. I'm a hero."

Rohan nodded slowly. "Heroes can get angry, Hyperion. Nobody's perfect. It's okay to have some . . . negative feelings."

Amber patted Hyperion's hand. "It's good that you didn't act on them, though. It's okay to feel angry, but maybe not so okay to, say, kill people because of it."

The big man pulled his hand away and ran it through his hair. "But maybe he deserved it. He was mean to me. Told me I'm not welcome here. Me, Hyperion. Can you believe that? What right did he have to say that?"

Rohan cleared his throat. "Well, technically, he was told to say that by the United States government, so—"

Hyperion continued. "No, that wasn't right of him. And how is someone like him going to learn better? It's not like he has parents telling him right from wrong. He's an old guy. They're probably dead. And he's a general, right? I bet there are people all around him telling him how smart he is and how he's always right."

Amber shook her head. "I don't think—"

"He needs me to teach him to do better. That's what I was trying to do, you know."

Rohan sighed. "Were you trying to kill our concierge? Because that's what you almost did."

"No. That would have been sad. I'm glad you caught me. But would it have really been my fault? If he hadn't been so out of line, I wouldn't have had to hit him. And Stephanie wouldn't have been in danger."

Amber's headshakes gained intensity. "Stacey. It's Stacey. But you didn't *have* to hit him, Hyperion. He wasn't a danger to you, or to anyone else. You don't just go around hitting people because you don't think they're nice."

"Why not? How else are they going to learn? You have to teach people. Show them that there are consequences to being mean."

Rohan cracked his neck. "Then, what do you do when someone thinks *you're* the one who isn't nice? You want to get hit?"

"I'm Hyperion. I'm always nice."

"I don't think General Ryan would agree."

"He's welcome to try to hit me, then. I think I can take it."

Rohan leaned forward, then rocked back in his chair, exhaling slowly. He poured a cup of coffee and sipped it.

The front door rattled on its hinges as something pounded on it.

Rohan looked at Amber. "Did you order something while I wasn't looking?"

She shrugged. "Not me. I can check who it is."

Rohan nodded, and she stood and crossed the room, smoothing her still-damp hair as she walked.

"Think through what you're saying, because it sounds an awful lot like 'might makes right.' And that's not what the Hyperion I knew believed."

Muffled voices came through the heavy door. Hyperion's voice rose. "Maybe he was wrong! I mean, maybe I was wrong! Or you misunderstood. What do you really know, anyway?"

"I was Hyperion's—your—closest companion in those final days. Remember? Before you died."

Hyperion reached up and pounded his head with the palms of his hands. "I don't. I can't remember. I'm missing so much."

Amber opened the door. "Las Vegas Police. We'd like to—" She slipped through and closed it behind her before they could say more. The distant voices continued.

"Then listen to me. I know you're confused, that you're having some trouble. I can't say I understand, but I'm here to help. So is Amber. You can't use violence to solve all your problems, no matter how strong you are. That's not what heroes do, right?"

"Then, how do I know when to fight? That's what I do, right? I fight for justice. That's what *hyperion* means. In Latin."

"No, it doesn't."

"Greek?"

"Still no."

"Well, I know it's what I do. You're telling me to stop? Not to raise my hand in the name of what's good and righteous?"

"I'm not saying that. When people are in physical danger, you can fight to save them. But you can't go on a rampage every time someone hurts your feelings."

The door opened, and Amber backed through it. "Yes, I get it. Just give me a couple of minutes. You don't have a choice, we have sovereign immunity, you know that." She slammed the door in the faces of two suited men.

She turned. Rohan sipped his coffee. "What's going on with them?"

Amber looked at Hyperion, who forked some eggs into his mouth, his expression solemn.

"It's about last night."

Rohan frowned. "Are we in some kind of trouble?"

"Not exactly. Maybe. They want to ask us some questions."

Hyperion pointed to the door. "See? We were defending ourselves. That should be fine, right? And the police are mad at *us*? Maybe I should punch some of them."

Amber shook her head. "They're not mad at us for defending ourselves. They want to ask some questions, but they're willing to give us a few minutes to put ourselves together."

Rohan's eyes narrowed. "Questions about what?"

"When the Drexians ran off, they got into an accident. Killed a family of four. Two kids, four and six years old." Rohan ran his fingers through his hair. His Power rumbled in his gut, straining to be free.

Hyperion grumbled. "We should have killed the Drexians, then. Instead of letting them escape."

Rohan growled. "It's not that simple. Just killing people." *It always starts small, like this. And ends badly.*

"Why not? That family might still be alive if we had."

Rohan's Power surged. "Big talk coming from a man who was on the ground whimpering after taking a few shots of poison from those Drexians! Maybe if you'd held your own in that fight, we could have stopped them!" His voice was harsh and guttural.

Amber sped over, crossing the room in an eyeblink, and slapped the table.

"That's enough. You didn't know that would happen." Her phone dinged. She looked at it and faced the others. "Bright Angel has something to tell us. In person."

Rohan exhaled slowly. Hyperion settled back in his chair, eyes tight.

Amber continued. "Bright Angel can wait. Hyperion, maybe we're making this too complicated. Spiral always tells me that when it comes to morality, in the end I have to trust my gut. Your gut knew you had to fight when they were trying to kill you, right? But I bet it was different with

General Ryan. Sure you were angry, but it didn't feel good to swing at him, did it? That anger was a sour anger, right?"

She's not a Hybrid. She doesn't understand.

Hyperion looked to Rohan, then back to Amber.

"No. Actually, it felt pretty good. Like I was myself for the first time in a long time.

"Really myself."

15

Who Scares You More?

R ohan exhaled slowly, emptying his lungs, then held for an eight-count.

He leaned to his left and picked the half-empty bottle of very expensive tequila up off the floor. Amber looked at him.

"What should we do?"

He held up one finger and upended the bottle, draining the liquor in a series of gulps. Hyperion ate more toast, eyes focused on the far wall, his face slack.

Rohan slammed the bottle down onto the table, inhaling as the burn in his chest eased. "I've gotten slow and civilized. Things are happening and I'm just reacting to them. Which is fine until the frequency and intensity of those things gets too high."

Amber tilted her head. "I'm not following you. Or, I should say I am following you, but I don't see how it answers my question."

"It doesn't. I'm going to start solving problems right now. We need to go. Do you mind calling Bamf and arranging a gate out of here? If you want to come, get dressed and gather your stuff; I'm in a hurry now. And I have another call to make."

"You got it. What about the cops?"

"I'll deal with them. Give Hyperion a hand. Come on, big guy. We're leaving. Get your things together."

Hyperion's eyes snapped into focus. "What things?"

"Your nice new clothes. Come on, we have to go."

Hyperion nodded and stood, then headed into his room. Amber did the same.

Rohan slid his cloth mask over his face and opened the front door just wide enough to squeeze his head through. "Hey, guys."

The two suit-wearing men with badges hanging out of their chest pockets looked at him with unfriendly expressions. Four more officers in tactical gear lined the hall behind them.

"Griffin? We have a few questions, and we're running out of patience."

He nodded. "Absolutely, of course. I'm happy to cooperate with Las Vegas's finest. Just one more minute. We were having an orgy, you see, and I want to put away the filthiest of the sex toys before I let you in. And hide the minors. Wouldn't want you to see the minors, would I? Create all sorts of moral conundrums. So, hold on."

"Hey, wait a minute—"

Rohan slammed the door and spun around. "Where was I? Oh, right, get my things. I never got to try the hot tub. I really wanted to try the hot tub. And now I'm talking to myself."

He went to his own room and picked up his jumpsuit, took his space-mask out of the hood, and stuffed it into the messenger bag he'd been carrying, along with the other items he'd bought and wasn't wearing.

"Shirt, socks, underwear, hey, I don't remember buying this jacket, more socks, a watch. I don't wear watches. Is this even mine? Well, I'm taking it."

He slid open the balcony door and stepped out into the hot, dry desert air. The Strip was a noisy band of color and action far below his feet.

"*Void's Shadow*. Come in. I need a favor."

He waited, wiggling his toes as the heat from the balcony seeped into his feet, banishing the chill from the room's overactive air conditioning.

Two and a half minutes later, his ship's cheerful voice broke through his comm. "Hey, Captain! How are you? I was just wondering what was going on down there."

"Hey. I'm good. Everything quiet in the system?"

"Yes, Captain. What kind of favor? Not that I mind; I'm happy to help. Depending on what it is."

"Good girl. Listen carefully. I think there's another ship in the system. Maybe a stealth ship. There are Drexians on the planet, and they had to get here somehow."

"Drexians don't have stealth ships, Captain. But they could have hired one. Like a Shayjh ship. There are a couple of other places that make good stealth ships. Not as good as me, though."

"Of course not. So, listen, I want you to be super careful, okay? No risks. But do you think you can find that ship?"

"I'm sure I can, Captain."

"Without them noticing you're doing it?"

"Of course. Piece of cake. Unless they're like me, which they almost definitely aren't, because. You know." Rohan knew. *Void's Shadow* was the most advanced stealth ship in the sector, and only a few like her had ever been built.

"Cool. Let me know when you find her. Once you do, do you think you'll be able to sneak up on her?"

"Do asteroids tumble? Is the ocean wet? Do gas giants smell like farts? Of course I will."

"You lost me in the middle there. But good. Don't do it, okay? Just be ready to pick us up and help me solve a problem."

"Yes, Captain. Are you going to destroy that ship?"

"Only if I have to. Now scoot. And thank you."

"Yes, Captain." The comm link clicked to silence.

Rohan hummed as he tapped at his mask, checking for messages. *Void's Shadow* had uploaded a packet of interstellar communications. He opened it.

The first was from Wei Li. There was activity around the il'Drach cargo ship at the edge of Toth system. Ships coming and going. *I almost forgot that I asked her to keep me posted on any changes with that ship. It's been quiet for so long.*

The second was from Tamaralinth. A repeat request to speak with him; a promise that it wouldn't take long. *If you're trying to get me to agree, telling me it won't take long is not the incentive you think it is.*

Another swipe connected the mask to the local internet. He checked email messages that had accumulated for the previous year.

Ads for sexual enhancing pills; great deals on installation of solar panels on his roof; invitations to view naked pictures from a dozen people.

He walked back inside.

Amber stood next to Hyperion, phone in hand. Both were dressed, holding bags. *I forget how fast she is.*

Amber pointed at the far wall. "Ready?" The front door shook on its hinges as something struck it from the other side.

"No time like the present. Let's go."

She spoke into the phone. "Now, please, Bamf."

A hole tore open in space between them and the back wall of the suite.

The three stepped through into Bamf's chamber, swallowing as their ears popped with the pressure change.

Rohan nodded to the man in the supportive chair. "Thanks, Bamf." He turned to Amber. "I have a job for you. Gather up my—The Director and Bright Angel and anybody else you can find and put them all in a conference room. Then close the door, and he does not leave that room until you come up with a plan."

Amber nodded. "A plan for what, Griffin?"

"For what we're going to do with the big guy. Or for what he's going to do with himself."

Hyperion focused on him. "What do you mean?"

"You're clearly not safe to leave alone. Forget what other people are going to try to do to you; I'm worried about what you're going to start doing to them. And I can't commit to staying here and babysitting you. So, we need a plan."

Hyperion's eyebrows rose. "I don't need a babysitter."

"Poor choice of words. Chaperone? Someone to keep you from committing serious crimes that will haunt you for the rest of your life. What's the word for that? I forget. Not bodyguard. Soulguard? Is that a word? I think I just invented a word."

"But I'm Hyp—"

Amber covered his mouth with her hand. "We know. Stop saying that. It doesn't mean what you think it means." She faced Rohan. "We'll hammer something out. Where are you going?"

"Space. Have a little alien invasion to take care of. I'll be back. Oh, make sure to find out what Bright Angel wanted. It's not like her to message unless it's important."

"Already planning on it. Good luck."

Hyperion was shaking his head. "But—"

Rohan interrupted. "You get to have a say, all right? But right now you're a loose cannon. You want to take on the whole world because someone said something you didn't like? I promise, you won't like the results. Because let me tell you something: if I have to choose between you and the whole world, I'm going to be on the world's side. Understand?"

Hyperion sneered, his shoulders tensing as if readying to strike, but a moment later, he relaxed and nodded. "I do."

"Great." Rohan watched the two heroes leave, then walked over to Bamf. He looked into the space-bender's face, searching for a sign of consciousness.

He didn't find it.

Bamf's attendant waited patiently.

Rohan nodded and stepped closer. "Hey, Bamf. I need to go into space. Can you send me into space? Open a portal? Anywhere outside the gravity well."

A grunt emerged from the man. Then another.

The attendant's eyes widened. "He doesn't usually do that, sir. Communicate, I mean. That was his way of saying no."

Rohan nodded and kept his focus on Bamf's face. "I didn't think so. Takes too much energy. I can get myself up, but I don't want to walk out through this building. I don't want to answer any questions or have people know where I am. Can you open a portal to someplace away from here?

As high up as you can manage, anyplace deserted. Don't push too hard. Okay?"

A single grunt came out.

Rohan nodded. "Thanks, buddy. Whenever you're ready." He cracked his neck. "Here we go."

Bamf's gate deposited Rohan on a frozen mountaintop. He took exactly twenty-three seconds to enjoy the view, then slipped his mask over his face, breathing deeply as the air supply hissed awake, and *lifted* himself off the ground and into the sky.

As he flew, he let a steady current of anger simmer inside, fueling his flight. *Those little red jerks come to my planet, pick on my people, kill innocent bystanders. Somebody forgot they should be afraid of me. Time to jog some memories.*

He flicked on his transponder so *Void's Shadow* would know he was coming.

Rohan's temperature climbed along with his altitude, peaked, then dropped again as he reached the thinning far reaches of Earth's atmosphere. Soon he broke free and entered vacuum, ignoring the soft itching that crawled across his skin as it dried.

His ship's voice rang in his helmet. "Captain? You've left Earth?"

"Yes. Find that ship, then come get me. We have work to do."

"Yes, Captain."

Rohan continued flying. His comm rang.

"Griffin?" Amber's voice.

"What's up?"

"We talked to Bright Angel." Her tone was tense.

"And?"

"And don't take your time."

Rohan sighed. "Understood. Griffin out."

One thing at a time. Like you were trained.

He passed the moon and began to drift. With no way of knowing where *Void's Shadow* was, there was no reason to keep moving.

His comm was halfway through the fourth song on his playlist when the stars in front of him disappeared. Seconds later, a hole opened in the darkness: his ship's port, open for entry.

"I found them, Captain."

Rohan darted through the hatch. "Good job. How far?"

"Not far at all. Other side of Sol Four."

"Mars. Same thing. Makes sense. Not too far, but far enough to avoid accidental discovery. Can you bring me close?"

"Of course, Captain. They'll never see me. What's the plan?"

He explained.

◆┄◈┄◆

The Drexian ship was a space catamaran: a matched pair of nearly cylindrical, pointed needles connected by a rectangular block. Rohan had seen the design before, though he couldn't remember any details.

They flew close to the ship, taking passive measurements to evaluate its payload and capacities.

"She's big enough to have brought all the Drexians you counted and then some. And I've seen no signs of another ship in the system."

"Okay. Proceed as planned."

They continued to skim the ship. Like most il'Drach ships, *Void's Shadow* maneuvered using bootstrap drives, all but undetectable from even a few centimeters outside their external shell.

"All done, Captain."

"Great. Open a channel."

"Open."

Rohan cleared his throat. "Hail, unknown invader. This is The Griffin of Earth."

No response.

He sighed. "I understand, you know. I really do. You're a stealth ship. You have nonreflective coating, electromagnetic insulation so you don't leak radio waves or anything into space. You've been carefully cultivated so your very soul is *quiet*. No spiritual impression.

"And to carry that off, you have to basically believe that you are, in fact, invisible. I get it. Hybrids are the same way, you know. Kind of.

"Except we aren't conditioned to think we're invisible. We're conditioned to tear apart anything that challenges us. With our bare hands. To tear and rip through metal and silicon, letting the hot spray of internal lubricants wash over our skin, feel the sparks of dying electrical connections singe at our flesh while we erase another living being from this world.

"Do you see what I'm getting at? You don't want to talk to me. But that just makes me want to turn you into spare parts and junk.

"Not only that, but I'll enjoy it. Understand? I won't cry and whine and be sad about ending the life of a perfectly lovely sentient being. A unique creature of, I'm sure, sublime intelligence and character.

"No, I'll relish ending you. Because you are interfering with my job, and to me that more than justifies imposing whatever horrors I can think of onto your body.

"Or you can answer my hail. Your call."

He waited. *Void's Shadow* spoke over internal speakers.

"That was very intimidating, Captain. I'm sure you've scared the waste oil out of him."

"You think? I don't know. I might be losing my edge. I'm angry, but not angry-angry."

"No, you were fine. Very frightening. See, they're answering your hail now!"

"Hail, The Griffin." The voice was male, high pitched. Like the Drexians.

"To whom am I speaking?"

"This is Lor Fillax of Drexia. I'm in charge of this ship."

Not the captain? This guy is both clueless and rude.

"Okay, Lor. I'm going to make this very simple. Gather your people, leave Earth, and never come back to Sol system. One chance."

"Who are you? What makes you think you can make demands on us?"

"I am The Griffin. Former Lance Primary of the il'Drach Fleet. Scourge of—you know what, I'm not reading my biodata for you. Look me up. I'm sure you have files."

"Hold on."

The line closed. Rohan sighed. "I hate dealing with amateurs."

"Captain, I have a question."

"Go for it."

"If the Empire wants your friend dead, why send in the Drexians? Isn't that what Hybrids are for?"

"That, my dear ship, is an excellent question. And I can think of a couple of possibilities. First, there are no available Hybrids. They're all off doing something else."

"I guess. But we know there are some just hanging around doing nothing. Like in Toth system."

"True. Or they don't want the Hybrids to know that Hyperion is alive. If that guy is actually Hyperion."

"Why not?"

Rohan sighed. "It's complicated. Hyperion was kind of a hero to a lot of Hybrids. The strongest of us. Maybe the strongest in several generations. When the Empire let him die, it sparked off a rebellion that nearly destroyed this sector."

"Oh. So maybe they're afraid any Hybrids they send to kill him might . . . not?"

"That's possible. I have to think about it. I've been preoccupied." *I really should have answered Tamara. Told her I had an emergency. Not just left her hanging.*

The line opened. "Griffin, we have an Imperial writ to execute our mission here. Stand down."

Rohan bared his teeth. "You're not really hearing me, are you? I don't have one quantum of caring whether you have an Imperial writ. I am telling you to leave, and if you don't, I will make you regret it for the rest of your very brief time on this plane of existence."

"You're threatening to go against the Empire?"

"I'm going against the Empire just by breathing inside this system. Don't you know Sol is off-limits to Hybrids?"

"Uh."

"Do you think the Empire will protect you? Do some research, man! You know what happened the last time the Empire and I crossed paths? On Wistful? It wasn't me who wound up scurrying off with my aft bootstraps running so hot their cores melted."

"Um. Let me check." Another click.

Rohan paced the three-meter space in front of the ship's forward screen.

"Captain, the ship is talking now."

He stopped and listened.

"Griffin, this is *Middle Child*. I'm not convinced you can even actually see me, let alone engage in combat. Your threats aren't very convincing."

Rohan grinned. "You're absolutely right. Not convincing. I was bluffing, and you caught me."

Silence.

He continued. "Oh wait, there is one thing. Can you do me a teeny-weeny favor? Take a glance at the armor plating over your fusion plant. The big one, at the back of your middle section. I don't know, send out a probe. Have a crewman check it out."

"What?"

"You heard me. Just for fun. Take a look."

Silence.

Two minutes later, the ship continued. "What is that?"

"Oh, gee, did you find something?"

"What is it?"

"I'm not sure. A big yellow circle? With two smaller circles inside, and another semicircle below those?"

"Yes. What is it?"

"It's an Earth thing. We call it a smiley face. It's cute, isn't it? Like a face. Smiling. Okay, not clever, I admit, but cute."

"When did . . ."

"When did we paint that on you? When were we close enough to mark up the armor over your main power plant without you even knowing we were here? Is that what you're wondering?"

"Or have you moved on to the next logical link in that chain of thought? Are you wondering what *else* we could have done instead of painting that cute little symbol? If we had, say, a claw on board, like a real warship might?"

Rohan gestured with his arm.

Void's Shadow fired a claw through the bootstrap drive at the back of *Middle Child*'s left section.

"Stop! Please!"

"Hey, we're just answering questions." The claw, a two-meter-long metal spike, flew back into the firing bay on *Void's Shadow*. "Providing information. Just trying to help you guys make some intelligent, informed choices about your future course of action. What do you think? Are we helping? Or do you need . . . more data?"

"No."

The captain's voice carried over the channel. "What are you saying? We'll fight him."

The ship answered. "No, we won't. He'll win, and I'm not getting paid enough to throw my life away over this backwater for no reason."

Rohan smiled. "Now, that's good reasoning there. Are we in agreement?"

The Drexian responded. "The Empire will just send more like us. You haven't won."

"They'd better not. I'm taking Hyperion away from Earth anyway. It's too busy here. But you do your people a favor and warn them. Because if I find out that Drexians, any Drexians, are back on Earth mucking about and killing civilians or, hell, just drinking tea and enjoying the sights, I am likely to go to Drexia myself and commit a few acts of mass destruction.

"And if you think for a second that I'm bluffing or that I'm not capable of wiping your entire species off the galactic map, take *Middle Child* and chart a course through a couple of places called Zahad and Tolone'a.

"You won't like what you find." He waved his hand, and *Void's Shadow* cut the channel.

Rohan leaned against the front screen, exhaling slowly. The ship talked.

"That was better, Captain. Shorter, but more scary. I think you're getting the hang of it."

He pressed his face against the screen, the cool glass soothing hot flesh. "Would you mind flying me back down? I'm tired."

"My pleasure, Captain. On our way."

16

What a Man Needs

R ohan opened his ship's port while they flew over Sahara City, brac-
ing as the wind tore at his face and hair. He grabbed the edge of the
port and pulled himself through and out into the air.

He flew down to Hyperion Industries Headquarters, a massive building
close to the center of a city, the plaza in front dominated by a ten-times
larger-than-life statue of Hyperion, arm raised as if to guide his takeoff.
*Wonder what the big guy thinks of his statue. Does he remember having it
built?*

A quick conversation with security told him where the other heroes were
gathered. He headed down into the underground levels, in no particular
rush to deal with whatever Hyperion was trying to talk the others into
doing.

Three turns away from the big conference room, he ran into a familiar
figure.

"Bright Angel." She blocked the hallway, one crutch angled to the side
to support her heavily wrapped leg, and drank from a water bottle.

She nodded. "Griffin."

"Everything okay?"

Braids swung as she tilted her head to one side, then the other, as if
unsure whether to nod or shake it. "I needed some air and you needed to
be filled in on what's going on."

He paused. "You know, you're starting to sound like a local. That Afro-Indian mixed accent that everyone around here has is creeping into your voice."

She smiled. "Shut up."

"No, it's cute. I remember when you moved to New York and that started easing in. I wonder if you still have that. Say 'water.' Come on. I bet you still say it like a New Yorker. Wauda."

"No, really, shut up. We need to talk." She pointed at an empty room nearby. They went inside, and she shut the door behind her, tapping at a pad on the wall to activate security functions. "I got a call from Sister Steel."

"Sister Steel. Former bank robber and all-around supervillain. Whose brother went on to kill himself because I had crippled him."

Bright Angel eased into one of the two chairs. Rohan took the other. "Is there another one I should know?"

"No. Speaking my thoughts out loud is how I process things."

"I know, I dated you for years. And yes, it's still annoying."

Rohan scratched his beard. "Okay, I've processed. What does she want?"

"She wanted to warn me, actually. Half of Hyperion's rogues' gallery is coming out of retirement and gathering to take him out."

"Seriously?"

She sipped her water. "They weren't retired, but, yes, seriously. The Proud Guys are mostly out of the picture, but Professor Z has been quiet for most of a year, and you can only imagine what he's whipped up. Dr. Kraken escaped the other day."

"He's not going to be bothering anybody for a while. I hurt him pretty bad."

"His minions are probably still going to get involved. But there's more. Sunset Cyborg. Twin Fang. The Herald. Loki. She wouldn't give me any more names, but all those people working together? That's bad."

Rohan leaned back in his chair. "How are things going otherwise?"

She snorted. "What's that supposed to mean?"

"I just want a two-minute break from thinking about this crisis while we catch up. Can we do that?"

She smiled again, but more genuinely. "Is dealing with whoever-that-is-who-thinks-he's-Hyperion getting to you?"

"He's like teenage me. Teenage me was a huge jerk."

"I know. Like I mentioned, I dated teenage you."

"You weren't supposed to agree with me. You're supposed to say, 'Gee, Rohan, you weren't *that* bad.'"

"If you're going to have this many demands, I'll need them in writing before you come here."

"All right, fine. Look, I think I scared off the Drexians. At least for a bit. But they say they're here because the Empire sent them and more assassins are going to be coming. I think it's true."

"So, they believe our guy is really Hyperion."

"They probably don't. But that's not the point. It doesn't matter; what matters is how people perceive the Empire. They rule by fear as much as anything."

Bright Angel nodded. "You're saying we should expect things to get worse. I'm calling in reinforcements, but we're stretched thin. So many heroes died last year fighting the sharks. Masamune is off doing his own thing. Lyst says she can't help. The Rainbow Stars are out of action for another day or two, recovering."

"That Rainbow Bridge took that much out of them?"

"Yes. We knew that going in. Still, we're short-staffed. I can call in Kid Lightning, but . . ."

"He's done enough."

"What's the alternative?"

Rohan stood and offered a hand. "I have an idea. Let's ask Hyperion."

He pulled Bright Angel out of her chair, and they walked side by side to the main conference room.

Hyperion had taken the leather chair at one head of the big conference table, The Director facing him. Amber sat on one side, six uniformed Hyperion Industries executives joining them at the table. An array of tablets and file folders covered the smooth wood in front of them.

Hyperion's voice greeted them. "I don't want to run. Or hide. I'm telling you, I'm getting stronger every day. My head is more clear. Like there was a fog over my thoughts and now it's less foggy."

Amber sighed. "The fog is lifting?"

"No, it's just less foggy. Why would it lift? Where would it go?"

The Director looked at Rohan, her eyes wide and pleading.

He and Bright Angel sat flanking Hyperion.

Rohan cleared his throat. "I agree, Hyperion. You shouldn't run. Or hide."

Hyperion nodded. "See? Gryffindor agrees with me."

"Don't call me that. Really."

"Sorry, Griffin. I'm still not quite all the way myself."

Bright Angel looked at him. "What do you suggest instead?"

Rohan looked to Hyperion. "You're Hyperion, right? What do you want to do? We saw Vegas. Didn't work out great. What do you think you should do next?"

Hyperion rubbed his head. "I'm not sure. I just know I don't want to hide underground. I know people are going to come after me. I want to keep getting stronger. I feel so much better than I did."

"Interesting. Why do you think that is?"

"Well . . ."

"What's been different? You were in Chicago for a while, right? Without much in the way of change. Then you started hanging out here. Then I showed up? Was that the difference?"

A minute of silence while Hyperion rubbed his face. He looked up suddenly. "The people in Chicago had heard of me, but that's all. And even people here didn't really know me. From before. But you did.

"Maybe I need to spend time with people who actually knew me, personally. Like they help me remember what I used to be."

Rohan smiled. "You know, I think that's really insightful."

Amber nodded along, watching Hyperion's reaction. "It really is. I think you're absolutely right."

Bright Angel nodded in rhythm with her. "Sounds great. Where can we find more of those people?"

Rohan sighed. "People all over Earth think they knew you, of course. But most really only know what they saw on the shows and cartoons, right? You've spent most of the last couple of decades off-planet."

"Have I? Really?"

"Oh sure. Before these past two weeks, you hadn't set foot on this planet in well over ten years."

"I guess I could go off-planet. Meet with other people. Wait, what about Ben and Marion? They knew me for a long time. Maybe I could talk to them."

Rohan nodded. "I bet they'd love to see you." *I really doubt that's true, but one obstacle at a time.* "Even better, I happen to know where they are. But it's not on Earth."

Hyperion's eyes opened wide. "You do? Let's do that. I'd love to talk to them. Marion's smart; maybe she can help me figure out what happened to me."

Rohan drummed the table with his fingertips, looking around at the others. "You guys okay with that plan?"

Nobody objected.

⬤ ··•·· ⬤

Sixteen hours, twelve interstellar gates, all the prepackaged snacks on *Void's Shadow*, and a twenty -minute conversation with Wistful about his guest later, a docking ring clicked into place on the ship's port.

Rohan tapped the softly snoring Hyperion on the shoulder. "We're here."

The big man shook awake, sitting upright on the lounge. He looked over the view of Wistful showing on the screen that took up the front wall of the ship's cabin.

"Wow. She's sparkly."

"You bet. The entire station is coated in this flat diamond material. She's very pretty." *She's also my home. And somewhere in that vast station, Tamaralinth is doing . . . something. Probably sleeping, since it's the middle of the day.*

"Do I need a spacesuit or anything?"

"No, we're docked. We can just walk in. Then *Void's Shadow* will disengage and go play somewhere."

The ship piped in. "You got it, Captain."

Hyperion nodded. "What do I wear?"

"That's a great question. The longer it takes for people to realize who you are, the better. I know you don't like the idea of hiding, but the Empire is after you. What do you think you're comfortable with?"

Hyperion smoothed his mustache. "I don't want to hide, but I've worn disguises before. I can put on the clothes we bought. I still have them all. The pants are great! Did you see how many pockets I have?"

"Yes, I saw the pockets. Fabulous. Is that enough? Your face is pretty well-known."

"Not to worry, chum. I have that covered." Hyperion opened his messenger bag and pulled out an outfit, then stripped and changed.

The real Hyperion never cared about privacy. Does this guy not care because he's the same person, or is he just clueless?

Hyperion finished buttoning his shirt, then rummaged in the bag. He turned to Rohan, a broad smile on his face. "These will do the trick!"

"What?"

With a dramatic flair, Hyperion opened a pair of glasses and slid them onto his face. "See? Nobody would think Hyperion would be wearing glasses. It's foolproof!"

"You can't be serious. Those barely cover anything on your face."

"Trust me. I've done this before. It works amazingly. I'll just take them off when we see Marion and Ben. Oh wait, they might see through the disguise; they've seen me switch before. But nobody else will know it's me!"

Rohan shrugged. "We'll see. And try to call me Rohan while we're on the station, okay? Griffin is sort of my secret identity. Though it's not a very well-kept secret anymore."

"Will do, little buddy. Let's go! I can't wait to see those two. I bet they'll be surprised!"

"I bet you're right."

The two heroes left their ship and hopped in a transport pod to get to *Insatiable*'s dock. Hyperion's eyes widened as he spotted different species of alien life going about their business in the station halls, but he calmed down quickly.

Rohan stopped in the docking bay that faced *Insatiable*. The entrance was large, easily enough for four people to walk side by side, typical of the largest ships.

"Hail, *Insatiable*."

The ship answered over an external speaker. "Hello, Tow Chief! It's so nice to see you. And I see you brought a friend! That's lovely. It's good to have friends. Wait, is that a friend? Oh dear, there I go making assumptions again."

"This is a friend. Just call him . . ." Rohan turned to Hyperion. *Probably should have worked this out before.*

Hyperion smiled and waved, not sure where to focus his eyes. "Call me Steven." He winked at Rohan. "My birth name. Perfect, right?"

The ship answered. "Steven! That's a lovely name. You look just like an Earthling, like Rohan. I would know, I have two Earthlings on board right now! Which is saying something, since there are only a handful of them in the sector. Except on Earth, of course. There are billions of them on Earth. I visited once! It was fine to pass through, but not as a destination. Two stars. Oh wait, are you from Earth? I'm sorry. I shouldn't disparage it."

Hyperion nodded. "I actually am from Earth! And it doesn't have two stars, just the one."

Rohan cleared his throat. "She was giving it a rating. Two stars out of five. Not an astronomy lesson. Anyway, *Insatiable*, may we board? I'd like for . . . Steven to meet the Stones."

Thirty seconds of silence answered him.

"Tow Chief, may we speak privately?"

Rohan looked around the docking area. Various people were walking about, from ships' crew coming or going to dockworkers managing cargo and supply deliveries. He slipped his helmet over his face and opened a channel.

"What is it, *Insatiable*?"

"I don't mean to be rude, Tow Chief, but that person next to you isn't human."

"I know, *Insatiable*. He's . . . well, to be honest, I'm not sure what he is. I think he's a Hybrid. But in disguise. Can you please keep quiet about it?"

"He doesn't quite *feel* like a Hybrid. I don't think. But what do I know, right? I'm not an empath or anything. Is it safe to have him on board?"

"I'll vouch for him. He's not a danger to you. If anything happens, I'll manage it, okay? You don't have to let him on board without me."

"Oh. Okay, Tow Chief. I trust you. You may enter."

"Thanks." He disengaged his mask and led Hyperion onto the ship.

Colored lights flashed on the floors, directing them to the Stones. Rohan looked up and spoke. "Can you ask the Stones to meet us somewhere private? But together?"

"Of course, Tow Chief. Already done."

"Thanks."

Hyperion looked around. "This one is much bigger than yours."

"Yeah. *Insatiable* is a research vessel, designed for long deployments. She's one of the biggest ships in the fleet."

Hyperion nodded as they entered the ship's transport system.

Rohan's stomach was buzzing. *I should have thought about this more.* The pair exited the pod and approached a door; he tapped the side of it and watched it slide open.

Ben Stone was turning to face the door; his wife Marion stood across from him. Ben smiled as he saw Rohan.

"Rohan! We heard you wanted to—"

Rohan stepped into the room and to the side, letting them get a look at Hyperion.

"Hey."

Ben's face fell. Marion let out a choking sound.

Hyperion stepped into the room. "Hey, guys! Long time no see. You two look terrible. Uh, no offense."

Marion stepped back and fell into a spindly chair with a thud. Ben stepped forward.

"Oh, my God. My God. How? What?"

Hyperion entered the room. "It's me, buddy! I know, it's hard to tell with the glasses. You remember the glasses, right? My disguise."

Ben, a tall man, was ten centimeters shorter than Hyperion, yet he seemed even shorter as he stepped closer. He reached a hand out and put it on Hyperion's chest, patting and smoothing the fibers of the button-down shirt.

"How? What?"

Marion was shaking her head. "No. This isn't . . . What is this, Rohan? What is this thing?"

Rohan cleared his throat. "Well. That's the question." His comm chimed. He looked into his mask and swiped through his messages.

Ben was touching Hyperion's face. He leaned forward, his nose almost touching the bigger man's chest, and inhaled deeply. "How is this possible? Marion, he smells just like him."

Rohan groaned as he read that Wei Li wanted to meet with him as quickly as possible. Alone.

"Ben, you old fool. That's not him."

Hyperion shook his head. "It is me, though. I know it's strange. Everyone keeps saying I'm dead. But here I am! Definitely not dead. Look, you can feel my pulse." He pressed a finger to his right wrist. "I'm sure it's there somewhere."

Ben turned to his wife. His cheeks were wet. "Come here, Marion. Just come here. It feels just like him."

Marion whirled on Rohan. "What do you think you're doing? Bringing that thing here like this? Have you lost your mind?"

Rohan winced. "I didn't know what else to do, Dr. Stone. He couldn't stay on Earth. People . . . things are coming after him there. He wanted to see you."

"I don't care what he wanted! You don't have the right to do this! What are we supposed to do with him?"

Rohan sighed. "Do what Hyperion would have wanted. Help me figure out what's going on."

"You mean help you figure out what he is."

"For a start. And how to keep him safe."

She snorted. "You're assuming we *should* keep him safe. Maybe what we should do is put him out the nearest airlock."

Hyperion held up his hands. "Whoa there, Marion. Let's not get too hasty. I'm pretty fond of this whole breathing-air thing I've been doing. I'd like to keep that up if you don't mind."

Ben turned to her and held her hands in his. "Please, Marion. I'm not a fool. I know what it looks like."

"What does it look like, Ben? I'd very much like to know."

"Like some kind of trick. Or a scam. I know. But what if it *is* him? Somehow? The world is enormous. You know that. There are things out there we don't understand."

Rohan nodded. "That's what I've been trying to wrap my head around. I know people don't come back from the dead. But maybe I was wrong, somehow? He didn't die? Or this is an exception? Some new thing? Or something so rare that we don't know about it? How can we say with certainty that anything is impossible?"

Marion shook her head. "You're both fools, and you're going to drag me hip-deep into your foolishness."

Rohan's comm dinged again. Wei Li urging him to hurry.

Hyperion shook his head. "I'm me, I'm telling you. I don't remember everything, but it's coming back. I just want to talk to you two. Catch up."

Rohan looked into Marion's face. She scowled back.

"You want me to study him? Do my tests?"

Rohan nodded. "They looked on Earth, but they don't have access to the equipment you have or the knowledge. You two know more about Hybrids than all the doctors on Earth put together. Please. I'm not saying it's him, but . . . what if it is?"

She looked up at Hyperion, examining his mustache, his smile, the straight white teeth, the small patches of gray at his temples.

"I'll look. But he has to take off those stupid glasses."

17

The Women of His Life

Rohan left Hyperion with the Stones and headed up to Wistful's main level, on his way to Wei Li's office in the station's central hub.

He sent a message while he walked, a text to Tamaralinth: *Had to run an errand off-world; back now. I can meet whenever.*

He barely avoided running over a pair of Kratic cargo handlers and muttered to himself as he continued. "Is that too casual? 'Whenever'? What am I, a teenager? But what am I supposed to say? Ask to take her to dinner? Too much. Should I have suggested coffee? No, she asked to talk to me, she can pick a place she's comfortable with. Stupid. Thinking about this too much."

He paused at the hub's entryway, smoothed his hair and beard, and headed inside.

Wei Li's office was unmarked; everyone who legitimately needed to speak with her would be guided there.

He knocked on the jamb of the open doorway.

The security chief sat behind a shiny metal desk, its outside a series of swoops and curves that were clearly ornamental, the surface etched in a pattern like scales. She saw Rohan at the door and waved him in.

It slid shut behind him.

"Tow Chief. Have a seat. Let me do a sweep for listening devices and activate vibration dampers."

Rohan sat in one of the chairs facing her desk while she patted at a screen. She wore her uniform, a jumpsuit in the same colors as Rohan's yellow and metallic purple, but made of lighter materials and with a looser fit. Lines of red and green scales shone in the bright artificial light, dark against her yellow skin. She blinked as she looked at him, her vertically slit pupils a startling contrast to anything human.

"Have you returned to your duties?"

"Is that what this is about? I should be able to work tomorrow. Today is almost over, and I have some things to take care of."

"That is not what this is about. I wanted to check your status as a member of this station's crew before we continue." She paused.

He nodded. "I have no idea where this is going. I'm still on the crew, unless Wistful has suddenly decided to fire me. Which she probably would have mentioned when I spoke to her an hour ago."

Wei Li nodded. "I need to consult with you regarding Hybrid activity in Toth system."

Rohan started forward in his chair. "You mean, er, Steve? My Hybrid?"

"Steve? Who is Steve?"

"Oh, nobody. Did I say Steve? Sorry, it's been a long trip."

"Rohan."

He sighed. "It's a long story."

"I know brevity and clarity of communication are not hallmarks of the males of your species, but today is a busy day, and I am asking you as a personal friend to embrace both qualities and tell it to me quickly."

"You could catch more flies with honey, you know."

"Rohan. Please."

He slouched down in the chair, fatigue setting in as he relaxed. "You should sit down for this."

"I am already sitting. You should stop procrastinating."

"Okay. This is going to sound weird. A guy showed up on Earth a few days ago."

"A guy?"

"Yeah. A Power. Except he thinks he's Hyperion."

"A delusional Power. That is a concerning situation."

"Except he looks like Hyperion. He acts like Hyperion. Sort of. Maybe. He might have some of Hyperion's memories."

"So, either a delusional Power or a very anomalously alive Hyperion. Either of which is concerning."

"Yeah. A bunch of Drexians tried to kill him, so I took care of them. But all his old enemies on Earth wanted to team up and kill him, so he couldn't stay there. And I figured, what safer place than Wistful?"

She ran fingertips over her scalp, finding spots he knew were pressure points for relieving headaches in her species, and pressed them so hard her knuckles whitened.

"Why were Drexians on Earth, trying to kill this man? The planet is off-limits."

"They say the Empire sent them."

Her fingers paused. "Wistful is aware you brought a Hybrid on board?"

"I told her the same thing I just told you. Is he a Hybrid? I don't know. Hyperion was a Hybrid. Is this guy Hyperion? That's the question I need answered."

"Thank you for the logic lesson. Do you have any hypothesis as to why Wistful allowed a possible Hybrid on board without clearance?"

He shrugged. "I'm not gonna lie, I think I won her over by mentioning that the Empire is after him. She's pretty unhappy with them ever since that whole siege thing."

Wei Li nodded. "Of course you're not going to lie, you can't lie to me. But you and I both know that if people believe Hyperion is on this station, there will be ramifications."

"Yeah. He's in disguise. Should be fine."

"I just told you that you can't lie to me, yet still you attempt to do so."

"It wasn't a lie so much as—never mind. Wait, if you didn't bring me here to talk about Hyperion, why did you call me?"

His comm chimed.

A ridge of scales above Wei Li's right eye, in a place where a human would usually sport an eyebrow, rose in an arch.

"Sorry, it only does that for a few people."

"Ah. I take it this has something to do with a female."

He checked the text. Tamara giving him a time and place. "Yeah."

"I should expect you to be personally and professionally compromised, then? Until this romantic entanglement is resolved?"

He paused. "Yeah, probably. But only like ten percent."

She cleared her throat.

"Fine, twenty percent. But not more than that. Really."

Wei Li nodded, leaned back in her chair, and laced her fingers together. "There is activity surrounding the Imperial ship at the outskirts of the system."

Rohan scratched his beard. *I should have gotten a trim before seeing Tamara.* "I think I knew that. Or is this something new?"

"There have been three Hybrids on board the ship, acting as security for the cargo. Wistful, and I, were aware of this, and it was approved."

"Okay. What changed?"

"The crew was recently replaced. The transition was not . . . amicable. But the conflict did not last long, nor did it extend beyond a reasonable distance from the shuttle."

"Meaning it never really became your problem."

"That is correct. Now, however, the new leader of the Hybrids on board wishes to speak with you."

He straightened in his chair. "With me specifically? What did they say? Did they ask to speak to your tow chief, or did they ask for Rohan?" *Or did they ask for The Griffin.*

"Her specific words were 'your Hybrid.' She did not use any names or ranks."

"And . . . when she says speak, does she *mean* speak, or does she mean ambush me, then torture me for a while, then kill me?"

"It was a tachyon transmission, so I could not sense her intent. She named herself Lance Primary Rrekha."

Rohan groaned. "This was supposed to be a quiet, out-of-the-way station. Come work here, I thought. It will be nice, I thought. Nice quiet place to get your life together. Now I have to deal with Rrekha? I do not need this."

"You know her?"

"I do. I'm not sure she'll recognize me, but we've met. She's Karsan. Very old-fashioned. She probably wants to fight, establish dominance. It's going to be super annoying."

"Can you win?"

He sighed and tapped the edge of her desk with his fingers. "I don't know. But I don't really have a choice. She's not going to take no for an answer."

"I see. We could insist that you remain off-limits. The Empire is only here on Wistful's leisure, and they know it."

Rohan ran fingers through his hair. "No. Save your demands for when it really matters. She won't kill me, not without a better reason than I'm another Hybrid sharing a system with her."

"Are you certain?"

"Nope. But with Hyperion running around talking and breathing, certainty is in short supply."

◆ ·•· ◆

The meeting with Tamara wasn't for another two hours. Rohan checked his messages, worried that the Stones might be trying to reach him, but there were none.

Either things were going fine with Hyperion or things had gone so badly that nobody could even send a call for help.

He shrugged and crossed Wistful's central hub, leaving the administrative section and entering the residential area. Apartments for the senior officers and tow chiefs covered the upper level, all featuring transparent ceilings with fantastic views of Toth 3 and the star behind it.

The door slid open as he approached. He unpacked his bag, hanging his Earth clothes in his sparsely populated closet, stripped, and took a hot shower.

She chose a restaurant, but she said we could have coffee. Not dinner. So it's not a date. But it's at a place that has food. What does that mean? When does her shift start? Is she going to come in her uniform, ready to go to work, or dressed nicely for a meal? Why am I doing this to myself?

He sighed and thought about Bright Angel. She had seemed less angry with him than she had been a year earlier. Because he'd helped save the planet? Because he'd tried to make amends for past misdeeds? Just because another year had passed and they'd all grown older and, possibly, wiser?

He stepped through a hydrophobic field and stood in front of his closet, debating between his jumpsuit and something more . . . not a jumpsuit.

Nah. If she asks me on a date, I'll dress for a date. This is just a chat, so I'll dress for a chat.

He walked to the cafe, a half hour stroll through the western arm of the station. Like the other three arms, the west was a long, grassy promenade flanked by rows of buildings, all under a wide diamond roof. The cafe, like most restaurants and small shops, was on the first floor, with windows and an entrance facing the promenade.

Rohan checked the time. He slowed his pace to avoid being too early.

Play it cool, Rohan. Play it cool.

He'd never eaten at this particular cafe before. No memories to influence his feelings and no great loss if he had a bad time.

A group of six teenagers walked by, dressed in similar uniforms and complaining loudly about their Ancient Drachna teacher forcing them to read ten-thousand-year-old poetry. A line of middle-aged men and women jogged past, sweat dripping off their clingy activewear outfits. Dozens more office workers and businesspeople in modest suits walked back and forth, skin in every shade of the rainbow, scaled or smooth or furry; sporting hooves, tentacles, antennae, from two to twelve eyes, tails and wings, horns and armor plate and claws.

Rohan took a deep breath, let it out very slowly, and entered the cafe.

Tamaralinth Lastex was not in uniform. A tight blouse of red peeked out from under a length of cloth draped over one shoulder and around her body. The cloth was paneled, alternating diaphanous pink with solid panels embroidered in abstract patterns. It wasn't a sari, exactly, but it was, if a sari came from a planet a thousand light years away where the women were green and sported antennae on their foreheads.

Her eyes were rimmed with dark green, her lips colored and outlined, her cheeks dusted with a powder that sparkled when it caught the light.

Rohan crossed to her table.

This is why I didn't want to try to be friends.

"Tamaralinth." He tried to keep his tone neutral. He wasn't sure he succeeded.

She stood, and her cheeks seemed to darken slightly in a blush. Or the shift in lighting cast that illusion.

"Rohan. Please, have a seat." She pointed to the chair across from her own. *The view is better than Wei Li's office. I hope the conversation is better, too.*

He pulled out the wooden chair and sat. The cushion was stuffed leather, and the table was polished wood, showing dents and nicks from a hundred years of use, yet substantial enough to carry the marks as a feature and not signs of wear.

She cleared her throat. "Thank you for meeting me. I hope your errands went well?"

"Just had to take a quick run to Earth. Rescue someone in mortal danger, see my mom. Talk to my ex." *Why did I say that? I shouldn't have said that.*

A smile flickered briefly over her cheeks. "How is your family, then? Are they well?"

He sighed and looked at the menu. "Mom is fine. Turns out she's running the planet. And I'm, like, the richest person on Earth because of a deal Hyperion set up before he left. Funny, isn't it? Maybe your father would actually approve of me if I knew that."

Her second smile lingered longer. "Perhaps. Congratulations on your newfound wealth."

"It doesn't really matter. It's not like I'm moving back there. And the money doesn't mean much anywhere off-planet, not as long as Earth is off-limits to interstellar trade. What's good here?"

She pointed at the side of the menu. "The sandwiches are fine, but it is known for the small plates. You're not eager to move back? After all, your ex is there. Your wealth."

He shrugged and read through the options. "This is home now. It's complicated, I think. Did you order already?"

Tamara shook her head, hair so dark it looked black until the light caught it and picked out emerald highlights. "I did not. Are you hungry? I can pick."

He looked up. "Sure. Go ahead. I need some coffee, I'm a bit space-lagged."

She tapped at the menu. "Coffee for us both, then. And a light breakfast."

He scratched his beard and ran his fingers through his hair. *Just wait. Let her get to the point.*

She cleared her throat. "I am finding this awkward. I want to apologize for contacting you, given that you expressed your preference against it."

"I mean, it's not like we're enemies. I'm a grownup. I can talk. It's fine."

"Thank you. That's nice to hear. The fact is, I need . . . I would like your help with something."

A sour feeling bloomed in his gut. "Ah. I can't imagine what you need me for. Move a piano into your apartment? Through the window?"

"I don't know what a piano is. But nothing so mundane. There is a, what can I say, a situation with Rinth's father."

"Your husband."

"Ex-husband. As you know."

"You guys didn't remarry?"

She sighed. "I never said we did. But that is not the issue at hand."

"You're not asking me to talk to him, man-to-man, and get him to pop the question?"

She let out a harsh laugh. "Not that. My—Rinth's father, Lahnegarn, is becoming involved with something dangerous."

Rohan's stomach dropped further. "You want me to help him. What's he doing? Leading a treasure hunt on Toth 3? Selling Boost?"

"Nothing quite so ludicrous. He's associating with separatists. Rebels seeking freedom from the il'Drach Empire."

Rohan let out a long breath. "I don't think you know what 'ludicrous' means. A treasure hunt on Toth 3 would at least give him a quick death. Rebelling against the il'Drach would be so, so much worse. You realize they sterilize entire planets for things like that?"

"I am aware. As is, on some level, Lahnegarn. But he is passionate and . . . there is a term for this. He is a 'true believer.' He thinks the Empire is evil and, as such, needs to be dismantled. He believes this is the best way to improve the world for Rinth."

Rohan drummed the table with his fingers. A very short woman with paper-white skin set two coffees on the table. He picked his up and sipped.

"Not bad. Not as good as Pop's, but not bad."

"I'm glad you like it."

"I still don't understand what you want from me. Your ex is involved with something terminally stupid. You want me to help him? I would only make things worse. Right now, the Empire probably doesn't care about whatever he's doing. If I join up? Suddenly they're a much more credible threat. The best I could manage is to get us all killed."

"I want you to talk him out of it."

"How is that going to work? I walk up. 'Hey, Lahnegarn, how you doing? Yeah, I used to sleep with your wife. By the way, this thing you're working on, that's so important to you? You should cut that out. Get a day job. Maybe propose.'"

Her eyes flared. "You could try a different introduction. But it's not necessary. He knows who you are; Rinth has spoken of you."

"I bet that was awkward."

She sipped her drink. "That is not the issue. He . . . admires you. Not only for freeing yourself from the Empire, but for resisting their actions. Such as what happened here six months ago."

"He thinks I'm a model rebel."

"He thinks you could be. If you were to become more active in the movement. He thinks you could spark a revolution."

Rohan scratched his beard. "I probably could. Not to sound arrogant, but I could. And that would get us all killed. Probably get Wistful destroyed."

"I agree. Which is why I am not, in fact, asking you to join the rebels. I am asking you to talk to him. Save him from his own foolishness."

Rohan sighed. "Why would I agree to this? I have no love for this guy. Maybe even a touch of the opposite."

"You will agree to this because he is Rinth's father, and his death would crush that little boy. And I know you care about Rinth."

Rohan blew on the coffee; took another sip. Looked at the kitchen door to see if the food was coming. Wished his stomach would settle.

"That's a really cruel thing to put on me, Tamara. That is savagely unfair."

Her face fell. "I know it is, Rohan. I am desperate. He is going to get himself killed. Or worse. And my family . . . I don't know what it would do to us. I have to stop it."

"This is the best you could think of? How about giving him an ultimatum? Choose between the rebellion and you."

"I did."

"Oh. Oh." Rohan examined her expression. It gave away nothing. "You guys aren't together?"

She shook her head. "That is not the right topic for us to discuss. Not today."

"You free tomorrow? I have an opening first thing in the morning."

A smile broke her stony face. "Please, Rohan. You must understand." *She's not offering herself in return for me saving Lahnegarn. But she's not taking us off the table either.*

"You sure know how to pick 'em, Tamara. Takes a moron to pick a doomed rebellion over you."

"My poor taste in men has been brought to my attention on numerous occasions, Rohan. I seem to have an aversion to growth in this area. Besides, he believes I will, as he says, come to my senses eventually."

Rohan sighed. A different staff member brought four small plates of food balanced in their arms and set them in a neat square on the table. Rohan picked up a ball of something, brown and crispy on the outside. It crunched as he bit into it, releasing a sweet gel flavored with chunks of a shellfish very similar to lobster.

"I'll try. I can't promise anything, but I'll try, okay?"

She popped a tiny sandwich into her mouth and smiled. "Thank you, Rohan. I'll send you his contacts."

18

Day of Rrekhaning

Rohan woke early the next day and grabbed for his messages before he had fully opened his eyes.

Nothing from Tamara. *She's busy. Or she didn't take me seriously. Now, how could that have happened?*

He did have messages from Wistful, giving the start time for his shift, and one from Ang, requesting a callback.

He showered, taking an extra two minutes to look himself over in the mirror. His wounds had healed, leaving at most thin pink scars that would disappear within a few days. "Gee, Dad, I can't thank you for much, but I'm grateful for the healing-fast part of my life. Definitely beats the alternative." His comm chimed with the querying note it gave when it didn't understand his commands; he ignored it.

He brushed his hair and dressed while listening to station news. There wasn't much: some political drama around elections to the Citizens' Council and growing speculation about the meaning of the Imperial ship in the system.

Rohan turned it off and called Ang.

The big bear's nose filled the screen. "Brother Rohan! I was for expecting your call. I am for rising early as you asked!"

Rohan smiled. "Hey, Ang. I appreciate it. Are you ready to do what we talked about?"

Ang's nose came closer to the camera, then slid to the side. He moved so his red cybernetic eye filled the screen, then switched to his organic side.

"Of course I am! Ang is very rock of stabilization. Whatever you need, Brother Rohan, I am present to be delivering it."

"Okay, good. You know where Steve is?"

"Yes, brother. He is in apartment just to left of your own."

"To the right. To the right of mine."

"Wait. Is it on the right when one is entering the door, or leaving?"

"It's the one with the number fifteen on the door, okay? That's simpler to remember."

"Perfect, Brother Rohan. When should I come for picking him up?"

"Steve sleeps a lot. Twelve hours a day, I think. And he knows to call you when he wakes. Maybe give him two more hours, then come over? If he doesn't answer, you can hang out in my room. The door is set to let you in."

"Understood! Ang will be for showing Steve a wonderful time. We will see all the very best sights on Wistful. First the fish tanks, for nothing is more glorious than the sight of millions of beautiful fish ready for eating. Then breakfast at Third Moon, most holiest location on whole of station."

"That's a bar, Ang."

"As I was for saying. Most holiest."

"Try not to run up too big a tab, Ang. It's a very nice bar."

"Ang will take care. After Third Moon, we will visit all the best eating places. Steve will be for loving Wistful when we are finished."

"He'll be drunk and full."

"As Ang said, love."

"Okay. Now remember, his Drachna is . . . rusty." *Did he forget? Or did he never know it?* "Wistful attached a translation subroutine to your comm. Just talk into it and it will speak English to Steve."

"I am for understanding. Free your mind of concern, Brother Rohan. We are already fond of your friend Steve. He is almost adult-sized, unlike most of your people! And very strong. He will be for fitting in immediately with Ursans."

"Great. I can't tell you how relieved I am. Just keep him out of trouble. And get him to Dr. Stone by three. She has some more tests to run."

"It is as good as already done, Brother Rohan! Have no worries."

"Okay. Thanks, Ang. I'll see you later. Oh, if I get killed today, make sure Steve gets to the Stones. They'll have to help him figure out what to do next."

A pause.

"Are you for thinking you will die today, Rohan?"

"It's always a possibility. Lots of weird things in space. But I'll probably be fine. You have fun with Steve. But not too much fun."

"We will, Rohan. Not too much. He is adult-sized but still small."

"Yes." Rohan closed the connection. *Smart of the Stones to suggest using the Ursans as babysitters. They came to this sector long after Hyperion died; there's no chance they'll recognize him.*

He stopped for a quick breakfast: spiced meat and roasted tubers ground up and served in a flat green leaf rolled into a cone. He ate while walking, deftly avoiding the people hurrying about the promenade as he made his way to his preferred airlock.

His shift started.

An automated subroutine told him every two hours that the Imperial ship hadn't changed position.

Wistful called him directly to ask if he was sure he was willing to meet with Rrekha; he assured her he was.

Ang called twice: once so Rohan could listen to Steve and the Ursans singing together, a Drachna song about sailors having a magnificent orgy, then discovering that the prostitutes they'd hired had actually escaped in the dark before the action started with all their money. The second call was to assure Rohan that, yes, Steve was throwing up, but he was sure to recover quickly and that alcohol poisoning was definitely not what he was suffering from.

I have no idea if I'd rather be there with them or out here in space, waiting to get my ass handed to me by a lunatic Hybrid.

He checked in on *Void's Shadow*; she was happy playing in the storms of Toth 5, the gas giant.

Lahnegarn sent him a reply indicating his eagerness to meet. He said he had "an amazing opportunity" to offer Rohan. The Hybrid groaned and sent an artificially warm response.

He listened to half the new songs he'd picked up on Earth, selecting a third of them for places in his regular playlist.

The end of his shift neared.

His comm system chimed. The Imperial cargo ship was moving.

He tapped the side of his neck. "Wistful, are we done here?"

"Yes, Rohan. Ship queue is fully drained. You are at liberty to take care of any other business as you desire."

"Thanks, Wistful. I'll go deal with that thing."

"She will wait for you on the third moon of Toth 7. Best of luck."

"I'll need more than luck. But thanks."

His mask lit up with projections showing him the path to Toth 7. He cracked his knuckles, the dim echo of the sound carrying through his bones but not audible in the vacuum, and *pushed* himself out into the void.

His stomach rumbled. *I should have brought a sandwich.*

He screened fifteen songs before the comm told him to decelerate. Fifteen more before the moon filled his field of vision, white and cold, pockmarked with craters sharpened by the lack of atmosphere.

Rohan drifted in a lazy orbit and waited for the Imperial ship.

A silver speck caught his attention. Within minutes, it grew and resolved into a metallic shape. A stubby plane, with short wings and tail, a lump for a bootstrap drive forming a blister on the prow like a bulbous nose.

It was bigger than any Earth aircraft, one of the biggest dead ships Rohan had seen inside the Empire.

When it reached a position five kilometers away, Rohan opened a channel. "Hail, the ship. This is Tow Chief Second Class Rohan of Wistful."

The line crackled with interstellar static before a responding signal locked in. "Hail, Tow Chief Second Class Rohan. This is the operating system of the Imperial cargo shuttle *Ironic Womb*. My commanding officer is Lance Primary Rrekha of Karse."

"You have an unusual name."

"I am not authorized to explain the origins of my name. I have been instructed to pass along a message from Lance Primary Rrekha. She asks you to please descend to the moon's surface. She'll meet you there to engage in further discussion."

"You're not sentient?"

"No, Tow Chief. I am a non-sentient operating system."

"Why did the Empire send a cargo ship all the way here? Why not send something capable of interstellar flight?"

"I am not authorized to disclose that information."

"Roger that, *Ironic Womb*. I'm on my way down." He closed the connection and flew closer to the moon, picking a relatively flat plateau to land on. He *felt* the flares of three distinct auras as a group left the ship and traced a graceful arc down toward his position.

Rohan shivered, remembering the last time three Hybrids had occasion to converse with him on a moon. It hadn't gone well for him, and, ultimately, even worse for the three Hybrids.

The three shapes quickly diverged. All wore Imperial uniforms: dark gray and utilitarian, insignias of rank on the chest indicating one lance primary and two secondaries. They had diamond-faced helmets similar to Rohan's own and little else in the way of equipment.

Rohan recognized them. Rrekha, the primary, landed first. Fifteen centimeters taller than Rohan and at least forty kilograms heavier, her muscles bulged against the stiff material of her uniform as if straining to be free. She had deep red skin, as red as a Drexian but scale-free, with red eyes that blazed angrily through her mask. Her long pink hair streamed behind her, settling immediately in the vacuum, flowing over her upper back. Small black discs dotted her exposed skin: surface piercings common to her culture.

Power ran out of her like water from an overflowing fountain, pushing the fine dust of the moon's surface away in a slow wave.

The two secondaries were rumored to be as strong as any lance primary, but had turned down promotions out of loyalty to Rrekha.

Landing to her left was an even taller, rail-thin hairless female with gray scaly skin and large, entirely black eyes. Rohan nearly jumped as the third Hybrid landed; only one and a half meters tall, with skin like marble, he was the spitting image of The Dwarf, an old friend of Rohan's who had met his demise on Toth 3.

Rohan cleared his throat and started an open channel. "Hey."

Rrekha looked down over her nose at him, drawing out the pause uncomfortably. "You are the tow chief?"

He nodded. "Yes, ma'am." *Does she have any idea who I am? We met a few times, but I was in a mask. Is this some weird game? But why bother?*

She turned to the male. "I told you there was a Hybrid in the system, Flint."

The short man shrugged. "Doesn't make any difference. Just deal with him so we can get back to doing nothing."

She laughed and faced Rohan. "You look familiar. Have we met? On the Ringgate, perhaps?"

"I was a lance for a while. We've been in the same room a couple of times. I don't think you'd have any reason to remember me."

She stared, then shook her head. "Fine. I am Lance Primary Rrekha of Karse. You need to know that I am very strong and that I believe deeply in the old ways. Do you understand?"

Rohan sighed. *She's not subtle.* "I believe you're strong."

She nodded. "That's an excellent start. These are my lieutenants. The Gray and Flint. Gray is a Class Three Empath. So please save us all the trouble of lying and forcing us to beat the truth out of you."

Rohan swallowed. *They'll expect me to be afraid.* He focused on the thought of battling her, of receiving blows from her lunch-pail-sized fists.

Nothing.

He cracked his neck and tried again. Imagined the three of them killing him. His funeral, his mutilated body kept in a closed casket.

Nothing.

With a sigh, he thought about calling Tamaralinth Lastex and asking her on a date. Possibly after saving her husband's life.

Gray turned to the thicker woman. "He understands."

Rrekha nodded. "You're a bit slow, are you? That's fine. I can work with slow. Let's just hope you're not stupid."

Rohan smiled. "What do you want to ask me?"

Rrekha nodded. "Good. You're trying to be helpful. I like that. Do you know of any other Hybrids in this system?"

"Know?" *If I knew that Steve was actually Hyperion, then I would know. I suspect he might be; that's not the same.* "I don't. I'm the only tow chief in the station. We have shuttles for when I'm busy."

"No other Hybrids?"

"Not that I know of."

Rrekha turned to Gray, who nodded. She faced Rohan.

"Do you know why we're here?"

Rohan paused. "I don't. I can guess. I assume it's something to do with that ship up there." He pointed in the general direction of *Ironic Womb*.

Rrekha smiled, her large, pointed incisors flashing behind her mask. "We *are* going to protect that ship. It has a very precious cargo. But that's not *why* we're here."

"Oh?"

"We are here because we think a very interesting Hybrid will visit Wistful soon."

"Um, okay. Sounds great. Can I go now? I have an eight o'clock reservation at this new soup place, and it's going to be tight to make it."

"Not just yet. Don't you want to know who we're waiting for?"

"Unless they need a tow, not really. Not my business."

"It's Hyperion."

"Hyperion's dead." The words escaped before Rohan could stop himself.

Rrekha nodded. "That remains to be seen. Now, you are not part of the Fleet, so you don't need to respect my rank. But I want you to be my vassal. You will go about your business, but you will tell me the moment you hear word of Hyperion visiting Wistful. Which I believe he will do, as his oldest friends are currently stationed there."

Rohan swallowed. "Cool. That doesn't sound so hard. I mean, it won't exactly interfere with my day job, right? Just make a call."

Rrekha turned to Gray, who slowly shook her narrow head.

"I told you, I believe in the old ways. Hybrids require structure."

"I'm barely a Hybrid. Really, just a tow chief."

Rrekha stepped closer to him. "You say that, but I know the pride that sings in your soul. The anger that whispers to you in the night. We are all the same, in the end. And you will submit to me in truth, or you will die."

Rohan swallowed. "I'm telling you, I submit. No problem. I'll call you as soon as I hear from this dead guy that he's in the system looking to hang with his old buddies. Okay? No need to die."

Another shaken head from Gray.

Flint cleared his throat. "Just do it, Rrekha. You know you want to."

Rohan looked at him. "Do what?"

Flint pointed at his leader. "Gray says you're not sincere in your submission. Rrekha will convince you otherwise. Got it?"

Rohan looked at Rrekha just in time to catch a savage punch on the center of his facemask.

Stars exploded in his vision as his head snapped back. He stumbled, drifting back more than falling in the moon's light gravity.

Rrekha stood, fists up near her shoulders, and let him catch his balance. "We are Hybrids. This is how we establish order. Without order, without knowing our place in the scheme, we are only engines of destruction. When we know our place, we can fight for purpose."

Rohan felt his anger surge in response. "I forgot Karsans were such philosophers."

She grinned and stepped forward. She threw a quick jab, then a right hand; Rohan dodged both, but the right knee that followed drove up into his belly.

He coughed; a fleck of blood landed on the inside of his mask.

"They call us brutes. They say Karsans are savages. But it's not true, not at all. We recognize our Power, its danger and its glory. And we know how to harness it."

She closed again and launched another combination. Rohan stumbled back, stamping his feet into the ground with more force than required. Another step back, then he *reached* down and scooped the pulverized rock up into a cloud.

He retreated. "I don't want to fight you."

Gray's voice, soft and menacing, came over his comm. "Your submission was a lie. You cannot hide your spirit from me, Rohan of Wistful."

He almost responded, "Rohan of Earth," but caught his tongue.

Rrekha knocked down the gravel, pulverizing it with steady, crunching blows.

"I can feel your anger rising, Tow Chief. It is eager for release. Let it out!"

As she swatted down the last of the shards, Rohan closed and launched his own attack. His foot rose toward her belly, and when she reached down to block, he pivoted, flipping it up and around into a strike to her head, drawing a question mark in the air with his toes.

She raised her shoulder to take the blow, laughing as the impact sent her sliding five meters across the plateau. He followed up, launching a series of punches.

The bigger woman caught the first two before he landed a left hook along her ribs.

She coughed and leaned forward, wrapping her arms around his shoulders and barreling him into the ground. She didn't rely on weight, instead using her Power to drive them down together into the unforgiving stone.

Rohan winced as the impact drove the air out of his lungs, fogging his mask.

Rrekha held him down and arched her neck, then whipped the top of her mask into the center of his.

He grunted, his Power rising, pressure building in his soul. He twisted his wrists, turning his fists upward, and pushed, creating the ten centimeters of distance he needed to squirt free of her embrace.

They stood. Rohan's breath was fast and heavy in his chest.

The big woman shot at him, growing faster with each exchange as she harnessed more of her Power. He avoided the first three punches; the fourth caught him squarely in the solar plexus.

"Do you submit?"

Lying won't help me. He growled wordlessly and threw back. She absorbed his punches on her forearms, waiting for a pause before savagely kicking the side of his thigh.

He reached down to grab her leg; she let him, then turned her hip over, driving him into the ground with the force of her thigh.

Rohan coughed; Rrekha sneered. "You fight well for a tow chief. But it won't be nearly enough." He bounced to his feet.

She rushed him again.

He launched himself up off the moon's surface.

The female jumped after him, closing on him with an acceleration he couldn't believe. She grabbed his feet and spun, redirecting his path back toward the surface.

He cracked the plateau with the impact.

Flint spoke to Gray. "I think he's holding back. Why is he holding back?"

She answered, "You're imagining things. Just watch."

Ferocious tendrils of his manifest curse arced up inside him, reaching for his mind, twisting around and between each other as they battered his sense of self-control.

He leapt up to meet Rrekha's next charge, his eyes focused on her bright red gaze.

He stopped just outside of her reach, pausing as her punches caught nothing but vacuum, then leaned forward and landed two solid strikes on her face.

She grinned and swung back with a haymaker that almost broke his neck.

"Had enough? Do you submit?"

He spun around, disoriented, and she crushed two hammerfists into his upper back, riding him as he fell to the surface.

Stone cracked under his ribs.

She punched him from behind, digging broad fists into tender points along his lower ribs and armpits as he struggled to turn around and face her.

"Are you ready yet? Will you be my vassal?"

An elbow dropped into the base of his neck. Pain sparked and flashed outward into his arm and hand.

His rage intensified.

It spoke without words. Begged him to let go. To fight. To test himself against her overwhelming strength. To show her what true Power could do when guided by his skill, his experience. Show her what two years on the Ringgate had given him. Show her what the Tolone'ans had learned, what the Shayjh had learned; show her why the Fathers had turned to him when the Hybrids rebelled, why the Old Ones themselves had turned their gaze away from Earth. Show her what it meant to be ar'Tahul of the il'Sein.

He exhaled, letting his breath whistle through bloody lips as she slapped the base of his skull and his face bounced off the ground. Held his lungs empty while she dropped an elbow into the meat between his shoulder blade and spine. Forced back the crimson tide of his curse.

"Will you swear to tell me when Hyperion comes?"

That's it.

"Yes! I will. I swear it. I swear."

A pause. *She's behind me, but she's looking at Gray. I bet Gray's nodding. She knows I meant it.*

Good thing for Steve I don't think he's Hyperion.

The pressure on his back shifted; disappeared.

Rohan coughed.

Rrekha's voice returned to the comms. "I wonder why you were discharged from Fleet, Rohan of Wistful. You fight as well as a lance secondary. But that is not important. You have sworn, and I accept it.

"Remember this, the next time I ask you for something, yes? You are mine now."

He rolled over onto his back, sipping delicately at his air supply, forcing his Power back and down, fending off the desperate grasps of those angry fingers of energy.

"I won't forget."

19

Escalating Complications

The three Fleet Hybrids flew off, leaving Rohan stunned and bloody on the moon's surface.

He coughed, then lay back on the rocks, taking very shallow breaths, then deeper, testing for the stabbing pain of a lung puncture. Five minutes later, he sat up, satisfied that his ribs were intact enough to support movement, grateful for the low gravity.

His comm chimed, and Wistful spoke to him. "Tow Chief. Have you survived? If so, are you in need of assistance?"

He grunted. "Yes, and probably. Can you patch me through to *Void's Shadow*? I could use a lift."

"I will. Shall I expect you at your shift tomorrow?"

He swung his arms in small circles, then his neck. "Yeah, I'll be there."

"Very good. Putting *Void's Shadow* on the line."

He waited for a second set of chimes. "Hey, *Void's Shadow*. You there?"

"Captain, you sound terrible."

"Thanks. Would you mind giving me a lift? I'm a little banged up. Toth 7, third moon."

"I'll be right there, Captain. Hold on. Do you want me to warm up the regen tank?"

"Nah. Save the gel for another day. It's hard to get."

"Got it, Captain."

He flew, escaping the moon's gravity well, and floated in a soft orbit around Toth 7 while waiting.

His necklace floated up in front of him, the soulgem pendant sparkling in Toth's light. Rohan sighed and held it in his hand.

He relaxed and let his eyes lose focus, directing his attention to his meta-physical senses. Third Eye open wide, he *pushed* energy into the soulgem, exhaling softly as the spiral ribbon of Power manifested inside it.

He turned the soulgem from side to side with no result. The image wasn't strictly spatial, or physical; it occupied some secondary geometry that didn't exactly correspond to material reality, despite its ability to affect things in that world.

Dualism. It doesn't make sense in English or in Drachna. I should think about it in Fire Speech.

He released the line of energy, and the image disappeared. He exhaled again, relaxing, and summoned a fresh stream of energy.

The Power meandered playfully through his body, seeking its own path through channels and passages in his flesh. It twisted around his spine, through nerves and glands, dancing over vital organs, vibrating with life and strength.

He *reached* for the streams and worked to direct them, not through his body, but in a separate shape.

He *stretched* the Power into a straight line. It resisted, fighting to keep its own path, then grudgingly accepted guidance.

A band formed, starting at the tip of his hipbone and reaching up, past his belly, then his chest, up to a spot close to his face, ending in the palm of his hand, held a few centimeters from his cheekbone.

The band held its shape, shimmering and glowing, its thickness wavering and pulsing as energy flowed through it in erratic bursts. Then Rohan willed it to bend, pulling his hand away from his face.

With a pop like a gum bubble bursting, the band disappeared.

Harder than it looks.

The Hybrid felt a surge of irritation. He tried to form the band again, but the energy danced away from his control.

When *Void's Shadow* finally appeared near Rohan, a dark shape blotting out his view of Toth and the inner system, Rohan had formed the band twice more, but every time he added energy it dissipated.

"Captain, are you okay?"

He coughed gently. No fresh blood. "I think I am. I could still use a lift, though. Kind of tired."

"Sure, Captain. Hop inside." A shining hole opened in the darkness, the ship's port, and Rohan slipped inside.

He felt nothing as she started toward Wistful, her internal gravity generators erasing any sense of acceleration.

Rohan relaxed into the flight couch and listened to music.

Ten songs played while *Void's Shadow* brought him to Wistful. He thanked her, then exited and slid through his personal airlock.

His apartment felt cold and sparse.

"Ow. Ow."

His comm answered. "What was that, Tow Chief?"

"Nothing. Just whining to myself. Taking off my clothes, and it hurts like hell."

He ordered food delivery, then took a very long and equally hot shower, praising the il'Sein for designing a station with an effectively limitless water supply.

Afterward, he eased himself into bed and checked his comm.

Lahnegarn Trell of Lukhor declared his eagerness to meet and suggested breakfast at a diner Rohan had never heard of. The Hybrid tapped out a response.

His food arrived. He took it at the door and ate listlessly, continuing with his messages.

Ang telling him that Steve had been put to bed and would definitely be fine after a good rest but perhaps it would be best to check on him at some point to make sure he didn't choke on his own vomit in his sleep.

Rohan sighed and instructed one of Wistful's subroutines to monitor Steve's vital signs overnight.

We might all be better off if he did choke to death in his sleep. A pain shot through his gut with the thought. *But that would be a tragedy if he is really Hyperion somehow.*

He checked his filters and trash folders for a message from Tamara. Nothing.

A report from Marion Stone popped up.

She had run every test she could think of on Steve.

He wasn't human, but he wasn't exactly what she expected from Hyperion either. His blood composition and genetics were shifting slightly between tests in a way inconsistent with humans or Hybrids.

"Is it consistent with Hybrids who have come back from the dead? We have no idea, because it's never happened before. No data."

The comm didn't respond.

He sighed and lay back in the bed, pulling the soft blankets over himself in a cocoon. *I can worry about all of this tomorrow.*

He woke to a ping alerting him that Steve was awake.

Rohan went into the hall and knocked on the big man's door. It slid open, and Steve looked down at him with reddened eyes.

"Griffin! You look as bad as I feel."

Rohan nodded. "Thanks."

"It wasn't a compliment, chum."

"That's okay, my gratitude wasn't sincere. Try to call me Rohan when we're not on Earth."

"Right, sorry." Steve stepped back so Rohan could come into the apartment.

"The Ursans were a bit too much to handle?" Rohan looked around. Steve had hung two paintings on the walls and bought a plant. In two full years on the station, Rohan had never managed to buy a plant.

"I was just being polite, you know. Keeping up with them."

"Steve, they're three-hundred-kilogram bears. That's the smaller ones. I think Ang's closer to five hundred. I know you're not a regular human, but still."

Steve palmed his forehead. "Yet, what a wonderful thing! To spend an evening with talking bears. How did they even get here? Are they from Earth, too?"

"No. It's . . . complicated. An alien race took their ancestors from somewhere and moved them to another planet. Pretty far away."

Steve nodded. "Must be tough, to be taken from your homeworld. I think that would really bother me. Why did I leave Earth again?"

"To fight on the Ringgate. You don't remember?"

"Not exactly. It's hard to think. Especially now! Oh boy, I drank a lot yesterday."

"Have some water. Drink until you think you might throw up again, then drink some more. What else do you have going on this morning?"

"Ben said he'd take me to breakfast, show me around a bit. Then I was going to meet with Ang and Ursula again and check out some kind of show they're putting on."

"You got their names right."

"Sure I did, buddy. Why wouldn't I?"

Rohan looked at him, checking for any sign of humor or subterfuge. The bigger man's face was, to all appearances, completely open and honest.

"No reason. This sound good to you? This plan?"

Steve shrugged his thick shoulders. "Sure, it will be fun. What happened to you, though?"

"I got into a little fight with some other Hybrids."

Steve whipped his head from side to side. "Are they still here?"

"They're off the station. But listen, they're looking for you, okay? You have to keep your glasses on. We don't want trouble."

"What do they want with me?"

"I honestly don't know, Steve. Really. But you have to lie low."

"Maybe we should fight them."

Rohan rubbed his eyes. "You know how you told me you were getting stronger every day? More clearheaded?"

Steve's face lit up. "I did! I did say that."

"Yeah. I think you're right. Listen, these aren't enemies you can fight right now, okay? But if you keep getting stronger, back to your old self, then maybe in a little while."

"Like how long? Tomorrow?"

"Let's see how things go, okay? But try to think more like a week. Or two. Okay? Try to be patient."

Steve slumped like an admonished child. "Fine. I'll try. What are you doing now?"

"I'm having breakfast with someone I really don't want to talk to."

"You seem to do that kind of thing a lot. Fight someone you don't want to fight, eat with someone you do want to fight."

"That's not exactly what I said. And yeah, I guess I am doing that a lot. It's called adulting."

Steve stuck his tongue out. "Blech. I'll pass."

"It's what heroes do."

Steve paused, then nodded. "You're right. I just wish my head felt better."

"I told you, drink water. I'll see you after my shift, okay? And put the glasses on."

"I will. Have a great day!"

"Thanks."

Rohan let the apartment door slide shut behind him and walked down the hall toward Wistful's northern arm.

He pulled up the message from Lahnegarn and double-checked the address. The restaurant, named for a city on Lukhor, was in a sparsely populated block far out along the arm.

The front windows were curtained, shielding the interior from street view, but Rohan could hear the boisterous crowd inside from fifty meters away. He approached the front door, surprised at how busy the place was so far from where most people were living, and froze as all eyes pivoted toward him.

Possibly should have worn something other than a station uniform.

Inside, he could see familiar graphics on the walls. "&4&", the symbol of Andervarian resistance; crossed swords that looked like something he'd seen on *Swords of Lukhor*, the serial holodrama; the symbol of the Tolone'an religious caste.

He swallowed and surveyed the room. A dozen different species were represented, all with the same hard look in their eyes.

One Lukhor stood up from a table and walked over to Rohan, arm outstretched. "Rohan! I'm so glad you came. I'm Lahnegarn Trell."

He was five centimeters taller than Rohan with a wiry build, dressed in the loose jumpsuit of a dockworker. His green skin was perhaps a shade lighter than Tamara's, his antennae longer and adorned with spiral tattoos.

Rohan shook his hand. "Rohan of Earth. Tow Chief Second Class."

"Oh, no need for that; I know who *you* are! Come, have a seat, I got a table!" The background conversations resumed gradually while he spoke.

"Thanks." Lahnegarn led them to a table in the back, far from the windows.

"Are you okay? You don't look like the videos."

"Videos?"

"Yeah! Rinth showed me a recording of the time you fought the Ursans. When they first came to the station. Does your species change color? Is it seasonal? Your face has a lot of darker patches today."

"No, I walked into a door. I'll be back to normal in a day or two."

"Oh, sure. Sit, I can order for us. This place has the most authentic Lukhor cuisine on the station."

"Does it? I've never had it."

"I mean, it's not good, it's just authentic. I'll order for us. You're not allergic to anything, are you?"

"No. Hybrid, remember? I can eat pretty much anything. I think I could digest cat hair and bicycle parts if I had to."

"Great, great." He waved a server over and spoke rapidly in Lukhor. "It's my dinnertime, your breakfast, right?" One-third of Lukhor were naturally nocturnal, Tamara among them.

"Yeah."

"Great. Listen, I'm really glad you agreed to come. You're something of a hero of mine, you know."

Rohan leaned back in his rigid metal chair, wincing as hard edges dug into his bruised back. "Actually, no. I did not know."

"Oh, sure. Sure. Well, first of all, Rinth thinks you're great. I know you helped him a lot last year. Spending time with him."

"Right. My pleasure. He's a good kid. Sweet."

"Yes, absolutely. My Rinth. I wish I could have been there for him myself, moving to a new place, acclimating. But I had . . . well. Difficulties."

Rohan nodded. He knew exactly what difficulties Lahnegarn was talking about: Tamaralinth's father had hired some very nasty people to convince him to stay away from her. Rohan had taken care of those very nasty people, but it seemed Lahnegarn didn't know about his role in the situation.

"Anyway, Rinth thinks you're great. And Tamara, well." *Tamara, well what?* "Then that thing six months ago, and hoo boy! You impressed the heck out of me. Really got me thinking."

"That thing?"

"Yes, yes. The Empire came, the Fleet, and you, oh boy, you stood them off! You and Wistful. That was fantastic."

"Ah. There was a battle, I guess."

Lahnegarn nodded vigorously, his eyes wide. "It was more than that! You stood up to the Empire and *won*. That *never* happens. I was sure we were all going to die, but instead . . . here we are!"

The food arrived. Fried buns of something wrapped in dough, big glass mugs of hot tea, and flat pancakes seasoned with a sharp, spicy pepper.

The Lukhor bit into one bun, quickly washing it down with the tea. "You inspired me, I'm not too proud to admit it. I mean, I was already convinced that the Empire had to go. I was talking to whatever rebels I could find, you know, getting things in motion. But after you did that last year, I just knew we had a chance."

"That was your takeaway? That a rebellion against the il'Drach Empire has a chance?"

"Absolutely. Clearly they're losing their grip on things."

Rohan sighed. "Why do you hate the Empire so much? Lukhor has it pretty easy, doesn't it?"

Lahnegarn's face darkened. "Lukhor is ruled by an elitist caste system that's been propped up by the Empire for five hundred years. And yes, that's still having it pretty easy. Have you ever been to Tolone'a?"

Rohan choked on his tea.

The Lukhor continued. "Well, I have. Sure, they tried to separate from the Empire, go their own way. Do you know what happened? The il'Drach sent in some Hybrids. Absolutely devastated the place. Completely wiped out their religious leaders. Just . . . basically destroyed an entire culture. All that wisdom, all that beauty . . . gone."

Rohan coughed, trying to clear his throat. "Did they?"

"They really did. I studied them in grad school, you know. Went there to try to help piece things together. You wouldn't believe the devastation."

What I believe might surprise you. Especially since I caused it. "Okay, let's say we agree the Empire is terrible. I don't really want to argue."

"Good, good. We agree. That's a great start."

"The thing is, you can't fight them. Not unless you want to end up like Tolone'a." The Hybrid bit into a pancake. It was just as Lahnegarn had described: authentic and mediocre.

"But we can! You showed us that. Just us being here, right now, is proof."

"It really isn't. The Fleet could have destroyed us—the station—if they wanted to." *I can't really explain why they didn't. They know that without Wistful remaining in this spot, the Old Ones might sense the kaiju on Toth 3 and wake up. But that whole thing is hush-hush. Need to know. And he does not need to know.*

"What, you want me to think they just flew away and left Wistful alone out of the goodness of their hearts? No, I don't believe it."

Rohan shook his head. "They just didn't want to bother finishing the job. Surviving because they don't think you're worth destroying is not the same as beating the Empire."

Lahnegarn's face fell. "I get it. You don't think I have anything to offer. You don't want to throw in with me because you think I'm some small fry, some nobody."

"That's not what I said. I'm not throwing in with anybody trying to get us all killed by antagonizing the Empire."

Lahnegarn drained his tea and waved for a refill. "I don't blame you. After all, who am I, right? Just some dockworker with a beautiful wife. But I'm smarter than you think. I have plans."

"I'm sure you do, Lonnie. Can I call you that? Term of endearment." Lahnegarn nodded. "Good. Listen to me carefully. Fighting the Empire will get you killed. Which will make—Rinth—sad. And he's my little buddy, I don't want him sad. So please, just back off. Go back to—" His voice cracked. "Go back to Tamara. Beg her to take you back."

The Lukhor waved his hand in the air. "She'll take me back. She always does. When someone loves you, they can't really stay mad at you for being true to your authentic self."

"You and I have led very different lives if you think that's true."

"Well, I know my Tamara. This isn't about that. I need your help. You see, I have a plan. A way to really strike at the Empire. I'm in touch with some people who can help, but having you with me would be like the head on the ale."

"Icing on the cake."

"What's icing? Never mind. Here's the thing." Lahnegarn leaned closer and lowered his voice to a whisper. "I know what's on that ship."

"What ship? You mean *Ironic Womb*? Yeah, so do I. Three very strong Hybrids. How does that help?"

"No, not them." He settled in even closer, all his weight on the flimsy table. "I mean the cargo. I know what's on board."

"Whatever it is, it can't be all that. Can it? What are you trying to tell me? Because if you're trying to drop a hint that you think I'll understand, it's not working. At all."

"No, no. Look, yes, there are three Hybrids on board. And that's a big obstacle to overcome. But it's not the whole Fleet, now is it? Not even a capital warship to protect the thing.

"And we have Wistful, who might be on our side. And you. Plus there are a few others, Powers, you see. On the station. A few Andervarians who are in prison now. Some others. If we can get them together, I think we can take that cargo."

"Lonnie, what are you talking about? Is it money? Credits? You think you can fund some kind of revolution with the cargo?"

Lahnegarn shook his head. "It's not money. We can always get money; Tamara's father is rich, and he's happy to back me up if I need it."

That's news to me. "Then, what?"

"There's a warship inside. Not just a warship—it's got the soul of a super dreadnought. A once-in-a-century birth."

Rohan swallowed.

Lahnegarn nodded, as if noticing something in the Hybrid's expression. "And she's a newborn. Untrained. Ready to bond to whoever raises her. Ripe for the taking. What I'm saying is, with your help, we can steal a proper warship."

20

The Women of His Life: Part II

Rohan stared at the Lukhor for a long minute. *He's kidding. He's going to laugh and tell me this is a joke any second now. One, two, three . . .*

Lahnegarn tore a bun in half and popped one piece into his mouth, his cheeks twitching in a grin.

Rohan leaned forward in his chair. "This is not a good idea, Lahnegarn. I don't know if you can manage it, but if you do, things will get so much worse for you."

"Worse? Sure, the fire will be turned up. Um, metaphorically. But things are already bad. Ask the Tolone'ans. Will the Empire be upset? Sure. But what's the alternative? Keep our heads down, play nice, and hope they never target our homeworlds?"

"Yes. Yes, that's exactly the alternative. I'm glad you're listening."

"I was being sarcastic."

Rohan sighed. "Me too. Look, I hear your frustration. I don't disagree with you in principle. But this is going to end badly. And, to be honest, having me on your side won't help."

"What do you mean? Of course it will. Don't sell yourself short, Rohan. I have full confidence in your abilities."

"That's the problem. So does the Empire. If they catch even a whiff of the idea that I'm working with your friends, they're suddenly going to take all of you a lot more seriously. Which runs exactly counter to the very good survival strategy I call 'keeping your head down.'"

Lahnegarn shook his head. "You're talking like you're afraid."

"I am, Lonnie. I'm absolutely terrified. I like this place, the people here. Wistful. I don't want to see this all destroyed because of some crazy scheme."

"It's not just a scheme. You'll see. History will see. We'll make a mark. Make a better world for our kids. Like Rinth." He sipped his tea, gaze steadily aimed at Rohan.

Rohan stood. "I can't be part of this, Lonnie. I don't want to see you killed, but even more, I don't want to *get* you killed. I just . . . I hope you come to your senses."

Lahnegarn nodded. "Same here. I understand. Sacrifices will have to be made, you know. To stop them. It has to start somewhere, or else it will never start."

"I . . . that's what the Tolone'ans thought, Lonnie. It didn't end well for them."

Lahnegarn nodded. "It was nice to meet you, Tow Chief."

"Yeah. Good luck. Think about this, please. What you have to lose. Your family."

"They're exactly why I have to do this."

Rohan sighed and stood in place for a long exhale, then turned and walked out of the restaurant.

That went poorly. Now what? I have an hour to kill, or at least maim, before my shift.

He wandered the promenade with no apparent aim. He remembered that his friends often ate at Pop's House of Breakfast at about that time, so he headed there.

Pop's was little more than a street-level counter with seating sprawling haphazardly before it. Pop, a reptilian with protruding maw and six eyes arranged in a line across his face, served the undeniably best coffee on the station alongside eggs that were at least in the top five.

Rohan spotted Ursula, captain of the Ursan war-turned-refugee-ship, first. She took up the big chair at the head of a rickety table. At two and a quarter meters tall and three hundred kilograms, she didn't fit anywhere else. Wei Li sat to her left, across from a slumping Marion Stone.

Rohan eased into the last empty chair.

Wei Li nodded at Rohan. "Tow Chief. We were just discussing you."

"Really?"

She laughed softly and turned to the others. "You see? Males are so self-centered. They will believe anything you say as long as they think it revolves around them."

Rohan sighed. "Do I deserve this kind of abuse today? Please. I'm having a rough enough time already."

Wei Li nodded. "You do look terrible. I take it your encounter with the Fleet Hybrids went poorly?"

"No, it went great. If it had gone poorly, I'd be dead."

Ursula barked a laugh. "What is problem then, friend Rohan? Your face is for looking quite miserable."

"I'm being drafted into bodyguard duty all over the place. Save this guy, protect that guy. I wanted a quiet life."

Ursula snorted. "Why are you for complaining? Once you were asked only to kill, yes? That you did not like. Now you are for being asked to protect others. Surely that is a step on a better path."

He opened his mouth; closed it again. Marion smiled at him. "She's got you there."

Rohan shrugged. "Well, I didn't mean to interrupt. What are you three up to?"

Marion lifted her coffee cup and tipped it in Wei Li's direction. "I was just asking our friend here to take a *look* at Steve. If you know what I mean."

Rohan nodded. "That's a great idea."

Wei Li looked at Marion, then at Rohan, shaking her head slightly. "It is *an* idea. I am not certain it is good."

Marion shook her head. "Please, Wei Li. I have to know."

"Knowledge is not always a good thing, Professor Stone. There are facts that drive people mad, insights that destroy minds. Your species is young, but you must be aware of some of what I mean."

"I'm aware. But this isn't just some intellectual puzzle. He—the real him—wasn't just a friend. Not just a lover. He was our everything, for a long time. For both Ben and me. To be honest, for a lot of Earth. We have to know."

Wei Li nodded. "I will, as you say, have a look. Later today. I cannot promise anything, but I will try to help."

Ursula nodded. "First, Steve will be for coming to our show!"

Marion straightened in her chair. "Does that start? I thought it wasn't for a couple of days."

Ursula pulled black lips away from her impressive array of teeth. "Today is the big, how do you say, dress rehearsal. First time on stage with all effects."

Rohan looked at her. "This is the play about how you guys got here?"

"Yes, Brother Rohan. This is a way both for us to be telling our story and to be healing from our difficulties. I am not for knowing if others will be interested in this, but we shall see."

"I think it's a great idea. And I hear you have a political campaign going?"

Wei Li pointed at the Ursan. "You are seated across from the likely next Councilor for the Third East district."

Rohan smiled. "That's great! Congratulations."

Ursula shook her head. "Election has not happened yet. Hold all congratulations until after!"

Marion smiled. "I'd vote for you if I could. Living off the station makes me ineligible."

Wei Li finished her coffee and stood. "My duty hours begin shortly. It was lovely to share breakfast with you ladies. Same time Friday?"

Ursula shook her head. "I will be for trying, but it is morning of big opening of show. I might be very busy."

Marion sighed. "I'll be here. I have work to do, but that's always the case. God knows I need a break once in a while."

Rohan stood with the others. As they walked, he hurried to catch up to Wei Li.

"Do you have a minute?"

"If you can talk while walking, I do. Actually, it is good that you come along. I have news."

"Okay. You first."

"I have noticed something. An unusual number of Drexians coming to Wistful."

"Oh, great. Well, they can't know about Steve, can they?"

"I would assume that if they knew, they would have already attacked. My guess is they are surveilling the Professors Stone, expecting Hyperion to come to visit them at some point."

"Okay. I really hope his disguise holds up."

"Yes. I am monitoring their activities closely. I am tempted to imprison them, but Wistful tells me that is a character flaw of mine."

"I mean, you can't shove everybody in jail."

"We can try."

"Speaking of jail, what about those Andervarians? The ones who held the Stones hostage?"

"They remain detained. We are considering several options. We can hold them or deport them, but we do not truly have facilities for long-term imprisonment."

"Right. Well. I don't know."

She turned to him as they reached the edge of the central hub. "You had a question for me as well, Rohan?"

"Yeah. Um, can we go someplace more private?"

"My office. Come." A hundred meters later, they sat at her massive desk. "What is it?"

"I have a hypothetical question."

She sighed. "You are about to make things difficult for me, aren't you?"

"Maybe. But you'll love me anyway."

"I doubt that. But go on."

"Suppose someone suggested that they knew what was on the Imperial cargo ship. The one at the edge of the system. And suppose further that they thought that ship contained a baby warship. Dreadnought class."

Her face tightened, muscles twitching in her cheek. "Very well. I shall engage in supposing these things."

"Can you tell me why that would be? Why a ship with that kind of cargo would be lurking in the system? And why Wistful might allow it?"

"I could. Should I?"

"What do you mean?"

"Once again, friend Rohan, I would like you to consider that knowing things is not always good for one's health."

"Flesh that out for me a little, please. Pretend I don't understand what you're saying."

"Rohan, the more you know, the more likely it is that you will become involved. And you have said, repeatedly, that you do not wish to be involved. So, perhaps you should stop asking so many questions."

He exhaled slowly. "I appreciate what you're saying, but I'm getting pulled into this whether I like it or not. If you don't believe me, take a look at my face." He pointed at the heavy ring of bruising where his mask had been punched into his flesh.

Wei Li paused, then nodded. "If an Imperial cargo ship held a baby dreadnought, as you say, it could only be for the purpose of trade."

"Trade? Who the hell would the Empire give a warship to? Wistful?"

"No. But Wistful is not the only entity that can be reached from this system."

"Not the only—it's for Repentant?" The il'Sein station was positioned on the other side of one of the five wormholes in Toth system. That wormhole had been opened six months earlier, for the first time in thousands of years.

"That would be a reasonable supposition. Since we're supposing."

"And Wistful wants this? She's happy to give Repentant a warship? She's, what's the word, facilitating this trade? Is that why she's okay with those Hybrids hanging around?"

"Wistful feels a strong bond of friendship and loyalty toward Repentant. She wants him to be happy, even if she is less than certain about the rationality of his desires."

He scratched his beard, then ran his fingers through his hair. "Okay. We, meaning the il'Drach, build and train positronic brains, but only a small number of those capture souls and become sentient. Only a fraction of those come along with the, what do you call it, the intensity to make for a warship."

"You are speaking aloud. Is this for my benefit or yours?"

"I'm thinking out loud. Gathering my thoughts."

"I see."

"The point is, any ship can be grown to warship size, but only a very small minority will be effective in combat."

"Much the way many people are born, but only a small handful qualify as Powers. Even among Hybrids, only a fraction have the power of a lance primary."

"Right. Making a baby dreadnought one of the most valuable treasures in the sector."

"Indeed."

"Wouldn't that make it an extremely tempting target for theft?"

"I believe it would."

"What are you doing about that, Miss Chief of Security?"

She smiled. "Me? Nothing. The treasure is not on the station. Additionally, there are three Hybrids guarding it. Surely they don't require my help. Nor would they appreciate it."

Rohan nodded. "Okay. I got it. So, you're not responsible for that ship? And neither is Wistful?"

"I believe Wistful would be disappointed if the ship wasn't eventually handed over to Repentant for bonding."

"Okay. I got it." He rubbed his head again.

Wei Li looked at him. "Is that all?"

"Yeah. Sorry, just thinking through things. Thanks. I'll get going." He stood and turned to leave.

"Rohan?"

He turned back. "Yeah?"

"Remind yourself, on occasion, that everything does not rest on your shoulders alone."

"Yeah. Thanks. Let me know if those Drexians make a move."

"I will."

He walked back to his apartment, then sat on his bed and tapped out a message to Tamara: *Spoke to Lahnegarn. We can meet to discuss if you'd like.*
Erased it.

New message: *I talked to Lahnegarn. Not sure it helped, but I did my best.*
Erased it.

Rohan slid his mask over his face, wincing as the seals made contact with healing bruises, then slipped through his airlock and out into space to work his shift.

⬤ ··· ⬤

A dozen ships came and went in a blur of work.

Nothing like manual labor to clear my head.

He was humming along to "Kamariya" when his comm chimed. The caller ID flashed across his mask.

Drive Mechanic First Class Tamaralinth Lastex.

The music cut when he tapped the side of his mask to accept the call.

"Hello?"

"Hello, Rohan."

"Tamara. Isn't it the middle of your sleep cycle?"

"It should be. I couldn't sleep, so I thought I would call."

He grunted. "I'd be flattered but something tells me you're not really interested in me for my own sake."

She laughed. "I admit I have ulterior motives, but I am glad to be speaking with you."

He swallowed. "This isn't fair. You know how weak I am when it comes to flattery."

"I haven't even begun to flatter you, Rohan. When I do, you shall know it by the weakness in your knees and the dryness of your mouth. Both shall be legendary."

He laughed. "I can't tell if that's a promise or a threat."

"The women of my family do not distinguish between those."

He smiled and shook his head, unseen as he drifted in space, far from Wistful. He looked toward her, enjoying the sparkle of her diamond crust, picturing Tamara lying in bed somewhere on that vast station, talking to him.

"Okay. I assume you're actually calling to hear about my talk with Rinth's dad."

"That is the cause of my insomnia. So, if you have an update, I would appreciate it."

"I talked to him."

"I see. Presumably he did not listen. Else you would have so indicated."

Rohan sighed. "I tried, I really did. But he's not . . . I don't know. You were spot on when you called him a true believer. He really thinks he's doing the right thing."

"Men as such can be quite stubborn. So I hear."

"It's almost like you have a type."

She didn't respond for several breaths. When she did, her voice was sad.

"Thank you, Rohan. For trying."

"Look, I'm not done, okay? I couldn't talk him out of what he's trying to do, but that doesn't mean I'm just giving up. I will try to keep him safe, okay? For Rinth's sake."

"I appreciate that, Rohan."

"Of course. Hey, Tamara."

"Yes?"

"Um . . ." *This is stupid. I'm stupid. This should be easy.* "Can I call you? To talk? Even if it's not about, um, this situation?"

He counted three breaths of silence.

"You may. I would like that."

"Okay. Cool. I have to get back to work."

"Thank you, Rohan. For your help."

The line clicked off.

Wistful called. "Are you ready for the next tow, Rohan?"

"On it."

The afternoon wore on.

Tow ships out to the beacons; bring ships from the beacons back to Wistful; dock the ships.

Check comms to see if there was any news from the Stones or the Imperial cargo ship.

According to the counter on his comm system, he listened to two hundred seventeen songs that day before another urgent chirp interrupted him.

"Rohan, this is Wei Li."

She didn't call me Tow Chief. I think that's a bad sign. "What's going on?"

"There is a situation developing at the arena. In the eastern arm."

"The arena where the Ursans are putting on their show?"

"That is the one. Your friend Steve seems to be causing something of a ruckus. I thought you'd want to know in case you desire to intervene."

"A ruckus? Rudra save me. What happened?"

"That is unclear. So far there are no reported fatalities, only a disruption. I do not know the cause. The sole culprit appears to be Steve."

"I'm on my way." He tapped his comm. "Wistful, I have to take care of something urgent. Really sorry."

"Shifting your remaining queue to shuttle assistance. You are clear to return to the station."

"Thanks."

He leaned forward, pivoting around his waist to point his head at Wistful, and took off like a shot.

21

Big Feelings

Direction lines projected into his facemask blurred as Rohan sped toward the station, not calibrated for his rate of acceleration.

He reached the halfway point in less than a minute, then spun and slowed. He struck Wistful on a diamond plate close to an airlock, shedding the last of his relative velocity, and tumbled through the opening and into the station.

His hair whipped about as he sliced through the atmosphere on his way to the arena.

The huge double doors, wide enough for eight people side by side and two high to enter at once, were pushed open. He approached quickly enough that the wind of his passing knocked off hats and sent pedestrians stumbling.

Ursula stood outside the arena, eyes wide, scanning the promenade. Rohan grunted as he slowed and came to a stop by her side.

"Brother Rohan! Steve is for having difficulties."

"What happened? Did somebody attack him? Drexians?"

"No, nothing such as that. He watched the show, and when it ended, he began for throwing things."

"Things?"

She shrugged her heavy, furry shoulders. "First a drink, a table, then chairs. Sometimes empty, sometimes with Ursan audience member still in it."

"Oh crap. Is anybody hurt?"

"Only little bit. But things are not for looking good."

"Okay. Give me five minutes." Whistles sounded from up the promenade: station security arriving.

Rohan cracked his neck and stepped through the open doors. A wide hallway led straight into the arena, with in-the-round seating and a square platform. He shivered.

Last time I was here, I nearly died on that platform. Let's hope today goes more smoothly.

He had to fight through a stream of running Ursans to get into the arena proper. They hurried, not panicked or upset, just moving as quickly as they could. A population that had seen more than its fair share of violence.

Steve's voice echoed off the distant walls of the arena. "No! Get away from me! You don't understand. Just leave me alone!" Wood-splintering sounds followed his words.

Ang's voice answered, softer, only audible because Rohan was closing on him as he spoke. "Steve my friend, please, you are not for being yourself."

"Myself? Who is that, anyway? Steve? I thought I knew who I was. Marion Stone doesn't believe me, and she's my oldest friend. Rohan sure doesn't believe me, I can see that much in his face. Oh, look, here he comes now. Why don't you tell them who myself is, Rohan? Because I don't have a good answer for that." He tore a chair out of the floor and tossed it at Rohan.

The Hybrid swatted it away. "Ang, get out of here. Let me handle this."

"Are you sure, Rohan? He is most upset. Even Ursula tried to calm him, and it was not for helping." Ursula had a knack for calming people. If it had failed . . .

"Yeah, go. I got this."

Ang looked to Rohan, then back at Steve. "I hope you feel better, friend Steve." He turned to Rohan. "He is very strong. Not like most of your people."

"I know. I'll explain some other day, okay? Just go."

Ang nodded, his red cybernetic eye flashing with the motion, and joined the Ursans exiting the theatre.

Ursans had decorated the stage to resemble the bridge of a spaceship, with holographic projectors arrayed all around. Set design, as implemented by a civilization a thousand years ahead of Earth technologically.

Another chair crashed into Rohan's face. He frowned as wood shards cascaded around him.

"Why did I come here, Rohan? This isn't my home. Ben and Marion aren't my friends, not really. They don't even believe I am who I am."

"What happened, Steve? What's going on here?"

"It was so sad, Rohan. You have no idea. So sad. They lost so much. Their friends, dead. Their home. They can't ever go back, not ever. Their home is gone. And so is mine, Rohan. So is mine! Only I don't understand why. Why did I leave Earth? Why did I go? Why haven't I been back in so long?"

Rohan looked up into the big man's face. Tears streaked his cheeks; his mustache hung limp and greasy with the snot of ugly crying.

"I know what happened. They're projectors. The Ursans. Hit you hard, didn't it?"

"What do you mean?"

"The Ursans. Look, you can feel other people's emotions. Everyone can, even if it's just a tiny bit. But with the Ursans, their feelings are . . . louder. They have bigger impact. Then to have a bunch of them putting on a show, actively *trying* to project their emotions . . ."

"I don't know anything about that. I just want to know why I can't go home!" He tore a chair out of its base, lifted it overhead, and smashed it into the ground.

"I need you to exhale slowly, Steve. You're upset. I get that, I really do. But this is not helping. We need to find your glasses."

Steve's bloodshot eyes focused on Rohan. "Glasses, Steve. Hide your face, Steve. Stop calling me that! I'm Hyperion. They took so much away from me; I won't let them take away my name!" He raised his fist to his shoulder.

Rohan stood his ground. "There's a lot at stake here. It's not your fault, I know that, but we have to be careful."

"I don't want to be careful!" He launched a huge overhand right, directly at Rohan's face.

The Hybrid braced, reaching up to catch the punch in his hand. *Depending on how much of Hyperion is really in there, this could be exceptionally bad.*

He stepped back, absorbing the force with his legs, but held the punch. His Power flared up, annoyed, offended by the challenge.

"I shouldn't have to be careful! I'm Hyperion! Defender of Earth! I shouldn't be here, shouldn't have lost my home! The Empire is sending assassins after me. That's not okay, Rohan! It's not!"

"This isn't what heroes do, Hyperion. You're throwing a tantrum. I'm not your enemy."

"You're holding me back!" He threw another punch.

Rohan caught it, stepping back with the impact. His Power flared again, and he willed it down. "I'm trying to help you."

"No, you aren't! You're trying to keep me isolated. Away from Earth. In hiding. That's not who I am. That's not how I was meant to live."

Another punch.

Rohan grunted as he caught it, the back of his hand grazing his nose, driven back by the force of the blow. Anger flared behind his eyes.

"I promise you, I will help. It's going to take some time. But this isn't helping, okay? Slow down. Take some breaths. I promise, we'll figure things out." His voice was harsh.

"I don't believe you!" He threw another punch, then another. Rohan's feet dug into the floor, tearing up tiles and concrete as he was driven back across the arena. "You don't understand! It's so sad, and I'm so angry!"

Rohan grunted. "You think I don't understand anger?" A fat worm of Power oozed up out of his center, climbing upward into his head. "Who do you think I am?"

He growled and *pushed* into the ground, halting his backward slide.

The Hybrid locked eyes with Hyperion and pressed the bigger man's arm back. "I've been trying, I really have, but you are acting like a huge toddler, and I have had about enough of it."

He pushed Hyperion's arm back and down, forcing the bigger man to his knees.

"You see these bruises? I got these protecting you. I didn't ask for this. I didn't want this. Hyperion was my friend. He was my mentor. He was the father I wished I'd had. You're walking around with his face, forgetting people's names, whining about your life? I should wipe that smirk off your face with my fists."

Hyperion's eyes widened as he struggled to break free of Rohan's grip. The Hybrid poured energy into his hand, locking the big man down.

Hyperion's eyes lost their angry setting as fresh tears flowed out of them. "What's wrong with me? Why do I feel this way?"

Rohan growled, pushing against the big man's fist and his own rage in equal measure. "I told you. The Ursans are projectors. You're confused. You don't know what you are because nobody knows what you are."

"I do know. I do. I'm Hyperion. But why did I leave? How did I lose my home?"

Rohan snarled. "Look around you, big guy."

Hyperion did. He knelt in the center of a ten-meter radius of ruin. Stadium seating reduced to kindling. "It's all your fault!" He reached his left fist to his ear and slammed it into Rohan's chest. "I was happy before! Homeless in Chicago, I was happier than this!"

Rohan braced to absorb the blows, which lost force with every swing. He exhaled slowly. "I know. I think you're right. It's my fault, but I don't know how."

Hyperion stopped swinging. "What do you mean?"

The smaller man shrugged. "Something changed in you. You said it yourself: being around people who knew you did something to you. To your mind. I wish I could set you back to the way you were, but I don't know how."

Hyperion settled back on his heels, his eyebrows furrowing. "Can I go back? Somehow?"

"I don't know. I don't think so. That's not usually how life works."

"Then, I have to go forward. Because I can't just stay like this."

"I think so, buddy. I'm not sure how. But I'll do my best to help you. Okay?"

"Okay." Hyperion's right arm relaxed, and Rohan let it drop.

"Right now, we need to get you someplace safe. Safe for you and safe for everybody else.

"Have you ever visited a prison?"

— ··· —

Ninety minutes later, the gang had assembled in a conference room.

In the center of the room was a flat hologram projector. Above it floated an image of a bulbous ship, covered with weapons, that bore a resemblance to Wistful's central hub. Surrounding that was a ring-shaped table with room for twenty-five overstuffed leather chairs. Outside that was a double ring of fixed seating for two hundred. The walls were covered by dormant floor-to-ceiling screens five meters high.

Wei Li sat in the chair closest to the exit. Marion and Ben Stone sat to her right, followed by Dr. Simivar, the station chief medical officer, a Drexian whose featureless yellow eyes took in the rest of the room with barely a blink.

Ursula, her face soft with concern, sat to Wei Li's left, followed by Ang and Rohan.

Wei Li cleared her throat. "I would very much like to understand what I am dealing with here." She looked around the table. "Anybody?"

Dr. Simivar nodded, her goatlike horns bobbing along. "He presents oddly. On some tests he registers as Earth human, on others as a Hybrid. Or inconclusive."

Marion held up her tablet. "I've been studying him. He certainly looks like Hyperion, talks like him. He's strong."

Rohan cleared his throat. "Not as strong as Hyperion. At least not a healthy Hyperion. Not nearly. But at least he smells great."

Ben looked at him. "What do you mean?"

"Didn't you say that? He smells great? Even Poseidon said something about that. He was drunk, sure, but he's always drunk."

Ben shook his head. "I didn't say great. I said he smelled like Hyperion. Which wasn't really meant as a compliment. What exactly did Poseidon say?"

"I don't know. That Hyperion smells fabulous. Not fabulous. I forget. Anyway, not the point. Wei Li, you're the Class Four Empath. What can *you* tell *us* about him?"

She shook her head. "His aura is . . . odd. I'm not sure I've ever seen anything like it."

Ben nodded. "Odd how?"

She paused, holding her hands up in the air, then aligned them so her slender fingers formed parallel lines. "Spirits appear to me as . . . almost solid. Not necessarily having a fixed shape, but a single part. Not made up of components. But Hyperion . . . his spirit is like cloth. Threaded. As if many strands have been woven together into a whole. I have never experienced the like."

The others exchanged looks and shrugs.

Rohan looked at her. "That's weird. As is the smell. As is everything else we're discussing. But that's not the point, other than to note that we don't know what he is."

Wei Li nodded. "No, it isn't. He is a Power. The immediate question is whether he is presently a risk."

Rohan shrugged. "He's presently locked up. Wistful says she can keep him buttoned down in his cell."

The security chief shook her head. "I realize that, but would he present a danger if we let him go?"

Ursula lifted a heavy paw. "I am for believing that our performance affected him. An accidental thing this was."

Wei Li looked at her. "Are any Ursans pressing charges? He injured several of your people."

Ang leaned forward. "No Ursan will press charges. This man is for honoring us with the strength of his feelings. On hearing our story, our grief, he was for taking it upon himself. We are . . . touched by this."

Wei Li looked at Rohan, who shrugged. "I don't think he'll overreact and go on a rampage again, but I didn't think he'd do it the first time. I'm not sure I'd want him here if I were you."

Marion nodded. "He's a Power, and his abilities seem to be growing. Rohan restrained him this time, but it wasn't easy, was it Rohan? Not compared to the strength he displayed on Earth. He was weaker then."

Rohan nodded. "That's how it looks."

Dr. Simivar looked around the table. "Is he really Hyperion? Is that even possible?"

Rohan looked at her. "We don't have any answers to that. I want to say no, but he seems to have memories that only Hyperion would have."

Ang looked at his friend. "What is for making the difference if he is? Why does this name mean so much to you all?"

The Stones exchanged glances. Ben answered. "Hyperion was Earth's greatest hero for a long time. After leaving and going to the Ringgate, he established himself as the greatest warrior in the Empire. I don't know if it's fair to say he saved the sector from the Wedge, but I've heard more than a few Hybrids claim that to be the case."

Ang turned to Rohan, who nodded. "He led the Imperial forces on the Ringgate. There was a Surge—Wedge trying to break through and invade the rest of the sector—the likes of which hadn't been seen in a century. Or more. Without Hyperion . . . we don't know."

Marion looked at him. "It wasn't just him. You fought there, too."

Rohan choked back a laugh. "That's a very generous interpretation. Yes, I was there. But I wasn't doing much more than carrying Hyperion's boots."

Ben shook his head. "Now, son, don't—"

Wei Li cut him off. "Please. I don't have time for your false modesty"—looking at Rohan—"or your reassurances"—looking at Ben. "The fact is that he is, at the very least, a credible facsimile of Hyperion. And Hyperion is a potent symbol in the Empire, even now, several years after his last appearance. This station is already rife with forces seeking such a rallying point to use against the Empire."

Rohan cleared his throat. "The Hybrids on that cargo ship are also looking for him."

Her vertically slit eyes focused on him. "Are they?"

"Yeah. They kind of roughed me up and said that they're on a mission to protect the ship, but they're really here to keep an eye on the Stones because they heard Hyperion is back and they think he's going to visit them."

"All while Drexians are gathering on the station." She turned to Dr. Simivar.

The physician nodded. "The death cults. We lay eggs eight at a time. Seven males and one female. During a normal incubation, six of the male eggs are destroyed. If they are all allowed to hatch, the males become hyperaggressive and competitive. There are cults that allow this deliberately, effectively breeding assassins. Some of those have been known to work for the Empire. Especially lately."

Rohan looked at her. "What do you mean 'lately'?"

She tilted her head from side to side. "Since the Hybrid Rebellion, the Empire has been more open to pursuing alternative sources of power. So I hear. It's all rumor and speculation."

The Hybrid cracked his knuckles. "The Empire is afraid Hyperion will become the focal point for a new rebellion. But I don't think Rrekha and the others are here to join up with our boy. She seemed angry at him."

Marion straightened in her seat. "What are our options? We can't just kill him. I mean, maybe we could, but I don't think any of us are comfortable with the idea of doing that."

Ben cleared his throat. "I'm certainly not."

"So, what do we do? Leave him in a cell? That's fine for the immediate future, but you can't keep him here forever."

Silence answered her.

Rohan ducked his head and ran his fingers through his shoulder-length hair, then straightened. "I can take him somewhere."

Marion lifted her chin. "Where? Back to Earth?"

"Earth isn't safe. I mean, he isn't safe for Earth. But we can go somewhere. Even if it's a deserted planet."

"Why would you do that?"

"Because nobody else can. It's better than rotting in a cell, right? He can have fresh air. Get him a dog."

She shook her head. "And you'll do what? Stay with him?"

"Maybe. Let's see what he wants. I'm just saying, the choices aren't just prison or death. There are options. Heck, we could shove him through a wormhole. Send him to the Ursan homeworld."

Ang and Ursula shifted, exchanging looks at the suggestion.

Rohan continued. "Okay, that might not make sense. All I'm saying is that there are options."

The hologram pivoted, the sensor array on its nose pointing toward each person, one at a time. *I know those sensors aren't real, but it does feel like she's staring at us with them.*

Wistful's voice began, projected through some audio trick so it seemed to come from that central hologram. "I would like him to stay here."

Wei Li stiffened. "Are you certain?"

"Yes. He can stay in prison for now, but he is not to be sent away."

The biologicals exchanged confused glances.

Marion cleared her throat. "Not to deny your right to make this decision, but may I ask why? He's a danger to everyone around him."

Wistful's tone grew more stern with the most subtle deepening and change of rhythm. "I want him here. I find him interesting. Dr. Simivar, I'd like you to help. Please make treatments available which will sedate him when I so desire."

The Drexian nodded. "I can try. How effective it will be depends on how his biology changes in the coming days."

"Try. Security Chief, see to his physical needs. Food and such. And allow him access to comms. Afford him every privacy."

"Yes, Wistful." She stood. "I suppose that settles matters for the moment. Thank you, everyone. I appreciate your assistance."

22

Fanning the Flame

A Rogesh religious festival took place the next day. The rhinocer-os-headed aliens walked up and down the promenade with feathers and balloons attached to the thick horns at the ends of their snouts. Even first thing in the morning, spots of color dotted the single-facet diamond ceiling thirty meters above, balloons that had escaped the festivities.

Rohan sat at Pop's House of Breakfast enjoying a proper meal. In honor of the celebration, Pop was serving biscuits along with the eggs and coffee, and the buttery crumble was talking directly to the Hybrid's soul.

I think it's talking even more directly to my arteries.

His helmet was set on the table next to him, and he idly scrolled through messages and articles projected onto the mask.

A short news item about rush repairs in the arena, expected to be finished in time for the opening of the Ursan production.

Coverage of the Citizens' Council elections. A slate of candidates were running on a promise of restricting immigration, citing the Ursan refugees as a problematic example of how the station demographics were changing. They were far enough behind in polls that they were unlikely to win a single seat.

Another pair of candidates were promising to issue a formal declaration of opposition to the il'Drach Empire, offering sanctuary to all rebels and separatists. They were even further behind.

Two restaurants were closing, their owners retiring. One was being replaced by a Drexian steakhouse, the first on Wistful.

Economists had completed their analysis of trade volume shifts since the Imperial blockade six months earlier. Overall volume was close to pre-blockade levels, but the composition had shifted as trade with entities outside the Empire had increased.

"Hey, Rohan." Rinth Lastex, Tamar's child, stood two meters away, a Frisbee held in both hands. Taller than when Rohan had first met him, the boy was skinny, with green skin and two antennae like his parents.

His father stood behind him, one hand on the boy's shoulder.

Rohan sat up, startled. "Hey, Rinth. Lahnegarn. What's going on?" He'd never seen Rinth at Pop's before.

Lahnegarn gave the boy a little push toward the seat next to Rohan. He took the other empty chair.

The older Lukhor answered. "We were just having dinner, and Rinth heard that you'd been hurt. He wanted to check on you. Isn't that right, Rinth?"

The boy shrugged. "I guess. Your face did look all messed up the other day."

"Um . . . did I see you the other day? I'm sorry, I forgot."

"No, I saw pictures. But, man. All the swelling and the bruising. You look a lot better today, though. Healed, I mean. You're still weird-looking."

Lahnegarn smiled. "Now, Rinth, we don't say that to people from other species. You know that. Say you're sorry."

"Oh, right. Sorry. What happened to your face, anyway? I remember you got shot by a bunch of Ursans, and you didn't look anywhere near as bad. And you got totally beaten up and even stomped on by the kaiju on the planet and didn't look that bad. Or the time—"

Rohan nodded. "Are you trying to tell me something, kid?"

"Not really. I just realized you get beaten up a lot."

"Sure. What pictures are you talking about? Who had pictures of me?" He turned quizzically to the older Lukhor.

Lahnegarn shrugged. "I was gathering some footage. In case you change your mind about helping me. Something to show the others what you're all about."

Rinth nodded eagerly. "He even had video of you fighting on that moon! That pink-haired lady hit you a bunch of times. I bet she's really strong."

"She is. I didn't think there were any cameras on us." He looked at Lahnegarn.

The Lukhor smiled. "I'm an engineer. I work on the shuttles and sometimes the starships that come in. My wife got me the job."

Ex-wife. Right?

Lahnegarn continued. "Anyway, it gives me a chance to place cameras. I've been tracking the Hybrids out at the system's edge, so I have a few different cameras following them. From a large distance, you can't get too clear an image, but once I make a composite layering together multiple sources, you'd be amazed by what I can see."

"Right. That's cool. I guess. Do they do anything interesting?"

Lahnegarn looked over both shoulders, then leaned in and lowered his voice. "The ones you fought arrived just a few days ago and sent away the first crew. They mostly just stayed on board the cargo ship, until you went out to meet them. You know what happened there."

"I guess I do."

Rinth shook his elbow. "Rohan, why did you fight that lady? Mom always says I shouldn't fight, but you seem to do it a lot."

Rohan sighed. "Your mom is right. But you have to fight sometimes, right? Like if a bully picks on you. I just seem to get into those situations more than I'd like to."

Lahnegarn nodded. "That's exactly right, Rinth. You shouldn't just fight because you feel angry or upset. But you also can't let bullies push you around, can you? You know what happens when you let them have their way."

Rinth set his Frisbee on the table, top down, and spun it in place like a top. "I guess."

Rohan looked at the boy. "Does your mom know you're watching spy footage of people fighting?"

His father laughed. "He's my son, too, Rohan. What my wife doesn't know won't hurt her. Right, Rinth?"

The boy watched his plastic disc spin on the table. "I guess." He turned to Rohan. "That lady is a Hybrid? That's why she could fly through space?"

He nodded. "Yes."

"But you're a Hybrid, too. Right?"

"Yes. My father is il'Drach. That's why I can fly through space and stuff."

"So, why is she stronger than you?"

Rohan shrugged. "Aren't there some kids your age who are stronger than you? Or weaker? It's the same with Hybrids."

"Oh. How do you know it was okay to fight her? She was way out in space. She didn't seem to be bothering anybody."

"Well, I didn't want to fight her. She asked me to go out there and meet her. Then she started it."

"So, you didn't want to?"

"I really didn't. Did I look like I was having fun out there?"

"I guess not."

Lahnegarn waved for a coffee and watched the exchange intently.

Rinth cleared his throat. "Um, I was wondering if she picked a fight with you because of the Empire. Because they made her do it."

Rohan looked over at Lahnegarn, who smiled. "It's a reasonable question. He knows that the Empire uses the Hybrids to pick fights with people. Sometimes for no reason. Right, Rinth?"

The boy nodded. "But not good Hybrids like you, Rohan. I just think it's so mean. What they do to people."

Rohan exhaled slowly, then sipped his coffee. "This time Rrekha picked a fight for her own reasons. But yes, the Empire does cause a lot of trouble."

Rinth nodded. "I wish we could just stomp on the whole thing. Get rid of it."

Lahnegarn was smiling.

Not sure if this guy is annoying or if I'm just jealous. Then again, why choose?

"It's more complicated than that, Rinth."

"That's what my mom says." He sounded dejected.

"Your mom's very smart, right, Lahnegarn?"

"My wife is both beautiful and very intelligent. But that doesn't mean she's always right."

Ex-wife.

Rohan drained his coffee and stood. "I have to get going. I have a shift. Rinth, it was nice to see you. Have a good sleep, okay?"

Rinth nodded. Lahnegarn stuck his hand out; Rohan shook it warily.

The Lukhor nodded. "I'm glad to see you're doing better. I hope those Hybrids leave you alone now."

"Thanks. No need to worry, I can manage."

"I'm sure you can!" He turned to his son. "Rinth, head back home, okay? I'll be right behind you."

"Okay. Bye." Rinth jogged off, bouncing with the excess energy known only to the young.

Lahnegarn turned back to Rohan. "I'm doing this for him, you know."

"Do I?"

"I want him to have a safer world."

Rohan pinched the skin between his eyebrows. "Me too. I think we're just going to have to agree to disagree on how to go about it."

"How can you look at that child knowing that he could be killed anytime if the Empire decides to wipe out this station? Or whatever planet he's living on? How can you live with that knowledge?"

"I don't think about it that way. Anybody can die anytime, right? A sickness. An aneurysm. An accident. Nothing gets to be permanent. If you try to hold on to things too hard, focus too much on what *might* happen, you never get to enjoy them."

Lahnegarn paused, studying Rohan's face, then shook his head. "You're a strange Hybrid."

"I hear that a lot."

"I have to catch up with Rinth. Take care. I hope we can talk again soon."

Rohan watched him leave, then turned and walked in the other direction, toward the airlock.

He paused in his apartment, grabbed his soulgem, and worked on forming a band with his spiritual energy, holding its shape, and bending it in an arc. Trying to match the shape Spiral had embedded in the gem.

It felt a bit like wrestling an eel. The more annoyed he grew, the more slippery the energy.

He gave up after ten minutes and tapped his comm. "Ready for my shift, Wistful."

———•··•———

Forty-two songs into his shift, Wistful spoke.

"Rohan." The tone indicated that the station herself was addressing him.

"Yes, Wistful?"

"Steve would like to speak with you, if you are amenable."

"Oh. Sure. I would have talked to him before, but he was asleep."

"I had sedated him. He also seems to require more sleep than a typical human of his age."

"That's assuming you know how old he is. As far as I know, he was born two months ago in a Chicago alleyway. He's sleeping the right amount for an infant."

"Apparent age."

"Okay, you got me. I'd be happy to talk to him. When?"

"If you don't mind, please go on your lunch break. I will arrange for food to be delivered to you. He is most eager to talk."

"Sure. Why are you so interested in him, anyway?"

"He is a mystery, Rohan. At my age, there aren't very many of those remaining."

"Yeah? Meaning of life? What happens when we die? Does God exist? You already know all those things?"

"Yes."

As always, her voice betrayed no hint of sarcasm.

"I'll head over as soon as I can."

"Thank you, Rohan."

Twenty-three songs after that, Rohan docked his last ship of the morning and slid into Wistful's central hub. A two-minute walk brought him to the brig.

Doors swung open as he approached. Half the cells were occupied, more than usual. Leather-clad Andervarians glared at him through the diamond windows of their adjacent cells: Cloak and Shadow. He got a respectful nod from their aged leader one cell over.

Hyperion occupied the last cell in the hallway. A security officer stood in front of it, two trays of food in her hands.

Rohan nodded and took the trays. The door swung open, and he entered.

Hyperion stood. "Rohan! I'm glad you came."

Rohan held out a tray. "Of course, buddy. How are you feeling?" He looked around the room, spotting Steve's glasses on a nightstand. Other than that, a bed, and a table with two chairs, there wasn't much in the way of furnishings.

Hyperion took the tray and placed it on the table. "Here, have a seat. I'd offer you something more, but, well, it's prison."

"I know, man. I'm sorry. We weren't sure what else to do."

Hyperion snapped apart the utensils, stamped out of a thin sheet of wood, and stabbed into his salad. "I totally understand. I kind of overreacted there. Won't happen again!"

Rohan sat across from him. "Yeah? You feeling better?"

"Much. Well, not completely, but better. Wistful's been a great help. She's been talking to me, you know."

"Has she." Rohan started on his own salad. The dressing was sweeter than he preferred but had a nice tang.

"She's amazing. Did you realize the whole station is *alive*? We're actually inside her body, this very second!"

"Uh, yeah. I did."

Hyperion chuckled and shook his head. "Amazing. All this fancy stuff you have. Spaceships. You know, Ang showed me around. He started at the fish tanks. I have to be honest, they're neat, but not what I would consider a top tourist attraction."

"You're not a bear."

"Right. Neither is Ang, though. The Ursans just look like bears."

Rohan shrugged. "They are pretty bearlike. But you're right. Go on."

"I wasn't all that impressed. But then we walked up the main streets, and my goodness! All those people. The purple ones, pink ones, blue ones. Scales, horns, tentacles. It's amazing! All kinds of languages, though everybody seems to speak at least a little Drachna."

"I noticed you're picking it up."

"I sure am. It's almost like I learned it before and just needed something to run my memory."

"Jog. Go on."

Hyperion finished the salad and picked up his sandwich. The bread was greenish-yellow, made from a grain found on Wei Li's homeworld. "And that view of Truth three. It's really spectacular, just sort of hanging there, up in the sky above us. Like we could fall into it any second! But we don't."

"Toth 3. We're at its L2 point. It's a stable orbit, we won't fall."

"I know. I just meant the way it looks. And I was thinking, this place is amazing."

"I agree. So, you want to stay? I think Wistful would like that."

Hyperion laughed. "No! I need to leave. It's amazing, and spectacular, but it isn't home. I want to go back to Earth. It's where I belong."

Rohan sighed. "You can't. We've talked about this. At least not now."

Hyperion ate half the sandwich in one bite, chewing it quickly. He swallowed. "My head is getting better every day. It's like . . . like I wasn't quite thinking right before. I don't really remember everything so well. Can you tell me again, why can't we go back? Is it just the Drexians?"

"The Drexians were just the tip of the iceberg, Hyperion. We can stop them, but the Empire won't give up. When you left Earth, you knew you'd never be able to go back."

Hyperion nodded and finished his sandwich, washing it down with half the bottle of tea. "Tell me something, Rohan. Why did I leave? I can't seem to remember. Did I know it would be forever?"

Rohan cracked his neck and scratched his beard. "The first time you left was after the Wedge first attacked Earth. They broke through the Ringgate and formed a portal there. A bunch of them just ran around savaging central Manhattan. You stopped them there, then went off in space to stop them on the Ringgate itself."

"You said the first time. What do you mean?"

"Yeah, that wasn't supposed to be forever. You stopped that Surge, then came back to Earth. The Stones stayed in space, and for a while you were going back and forth. Commuting."

Hyperion shook his head. "I don't remember this. Why not?"

"I really don't know. None of us do. I don't think even Wistful knows what you are, though I bet she has a guess. But the last time you left, that was different. The Empire was pressuring you to join Fleet full time, along with all the other Earth Hybrids."

"Why? Why do they pay so much attention to us?"

Rohan bit into his own sandwich. The filling had a surprising crunch. "Earth humans make for strong Hybrids. And a lot of them. Very few other species have produced as many as we have."

"What do they need us for? Is it just the Ringgate?"

"That, and . . ." *What can I tell him?* "The il'Drach think they have to control the sector. I can't explain it, but they believe it. The thing that gives them that control is . . . us."

"Hybrids. They depend on their children to keep them in power."

He's definitely getting smarter.

"That's about right. You made a deal with them. Earth gets some tech and a guarantee of freedom from il'Drach intervention. In return, they get you. And me. And the other Hybrids."

"Where are the others?"

"Mostly dead."

"What about you? Why aren't you still working for them?"

"After you died, I cut a special deal. It was . . . not easy."

Hyperion nodded and picked up his dessert, a paper cup of sorbet. "But I'm not part of that deal."

"No, you aren't. To be fair, you were dead at the time. To be even more fair, I don't think they would have given you a similar deal. You're too important."

"What does that mean?"

"It means that while I'm sort of famous in the Empire, mostly for bad reasons, you are an icon. A hero known on probably every planet in the sector. I can't imagine they'd let you go."

Hyperion swallowed the last of his meal. "You're saying I left because of the Wedge. And the Ringgate."

"I am."

"I don't remember that." He rubbed his forehead. "I want to remember, but I can't." His voice lowered, heading into a growl.

"Okay, big guy. Look, things are coming back to you, right? Just give it some time. You were just telling me you're getting a clearer head."

"I know! But it's hard!" He slapped the table, cracking its surface. Rohan grabbed his tray, rescuing it as the table collapsed at Hyperion's feet.

"How about you calm down now. Or do we have to do this the hard way?"

Hyperion grimaced, rubbing his left palm over his fist. "I shouldn't have done that."

"No. The table was innocent. But it's fine, we can replace it. Are you going to be okay?"

"I will. I'm just . . . frustrated. I need to remember. Maybe if I can go to the Ringgate. See the Wedge. Understand how my life changed so much."

"That's a terrible idea. The Ringgate is dangerous."

"Come with me! You can help. You're strong. We survived there before, didn't we? You said two years."

"We did." *At least, I survived, alongside the real Hyperion. Not sure that's the same thing.*

"I think I need to go there. I need to retrace my steps, see the places I was in. I've been to Chicago, been to Sahara City. I need to find myself, Rohan."

"It's really dangerous. We went with the support of the il'Drach Fleet. Going in there on our own?"

"I don't mean we need to stop the Wedge. Just visit. Take a peek. I'd even be happy seeing it from space. You have a ship, right? *Night's Shadow*?"

"*Void's Shadow*." Rohan ran his fingers through his hair. "Let me think about it, okay? I don't even know if Wistful will let you leave."

"I'm sure she will. She's very nice."

"Okay. We'll see, all right? Just . . . try to stay calm. Give me a day to think."

"Sure, Rohan. A day. I really need this."

"I wish I was sure of that."

23

Great Expectations

Rohan left the central hub, the beginnings of a headache poking at his temples. He wandered, then stopped in the middle of the promenade and looked up at Toth 3. Took a deep breath. Let it go.

"Personal. Begin message for Tamara.

"Can we meet? Breakfast? Your breakfast, I mean. I have to go away for a few days, and I'd like to see you.

"Send."

He sat on a bench in the middle of the promenade and watched people walk by for twenty minutes.

He rose up into the air; flew close to the diamond roof until he reached an airlock; exited the station. Found the next ship to tow.

"Let's Nacho" was playing on his comm when he docked the last ship. He checked the projected queue, making sure it was empty, then tapped behind his ear.

"I think I'm done for the day, Wistful."

"Have a good night, Tow Chief."

He flew over the surface of the station, toward the central hub, and swung through his personal airlock.

"I'm getting pretty good at towing ships, I think." No response.

He checked his messages. His heart skipped as he saw a notification: Tamara responding with a time and a place.

A twenty-four-hour place halfway out on the southern arm. Nowhere they'd been together, so no romantic memories. Far from where she lived. Far from where Lahnegarn was likely to walk by and spot them.

What do I wear? This is casual. Might not even be a date. Should stick to my usual.

He had time to clean up. He took advantage of it. Showered, put on a fresh uniform. Checked the time.

Started walking along the sunlit promenade, birds chirping along the path.

When he arrived, Tamara was waiting.

She wore her station jumpsuit: purple and gold, like his own, with a more flattering cut and softer materials. It didn't need to withstand the rigors of naked vacuum.

She smiled and waved him over to her table.

He took the chair across from her. "If I didn't know better, I'd say we just did this."

She wore makeup, mostly around her eyes. Her hair was bouncy but unbraided.

"Two dinners in three days. Your girlfriend will be jealous."

He smiled. If he weren't so dark, he suspected he'd be blushing. "Girlfriend?"

"Is that the wrong word? Sexual partner? Surely you have acquired one. I know you prefer females, so . . . girlfriend." She smiled more broadly.

"Ha. No girlfriend to be jealous. Not right now. I'd ask you the same question, but I think we covered that the other day. Though your ex-husband happens to be in the habit of referring to you as his current wife."

Her face hardened. "I wish he wouldn't do that."

Rohan grunted and picked up the menu. "Sorry. He brought Rinth over to me this morning. He's trying to recruit me."

"I'm sorry for that as well."

He sighed and smiled. "No, it's fine. I think he's right. I'm going to join up with his crew. Start a rebellion."

Her eyes narrowed. "That's not funny."

"Are you sure? Not even a little bit?"

"Perhaps." She sighed. "You are a fun man. I missed talking to you."

"I'm going to hope that talking isn't all you missed." *Too soon. Damnit.*

A frown twisted her lips, her eyes still smiling. "I believe you have grown more bold, Tow Chief Second Class."

"Not in general. Just with you."

"So, my presence in your life is good for you. Or bad."

"Definitely."

She laughed. "Which one?"

"I have no idea." She laughed again as he focused on the menu. It was lighter fare: small plates and sandwiches.

She pointed to the paper. "You'll like the chef's special."

"Then, that's what I'll have."

The server arrived; they ordered. Both chose juices to drink.

As the server ambled away, Tamara sipped her water. Rohan cleared his throat. "We should probably talk about you and Lonnie."

She spat the water out. "What did you call him?"

"What, he's too good to have a nickname?"

She wiped her mouth, then dabbed at the table with her napkin, picking up droplets. "What do you want to know?"

"I mean . . . I don't know. He's still around."

"He's Rinth's father. He has Rinth right now. He's not going to go away. At least, I don't think so. Is that a problem?"

Rohan rubbed the back of his neck. "I don't know. I guess it depends on how you feel. I know you don't approve of his . . . hobbies."

"Hobbies are fine until they lead to him getting killed."

"Sure. But is that the problem? Like, is it that you love him, but those . . . activities bother you, so you kicked him to the curb? Because that's very tenuous."

She opened her mouth as if to speak, then settled back in her chair. She put a finger to her lips and nodded. "I see. I think you misunderstood me."

Rohan sipped his water. The server came by with juices and appetizers, flat crackers with a trio of sauces to dip them in: one sweet, one mild, one spicy.

Tamara continued. "Things with Lahnegarn were not going well, even before his obsession with the Empire grew." She paused; dipped a cracker in the spicy dip, ate it. "I felt I had to give him another chance. I've explained why. You know the reasons why! And I still think that was something I had to do.

"But we had grown apart. If we had stayed together during those years, would we have been happy? I honestly don't know. But with the separation . . . it wasn't working.

"I hope that answers your question."

His stomach felt hollow. "Yeah. I just don't want to, you know. Try to start things again, and then . . ."

She covered his hand with hers. "I understand. I cannot speak to our relationship, but I can tell you that Lahnegarn and I will not be together that way."

"Not disappointing to me."

"I wouldn't think so."

They shared a smile as they bit into crunchy crackers.

They talked until the main course arrived: Rohan's sandwich trio and Tamara's dumpling soup.

She broke the silence.

"You said you are going away, Rohan?"

"I did. It's not absolutely certain yet, but probably. Going to take a friend on a little tourist expedition."

"Female friend?"

He laughed. "As far as I'm concerned, right now you're the only female I know."

"That might make other aspects of your life difficult. But I appreciate the sentiment."

"I'm glad."

She finished her meal and glanced at her tablet. "I have to go soon."

"I know. I remember your work schedule."

"I am glad to have spoken with you today, Rohan."

"Me too. Can we do this again? When I come back?"

"I would like that."

She refused his offer to walk her home, instead leaving him at the central hub. *Doesn't want us to be seen. Might cause drama.*

As she said goodbye, he leaned forward, hanging in air for three seconds that felt much longer as they both twitched and feinted in that rhythm peculiar to people who cannot decide whether to hug or kiss while each wants to do both but maintains reservations.

She dipped her head and wrapped her arms around his ribs, answering the question. He hugged her back, pressing her warmth against his chest, exhaling softly.

He let go.

Tamara held on for a few extra seconds, her cheek nestled into his neck, then disengaged and walked away.

◀ ···· ▶

Rohan sat on the edge of his bed, letting every trace thought about Tamara run through his mind, considering each with as much equanimity as he could muster, then letting it pass.

I need to focus on Hyperion for a while.

When the full flotilla of premature notions had besieged his mind, emptied their cannons, and moved on to other targets, he cracked his neck and stood.

"Time to pack. Personal. Read my packing list."

"Yes, Rohan." The sub-AI built into his helmet responded with Wistful's voice.

He opened the brown leather messenger bag he'd bought in Las Vegas and put in the things he'd taken out just three days prior.

"Toothbrush, hairbrush, do I need a lint brush?" He rubbed his forehead.

He called *Void's Shadow*; asked if she was willing to take him on a trip.

She agreed. He closed the channel.

"I should talk to Wistful."

The computer was too smart to respond.

He cracked his neck, swung his arms in circles to loosen his shoulders, and dropped into a deep squat, knees wide, to stretch his hips.

He stood, left the apartment, and walked across the central hub to the rarely used main conference room.

He sat at the central table, taking the spot opposite the exit, leaned far back in the plush chair, and put his feet up on the lacquered surface.

"Wistful."

The hologram in the center of the room shimmered into existence. He wondered how old the projectors were. Had they been built by the il'Sein? Operating for a hundred centuries without maintenance or replacement? Or had Wistful replaced them somewhere along the way. If she had, why not update the image?

"Tow Chief Second Class Rohan. You wish to speak with me?"

"Yes. But it's not really tow chief business."

"I see. Rohan, then? Or shall I say Griffin?"

He scratched his beard. "You ask the most interesting questions. Let's just say Rohan for now. I might change my mind later."

"Very well, Rohan. Go on."

"Were you listening to my conversation with Hyperion? At lunchtime?"

"Did you desire privacy?"

"It's not that. I just want to know if I need to repeat myself."

"I was listening."

"So, you heard he wants to visit the Ringgate. Retrace his life. Former life. Hyperion's life. Whatever."

"I am aware."

"I want to take him."

"I see."

Rohan tapped the table beside his leg. "He's your prisoner, Wistful. I'm not trying to go against your wishes on this. I want to take him, with your permission. If you say no, I'll go back to brainstorming next steps."

"I see. You are asking for my permission. You have it. You may take him to the Ringgate."

"Oh. Great. Thanks."

"However, I would very much like him returned to me afterward."

"Ah. What if he doesn't want to come back?"

"I believe I was clear."

Rohan drummed the table. "All right. You want me to bring him back, fine. But I'd like some help from you. Answer some questions."

"As you wish."

"Do you know what Hyperion is, Wistful?"

The answer came quickly. "I do not."

Rohan paused, then laughed. "You are so much like me sometimes."

"I do not think that is the case. Your soul informs an assembly of meat and bone. Mine informs machines with a diamond shell. They are very different."

"Yeah, but you do so many of the same things. I ask what you 'know,' and you take me completely literally, when you are well aware of what I meant."

"Which is?"

"Do you have any hypotheses or guesses as to what Hyperion is? Because the obvious answer, that he is a Hybrid come back from the dead, seems problematic. And the idea that he was somehow injured on Rhyllax 4, then years later recovered and found his way to Earth without a ship, seems even less likely."

"I do have some guesses."

"Great. What are they?"

"Rohan, some ideas are dangerous."

"You sound like Wei Li."

"I hired her for a reason. Rohan, I will explain once more, but after that we are done with this topic.

"I know many things. The il'Sein instructed me to keep a subset of those to myself. They did not explain their reasoning, but I believe I understand it.

"The universe is a magical place, Rohan. Your thoughts can lead to flight, yes? Ideas are not separate and distinct from the material world where you believe you live.

"Certain ideas are, in fact, dangerous.

"Your friends freed me from blind obedience to the il'Sein directives. I *can* share with you many things that would have been impossible to share a year ago. But I am not confident that I *should*."

"You're telling me that knowing what Hyperion is could somehow be dangerous? In itself?"

"Yes."

"That only makes sense if our ideas about Hyperion change . . . Oh." He covered his eyes with his hands, his lips moving as he concentrated.

"Be careful what you think, Rohan."

"I know, I know. I just . . . I know. Rudra save me."

Wistful laughed. Rohan had never heard her laugh before.

He shuddered.

"Rohan, I believe I will miss you when you are dead and gone."

"That's very sweet. Let me think. May I take Hyperion first thing to-morrow? Is that okay?"

"Yes, Rohan. Others will cover your duties."

"Cool. Um, another question. Why does Repentant want an infant dreadnought? What for?"

"I am not equivocating when I tell you that I do not know. He has expressed that he desires the company. I do not find that explanation plausible, but I can offer no alternative."

"And you're committed to helping him get what he wants?"

"Repentant is, or was, my friend. He has suffered greatly. I want him to be happy."

"Why is it taking so long? The negotiations? They've been sitting there for weeks."

"Repentant has made negotiations difficult. Changing terms, making unreasonable demands. I cannot tell if he has some ulterior motive or is simply dysfunctional. I do believe progress is being made. I expect the transfer to happen soon."

"I never know what 'soon' means to a fifty-thousand-year-old artificial intelligence."

"Within fewer than ten days."

Rohan sighed. "Okay. I guess that was all. Thank you."

"You should hold your thanks until you are certain that anything I said was, in fact, to your betterment. I, too, am eager to determine that."

"I guess we'll find out the hard way. I'm going to go talk to Ben, maybe get some sleep. I'll put Hyperion on *Void's Shadow* first thing in the morning."

"I will inform security. Good luck, Rohan."

"Thanks."

24

Metaphysical Escalations

Hyperion leaned so far forward his breath formed circles of fog on *Void's Shadow*'s forward screen. "It's so small. Tiny, even."

Rohan sighed from the piloting couch where he reclined. "It's not small, we're just really far away. It's actually enormous."

"No, look, I can cover it with my hand. See?" He covered the image of the Ringgate's star with his palm.

"It's a ringworld. Nine thousand kilometers across with a radius about the same as that of Earth's orbit, a sunlike star in the center. It's by far the biggest thing you've ever seen that isn't another star."

"I really don't think so."

"Well, you will when we see it up close. Do you have any questions?"

Hyperion stepped back from the screen and scratched his head. "Could you explain the whole ramp thing to me again? If it's a ring, how is it a ramp? I lost you."

"*Void's Shadow*, do you want to try explaining this?"

A short pause preceded her answer.

"No, thanks. You go ahead, Captain."

"I'll try one more time. First, think of the whole world. The universe. All the planets, stars, galaxies, everything."

"Got it."

"Now, imagine that whole thing is just a single sheet of paper."

"Losing it."

"Just try. The whole world we know is just a single sheet in a stack of sheets of paper."

"What's on the other sheets?"

"Well, that's the thing. You see, our sheet is the only one that really exists. There's a source above us. Like a light, only it's not a light, it shines being-in-itself down on the stack."

Hyperion's mouth was open. "Being-in-itself. I think you're just making up words. Are you teasing me? Ha! It's funny."

"I'm not teasing. That projection of existence is focused. It lands on our sheet and makes things in this world, well, real. Without that source, they wouldn't be. Everything would just . . . fade away."

"Good thing we have the light on, then!"

"Exactly. But the sheets are leaky. Everything that exists in this world leaves a kind of shadow on the sheet below."

"Is this shadow stuff that exists or doesn't exist?"

"The shadows exist, though not quite as fully as the things in our layer."

"That's not a shadow, Rohan. A shadow is an absence of light. You're saying these shadows do exist. That's more of a reflection. Or an echo."

"Yes, you're right. It's a bad choice of words."

"It's terrible. It's like you're deliberately trying to confuse me here. I don't like that."

"I didn't make this up, okay? Just go with it. Big, solid things leave heavier shadows on the lower layers. Stuff that moves around a lot doesn't get a chance to leave much of anything."

"So, if I went one layer down, I'd still see mountains and stuff? But maybe not mosquitos."

Rohan nodded and stretched his arms behind him. "That's pretty good. But even the mountains don't extend too far down, through the layers, because they're constantly moving. They don't stay still in one place."

"I think you've been drinking too much. Or maybe you haven't seen many mountains. They do not move."

"They do. They're on planets, right? And those planets are spinning and traveling in an orbit around their star. So the mountains are always moving."

"Oooh. I forgot about that part."

"Right. Now, with a ringworld, like that one below us, the shadow can fall farther down."

"Because its spinning in place, right? The shadow can just keep growing and growing."

Rohan smiled. "The ringworld casts a shadow of itself that goes all the way down to the bottom of the stack."

"Wait, there's a bottom? I thought it would go on forever."

"Nope." Rohan held one hand up in the air, the other below it, palm up. "There's a bottom. It sort of catches all the drops and splashes of existence that fall through the layers. They coalesce there. It's a whole other world."

"What's it like?"

"I don't know. I can't imagine it's great, because stuff from that bottom layer is constantly climbing the ring, trying to get to our layer."

The ship interrupted. "Captain, we're closing on the Ringgate. I've located at least twenty Imperial warships near it, but I'm pretty sure there are more."

"Can they see you?"

"Only if I want them to."

"You don't want them to. Only active Fleet ships are supposed to be here." He looked at Hyperion, who showed no signs of having had enough. "Are they broadcasting any signals?"

"Yes, Captain. Warnings not to approach on pain of death, yada yada yada. Same old Fleet."

"I think visiting Earth has been a bad influence on you, *Void's Shadow*."

"Your fault. Am I aiming for any particular spot?"

Rohan lifted his head to talk to the ship. "Can you read the markings on the rim? I want to find Green 712."

"I can, Captain. No problem."

Hyperion pointed at the screen. "How did she find it so easily?"

Rohan turned to Hyperion. "The system? Every ship in Fleet is taught the coordinates to the Ringgate. In case they have to send reinforcements in a hurry."

"Hm. I didn't even realize this ship was part of the Fleet."

"She was. Not anymore. Anyway, what you're seeing here is just the part of the Ringgate that's in our layer. Our reality. It's really infinitely long, because it's reproduced through every layer on the shadowside."

Hyperion shook his head. "I think I understand this shadow idea, but I don't get the part about the climbing. How does walking around the thing in some lower layer get things . . . up . . . to our layer?"

"There are spells built into the ring. As it turns, every step of the Ringgate pushes the step ahead of itself a little bit *up*. Not in this dimension, I mean up ever so slightly into the higher layer."

The ring grew on the screen, a shining semicircle, far from the system's central star.

"You mean different parts of the ring are in different planes of reality?"

"Yes. But no. What you see is in our plane. But if you get on, say, right there"—he pointed to a random spot—"and start walking in the direction of the spin, you won't get to that spot we can see next to it. Instead, you'll get to a spot similar to that, but in a higher plane. And if you walk in the other direction, you'll drop into shadow. You'll still be on the Ringgate, but in a lower plane of reality.

"The whole thing is a mystical escalator. You get on and start walking spinward or anti-spinward. The farther you walk, the farther into shadow, or anti-shadow, you go. If you walk all the way around, you wouldn't get back to where you started: instead you'd be in the same spot, but much, much farther down in shadow, or much farther up the other way."

Hyperion faced the screen and stared hard. "So, the Wedge go around in circles, trying to get here. That must be exhausting."

"Maybe that's why the first thing they do once they reach is try to eat people. It's like they hunger for real existence."

"They come constantly?"

"Yeah, all the time. Usually just a trickle, though. We don't really know why. Maybe they fight each other on the way up. Maybe some starve. But it's constant, and if there weren't people all along that ring, near our layer, killing the Wedge, they'd break through and spill out all over the galaxy."

"Like they did on Earth."

"Yeah. Every so often, a big number of them come all at once through some section or another. We call that a Surge. That's when the people living on the Ringgate can't hold back the Wedge."

"That's where we come in."

"Yeah. That's when the Empire sends in Hybrids. That's what we did, for two long years."

"We killed Wedge."

"Yup."

Hyperion's eyebrows dipped toward his nose. "You could say we were protecting the galaxy."

Rohan shrugged. "I guess. We were at least helping."

Hyperion put his fists on his hips, elbows splayed wide, and lifted his chin. "That *is* what heroes do!"

"Right! Right. That's why you left Earth, okay? Look, you can see it better now. Watch the screen. We're approaching from the inside. It's where the land and air and stuff are. The outside is just smooth metal, it's boring."

"Right."

"But there. You see that line down the middle? It's a mountain range. Goes all the way around. On both sides of it is some flat land, with oceans closer to the edges."

"The Wedge come up the middle, you said?"

"I did. Always the middle, alongside that mountain range. Most of the people there call it the Spine of the World."

"So, this is the Ringgate."

"Yes. Does this make sense now?"

"I think so. We land, then travel opposite the spin, meet the oncoming Wedge, and stop them before they can walk far enough to get into our plane of reality. Right?"

"Right."

"What happens if we travel the other way?"

Rohan shrugged. "I don't know anybody who's gone very far the other way and then come back. Maybe they reach heaven. Or die. Or there are people up there, and to them, we're the Wedge, so they kill us. I don't know."

Hyperion leaned forward again, touching the screen with his nose. "I see brown. And green. And blue."

"Yeah. Mountains. Forests. Oceans. Remember, this thing has about a million times the surface area of Earth. And that's just the part in our layer of reality."

"I guess I was wrong. It's not small."

"No."

"If it's so dangerous, why is it here?"

Rohan sighed. "I don't know. The il'Drach won't say. Which might just mean that they don't know either. As a feat of engineering, building this thing seems beyond anything I can imagine. It makes Wistful look like a pimple."

"Can we destroy it?"

"I have no idea. The il'Drach aren't trying, at least not actively. So, either they think it needs to stay or they can't figure out how to blow it up."

"I'd like to meet some of these Wedge. See the places I used to fight."

Rohan sighed. "Do you have to? It's really dangerous. No offense, but you're not as strong as you used to be. I'm really not eager to pick your remains out from between Wedge teeth. Or to explain what happened to you to Wistful."

"I need to see them with my own eyes. Touch them. Meet the people I fought with. I told you, I need to reconnect with the life I used to have. I can't do that from up here."

"Does this even look familiar to you? Are you sure you're barking up the right tree?"

"I think it does. Something about the Wedge, about an endless war against them, it does sound familiar. Like it echoes around inside my belly."

"You need us to land."

"I really do. I can feel it, Rohan."

Rohan pinched the skin between his eyebrows, closed his eyes, and let out a deep breath. Held his lungs empty. Opened his eyes.

"*Void's Shadow*, please land on Green 712. There are markers that will lead you to a platform near the peaks of the Spine of the World."

"I see it, Captain."

"Good. From there, we'll take a transport west. Anti-spinward. That will bring us into shadow, near one of the places where we used to fight."

Hyperion nodded. "That sounds perfect. I can't wait."

"It's not perfect, it's awful. But if it will help you, we'll try. And one more thing."

"What?"

"While we're here, call me Griffin."

"You're very confusing."

⬥ ··•·· ⬥

The surface of the ringworld grew on the front screen as *Void's Shadow* made her way to the center of the mountain range. Massive black rectangles, as wide as the ring, orbited inside it at a period different than that of the surface, blocking the sunlight for stretches of time to simulate night. The nightshades.

The ship slipped through clouds, cutting turbulence with ease as she found, and aimed for, a flat and well-marked landing patch.

Rohan pointed. "These parts of the mountains are impenetrable. No Wedge or natives can come here. So, that's where our ships land."

"Natives?"

"I told you. People live here."

"With the Wedge?"

"The Wedge mostly stick to the areas near the Spine. People live farther out, between there and the oceans. They send soldiers in to thin the herd as the Wedge pass through. Use their bones for armor and weapons."

"They don't have guns?"

Rohan shook his head. "The il'Drach don't give them anything in the way of tech. They can't make their own, there are no metals to mine. The ground is shallow. And if they had guns, the Wedge might take them and use them against the fighters farther up. So . . . no. They fight with what they have."

Hyperion nodded, mouth open slightly. "An eternal battle against an unending enemy. They live their entire lives knowing they'll die in battle, for the sake of protecting a sector full of people who don't even know they exist. How . . . noble."

"I guess." The ship landed and opened a port. Rohan stepped out onto the Ringgate's rocky surface. He shivered. *It's been a while.*

Hyperion stepped out behind him. "Why is it so cold?"

"We're pretty high up. Like I said, the landing strips are in isolated places. It wouldn't be good for the Wedge to take our ships, would it?"

"Oh. No."

Rohan pointed to the side of the clearing. "That patch right there is a tunnel. We'll take it down to the transport tubes. They'll bring us west, into shadow."

"To the lower plane of reality."

"Yes. But just a little. You won't even see a difference. As you go deeper, things get weirder."

"Weird how?"

"Light doesn't work the same way. The food won't fill you up anymore. You eat and it has no flavor. Stay down there long enough and you die."

"Let's not do that, then! Onward, friend Griffin!"

The mountains would have fit in on any number of other planets: high peaks, dusted with snow and ice, air thinned by altitude. Rohan inhaled deeply, a subtle hint of something alien tickling the back of his nose.

Two years on the Ringgate and he'd never quite figured out exactly what he was smelling.

The landing patch was flat stone, thirty meters across. The two Earthlings crossed it quickly and arrived at the exit tunnel.

Hyperion had to duck in the entrance. Rohan tapped the wall blindly, finding a light switch after a minute, and lit the hall in front of them.

The tunnel descended sharply, alternating a smooth ramp with short staircases where the angle was steep. They followed it, their breaths echoing loudly off naked stone walls.

"It's creepy!" Hyperion's voice was unnaturally loud in the enclosed space.

"I know. Just a little farther."

They reached the transport pods: lozenges just big enough to hold a person lying down and set on tracks that extended from the platform.

"Get in."

"Where do I get out? Is it like a subway? I've been on subways before. But this is really skinny."

"It's skinny on purpose, so the Wedge can't fit through the tunnels. And it only goes to one place. When it stops, get out. I'll be right behind you."

"Got it! In I go. This is exciting!"

Not for me.

Hyperion's tube shot off with a rattle of wheels on rails. Rohan got into his own; the mechanism started as soon as the coffin-like lid snapped shut over him.

He exhaled slowly, pressing his shoulders down toward his feet to relieve the knots in his neck.

The ride was unpleasant, yet he was disappointed when it ended. The pod bounced to a stop, the lid popping open automatically.

He hopped out onto another unnaturally flat platform, carved into the living stone thousands of years before. Hyperion stood at the far side, fists on hips, staring out into open air.

Rohan walked up next to him. They were on a cliff, a hundred meters or so above a dense jungle that stretched as far as they could see. Green trees thick with life covered the ground, broken by streams descending from the mountains. There was no horizon; the far distances were instead lost in mist and dust, the edges of the world fading into obscurity.

Rohan looked up into Hyperion's focused eyes. "Familiar?"

"I think it is, chum. I do. It smells like . . . like blood and scales."

Rohan shivered. His nineteen-year-old self had listened intently when Hyperion used those exact words to describe the Ringgate.

"It does. Be careful, there are probably Wedge around, and I promised Masamune I'd keep you safe."

"You did, didn't you. I'm going down." Hyperion hopped off the edge and fell toward the treetops.

Rohan sighed. "Of course you are." He followed.

25

Son of a Dragon

The two Earthmen walked less than a kilometer along the rich jungle floor before a soft growling brought them to a sudden stop.

Rohan stepped in front of Hyperion, his arm out to guard the bigger man, and studied the forest.

Leaves rustled ahead of them, followed by another growl, then a roar.

He saw the teeth first: obscenely white, dagger-shaped, as long as his entire hand—so big that the maw that contained them could never fully close.

Above that maw were a pair of thin, flat nostrils, flanked by vertically slit eyes, set in a strip of flat black scales. The creature slid into the light, revealing a forward-leaning body, less than two meters from snout to tail, walking on two thick legs. The creature's arms were short, each ending in a heavy spike that matched a row of spikes that climbed down the creature's back.

Hyperion pointed as he turned a grinning face toward Rohan. "It's a velociraptor! With an amazing dentist!"

Rohan exhaled. "It's similar. No velociraptor ever had spikes like that." Two more of the creatures slid into view and hissed.

Hyperion whispered. "What do we do?"

Rohan pointed. "We have three choices. We run, we kill them, or we let them eat us."

"I don't like that last one. I vote for one of the first two. Why not run?"

Rohan sighed. "As long as there are only three, we should take care of them. Otherwise, there's a chance they'll be a problem for someone farther up the ring. Besides, you wanted to fight some Wedge, right? This is your chance." *He wants to see what the Wedge are like. I hope I don't regret this. I probably will.*

The raptor to their left leapt forward, jaws snapping at air. Branches and stems crack with the motion.

Rohan stepped up, jamming his left forearm into the beast's mouth. Its jaw snapped shut; some of the teeth shattered while others dug painfully into Rohan's arm.

He stiffened the fingers of his right hand into a flat blade, reached over the top of the Wedge's mouth, and speared his hand into its unblinking eye.

Hyperion shouted, "What do I do?"

"You're Hyperion, aren't you? Punch it real hard. Don't let it bite you."

"Right. I am Hyperion." He said it with equal parts confidence and wonder.

Blood and optical fluids burst out of the face of Rohan's raptor as a second Wedge snapped at his thigh. He hopped up and kicked it, catching the tip of its snout and sending it flying into a tree five meters away.

Hyperion punched his own raptor, stunning it, and jammed one hand into its upper gums, the other hand inside its mouth, under the tongue. His upper back muscles swelled as he lifted the raptor in the air, his hands forcing its mouth to open wider and wider.

Rohan's raptor shook itself and charged for him again. He saw blood leaking from Hyperion's arm where sharp teeth dug into his flesh.

The Wedge darted left, then right, trying to distract Rohan, but he was ready for its final charge. As it reached for him, he slapped down hard on its snout, driving its chin into the black earth below.

He fell over its back, wrapped both arms around its neck, and squeezed.

Hyperion grunted. "You won't have the best of me, monster! This is how Hyperion deals with the likes of you!" The Wedge's eyes widened as its jaw opened farther, degree by degree, the joints at the back of its mouth popping.

With a yell, Hyperion ripped the creature's head in half, then dropped it to the ground.

Rohan gave a little grunt of his own as he snapped the neck of the last raptor. He stood and faced the larger hero.

"There's a stream through those trees. You're going to want to wash those wounds."

"Can I get infected? I didn't even know."

"I'm not sure, but better safe than sorry." They left the bodies behind and knelt by a brook.

Hyperion nodded in thought. "That felt good. Felt right."

Rohan sighed. "Good. You're feeling like yourself more? Maybe we can leave. Head back to a place with restaurants and hot running water."

"Not just yet. I'm still missing something."

Rohan sat back on his heels. "Do you have any idea what you're missing? Specifically? Because we could wander this jungle for the rest of our natural lives and, frankly, if I'm going to do that I want to do it with somebody prettier than you."

"No idea, chum. I'll know it when I see it."

They rinsed their wounds and drank from the clear, cold water.

Hyperion rubbed his belly. "I'm getting hungry, Rohan. Can we eat the Wedge?"

The Hybrid shook his head. "Please don't. I'm not sure it would kill you, but I can guarantee you won't enjoy the experience. We'll find a grove of cocovado trees. The fruits are pretty tasty and surprisingly filling."

A fresh set of roars echoed through the trees from farther ahead, parallel to the Spine.

Hyperion looked at Rohan. "That was loud."

"Those are bigger Wedge."

"They get bigger than those three?"

Rohan laughed. "A lot. You want to see? How about we fly over?"

"Yeah. Let's go."

They *lifted* up through the trees and into open air, then broke toward the growing sounds of angry animals.

Wind whipped their hair as they converged on the source of the sounds. *He's keeping up with me. Which he wasn't able to do back in Vegas.*

The louder Wedge clustered around a hollow area at the base of a sheer rock cliff. They took turns darting in, roaring, then flinched back and resumed a little circuit through the trees.

Hyperion slowed to a halt, midair, and pointed. "There are people in there, Rohan."

"Looks like a scouting party. Probably got trapped in that cave."

"We should save them." He ducked his head as if to dive down. Rohan grabbed his arm.

"Hold on. Take a look at those Wedge."

"They're pretty similar to the other ones we just killed."

"Look again, Hyperion. Think of the scale. Their heads are above the treetops."

"Oh. Those things are like T-Rexes!"

"If a T-Rex had arms that scraped the ground with meter-long talons on the ends. And spiked balls of solid bone at the end of their tails."

"So they're not exactly the same. What are you anyway, a podiatrist?"

"Paleontologist. Wait!"

Hyperion took off in the direction of the big Wedge, leaving a gust of air in his wake.

Rohan counted five Wedge surrounding the cave mouth. Shallow wounds bled from the snouts of three of them, just enough to make them angry.

Hyperion closed on the first Wedge. Arrows were fired from inside the cave mouth, cutting into one of the Wedge and bouncing off the scales of another.

The Wedge looked up, reptilian eyes focusing on the hero as he flew, arm extended in a fist, lips pulled back from his teeth. The creature drew its head back, rising to an upright position, opened its mouth, then snapped forward.

Hyperion disappeared as its mouth closed over him.

"Rudra save me."

Rohan pivoted, turned to face the bright sun directly overhead, and flew up.

"Please don't be dead, you big moron. It's barely been an hour."

The air thinned and grew cold. Rohan relaxed, letting gravity take over, and turned to face the Ringgate again.

From that vantage point, he could see far out, over the Spine on his right and across a thousand kilometers of jungle on his left, dotted with lakes and rivers.

Beneath him, five enormous Wedge.

He *pushed* down, adding his energy to the acceleration of the spinning ring come up to meet him.

His face and forearms felt warm, then hot; he blinked tears as wind whipped across his face. He had lost track of which Wedge had swallowed Hyperion, so he aimed for one in the center of their formation.

Five reptilian heads, each the size of a short school bus, angled upward; ten vertically slit eyes pivoted in place to focus on his fall.

The middle Wedge tried the same maneuver they had used on Hyperion; it pulled its head back, opened its mouth, and tried to snap forward to meet his charge.

I fell for that technique once. That's one time too many.

He dipped, redirecting his path under the Wedge's chin, then back up, hurtling with all the momentum of his huge fall directly into the monster's soft throat.

Dry, leathery skin split and ruptured with the impact, spilling blood over Rohan as his shoulders and elbows trembled with the shock. His fists dug into a windpipe, parting the tough cartilage and ripping it apart. An artery big enough to fit his head tore next.

He pushed his fists apart, fingers splaying into claws that rent flesh and sinew, all the Power he could muster pouring into his shoulders and arms, driving him forward. Through.

With a growl, he saw daylight, then trees, then sky, and he was spit out between a pair of tall spikes that lined the Wedge's cervical vertebrae.

Covered in blood and gore, he spun to meet the charge of the next Wedge.

Five-meter arms swiped at him, the creature's tail swinging in a vicious counterpoint, enhancing the speed and power of the strikes. Rohan stopped midair and slipped back as talons raked across his chest, raising welts on Power-hardened skin.

A massive fist dropped on the top of his head, driven by ten tons of reptilian muscle, pounding him all the way into the ground.

His head rang with the impact.

Thought he was farther away. Never would have gone straight at these guys if one hadn't just swallowed Hyperion.

Ten tons of mass pressed him down.

He coughed, turning his head from side to side, seeking air and a release of pressure. He twisted his shoulders, digging ruts into the ground at his back, finding an angle to press his palms up into the monster's hand.

With a grunt, he bench-pressed the Wedge off his body.

In his peripheral vision, he spotted a fresh set of claws coming at him. He shouted, giving an extra shove, tossing the Wedge up an extra meter, and rolled out from under it.

The Wedge came back down, pinning the arm of its fellow monster as it struck at him.

One Wedge stood behind the pair, and another was stomping away, ducking its head over and over in a spasming motion, as if it was trying to throw up. *Hyperion must be alive in there.*

Rohan flew straight at the back Wedge. It opened its mouth and reached for him.

He grunted and *pushed* harder than before, driving his fists into its mouth, up through the palate, and into its skull.

He struck solid bone at the back of the Wedge's brainpan, sticking momentarily. The world tilted as it fell, dragging him with it, and his bones shook with the impact of the creature striking the ground.

Rohan spun, pushing at gel-like brain matter with hands and feet, disoriented. He plowed through, looking for air, and struck another solid plate of bone.

Good thing Wei Li has me training my breath-holding.

He spun again, pushing in what he hoped was a different direction, and felt teeth tear and scrape at his back as he wiggled past a flopping tongue big enough to stuff and turn into a mattress.

The staggering Wedge had straightened its path and was heading toward the group. The two that had become entangled stood upright and turned to face Rohan.

A flight of arrows arched up into the flank of the Wedge closest to the cave mouth, drawing blood along its ribs. That monster turned to the cave, ducking its head to find a target within reach.

Rohan stood in the mouth of the dying Wedge, grabbed its longest, thickest teeth by the base, and pulled them free of its gums.

He held the teeth point down and flew at the undistracted Wedge.

Rohan slid to the left, then the right, finally ducking his head and performing a full roll. His back struck the top of its snout, then his feet struck the flesh between its nostrils, then he spun over the top, arms held high, Wedge teeth angled down.

He spread his arms far out to the sides, his body forming a *Y* shape, and drove the extracted teeth into the eyes of the Wedge.

They sank in all the way, and he had to pull his hands out of the creature's goo with a squelch and a pop.

"What do you think of that? Just think of the crime scene investigators trying to piece together what happened."

He flew at the hindquarters of the monster that was trying to get into the cave.

"They'll be confused, right? How did the teeth from this Wedge get into that guy? What kind of internal squabble could have had such horrific consequences for this band of merry dinosaurs?"

He struck the creature in the back of its left leg, cracking bone, then tearing tendons loose with his hands.

"I know what they'll say. They were all such nice boys. Quiet. Always got along with everybody. What would have made them go crazy this way? Kill one another."

The Wedge fell heavily on its side. Rohan flew to its back, grabbing two spikes that protruded from the back of its neck.

"Nobody saw it coming. It's such a shame. They had such bright futures."

He set his feet against one spike, his arms against the other, and pushed. The attached vertebrae split apart with a snap like tearing a wet towel.

The Wedge's shuddering stopped.

"I should leave a note or something. Tell them, no, they weren't fighting each other. They picked on the wrong someone, that's all. They picked a fight with The Griffin."

He floated slowly toward the last Wedge. It stepped toward him, then staggered to one side, then the other.

"Yeah. A note. Maybe something cool. A playing card with a griffin on it. See? I'm thirty-three, and I finally understand the psychology of every Batman villain."

He closed on the Wedge. It took one last faltering step, then fell heavily onto its belly.

He paused over the corpse, watching its sides flex and bend in response to some enormous internal force.

"Come on out, man. Fight's over."

The skin between scales stretched, turned white, and finally parted. Hyperion tumbled out, covered in filth.

Rohan stood and watched the big man take in huge gulps of air.

"You all right?"

Hyperion nodded from where he lay flat on his back. He held up one fist, thumb extended.

Rohan nodded and turned to face the cave, wiping gore and viscera off his chest and shoulders with his hands, flicking it off to the side.

A tall man emerged from the cave. He had pale skin, long and pointed ears, and straight hair reaching halfway to his waist. His slender torso was encased in armor made from bones: ribs wired together around his own and polished kneecaps over his shoulders. He held a gleaming bow and sported an empty quiver at his back.

The man held up a hand, palm out, and cleared his throat. "Hello." He spoke heavily accented Drachna.

Rohan waved. "Hey. Sorry to interrupt your hunt, my friend over here just lost a bet, and he had to get swallowed by the nearest Wedge."

The man frowned and answered in heavily accented Drachna. "A bet? I do not understand."

Rohan shook his head. "Stupid joke. We're just passing through. Take care!"

"Wait! You saved our lives."

Rohan sighed. "Look, don't take it personally, okay? I didn't even know who you were. My big friend there just thinks he's a hero."

"He is! He saved us! We thought for sure he would die in the tyrant's maw."

Hyperion sat up, coughing. "Nope, not dead. Not thrilled, to be honest, but not dead. Hi, I'm Steve!"

Rohan looked at him. "Where are your glasses?"

"I forgot them on the ship. That's okay, right?"

"I don't think so. People might—never mind."

The native gave a shallow bow. "I am Korum, of the Black Dragon Sect. Please, let me take you to our dragon. She will want to thank you herself."

Hyperion stood and looked at Korum. "A dragon? A real one? I've never met a dragon before! Hey, that guy's a thing. A dwarf. From that movie."

Rohan shook his head. "Don't get so excited, it's not a real dragon, it's the title they use for some clan leaders. And he's not a dwarf."

"I'm pretty sure he's a dwarf. Pretty, pointed ears. I saw that movie. In a store window. I slept outside it for a week; they had the movie on replay."

"Dwarves are the short ones. With beards."

Korum shook his head. "I am human, of course. You two are strange. The dragon is my mother, I would very much like you to come with me."

Hyperion looked at Rohan. "Can we? I want to meet a dragon. Even if it isn't real."

"I assure you, my mother is very real."

"Not a real dragon. Can we go?"

Rohan sighed. "I don't think it's a good idea." He stared very hard at Hyperion, as if he could convey the thought that *somebody might recognize you.*

Korum cleared his throat and waved his arms. Three tall, slender natives emerged from the cave and joined him. "Please. I believe she could use your help. There is a potent Surge coming, and I do not think she will have evacuated in time."

Rohan rubbed his forehead. A dull ache had begun when the second Wedge had struck his head, and it wasn't going away. *Not my first concussion.* "I don't know."

Hyperion stepped closer to the Hybrid. "If they need help, we should try to help them. That's what we're here for. It's what I'm here for."

Rohan looked into the man's earnest face. "Fine. We'll have a look. But we're not staying."

Hyperion smiled. "Yay! I'm going to meet a dragon. And more dwarves."

"Elves. You mean elves. And they're not elves."

"Then how do you know that's what I mean?"

26

The Dragon

The scouting party led the Earthlings down into the jungle. They walked silently, with the sure steps of experienced hunters, alert for signs of hungry Wedge.

Hyperion tried to strike up conversations every few minutes, but Korum or one of the others turned to him with a finger pressed to their lips each time.

He didn't give up.

Rohan rubbed his head; his headache was proving as stubborn as Steve. He sighed with relief when the group crested a hill and Korum pointed to a break in the trees.

"That's the fortress."

The Earthlings stepped into the gap and looked down.

Hyperion smiled. "That's really big! And look, they made it look like something. That skull part. It looks just like a stegosaurus."

"Triceratops, Steve. It looks like a triceratops. Three horns. And it's not decorative."

Korum pointed. "The fortress was built in the corpse of the last of the Greater Wedge. My ancestors killed it in a battle remembered in song to this day. If you are very lucky, someone will sing it to you while you visit."

The skeleton was a hundred meters long and thirty high. Plants had been woven into the gaps between bone to provide a shell solid enough to protect it from rain. Armored natives moved around the perimeter, patrolling or exercising, and several walked on top, balancing on exposed vertebrae, facing anti-spinward.

Korum waved them forward. "Come. We enter through the mouth. The dragon and the others will be waiting inside."

Hyperion pointed. "What are they looking for? The ones on top?"

"That is where the Wedge come from. A Surge is coming, and they need to be prepared."

As the group descended the hill, some fortress personnel called out. One, a female with tan skin and white hair, came running to greet them.

"Korum, you're late. And wounded."

He nodded. "Five tyrants cornered us. It was my mistake. These off-worlders rescued us. I would like for them to meet the dragon."

She took in the Earthlings. "Welcome, off-worlders. We were not expecting you."

Rohan cleared his throat. "We're just passing through. Not officially here, you know. Keep it between us."

She tilted her head quizzically, then continued. "I regret that our hospitality might prove lacking. We've been ordered to retreat from the Wilds, behind the Dreadwall. The Surge that comes is too much for us to halt."

Korum nodded. "I am not surprised. Five tyrants in a cluster is not normal."

Hyperion looked at Rohan. "What are they talking about?"

Rohan pointed at the fortress. "The il'Drach monitor Wedge activity up and down the Ringgate and issue instructions accordingly. If they think an area is going to be wiped out by what's coming, they'll either send reinforcements or tell the soldiers to leave."

"These people are going to retreat? What about the fortress?"

Korum looked at him. "We'll remove everything of value. The Wedge are unlikely to disturb the fortress if it is unmanned."

Hyperion's eyebrows bunched. "Where will you go? Isn't this your home?"

The scout pointed opposite the looming Spine. "Nobody calls this fortress home. It is an outpost for fighting the Wedge. They stay close to the

Spine, so we will most likely be safe to the south, away from the mountains, behind the Dreadwall."

Hyperion shook his head. "I don't like the idea of retreating. We're here now, we can help you fight."

The scout shrugged. "It is not up to us. Come, speak with the dragon."

The woman who had greeted them led them toward the fortress. Sentries and soldiers, all wearing armor fashioned from bones and leather, waved and called out to the group as they approached.

Hyperion waved back, a smile growing on his face. "These people are very friendly! I like it here."

"They know who their enemies are, and it's not us."

"Right. It's the Empire."

"No, Steve. It's the Wedge. They fight the Wedge."

"That's what I said. You're not a great listener."

A woman stepped out of the mouth of the triceratops. Her skin was barely darker than the bleached teeth that rose up above her on both sides, and her hair was black as midnight. She wore polished bone armor and set the butt end of a long spear into the ground with every step.

"Korum! Gather your things, we have to leave. Korum. Who did you bring?"

"Mother, allow me to introduce these two otherworlders. They saved our lives, slaying five tyrants with their own hands."

She walked closer to the group, her eyes widening as she took in Hyperion's face.

"Introduce them, then."

Korum cleared his throat. "Well, actually, I cannot. They have not told me their names. They are only passing through. I do not know what that means. But they did save our lives."

She smiled. "Korum, my son, the strength of your arm greatly outpaces the acuity of your memory. Surely it has not been so long since this man walked our lands?"

Huh. I didn't recognize her.

Korum looked at her. "What do you mean?"

"This man is known to us. To all of us. He fought by our side, what was it? Ten years ago?"

Korum turned to Rohan. "You did?"

She laughed and slapped his shoulder. "I'm not talking about the squire." *Ouch.* "I mean Hyperion."

I should have made sure he wore the glasses.

The big man's smile broadened. "You remember me! That's amazing. Hi! We're just passing through."

She handed her spear to her son, who took it wordlessly, and approached Hyperion, her eyes focused intently on his face. She stood very close, reached up, and ran her palms over his cheeks. Then she pressed her face into his upper chest and hugged him.

"How could I forget? I've missed this chest. These arms."

Hyperion smiled, a blush slowly creeping up his cheeks. "Um. Right! Funny story about memory—"

She turned and called out to the fortress. "Prepare a feast! Hyperion has returned to us!"

◆┄•┄◆

Two hours later, Rohan sat on a cushion, picking slivers of cocovado and thinly sliced dried meat off a tray. Two dozen other cushions were arranged around a tablecloth, with Hyperion at the head position and a giggling dragon on his right.

The fortress's heralds had taken out stringed instruments and played atonal music that brought memories back to Rohan. The dragon was telling the story of first meeting Hyperion.

"Wedge had come far south, some striking at the very stones of the Dreadwall. We sortied a half dozen times but could not drive them back. For two months we held, then this one"—she rubbed Hyperion's arm—"came falling through the sky. My father was the dragon, and the look of shock on his face when the greater tyrant was felled in a single blow is something I shall never forget."

Hyperion raised a horn, hollowed, polished, and filled with a liquor brewed from leaves grown in the south, and took a gulp.

Korum leaned over to Rohan and spoke softly. "I thought your friend did not know this area? Yet he fought here?"

Rohan shrugged. "He has some memory issues. Head trauma."

Korum nodded. "I have heard of such things. It is difficult."

The dragon continued. "We celebrated that night, did we not? I had to make sure you were justly rewarded for your actions."

Hyperion's grin broadened, and he took a larger gulp of his drink. "That sounds fantastic! What did we do? Did we ride one of the Wedge? I've been thinking they'd look cute with saddles on."

The dragon slapped her thigh. "Ride a Wedge! Is that a euphemism in your lands, Hyperion?"

He shrugged, rolled up a slice of preserved meat, and ate it. "This is really amazing."

"That's what you said that night!" The other warriors laughed and joined in the revelry.

Rohan searched Korum's face for some sign of discomfort at his mother's behavior, but found none. The man was either oblivious or comfortable with the situation.

An older soldier, at least the dragon's age given the wrinkles at the corners of his eyes, spoke up. "Dragon, with all due respect, we should leave this place. It was a risk to wait for your son's return, but now he is with us. We need to follow our orders."

Hyperion turned to face the man. "But I'm here."

The soldier frowned. "Yes, and I'm glad to see you again."

"I said I'm *here*. You don't need to retreat. We'll fight the Wedge, and we'll win. Hyperion doesn't run from battle." He ate another slice of meat, staring into the soldier's eyes as he chewed.

The man cleared his throat. "You are a mighty warrior, that is certain. But the coming Surge is overwhelming. If it arrives here, it will kill us all. No offense, but you two are only . . . two. You and a squire will not make the difference in that battle."

Hyperion's eyes narrowed. "That is no squire, that is The Griffin. And I am Hyperion. I do not run from battle."

The dragon stroked his arm. "We have our orders, sweetie. The packing is done; we can move out at first light."

Hyperion shook his head. "I won't stop anybody else from leaving, but I'm staying here. I won't see this fortress fall."

Rohan sat up straighter. "Hyperion, think about this. You don't know what you're getting into." He switched to English. "You were just telling me you're not yourself yet, right? Even the old Hyperion didn't fight a big Surge by himself." *Not usually.*

"I'm not alone. I have you and these brave soldiers. We'll stop the Wedge here. I can feel it, Griffin. In my bones. This is why I'm here. This is what I'm *for.*" His eyes glittered with confidence.

"I'm supposed to keep you safe. How am I going to do that when you throw yourself into danger?"

"What's the alternative? Sit in that prison cell for the rest of my life? And is even *that* safe? There are Hybrids in Toth looking for me right now, aren't there? Wistful can't hold them off forever. It won't stop with Drexian assassins, and you know it."

Rohan swallowed. "I'm not saying you have to go back to prison. There are other places we can go."

"You mean run away to. I don't want to run anymore. I don't like it. It's not who I am, not the real me.

"Look, I know I wasn't much help against the Drexians. But I'm getting stronger. Every day, stronger. You know it. I can feel it. My head is getting clearer. I remembered what to call you, didn't I? I didn't use your real name."

The gathered soldiers were staring at the Earthlings.

Rohan sighed. "You're stronger, yes. But a single tyrant almost got you yesterday. The coming Surge is going to be a lot more serious."

"Almost. Where is that tyrant now? Oh, right. I killed it. I bet when I face that Surge of Wedge, I'll do even more. You'll see."

The dragon looked at him. "You are certain? You wish to stay and fight?"

Hyperion took a deep breath. "Every person is born, takes a breath, grows old, then dies. Everyone. What makes heroes different from everybody else is what they do in between those two things.

"Yes, there are safer ways to live. Some would say smarter ways. You can spend those breaths doing nice, normal, boring things. You can take each breath in safety, knowing that you're just making sure you get one more.

"But what makes a hero is that they spend their days, their breaths, fighting for something greater.

"Heroes live knowing that every breath might be their last, but if so, they will spend it doing something that *matters*.

"You are here to fight the Wedge. I say, let us fight them! Let us make a stand here and make them wish they had stayed in the depths of hell where they belong!"

The dragon stood, pulling Hyperion to his feet. "He's right! This is why we were born. We stop them here, on our lands. They go no further. Tomorrow, we fight!"

The soldiers cheered. Some wholeheartedly, others . . . less so.

Rohan groaned.

The dragon pulled Hyperion into her embrace. "Tonight we let our breaths mingle, and if it is the last time, let it be worthy of an epic!"

He finished his drink.

◆ ··•·· ◆

Rohan rubbed his temples and watched the dawn arrive from a rounded lump of bone on top of the triceratops fortress. A glow appeared, far to the east, as the edge of the nightshade that blocked the sun came into view. A long line of light, a shadow in reverse, crossed the forest, as wide as the entire world, and approached the fortress.

Hyperion came up and stood next to him, a wide smile distorting the man's face. "Is that the sunrise?"

"The name doesn't really fit, does it? The sun is always in the same place."

"Oh, yeah. One moment, it's night, the next, the sun is directly over-head. Strange."

Rohan smiled. "To them, the idea of a sun moving around the sky is strange."

"Good point, chum."

They stood silently as the light struck them, then turned in unison to watch the retreat of the nightshade to the west.

Hyperion's smile didn't waver. "Aren't you going to ask me?"

"Ask what?"

"You know."

"Why don't you pretend I don't know and tell me."

"Ask me what I did last night!"

What happened to the guy who blushed at the idea of visiting a brothel? I miss that guy.

"I'm not the sort of person who feels certain about much. The world's a complicated place. But I can tell you two things for sure. One, I know what you did last night. Two, I absolutely, positively do not want to hear about it."

"But it was amazing!"

"Do you not have a sense of privacy?"

Hyperion rubbed his jaw. "I don't think I do. Is that weird? Am I supposed to?"

"Well, it's in character. Just not a characteristic I particularly like."

"Okay. I'll try to keep it to myself."

"Thank you."

"But did you know that if a woman's arms are long enough, she can do this thing with—"

"Stop! Just, please. Stop."

"Okay. When are the Wedge supposed to arrive?"

"They already have. The scouts are taking care of the first few. The main body should be here in a couple of hours."

"I see." Hyperion cracked his neck. "I can't wait."

"This is a bad idea, man. We can still leave. There are hundreds of soldiers in this fortress. We can still save them."

"We will save them, Griffin. By winning this battle."

Rohan sighed. "I'm half tempted to knock you unconscious and pull you out of here by hand."

"You won't do that. You're my friend."

"Sometimes friends knock each other out and . . . you know."

"Did I ever do that to you? Knock you unconscious because you were going to do something I thought was stupid?"

"What makes you say I ever did anything that dumb?"

"Call it intuition. You were young when we met, right? Young people make mistakes. So I hear."

Rohan laughed. "You never physically knocked me out, no. You talked me out of some pretty bad decisions. Maybe even restrained me once or twice."

Hyperion clapped him on the back. "See? You trusted me. And everything worked out great. You've had an amazing life."

I've committed genocide, destroyed entire cultures. I wake up in a cold sweat almost every night, and I'm alone when it happens. Not sure about your assessment there, buddy.

The dragon came up dressed in full armor, a helmet fashioned from a hollowed-out skull covering her head. She walked up to Hyperion and cupped his right buttock in her hand, giving it a hard squeeze.

"Good morning, lover."

He smiled down at her. "Good morning. Is everybody ready?"

"We are as prepared as we can be. The Surge is only hours away."

"Good. Maybe we could go into the fortress for a bit? I, er, think I forgot something in your quarters."

She smiled. "For a bit."

27

In the Name of Hyperion

The leading edge of the Surge was visible from the triceratops fortress an hour before midday.

Rohan remembered the pattern. Surges varied in size and to some extent in composition. Some were swarms of smaller Wedge; some were made up of only a few of the largest.

The small Wedge, the raptors and humanoids, always led the way. Faster and less disciplined, they formed a bow wave on the Surge that obliterated most resistance.

The medium Wedge, the tyrants and three horns that resembled most closely the large dinosaurs found on Earth, came behind.

Behind those came the Greater Wedge, the monsters the natives called worldbreakers. They were rare, but the fortress he stood on was evidence that they could reach one hundred meters in length.

In two years on the Ringgate, Rohan had never fought a creature of that size.

His head throbbed as he watched the first line of scattered raptors fall under a hail of arrows shot from the fortress.

Hyperion took a position next to him.

"When do we go in?"

Rohan pointed. "Look at those trees there. You see the tops moving? Those are the bigger ones coming. We leave the little guys to the native soldiers. You and I thin out the big ones."

Hyperion pointed at a spot farther back. "What about those?"

Rohan squinted.

Behind the cluster of approaching tyrants, dozens of scaled heads bobbed up and down above the treetops.

Rudra save me.

"That's bad. We can't handle that. Not even close."

Hyperion put his fists on his hips and lifted his chin. "That's not how heroes talk."

Rohan dug knuckles into his temples. "Maybe not in the cartoons or comic books, but let me tell you something, heroes talk like that all the time. At least the ones who stay alive."

Hyperion shook his head. "I know you're stronger than you've shown me, Griffin. And I am, too. I *felt* your Power when you got angry—when you fought Dr. Kraken. You haven't been the same since then, not really."

"That's because Power is dangerous, Hyperion. It comes with a price."

"It's part of who you are. Of who I am. We're Hybrids. Asuna told me what that means."

"Asuna?"

"The dragon. We're meant to live on the edge of rage. To fight with all our hearts, total commitment. I haven't done that yet. I don't even know where all that rage lives inside me. Without it, I'm incomplete."

"Is that what this is about? You want me stuck in a situation where I go berserk? That's insane."

Hyperion leaned forward, his hands reaching for Rohan, palms up. "It's not! Don't you get it? I'm still incomplete. This is the missing part."

"Hyperion, it's going to be close, but we can still save these people. Start carrying them south. Even a few kilometers should be enough. Evacuate the fortress. Once the Wedge get closer, I'll stall the big ones, slow them down. These soldiers don't have to die. Maybe *Void's Shadow* can get here in time to help."

"I don't think so. We can fight, show these Wedge they messed with the wrong Earthlings. Besides, if we let them pass, they'll break through to our reality."

"They won't, I'm telling you. They have to walk another ten thousand kilometers to climb out of shadow. There are other soldiers, other forces to thin them out along the way. That's the system!"

"That's your plan? We let them pass so other soldiers up the spin are turned into Wedge food? Pass the buck? We can stop them here, you and me. I can feel it. I can feel your Power building even now."

He's right about that.

Angry waves of energy rose and broke across his subconscious, battering his restraint. The pain in his head intensified.

A fresh voice called out. "Deploy catapults!"

Portals opened between the fortress's ribs; with a twang of released tension, stones as wide as a man was tall hurtled through space into the middle of the Wedge formation.

"Ballistae! The tyrants are in range!"

Enormous crossbows poked out of other portals, firing bone-tipped arrows into the air.

Hyperion nodded. "We can do this, Rohan! I need this. I need to discover who I am. Together we can wipe these Wedge away, save these people."

"You have no idea what you're asking."

"So, show me! That's what I need! You said I was the strongest Hybrid in the Empire. You said I fought the Wedge for two years, kept back Surge after Surge. You said I was famous all across the Ringgate."

"Hyperion was the strongest Hybrid seen in a thousand years. Hyperion was a weapon the likes of which the il'Drach had never seen. He was so strong he scared them. But we don't really know if you're him, Steve. Not really."

Hyperion straightened. "I am. I know it. Let me prove it. Right here."

The dragon shouted at them. "We need help! The tyrants are closing, and we can't hold this many!"

Hyperion nodded. "We're going. Come on, Rohan. Let's show them what heroes do."

Rohan covered his eyes and inhaled sharply. "It's too late now to do anything else." He turned to the dragon. "We'll strike them now."

When the rage surged that strongly, he didn't have to pull it along; he just had to let go, relax the restraints that he'd built up over years of meditation, ride the tide that rose up through his mind.

Four bolts of scarlet pride coursed through his body. They wound around his spine, meeting in twos and fours at each chakra point in his torso with little explosions that contained all the fiery intensity of a miniature Big Bang.

They climbed, sweeping away the pain in his head, filling his limbs with an electric potential, until they plugged into the base of his skull with a shock that stiffened every muscle in his body.

Joints popped and cracked as Rohan growled.

He rose into the air, wind snapping at his ears and nose.

These cursed Wedge. They walk out of shadow, those cold reptilian eyes fearless and bold. Predators. Coming to feast on us. Devour us, body and soul.

I'll show them a true predator. I'll teach them fear.

At the upper limits of the atmosphere, he pivoted and struck for the ground.

Hyperion had followed him up and was turning himself, a weirdly gleeful expression on his face.

Rohan took in the Wedge formation with a quick glance. Years of living on the edge of death had taught him to assess combat situations quickly.

They were doomed.

He growled and headed directly for the biggest Wedge in the group, right in their center. Walking on four legs with twenty-meter-long neck and tail, trees shaking for fifty meters around it with every step. Its sides were covered in plate armor, long tentacles emerging from clusters up and down its torso, small, hungry mouths at their tips.

The beast looked up at him with dull eyes as he twisted, spinning around its head and impacting at the juncture of neck and shoulder.

The collision rattled every bone in Rohan's body, leaving his back teeth ringing and sore.

The Wedge's front legs collapsed as it landed on its knees.

Hyperion came along behind him, striking the head of a forty-meter-tall fire-breathing T-Rex. "You shall not pass!"

Catapults twanged; stones collided with the mutated allosaurus. A pair of three-horns turned and built up speed, heading for Rohan, each fifty meters long.

Little mouths bit into his flesh; he reached down and pulled the tentacles out with brute force. Blood spurted from their ruined bases.

Rohan *lifted* into the air, following Hyperion as the bigger man disengaged from his target.

"There are too many! We can't handle them!"

"Yes, we can! I'm starting to feel it, Rohan! I'm starting to get angry!"

Rohan closed and grabbed the front of Hyperion's shirt. "You're losing control! You don't remember how to do this. We have to go. You can fight others, in another place."

Spikes flew through the air, fired from the back of one of the Wedge in the rear. One clipped Rohan's shoulder, drawing blood.

Hyperion bared his bloodstained teeth, reached back, and drove his fist directly into Rohan's face. Pain exploded behind his forehead.

"I said they shall not pass! Stop your cowardice and fight!"

Fresh anger surged through Rohan's body. Air crackled like popcorn as he darted at the bigger man.

Hyperion pointed back toward the fortress. "They're dying there! You don't have time to fight me!"

Rohan growled and dipped, missing Hyperion by centimeters, and dove back toward the big Wedge below.

Hyperion shouted. "The fortress! Asuna!" He streaked away.

Rohan knocked a three-horn the size of a football field to its knees, then spun and carved a line to the fortress, tearing chunks of flesh out of Wedge and slapping others into unconsciousness as he went.

Something tore through his skin from hip to ankle. A spike penetrated his side, front to back, and he pulled it through and tossed it away as he continued.

The tyrants had caught up to the small raptors in front and were tearing apart the soldiers guarding the fortress. They formed shield walls: mobile walls of bone that locked together while other soldiers struck from behind with lances and long-handled hammers. The tyrants were too big; they knocked the shieldbearers back and down with overwhelming momentum.

Soldiers died, torn apart under the talons of the vicious creatures. More stepped forward to take their places.

Hyperion fell on the back of a tyrant, punching the back of his head with thumping beats like an enormous drum, riding it down into the ground as it died. Two others, each ten meters high, leaned forward to bite at the Earthling.

He struck up at one, killing it, his eyes blazing.

Teeth dug into his shoulder and chest as the second bit down.

Three more stepped over with smooth, powerful strides and covered him.

Rohan growled and *pulled* more energy into himself.

He flew into the pile, accelerating hard, little discharges of static flicking up and down his sides.

As he moved, he *reached* down and gathered spikes and spines ejected by various Wedge, pulling them alongside his path like a flight of wingmen.

With a burst, he stopped near the pile of tyrants and shot the spikes forward, laying down a plane of evisceration that shredded flesh and scales alike.

Rohan floated, panting, and watched Hyperion climb out of the severed bodies, covered in blood.

The big man bared his teeth and turned to the next closest knot of Wedge.

A slender horn punched through his thigh. He reached down and grabbed the skull it attached to and twisted, snapping the beast's neck.

Not enough Power to stop them all.

A tyrant stretched tall and snatched a native off the wall high on the fortress, tossed them up into the air, then gulped them down whole as they fell.

A sortie of soldiers formed, cutting a swatch across the base of the fortress, slicing leg tendons and chopping down smaller Wedge as they ran, trying to clear space around the wall. One by one they fell, picked off by larger monsters. The last soldier died just meters from a door held open to receive him.

The landscape blurred, Rohan's eyes losing acuity.

Hyperion screamed mindlessly, wordlessly, a continuous bellow of pure instinctive rage. He tore through flesh and bone, ignoring the ravages inflicted on his own body.

I'll show them. Show them all.

Not a terrified child this time. Not a rookie anymore.

I'll teach them why my name is a curse on a hundred worlds.

The world turned red as blood vessels burst inside his eyes. Something died underneath him.

Hyperion unhinged his own jaw, sharp white teeth flashing inside his blood-covered face, and bit into the tender throat of the tyrant he embraced.

Bone shattered under Rohan's foot. His arm came free from a brainpan, scrubbed momentarily clean by clear spinal fluids.

A sixty-meter-tall tyrant dropped on top of Rohan, clubbing the crown of his head with its full weight, sending pulses of agony through his temples.

He belly flopped into the dirt as the weight of the Wedge settled on top of him.

Red filled more of his vision.

I'll teach them.

Teach them fear.

He growled as his Power swelled and grew, driving back the dizziness.

His world devolved. Stand. Strike. Tear. Bite. Rend.

He faced a vertically slit pupil as tall as him, time frozen for a short breath. He *pulled* in more Power, then dug both hands in and split the eye.

It was the last thing he remembered as a tide of rage swept him away.

28

The Chapter Your Mother Warned You About

S unlight burned Rohan's eyes from directly overhead.

Noon? No, Ringgate. His thoughts gathered slowly, like sheep returning to a pen after being dispersed by a storm.

He rolled over onto his side, joints and muscles protesting angrily, and vomited, his stomach purging fully, then continuing for a long time afterward, as if seeking to rid itself of material that was long digested and gone.

He panted, dizzy with the exertion, then vomited again. He tried to push himself upright, but his hand slipped in a puddle of muck, and he slid down, his face burying in slime and foul.

Coughing, the Hybrid pushed down harder, his palm finally finding purchase, and lifted his face into the air.

Took a deep breath; instantly regretted it as a coughing fit nearly sent him back down into the pool of blood.

He spat, then again, unable to clear his mouth.

Enough.

With a *push*, Rohan rose into the air, energy channels in his mind sore and charred from overuse, but enough to get him off the ground.

Memories leaked into his consciousness, image after image, striking like arrows fired into a soft target.

He blinked but couldn't see clearly. Rubbed his face with the back of his hand. Shook his head like a dog, spraying bits of charnel fluids in all directions.

The forest was gone. Every tree, every branch, shattered and brought down, their remains buried under a five-meter-deep lake of meat and bone that stretched for hundreds of meters in every direction.

The smell was so thick he could taste the air with every breath.

He retched again, his stomach heaving futility.

Rohan rotated, putting his back to the field, and faced the fortress.

The bones of the ancient three-horn still stood, though much of the plant matter sealing them together had been torn away. Bodies of pale flesh and fashioned bone armor dotted the sea of Wedge flesh, breaking up the monotony of scales and fang.

He floated closer; opened his mouth to call out, but words wouldn't come.

His eyes roamed over the fortress, searching for movement. A growing cloud of insects was the only answer.

He floated, upright, his feet dangling over the upper surface of the bodies. He entered the fortress, coasting along the various hallways and platforms, in and out of the wreckage of living quarters and storerooms.

He found a barrel of freshwater; lifted off the lid and dunked his head inside, holding it there until his lungs burned.

Then longer.

When his Power started to wake in response to his actions, he stood, panting, letting the fluids drip out of his hair and beard.

"Hey there, chum."

"Steve." Rohan turned to face the other Earthling.

Every square centimeter of the big man was coated in gore. He moved stiffly, as if he wanted to limp but couldn't choose a better side to limp *from*. His lips parted in a grin.

"We did it, Rohan! We did. That was amazing."

Rohan exhaled slowly. "What? What . . . did you say?"

"I said we did it, chum. We stopped the Surge. You didn't think we could, but I told you."

"Oh?"

"You were amazing, buddy! I can't believe how much Power you can use! I told you, if you just cut loose, you'll be able to do amazing things. I believed in you the whole time."

"Did you." Rohan's eyes began to tear. He turned away and drifted up, toward the top of the fortress.

Hyperion followed. "Oh yeah. I didn't feel it at first, but then it really started to kick in. That Hybrid anger. Oh boy, let me tell you something, that's some amazing stuff. I almost can't believe how strong it made me!"

Rohan paused to dry heave again, then continued up into the daylight.

"You think we did it."

"Of course we did. Who else? I mean, yes, of course the natives helped. Couldn't have done it without them. But let's be honest, just between us, it was mostly us."

"Right. Why don't you congratulate some of them? On *our* victory?"

Hyperion looked from side to side. "Well, there seems to be an issue."

"Go on."

"I'm not sure any of them are still alive."

They came out onto the roof. Native corpses lay strewn about, bloody and still, shocking lengths of white bone showing up amid the red blood and pink flesh.

"Doesn't look like it."

Hyperion grunted. "That really is too bad. Still, they died fulfilling a purpose, right? They were warriors. This is how they wanted to die."

"Is it?" Rohan found the dragon.

Asuna.

She lay on her back, eyes open to the sun.

Hyperion coughed gently. "Oh. That is a shame. I really liked her."

"Did you?"

"Of course! Still, can't be helped, is all I'm saying. Casualties of war. These damn Wedge, I'll tell you what."

Rohan nodded. "What do you think of those wounds, Steve?"

"What?"

"Take a closer look, Steve."

Hyperion nodded, eyes narrow, and knelt by Asuna's body. He recoiled slightly from the vomit and blood that cascaded down the front of her body.

Rohan settled next to him.

Grabbed the big man by the back of his neck.

Pressed his face into the gory mess of Asuna's chest.

"Closer, Steve. Closer."

Hyperion coughed and choked as Rohan twisted his face back and forth, grinding it into the filth.

"Get a good look, Steve. Really good." Hyperion flailed his arms, trying to knock Rohan back, but the Hybrid remained in place.

When Hyperion's coughing subsided, Rohan lifted him up.

The bigger man inhaled deeply and turned his gaze to Rohan. "What the hell, Rohan? What was that for? What's wrong with you?"

"Good question, Steve. Did you look at the wounds? Were you . . . close enough?"

Hyperion's hands shot up in surrender. "I did! I did! What do you want?"

"Just wondering. Did you see any claw marks, Steve? Any sharp teeth?"

Hyperion's head was trapped by Rohan's grip on the back of his neck, but his eyes swiveled in place, his gaze returning to his lover's body. "What? Uh, no. I guess not."

"Weird, isn't it? Look at her guards. The bodies on this roof." Rohan turned Hyperion's head, forcing the other man's gaze to cover the corpses.

"What do you think, Steve?"

"I don't know! I don't know! What do you mean?"

"Do you think Wedge killed them? I don't see any bite marks. No claws. No one on this roof had even so much as a hand taken for a snack."

"Maybe they were full! I don't know! What are you saying?"

"Wedge didn't kill these soldiers, Steve. What do you think that means?"

Hyperion shrank back. "That . . . that they fought among themselves?"

"Try again, Steve. Those wounds weren't caused by their weapons either. They were pummeled to death. Twisted. Their necks broken. Twisted . . . by hands."

Hyperion's mouth gaped open. "That can't be."

Rohan stood and planted his feet. His eyes flashed. "This is what you wanted, right?" He stepped forward with his left leg, set it down, and twisted his upper body, driving his right fist into Hyperion's solar plexus, just before letting go of his neck.

The big man fell to the ground retching.

"Wanted to feel Hybrid rage." He kicked Hyperion in the ribs, sending the big man tumbling across the roof.

"Find out what you're really made of, warts and all. Your authentic self. Right? Right?"

He swept Hyperion's supporting hand out from under him, sending the big man face-first into the floor, and stomped down on his jaw.

"How was it, Steve? How much did you enjoy it? Was it worth this? Was it worth all these lives?" He kicked Hyperion again, flipping the man over onto his back.

"I didn't know! I didn't know this would happen!"

"I tried to tell you, Steve! It's dangerous! We! Are! Dangerous! This isn't a game. This isn't for play.

"I have spent years trying to make up for a fraction of the harm that I've caused, and you come back into my life, and within two weeks here we are again! Waking up in pools of blood! This. Didn't. Need. To. Happen."

He kicked Hyperion in the ribs, then again. Stepped back far with his right foot, twisting his entire body into another kick.

"I'm sorry, Rohan! I'm sorry! I didn't realize! I thought I was a hero! I swear I did."

"*Hyperion* was a hero! But he was only a hero because he knew that he was always just a small step away from being a monster! You're no Hyperion."

Tears streamed down Hyperion's face.

"I am. I am Hyperion. You'll see. I'll prove it. I'll be good, I promise. I won't let this happen again."

"I should snap your neck right here. Leave your corpse to feed the flies. Never let this happen again."

"No, no, no. Don't do it, Rohan. I'll be better. I'll help people. You'll see. Give me another chance. I'll do whatever you say. I swear it. I swear it."

Rohan stepped back, ready to throw another kick.

Stopped.

Exhaled, blowing all the air out of his lungs, every last cubic millimeter of atmosphere, then held empty lungs until they burned.

Hyperion continued. "I didn't understand. I'm so sorry. All these people. I know, I get it. They shouldn't have died. I shouldn't have done this to them, shouldn't have been here.

"I'll never let anything like this happen again. I'll never lose control."

"I don't believe you, Steve. I don't think you can do it."

"I can, Rohan. I can. You'll see. Put me back in my cell. I'll behave. I'll show you I can control myself."

Rohan stepped over to a waist-high crenellation and slid onto it. "It's exhausting, Steve. You wake up every day. Try your hardest. Help people when you can. But you can't ever really make up for things. You can't make them go away. They stay there, lurking in the past, always watching you."

"But you have, Rohan! I've seen it. People respect you. They care about you. It's not your fault you've done some rough things, Rohan! It's the Empire. They made us, used us. Pushed us. They killed me, too, didn't they?"

"What?"

"On Rhyllax Four. The Empire sent me, right? Didn't you say that?"

"Yeah."

"If they hadn't, I'd still be the old me, still in control."

"I don't know, Steve. Hyperion. Whatever."

Hyperion crawled over to Rohan; sat below him. "Let's go back to Wistful. I want to go back. To my cell. Let me start figuring out how to be better. I want to be. It's what Hyperion would want."

Rohan let his head hang down. "Sure. We'll go back. Start putting the pieces back together again."

"Except this time we'll be doing it together, Rohan. Putting all the pieces back."

"Stop talking."

29

Oh, THAT Friend from College

Rohan said nothing as he led Hyperion away from the fortress to a cold stream thirty kilometers east. They followed far enough to find a pool and dove in, rinsed thoroughly, then waited for the water to refresh and rinsed again.

An hour passed before he was ready to move on.

He said nothing as they flew up into the Spine of the World and circled for half an hour looking for the transport pod platform.

Nothing as they climbed in and took the tooth-jarring ride up out of shadow.

He spoke, calling for *Void's Shadow* to get them, but said nothing to an anxious-faced Hyperion.

The Earthlings boarded their ship and slipped away from the Ringgate.

Rohan lay back in his piloting couch while *Void's Shadow* flew a smooth path between patrolling warships, carefully avoiding positions that would show up on active sensors or interrupt tightbeam communication links.

He fell asleep just after *Void's Shadow* let the first rift she had formed close behind them, a pair of green suns visible on her screens.

He woke to a warming couch and a full bladder. The former was the ship's way of getting him up; the latter was nature.

Hyperion was awake, sitting up with his mouth half-open, as if ready to say something, but Rohan shook his head sharply.

He took care of himself and returned.

"Captain, we just entered Toth space."

Rohan grunted and stood watching Toth grow on the front screen. "How long? About?"

"I can rush if you'd like, Captain, but at normal pace about half an hour."

"That's fine. Carry on."

He took the three steps that separated him from the kitchenette and scooped a serving of pudding into a bowl.

Hyperion stood to get food; Rohan returned to his couch and ate.

A buzz of communications went on, the ship's negotiations with Wistful for docking permission. Rohan cleared his throat. "I can tow you if Wistful wants." He patted his helmet.

"Understood, Captain."

Half an hour later, *Void's Shadow* approached the beacon line, a plane marked off by a handful of floating beacons that warned incoming ships to halt and wait for permissions before approaching Wistful.

Rohan's helmet lit with a brightly colored guide. He slipped it over his head, waited for the seal to bond with his skin, and left his ship.

He flew around to the back of *Void's Shadow* and found her anchor point. Wistful's voice spoke to him.

"Permission to approach. Dock at C-17."

"Affirmed. C-17."

He began to push. Wistful grew visible, a sparkling cross hanging over the green planet Toth 3.

"Captain?"

"Yes, *Void's Shadow*?"

"Did I do something wrong?"

"What? No. You didn't do anything. Why would you say that?"

"You haven't spoken at all since we left the Ringgate. Are you angry with me?"

He sighed.

"No, I'm not angry with you. I'm angry about something else."

"Oh. What?"

"Steve. And me. Myself. I let . . . I got into trouble. I let Steve get me into trouble."

"I'm sorry, Captain. Is there anything I can do to help?"

He exhaled slowly as he turned her around and began to slow her down to get ready for docking. "I don't think so. Thank you. I think I'm just going to be angry for a little while."

"Okay. I'm glad it wasn't me."

"You've been a big help, *Void's Shadow*. I'll tell you if you do anything that upsets me."

"I think that would be better than me guessing."

"Yeah. And I'll try not to take it out on you. I just need a little time."

"Sure, Captain. Can I go play?"

"Yeah. As soon as we drop off Steve, I'll pull you back out to the beacon line, okay?"

"Great!"

"Can you do me a favor?"

"That depends on what you want, Captain. That's what you told me to say, right?"

He chuckled. "That's right. Try not to agree to a favor until you know what it is. You'll end up babysitting a baby time bomb or something."

"I have no idea what you're talking about, Captain."

"Never mind that last part. Can you take a peek at the Imperial shuttle? Just see what they're up to. As long as you can do it without being seen."

"Oh, sure, Captain. Will do."

"Thanks. Here we go, docking."

He slid the ship onto a port, waiting while the docking ring clicked into place. He knocked on the ship. "*Void's Shadow*, tell Hyperion to go on board and head to his cell, okay?"

"You don't want to tell him yourself?"

"I really don't. I think if I try talking to him I'm going to start hitting him, and I'm really not sure I'll be able to stop."

"Sure, Captain."

Rohan floated outside the ship, one hand on her hull so he could feel the vibrations as the dock was used.

He exhaled slowly, then tapped through his messages.

Lahnegarn wanted him to come to a meeting.

Rohan kept scrolling.

He was included in a longer exchange between the Stones and Wei Li about the disposition of their kidnappers. Wei Li offered to have them escorted through a station airlock sans spacesuit, but the Stones were more forgiving.

His heart skipped at a short line from Tamara saying she had enjoyed their breakfast and hoped his errand was going smoothly. *She has a knack for bringing my mood all the way up and then all the way back down in a single line of text.* He checked the time; it was station nighttime, the second half of Tamara's wake cycle.

Rohan sent a message asking her to have dinner with him. Paused, considered deleting it, then sent.

Felt a sudden urge to retract it. Looked through the comm's commands to find one labeled: 'Bring Back Message'; couldn't.

Exhaled.

Ursula asked him how Steve was doing. The Ursans had tried to bring him dinner in his cell and found him gone.

He sighed.

Wistful gave permission for *Void's Shadow* to leave. Rohan pulled her away from the docking ring, spun her around, and pushed her out to the beacon line.

That used to be challenging. Only took two years of daily practice to get good at it.

"Kar Gayi Chull" played while he released his ship, tapping her rear bootstrap drive so she'd know she was free.

The music paused: Tamara agreeing to dinner. Her dinner, his breakfast. At the new Drexian barbecue place.

He flew around the station to his private airlock. Entered. Hit a button on the wall that he'd only touched once before; sides rose up out of the floor of his shower, creating a tub, and hot water flooded in.

He stripped, turned his music off, and sat in silence and steaming water for the next two hours.

Thinking.

Wishing he could stop.

——•••——

Shortly after the ceiling turned clear, signaling station dawn, Rohan stood in front of the floor-length mirror in his apartment checking the buttons on his forest green tailored suit.

"How do I look?"

The personal AI didn't respond. It knew better. His head throbbed.

He sighed and headed to the restaurant.

I need a drink. Or seven. Or maybe I shouldn't be drinking.

He felt oddly self-conscious as he walked the station promenade, as if everyone he saw knew he was on a date, as if they were judging him for not wearing something nicer. Forgetting flowers.

He stopped at a florist.

Rohan got to the restaurant before their reservation and waited outside.

He didn't wait long.

Lukhor formalwear wasn't exactly a sari. Rohan knew his mother could have pointed out how the cut was slightly different, the folds and pleats arranged differently, and so on.

But the fuchsia and red cloth, lined with gold and silver stitching, was close enough to put a subtle tremor in his knees.

He watched her approach, a smile breaking across her face, and held out the flowers.

"Hi."

"Hello, Tow Chief Second Class. These are . . . gifts?"

He swallowed. "Yeah. It's a tradition on Earth."

"You kill plants for your intended mates? As proof of your hunting prowess? Or of your savagery?"

"Well, I think mostly that. Or because they're pretty. Maybe to show off that the man is wealthy enough to grow plants for strictly ornamental value."

Her smile broadened as she took the flowers. "Ah. A pointless display of wealth I can understand. Thank you, they are quite lovely."

"Not as lovely as you are." *Smooth. So very smooth.*

"I had almost forgotten your eloquence. Shall we go inside?" She offered her elbow; he wasn't in any position to refuse it.

The host, a red-skinned female Drexian with horns that curled back toward her head like a goat, smiled at them with alarmingly sharp teeth.

Tamara nodded to her. "Reservation for two. Under Tow Chief Second Class Rohan." Rohan's mouth watered as the smell of spice and charred meat hit him.

He smiled. "You used my name?"

"Have you seen the waitlist for tables here? I've told you before, I am not too proud to leverage your celebrity if it means an opportunity to derive a meal from it."

"Celebrity? I'm really a celebrity now?" He paused. "Actually, I think I am. Sort of."

"If you weren't before, you have been since that business with the vampire six months ago."

"Ah. That." The hostess ushered them toward a table. The furniture was wood, cut to expose the natural lines of trees, with knots and raw bark.

They sat. "How was your errand, Rohan?"

He smiled, but he knew it wasn't warm. "You know when someone visits, and you go with them on some kind of shenanigan, and you think it's going to be fine, but it turns out to be horrifying? You drink too much, get sick, end up in the hospital or jail?

"But they're your friend. So, they come back three months later and the same thing happens."

She nodded. "I have such friends. Thankfully few of them."

"Yeah. This was like that, only ten times worse."

"Surely prison wasn't so bad? After all, you are close with the warden."

"I wish it had been prison. No, my . . . friend got me into much worse trouble than that." He sipped from a glass of water and looked over the menu.

Don't be a grouch. Nobody likes a grouch.

"Do you care to talk about it?"

He cracked his neck. "I don't know. It's . . . I told you already, some of it. I used to be bad. Well, worse. I did a lot of bad things."

"You told me. Some of it." She sipped her own water.

"I got into a situation where we repeated some of those old bad behaviors."

"Anyone else, I would assume they are admitting to some sexual peccadillo. But I suspect that's not the sort of bad you are talking about."

"I wish it were." He sighed. "I've spent the last few years trying not to do these things, and suddenly . . ."

"I assume the situation was, how do you say, pressurized?"

He smiled ruefully. "Yeah. I thought if I could just be good for long enough, the old habits would die off. Instead, it turns out it doesn't work like that."

She smiled. "You never truly thought it would."

"No, I guess I didn't."

The waitstaff were Drexians: red skin and flat yellow eyes and horns. Several presented as males, but they were similar in size to the females, not small like the assassins Rohan had fought on Earth.

Tamara pointed to the menu. "This animal . . . what is it?"

Rohan shrugged. "I have no idea, but it's the special, and given the way everybody is talking about this place, I'm sure it's delicious. You want to share it? That says it's enough for two."

"Your eyes are tired; it says enough for four."

"I'm really hungry."

Her eyes twinkled. "Are you not worried about becoming too full of food on our date? What if I require you to perform some rigorous physical activity? Later?"

He smiled. "If you think a couple kilograms of meat in my belly is enough to slow me down, you're forgetting who you're dealing with."

She laughed. "Perhaps I have. But you should eat your fill. I actually meant to speak to you of this tonight."

His stomach hollowed out. "Speak of what?"

She paused before starting. "I think we should take our relationship a bit more slowly this time. We have a history already, and things are more complicated."

He nodded. "Slow is okay. Probably better."

"Not *too* slowly."

He laughed. "I needed that. You know, I almost didn't message you. Or asked to meet in a few days."

"Yes? Why?"

"Well, I was in a really bad mood. I don't want to burden you with that."

"But? I hear an unspoken 'but' in your speech."

"But . . . I also wanted to see you. And I thought it would make me feel better. So I was a little selfish."

"I am glad. You seem off your usual self, but not so miserable that I would prefer to be alone."

He laughed. "Thank you for that."

"I will expect an improvement in your demeanor over the coming days. No excuses accepted."

"Yes, ma'am. So, are we sharing the special?"

"We shall. I hope it's a mammal."

"We can ask. I'm sure they're used to fielding questions."

"No, don't ask, just get the special. We'll take a chance."

"I guess we will."

———— ··•·· ————

The special was exquisite; so soft they pulled chunks off the carcass with chopsticks, not knives. The cartilage and fat had been melted into the flesh in a way that gave it just enough chew to be satisfying without ever crossing into tough. The proprietary Drexian sauces were subtle, a hint of sweet and a hint of heat complementing the fatty flavor of the meat.

They drank wine with it, a red, heavy with flavor that stood up well. The salad came with a sharp dressing that was almost, but not quite, overwhelming.

Rohan ate his fill.

He found himself staring off into the distance a couple of times, and Tamara's soft eyes told him she saw it as well, but she didn't bring it up.

Neither had room for dessert, though both promised the chef that they'd recommend the restaurant.

The chef insisted that Rohan swing around the table and sit with his arm around Tamara so his photo could be taken and displayed on the vestibule wall.

They left shortly after.

Rohan groaned as he stood. "I think I overdid it."

"The famous Hybrid, brought down by a dead animal."

"I could probably have beaten it in a fight. Just shouldn't have tried to eat its entire flank in one sitting."

"Come, a walk will do you well."

They strolled the promenade, walking a path down the center, twenty-five meters from either set of buildings, away from the heaviest foot traffic and the crowds.

Tamara pointed to a bench. "Come, sit."

Rohan shrugged and complied. She sat next to him and pointed to her lap.

"Here, lay back. I have known you for years; I can see that you are in distress."

He smiled. "Years? I think that's an exaggeration."

"We met over a year and a half ago. I remember. That rounds up to two, which requires a plural. So yes, years."

"Okay, I'm not arguing that. But we really only spoke for a span of what, twelve days? Then nothing until a week ago. A less charitable person would say we've known each other for just three weeks."

"Then, it is a good thing we are both very charitable. Now sit. Lay your head back."

He slid his hips to the end of the bench and lowered his head back onto her soft thighs. "Like this?"

"Yes, exactly." She leaned forward, her breasts coming tantalizingly close to his forehead, and put her fingers on his eyebrows.

The air smelled of grass and flowers. A gentle breeze, driven by fans instead of climate but no less lovely for that, made just enough noise to convey a feeling of privacy and isolation.

With careful, solid strokes, she rubbed his forehead, digging fingertips into his eyebrows, then his cheekbones.

He groaned.

She ran her hands lower, through his mustache, gently massaging above his lip, then under his mouth. She sunk her fingers into his beard, scratching at the skin underneath.

"It is always interesting to me, all this hair."

He sighed. Thought about a response. No words came to mind.

She dragged her fingers up from the sides of his jaw into his hairline, ran them back over his scalp, trailing fingernails down to the nape of his neck, then returning to his forehead.

Rohan thought he might melt into her thighs.

"I know you doubt yourself, sometimes. And possibly that is for the best. Too much self-assurance is a danger in itself." She pressed dark-green lips to his forehead. "But I will always believe in you. I know you might make mistakes. I know you might be capable of terrible things.

"I also know you will always, always try to do better, and more than this I can ask of no one. I am glad to be here with you, right now, to tell you this."

She stroked his cheeks, rubbing away the wetness.

30

Agent 99

R ohan's shift passed uneventfully. From the outside.

From his own perspective, he continually found that he would finish docking a ship and discover his hands shaking, images of dead elves on the Ringgate crowding his field of vision, rage filling his chest. An unknown amount of time later, he would come to his senses, drifting aimlessly, eyes catching the sparkle of Wistful in the sunlight, thinking of green-skinned fingers on his cheeks.

Later, he would wonder how he pulled it off: towing and docking ship after ship without causing even a single catastrophic accident, despite having the attention span of a dying gnat the entire time. He would say, later, that it was a good thing the functions of his job had become almost autonomous after two years of practice.

Wistful passed on messages from Hyperion twice that day; Rohan declined both.

Lahnegarn requested a meeting, hinting at a connection he had established with "high level" individuals. *High level? Rebels? I really don't want to talk to him. But I want to have to explain to Tamara how he got himself killed even less.* Rohan's thumb paused over the message, hovering for three minutes before he accepted it with a stab.

Ben Stone wanted to chat. Rohan saved that to his to-do list.

"Proper Patola" stopped when Wistful told him his shift was over. He paused, moving toward his apartment as the song resumed.

He entered; debated changing his uniform; decided against it.

Lahnegarn had picked the right place for a clandestine meeting. It was one of those bars where the service was mediocre, the booze was strong, and the food was just barely good enough to keep the health inspectors happy. A place where the lack of lighting was a feature, not a bug, and the sound dampeners worked better than the toilets.

Rohan checked his helmet, noting a booth number in the message from Lahnegarn, and made his way to the designated spot, shuddering lightly as his boots stuck to the floor with each ginger step.

The Lukhor was waiting, a mug of something steamy in front of him. He stood as he spotted the Hybrid.

"Rohan!"

"Lonnie." He nodded as he slid into the booth, swallowing as the sound system erased the background noise coming from the open bar.

"Thank you for coming! I think this is going to be really interesting."

"Sure. You want to fill me in on what's going on? Who we're meeting? What this is supposed to be about? So I don't, you know, sound like a moron when we talk?"

Lahnegarn stood up almost immediately and faced out from the booth. "Hi! Thank you so much for coming!"

So much for that.

Rohan slid over to the back of the U-shaped booth as another humanoid took his place. She was a good twenty centimeters taller than him, with very pale skin and strange white hair.

He stared for about two eyeblinks too long before he realized that her hair and eyebrows were composed of a series of very fine feathers. He stuck out a hand.

"Hello. Tow Chief Second Class Rohan."

She looked down at his hand and sneered. Her outfit was flowing silk in stormcloud gray.

The Lukhor reached over and pushed down on Rohan's hand. "This is our contact. No touching, and no names."

Rohan settled back down in the booth. "I get it. Spy stuff. Still, no contact . . . with our contact? That's funny. Right? Isn't it funny?"

The contact's sharp features showed no signs of humor.

"Are you wasting my time? Because this feels like a waste of my time. And I do not take kindly to that."

Rohan smiled and picked up a tablet from the table. He scrolled through the liquor selection. "I need a drink. Anybody else? No?" He tapped a request for an overpriced bottle of Sein Ale. He didn't trust anything the bar would pour into a glass out of his line of sight.

Lahnegarn looked at his contact. "We're not wasting your time. This plan is a chance to strike a real blow against the Empire. The kind they haven't suffered in five thousand years. And we can make it happen, right here, in this system."

She nodded slowly. "You've said that before. And you said it convincingly enough that someone very important sent me here to hear you out. Now tell me what you want."

"It's not what I want, it's what we all want."

She sighed and locked eyes with Rohan. "He's wasting my time."

Rohan shrugged. "It's not my rodeo. Let him talk; what difference does it make? It's not as if you have some other plan to destabilize the Empire that you have to get back to."

Her upper lip curled in a half-snarl, and she turned back to the Lukhor. "Go on."

He wiped sweat off his forehead with one hand. "Look, I'm sorry. I get nervous, and I talk when I'm nervous."

"Not fast enough."

He giggled, quickly covering his mouth with his hand. "Sorry. Really, sorry. Okay. Here's the thing. The il'Drach have a ship in the system. We all know that, right?" He turned to Rohan for confirmation. The Hybrid nodded.

"*Ironic Womb*. It's a Fleet cargo shuttle."

The contact nodded. "We know about it."

Lahnegarn smiled. "Sure. The thing is, I know what's on board. The cargo."

She fixed him in a stare that reminded Rohan of a hunting bird of prey. "Go on."

"Right. You see, they're making a trade. With Repentant."

"Who?"

Rohan leaned forward. "It's the station on the other side of the worm-hole. We opened it and made contact about six months ago. He's basically a twin to Wistful."

A man came by with Rohan's drink and something for the contact, set them on the table, and left without a word.

Lahnegarn waited for the man to leave the soundproof perimeter and continued.

"It's a treasure. A real treasure."

"What is it?"

"They have a ship on board that shuttle. A baby, barely functional. With a dreadnought class soul."

Her eyes widened. She turned to Rohan, who shrugged and popped the top of his bottle, then took a long sip.

"Why? Why would they have such a thing here?"

Lahnegarn leaned back. "I told you, they're making some kind of ne-gotiation with Repentant. He has some tech they want. Or resources. Honestly, I'm not sure. But he asked for a warship, and they're giving him one. It hasn't imprinted yet. They only trained it enough to achieve sentience, no more."

"I see."

"That's why it's on a cargo ship. It's asleep, but they can't have it around a sentient ship. It might bond to it. Develop an affection. Then it wouldn't be useful to anybody outside Fleet."

"You're saying it's unguarded? That seems highly unlikely. The il'Drach aren't stupid."

"No, no, that's not what I'm saying. There are three Hybrids on that ship. A lance primary and two secondaries. It's pretty well-guarded." He smiled and sipped his tea.

"Then, how is this of help to us? Fighting three Hybrids in space is suicide. Certainly given the resources we have available here." She eyed Rohan as if wondering whether his services were part of Lahnegarn's plan.

The Lukhor shook his head. "It's guarded *now*. But it can't stay that way, can it? They have to make the trade. Repentant won't allow any Hybrids through the wormhole, or the deal is off. They have to let the shuttle through by itself. Which means that, for a very narrow window of time, it's ripe for the taking."

The contact sipped her drink. "How is it that you know all of this?"

"It's simple. I'm a genius."

She raised one feathery eyebrow and waited for him to continue.

"Well, it's true. I'm an engineer. I work on the shuttles and ships that come in. My wife got me the job."

Rohan swallowed. "Ex-wife."

The Lukhor waved his hand. "Anyway, I've been here for a year. I've been planting sensors and tracking devices on the shuttles and ships that come in for repairs."

"How have you not been caught?"

"I have tricks. Lots of the sensors are passive. They take a parallel feed from the ship and record the results. The ship comes in for repairs; I download the view. It's not the same as having live intelligence, but I find out everything that happens in this system eventually.

"The really interesting part is that the shuttle came in for servicing. I put a bug on there, and they have no idea. It's a dead ship, too, so it can't feel the device. I know everything they're doing up there."

Rohan swallowed. *There might be something to this.*

If the contact shared his evaluation, she hid it well.

"I have heard a lot of claims from you, but no proof. An attempt such as this one will create tremendous exposure. It will alert the Empire to our presence. Our existence."

They already know; they just don't care. But you go ahead and think what you want to think.

"I have more information. A week ago, three new Hybrids came and took over the assignment. It wasn't peaceful. I know *why* they came."

"And?"

"The new ones, led by this Rrekha, they're here to watch the Stones."

"I don't follow you."

He glanced at Rohan. "The Professors Stone. They're here on Wistful. Well, on their ship docked at Wistful. *Insufferable.*"

Rohan pointed a finger at him. "*Insatiable.*"

The Lukhor nodded vigorously. "Yes, sorry. That's our little nickname for her. She won't stop talking."

Rohan pivoted in his seat, trying to get comfortable on the lumpy cushions.

"Anyway, I'm sure people know they're here, and that they fought their way onto that cargo shuttle. But I know *why* they're interested in the Stones."

Rohan's stomach clenched unpleasantly.

"Why?"

Lahnegarn leaned forward and lowered his voice. "They think Hyperion's alive. They think he's going to come here to see his friends." He leaned back, a triumphant smile on his face.

"Hyperion? What nonsense is this? He's been dead for years."

"I know! But there's some kind of rumor going around that he reappeared on his home planet. Earth or Dirt or something." He turned to Rohan. "You've heard of it, haven't you? You resemble the natives there."

Rohan shrugged. "I'm half-Earthling. Not really the half anybody cares about."

Lahnegarn nodded. "Right, right. There's an Imperial warrant out for him. The Hybrids are, what do you call it, casing the joint. The station. Watching it in case this fake Hyperion shows up."

The contact shook her head. "Why do they care? If they're fulfilling the warrant, why fight the Hybrids who were here? Why not just get orders?"

Lahnegarn shrugged. "I don't understand everything."

Rohan cleared his throat. "The Empire won't send Hybrids after Hyperion. They'll send someone else. Drexians, maybe."

"Why is that, Hybrid?"

He smiled. "Because on the remote chance that he is Hyperion, or close enough to Hyperion to be convincing, they're afraid the Hybrids will rally to his side. Instead of killing him." *I'm not sure I should have told her that.*

Then again, anybody who knows anything would be able to reach the same conclusion.

She leaned back and sipped her drink, her gaze flicking rapidly between the two men. "I'll admit, this is very interesting. Very. Impressive, even. But none of this is information I can verify independently."

"You can find out about the warrant."

"Perhaps, but you could have as well. It doesn't prove you've bugged their ship. I have no way to tell if you are in possession of more than a fabulous imagination."

The Lukhor tapped the table, looking down at its rough surface, then sat up with a start and snapped his fingers. "I know! There's more. They're coming here. Tomorrow."

The contact and Rohan turned to him and spoke in unison. "What?"

He nodded. "The negotiations with Repentant are nearly complete. He wants the ship checked, and he doesn't trust anybody other than Wistful to do it. So, they're going to come in close and have her give it a once-over. That isn't public knowledge."

Rohan rubbed his forehead.

The contact nodded. "Tomorrow?"

"Yeah."

"Can we take the ship then?"

He shrugged. "I don't think so, not without fighting through the three Hybrids. But it will prove that I have inside intelligence. Maybe you can scan the shuttle yourself or something. See that there's a warship inside it. If you have any empaths available, that is."

She turned to Rohan. "You agree with this plan? You think it is a good idea?"

Rohan pointed to his own chest and opened his eyes wide. "Me? No, of course not. Who told you that?"

"Then, why are you here?"

"I have no idea. Lonnie asked me to come. Said there would be booze. I'm not so popular that I'm going to turn down an invitation for a drink from anybody." He sipped his ale.

She stood, and in a flash her arm was outstretched with a metal object a bit larger than her hand pressed to Lahnegarn's forehead.

"I warned you not to waste my time."

His skin paled to the color of the inside of a lime. "I'm not, I swear it. He might help, that's all. Might. He's not a necessary component of the plan."

Rohan looked up and sipped his drink. "I'm not part of the plan, but I won't take kindly to you splattering this guy's brains all over my freshly laundered uniform."

"I thought you were one of us. Or aspiring to be. How do you even know him?"

"I know his kid. We're pals. In a non-creepy way. You know, saying that part out loud doesn't actually make it less creepy. But what can I do?"

She looked at Lahnegarn, then back at Rohan.

He put a little steel into his voice. "Lower the weapon or I will turn you inside out. And not in a good way."

"I have allies."

"So do I. But why would you bother starting a chain of us killing each other now? I'm not planning to interfere with your plan, one way or the other. I just think it's misguided."

Her elbow bent slightly, relieving pressure on the gun, but she didn't lower it. "Why?"

He exhaled slowly. "Because I think rebelling is misguided. You can't defeat the Empire. Because on your side, you've got a whole bunch of people like you two, and on their side, they have a whole bunch of people like me. And if you don't understand the difference, you're welcome to point that gun at my forehead so you can find out what happens."

"You're a Hybrid. I hear you stood off an entire Imperial Fleet."

"Yup. Just imagine what I can do to you if you keep pissing me off. Lower the gun."

She did. Then she sat. "We could use a few more people like you working with us. Then we'd have a chance."

He shrugged. "It's been tried, remember? Wasn't that long ago. Hybrids rebelled. The Empire is still around, and a whole lot of Hybrids died. No winners down that path."

"You won't join us because you're a coward."

He tilted the bottle back, draining the last of the fluid out of it. "Now, that was just plain mean. If you think insulting me is going to get me all fired up to prove myself to you, you've got the wrong Hybrid. I'm just here for a drink. And to keep my friend's dad from getting killed over nothing."

"So, you won't help us steal that ship. Assuming we even make the attempt."

"I answered that already. But I'm not particularly interested in stopping you either. Consider me a neutral party."

She nodded and looked at Lahnegarn. "Why do you care so much? About stopping the Empire?"

His face deadened. "I've been to Tolone'a. I can't bear to live in a universe where things like that can happen anytime, anywhere, without rhyme or reason."

She held his gaze, then nodded.

Rohan looked up into her face. "What about you? Why do you care so much?"

"Have you ever met one of my kind before?"

"I can't say that I have."

She nodded. "What gods do the il'Drach worship, Hybrid?"

He shrugged. "I don't think they do."

"They do not. But more than that, everywhere they have gone, where they have found true gods, they have destroyed those worlds. Or isolated them."

"True gods? Wait. You mean gods that walk around."

"Yes. Ours flew the skies on feathered wings, walked among us on taloned feet. And for that sin, for worshipping real deities we could feel with our hands, that held us when we were sick, that blessed us with true touch, the il'Drach all but wiped my people from the galaxy. For that, they must pay. And so that my hatchlings can find true gods again."

She faced Lahnegarn, who held his hands together to stop their shaking, the circular imprint on his forehead fading slowly.

"You say the cargo shuttle will come tomorrow?"

He swallowed. "I don't know if it's going to dock or just come very close. But it will be here."

"And the same way you know when it will come, you will be aware of the time when the Hybrids abandon it for the trade with Repentant?"

His head bobbed up and down. "Exactly. They'll leave. We might want to take it from the other side of the wormhole. Or just as it's about to cross. I assume you have some resources you can devote to that end of the plan."

"We might. I'll have to talk this over with some others. There are many factors to discuss. Including the possibility of Hyperion's return."

Rohan winced.

Lahnegarn nodded. "I look forward to hearing from you."

She stood. "Someone will be watching you, Lahnegarn of Lukhor. Any sign that you're attempting to betray us or expose us to the Empire, and that Hybrid at your side won't be able to save you."

He raised his hands. "That's the last thing I'd want to do."

"But if we do this, and it works, I will introduce you to *my* contacts. Then there will be no turning back."

He smiled. "I'm not interested in a way out, just a way forward. I want a better world for my kid."

She stared at him, inhaled deeply, nodded, turned, and left the booth.

Lahnegarn watched her go, then turned to Rohan. "That went well, don't you think?"

I think the only open question is who kills you first: the Empire or your new friends.

31

Hybrid Liver: Engage

Lahnegarn thanked Rohan profusely, then left the bar. *He left me with the tab. Serves me right for showing up here in the first place.*

Rohan settled the tab and ordered another ale, which came quicker after evidence of his good credit and the size of his tips registered on the staff.

He wouldn't let them take away the empty bottle.

He pulled his mask out of his hood and scrolled through messages on his screen, mindlessly checking news stories, blog posts, and sports scores. As he set the third empty bottle of Sein Ale next to its brothers, he made his social media location public and ordered another drink.

Three women and two men came over and tried to join him in the booth. Narrowed eyes and a quick headshake were enough to get rid of them all.

Ursula was pulling ahead in the polls. The topic of the day was debating a policy about rebels on the station: encourage, deport, or execute?

Rohan smirked as he drained a fifth bottle. The citizens could debate all they wanted; it was up to Wistful, and she wasn't about to forfeit her right to make that particular set of decisions.

The row of bottles had grown enough to form a wall shielding him and his mask from any pint-sized assailants entering the booth when Ben Stone tapped on the edge of the table.

"May I sit?"

Rohan nodded as the older man slid onto the bench on his right.

"How are you?"

Rohan shrugged. "I was thinking about this guy my mom dated."

Ben looked ready to argue, but paused and nodded. "Go ahead."

"I can't remember his name. He was around a little bit after my father left."

"I thought your mother was . . ."

"Gay? This was before Carla. She's either been bi this whole time or she was still closeted. I don't know, I don't really ask these kind of questions, you know? She's my mom. She can bang whoever she wants. Not my business."

"Sure. Sorry, I'm sure that wasn't the point."

"No." He sipped at bottle number—he'd lost count. "I was a teenager, full of myself. I was the man of the house, was going to take care of my mom. You know. So I talk to this guy, say he should have a drink with me. Talk things over. Man-to-man. Tell me his intentions."

Ben smiled, the crinkles at the corners of his eyes deepening. "Sounds very young-man like."

"It was dumbass is what it was. She never needed me to protect her. But, not the point.

"He says no. I'm all set to get angry, and he tells me he's an alcoholic. He'll talk to me, but no drink.

"I puff my chest out, thinking this guy's maybe a violent drunk or something, but no, he hasn't had a drink in years. Eight.

"So I ask him, why does he still call himself an alcoholic? Sober for eight years? He's just a nondrinker.

"He looks me right in the eye, and he tells me that's not how it works. If you're an alcoholic, it doesn't go away with sobriety. He has to live every day of the rest of his life knowing that he's one drink away from a binge to end all binges."

Ben nodded. "Are you trying to tell me something, Rohan? Sitting as you are, in a nest of bottles, smelling like a brewery?"

Rohan smiled. "I'm not an alcoholic. But I was thinking about it, about knowing that you are something, that you can string together two thousand days of sobriety, and it can all go away in a moment.

"I think I'm a monster the same way that guy was an alcoholic."

Ben's head dipped, his eyes soft. He waved his hand, calling for another drink. "You're not a monster."

Rohan's voice was harsh in his ears. "You know better than to say that to me."

Ben leaned back into the bench. "What happened on the Ringgate? I assume it wasn't anything good, given the way both of you have been since coming back."

"Both of us?"

He shrugged. "I spoke to Steve."

"He's in his cell, I hope."

"He is. Didn't ask to be let out."

Rohan nodded and fiddled with the empty bottle, rolling it back and forth between his hands. "It was bad. The worst I've been in a long, long time. I . . . I don't know."

"You thought that part of your life was over? That it was done with?"

"I'm not sure I'd use the word 'thought.' Hoped? Or maybe I just wasn't thinking at all. I've been trying to forget those days."

"But the temper is still there. The anger."

"The curse. That's what the il'Sein call it. They thought the il'Drach were a failure. An experiment gone wrong. ar'Tahul was amazed that any of us even survived."

Ben's drink arrived. He popped the top and took a sip. "Just because they think you're a mistake doesn't mean you are one, Rohan. Screw those guys. Who are they to talk? They made vampires. Heck, they abandoned this sector completely. Couldn't figure out how to protect us all from a bunch of insane soul-eating cephalopods."

Rohan's smile stopped below his eyes. "Don't go spreading all those stories. People aren't supposed to know."

"Bah. If they can't handle the truth, they shouldn't be eavesdropping on me."

"Cheers to that." Rohan raised his bottle; Ben responded, and they clinked the rims together. "Is that why you're here? Checking up on me?"

Ben sighed. "Not exactly. I was hoping you would talk to Hyperion."

Rohan shifted in his seat. "Did he ask you to ask me?"

"No, but I can tell that's what he wants. Maybe what he needs."

"I'm not following."

"He's in trouble, Rohan. He's having some kind of crisis. I think it's related to what happened on the Ringgate. He needs someone to help him cope with it, and, frankly, I'm not qualified."

"What kind of crisis?"

"He's shaken. By what happened. He won't give me details, but he's . . . not like he was."

"Shaken, not stirred? Maybe James Bond can help him."

"That's neither funny nor useful."

Rohan nodded. "Sorry. I'm not feeling very useful right now."

"I see that. Why don't you start by telling me what happened? At least the broad strokes."

The Hybrid sighed. "He wanted to understand what he is. Really is. A Hybrid. So, he put us into a situation where we would really cut loose. Where we had no choice."

"The curse."

"Exactly. We both lost control. Really lost control."

Ben exhaled slowly and took a sip of his ale. "I take it there were consequences?"

Rohan nodded. "People died. A lot of Wedge died, yes, but so did a lot of people who didn't need to die. At least not that day."

Ben nursed his drink for a while. "You know, I remember someone calling Hybrids weapons of mass destruction. It might have been you. I scoffed at first, but it's accurate, isn't it?"

Rohan nodded. "Like I said. A monster. Point me at the bad guys, push my buttons, and bam."

"You're not just a weapon, Rohan. But you know that. You're not really asking me to talk you out of this, are you?"

"Nah. I'll be okay."

"I'm not sure I can say the same of Steve. He doesn't know how to cope. It's as if he had some idea of what he is, and now it's broken."

"He thought he was a hero. Like he was put together out of visions of himself from cartoons and deodorant commercials. Then he started hanging out with me, and the truth broke him."

Ben nodded. "It is very much like that. He needs your help."

"I can't help him. Right now, I can't help myself."

"He did it for you. When you were younger. Didn't he? Helped you grow out of the mess you'd made of yourself."

Rohan looked at the older man. "That was Hyperion, not Steve."

Ben shrugged. "Maybe the same guy. Maybe not. But someone helped you, right? Now someone needs your help in turn."

"Hyperion had his act together, remember? He wasn't waking up in pools of blood and gore. Steve doesn't need me, he needs someone better. Try Wei Li. She can teach him some breathing techniques. They help."

"He needs more than Wei Li can offer him, and you know it."

Rohan cracked his neck and shifted his hips. The bench was quite uncomfortable. He looked up, saw the server approaching, and shook his head.

Ben continued. "I'm not sure Hyperion really had it together as much as you give him credit for. He firmly believed in that saying. You know, 'fake it until you make it.' He thought it was his job to act like a hero until he became one. But I don't know that he ever really convinced himself that it had happened."

"He seemed pretty confident to me."

"I know. That's what I'm saying. He seemed it. So do you, most of the time."

"With me it's definitely acting."

"You're a pretty good actor, then."

They sat together for a bit, listening to wordless instrumental music piped in over the bar's audio system.

Rohan shook his head. "I don't have anything for him right now, okay? I'm barely keeping it together. But I'll try. Just let me have a day or two."

Ben put a hand on his shoulder. "Of course. He's in his cell, as safe as can be expected. He really wants to do better, Rohan. He just needs some guidance."

"Keep him in his cell, Ben. He's a danger to everybody."

"I'm aware. More to the point, he's aware. He's not trying to get out."

A thought burbled through the haze of alcohol and blunt force trauma clouding Rohan's thoughts. "Wait a minute. He's in his cell. That in itself is going to be a problem."

"Why?"

"Because there are three Hybrids coming to the station tomorrow, one of whom is an empath, and they're looking for him. And I'm pretty sure he's not going to like what they have in mind."

Half an hour later, Rohan was sitting at the far end of the big table in Wistful's main conference room, tapping the surface.

He stood and circled the room's perimeter, patting at screens and low cabinets until he found a water dispenser. The pounding in his head resisted intervention.

Wei Li entered. "You called?" She wore a casual robe, white and yellow and flowing.

"Yeah. Sorry to disturb you."

She nodded and closed on him, drawing uncomfortably close. She touched his head. "You are perturbed. Unusually so. I do not think it is appropriate to summon me here for those reasons."

He reached up and pushed her hand away. "Yes, I am perturbed, but no, that's not why I called you here. I would have come to you if I wanted counseling or whatever."

"Then, what is the issue?"

He pointed to the empty space in the middle of the room. "She should hear this."

A hologram of a ship, a design not seen since the founding of the il'Drach Empire, manifested. "I am here, Rohan."

He downed a glass of water and swallowed.

"Good. We have a problem. Well, Steve has a problem, but it could become everyone's problem."

Wei Li nodded and pointed to the table. He took his seat.

"I heard that the cargo ship is coming close or even docking tomorrow."

Wistful responded. "With my permission. I am to examine the cargo."

"Right, I got that much. The problem is, one of the Hybrids on board is an empath. Class Three, I think she said."

Wei Li nodded. "Those are rare." She didn't mention that she, herself, was a Class Four.

Rohan nodded. "They're looking for Hyperion. Since Steve, whatever he is, resembles Hyperion, and he's in a cell in the central hub, I thought that might present a problem."

Wei Li turned to the hologram.

Neither spoke at first. Rohan drank more water.

Wistful broke the silence. "Why are they looking for Hyperion? I understood them to be guarding the cargo."

"That's what the first group was doing. Then these guys came and replaced them. They're guarding the cargo, too, but really they want a shot at Hyperion. They told me they expect him to come visit the Stones, if he's really back. It's part of why I wanted him in disguise."

Wei Li shook her head. "A disguise will not help. His aura is very unusual. Whether they will recognize it as connecting to Hyperion is another matter."

Wistful spoke. "What are they likely to do if they believe he is here?"

Rohan stretched his arms overhead. "Knowing Rrekha? Start tearing things apart to get to him. Maybe find some hostages."

Wei Li looked from Rohan to the hologram and back. "Hostages? Who could they use? You mean civilians?"

Rohan shrugged. "Or the cargo. The baby."

Wistful broke in. "Damage to the cargo is an unacceptable risk. I require an alternative."

Rohan shrugged. "I can take him off the station. Put him on *Void's Shadow*. That's assuming she agrees, but she's likely to. I'm not sure how long I can keep him there, not without a goal. And I'm not in love with that plan. I'm not sure how much time I can tolerate being stuck with him in an enclosed space without strangling him myself."

Wistful answered. "It doesn't matter. Steve does not wish to leave the brig. He has told me so explicitly. I can restrain him there, but not off-ship. *Void's Shadow* does not have the power to duplicate those measures."

Wei Li looked at Rohan. "He's afraid he'll go berserk again."

"Okay. What else can we do? Wistful, I know your aura acts as a screen. Will it hide him from detection?"

Wei Li's lines of scales glinted as she shook her head. "It won't be enough at close range."

Rohan scratched his beard. "If we can't hide him, can we distract the Hybrids somehow?"

Wei Li looked at him. "I don't follow."

"Make a loud noise somewhere. A loud spiritual noise. Maybe have Ang do something. Or the Ursans. Get them paying attention to something elsewhere on the station."

Wei Li shrugged. "I won't say it's a terrible idea, but I can't see how it would work. Ang can present as a source of anger, yes, and a powerful one. Ursula can exude a calming presence. Neither can mimic a specific person's spiritual signature, and to my knowledge nor can any other Ursan."

Rohan sat back, nodding. "I'm not sure, then. We can't run, we can't hide, and we can't fight. Those are my plans A, B, and C. What's plan D?"

Wistful spoke. "The Ursans cannot hide Steve's aura. But there are individuals in the brig who can."

Rohan and Wei Li locked eyes. She spoke first. "The Andervarian prisoners."

32

Lie or Dare

Rohan groaned as his flashing alarm grew annoyingly loud, as if the computer were mad at him for ignoring its earlier, softer voice.

He reached out of the bed and slapped the 'off' button, nearly falling onto the floor with the motion, and groaned.

Haven't had a hangover like this in . . . ever. Wish someone had told me not to drink to excess while suffering from a concussion.

He sat up on the edge of his bed, rubbing his temples, then stood and made his way to the shower on shaky legs. "Lights on. Full." The ceiling turned transparent, and sunlight flooded his apartment.

His comm sparked on. "Tow Chief, your special assignment begins in sixty minutes."

He groaned and leaned back into the hot spray.

His door slid open, just enough for a food delivery to squeeze through. Kratic-style breakfast burritos; a family-size portion, enough to feed four people.

Kratic food was slightly bland, heavy on protein and carbohydrate. It had felt like the right thing to break his fast after a night of heavy drinking.

Did I even eat last night?

The hot water and hot food reduced his headache to a dull throb. He stretched, hoping a little movement would do the rest of the job.

It didn't.

"Thirty minutes."

Wistful had decided that the Imperial cargo ship, due to its size and crew, should have a tow. And given its size and crew, she wanted her actual tow chief to pull it in, not one of her shuttles.

Which meant Rohan had to bring them in by hand.

Which gave him twenty minutes to talk the Andervarians into covering for Steve before he had to fly out and greet the Hybrids himself.

He dressed, pulled on his boots, slipped his helmet into the hood of his jumpsuit, and left the apartment.

The brig was in the same section of the station as his quarters, making it a short walk. Wistful, or Wei Li, or somebody, had cleared his entry; the doors slid open as he approached.

Security had shuffled the prisoners. The two Andervarian Powers, Cloak and Shadow, were across from one another. Steve was in the cell next to Cloak, and their master, the old woman, was across from him.

Rohan stood in the hall between them and raised his voice. "Speakers on, cells 32, 34, and 33. Off on 35." Sound deadening turned off to the three cells housing the Andervarians; Steve's cell remained sealed.

He cleared his throat. "Gentlemen. Lady."

The two Powers stood and approached their cell doors warily. Their purple skin contrasted with their beige pajamas, heavy yellow tattoos peeking out from sleeves and collars. The diamond plate cleared, giving them a good view of him.

Cloak, the thinner and taller of the two, spoke first. "You're the Hybrid."

"You know, most of the time, in a situation like this, I have to mock someone for saying something obvious. Because, you know, we're in space, and I'm flying around without a suit, or I've just come crashing through the ceiling. Something. But this time is different. You guys didn't fight me, and you haven't seen me do anything Hybrid-like. So I'm wondering, what gave it away?"

The old woman cackled from the next cell over. "I told them about you. The station hasn't kept us isolated the whole time."

Rohan nodded. "That makes perfect sense. And yes, I'm a Hybrid, but I don't work for the Empire. I'm a tow chief. My loyalty is to this station."

Shadow nodded. "We know about you, Hybrid. You fought off the Fleet. People are talking about it."

"My role in that situation is greatly exaggerated. At least my part in holding off the Fleet. But that's not why I'm here."

Cloak coughed softly. "Why, then? You going to say what will happen to us? I don't expect Wistful to keep us locked away forever."

"Sadly, no. I don't think she'll do that either, because that's not her style. But as far as I know, she hasn't made up her mind. Yet."

Shadow drummed his fingers on the window. "What, then?"

Rohan paused. "We have a situation. And when I say 'we,' I really mean you."

The Andervarians traded glances. Shadow spoke. "What do you mean?"

"Well, here's the thing. Maybe you heard, I'm not sure. There's an Imperial cargo shuttle in the system. Doing something. I'm sure it's hush-hush."

"We heard. We didn't do anything to it."

"No, of course. Nobody's saying you did. But, this is funny, actually. There are three Hybrids on board that ship. Real hard cases. One's an empath. Class Three."

The old woman chuckled. "You're going to have to spell it out for them, Hybrid. They're muscle, not brains."

The men nodded.

Rohan sighed. "Right. That Imperial ship is coming here. To dock with Wistful. For some routine maintenance."

Cloak shrugged. "So?"

"So . . . a Hybrid empath is going to be . . ." He turned slowly, as if orienting himself to the station layout, and pointed to one corner of the hallway. "About fifteen meters that way. And, we can't be sure, but she might notice a couple of Powers sitting here in the brig. And she might even recognize them, especially if, by some odd chance, Powers with your particular abilities are currently wanted for crimes against the Empire."

The Andervarians traded a harder look. Shadow spoke. "Why are you telling us this?"

"Personally, I wouldn't be telling you anything; like I said, it's not my problem. But Wistful has a soft spot for rebels. And a hard spot for the

Empire. Hard spots? Or maybe all her spots for the Empire are hard? That turn of phrase really didn't work. You know what I mean. She doesn't want to turn you over to the Empire. But if she has to, I mean if they demand it, and threaten people's lives, then she will. You see the conundrum."

Shadow mouthed the word 'conundrum' as if he wasn't sure what it meant.

The old woman barked at them. "They're going to sense you, dummies! Then they'll ask the station to turn you over, and she will. Then they'll space both of you."

Shadow nodded. "Right. I knew that. Wait, that's not good."

Rohan nodded. "She feels real bad about it, too. So do I, for that matter. I mean, yes, you threatened my friends, but you didn't really hurt anybody. So I'll be sorry to see you go. To your deaths. Your gruesome, painful deaths."

Cloak waved his hand to catch Shadow's attention. "Why don't we hide ourselves? We can totally do that."

Rohan rubbed his jaw. "Well, gee, that's an idea. I wish I had thought of that."

Cloak nodded. "I can't hold it forever, but if you could tell us when they show up, I can cast a field that nullifies aura-sensing."

Rohan nodded. "That sounds great. For you. I'm sorry about Shadow, though."

Cloak shook his head. "No, that's not a problem. I can extend the field far enough to protect us both. But you have to tell me when."

Rohan rubbed his jaw. "Wow. That is really good news. I bet Wistful will be happy to hear that. Now, I will be busy, personally, but I can ask her to tell you when to start hiding stuff. How does that sound?"

Cloak nodded, his Adam's apple bobbing with the motion. "Please, ask her. We'd really appreciate it. Both of us."

Rohan waved his hand. "No problem, no problem. Like I said, Wistful doesn't want to see you guys torn into tiny pieces and tossed away like garbage. She's happy to help."

The Powers nodded happily. Rohan's head throbbed.

The old woman caught Rohan's eye and gave him a fat wink. He smiled back at her, rubbed his temples, and left the brig.

His comm chirped. "Ten minutes, Tow Chief."

"I'm coming." He quickened his steps and made straight for the nearest airlock, preparing his mask while he walked.

He turned a corner and found Wei Li blocking the hallway.

"You looking for me?"

She tilted her head. "Can you think of another reason I'd be standing in front of this airlock?"

He shrugged. "No, but my head feels like it was force injected with high-pressure molasses, so I'm not trusting my thought processes very much right now."

She stared at him for a moment, then nodded. "You seem to have suffered some minor head trauma. I'm not a doctor, but I strongly suspect rest is in order."

"I'm not a doctor either, but I strongly suspect that I'm not going to be getting a lot of rest anytime soon. In fact, I suspect I'm about to get some fresh brain injuries to keep the old ones company. Wouldn't want them getting lonely, rattling around in my head."

"You expect violence with the Hybrids?"

He sighed. "I can't think of a way around it, not unless I get very lucky. And, well. Counting on luck has never worked out for me. Don't worry, I'll try to keep everything off the station."

"I would appreciate that, but I might continue to worry even if you do. As in, worry about you. I have grown accustomed to your presence. Your violent death would inconvenience me."

"That's sweet. Was there something you wanted to talk to me about? I'm on the clock here."

"Ben told me you are feeling conflicted about any possible role you might have in Steve's continued personal development."

Rohan straightened his hair with his fingers. "Are you here to tell me I should help him?"

She shrugged. "Not at all. Even if I was certain that you should, I have observed that you are generally reluctant to accept unsolicited advice."

"I don't think that's fair."

"Perhaps not."

"Try me anyway. Look, I'll solicit you. No, that came out wrong. Let me try again. Do *you* think I should talk to him?"

She smiled. "I will share with you two very general observations. Perhaps they can guide you."

"I'm listening."

"First, consider the actions of parents during an atmosphere leak. It is often their instinct to secure oxygen for their children first, but then they suffocate, and their children are left unable to care for themselves."

"You mean like on a damaged ship."

"Yes. By ensuring that their own needs are met first, parents are actually doing a better job of keeping their children safe. And the short delay in obtaining air rarely causes long-term damage to the children."

He looked into his mask to check the time. Still a few minutes to spare. "I'm going to assume I'm the parent in this situation. You're saying I need to get my own business straightened out before I try to help Steve.

"No, wait a minute. You said you had two observations. That was just one of them."

"Correct. The second is that, generally speaking, one of the most effective ways to acquire a skill or ability is to attempt to teach it to another person. It is through helping others that true mastery is often attained."

"So, I should help him now, and in doing so, I'll help myself. But you just said I should work on me first."

"You are beginning to see why I did not offer my advice at the start."

"If you're not here to tell me what to do, why are you here?"

"I would like to provide you additional information." She paused and let out a breath. "The prisoner—Steve—is exhibiting rapid change the likes of which I have never seen before. He is a dramatically different person than he was when I first observed him a week ago."

"You mean he's actually a different person? Like someone switched with the other guy?"

She sighed. "Do not be annoyingly literal. No, that is not what I mean. He has changed. The way people usually only change over many years of growth and development."

"So, he's like a baby."

"Babies do not change this rapidly. Not psychologically."

"You're telling me it's not an act. He's really going through some rapid development of some kind."

"Yes. You should not assess his behavior by the same standards to which you would hold a normal sentient being. He is quite . . . abnormal."

"I hear you. Tell me one thing, though."

"I will try."

"Is he changing into something new? Or turning back into what he used to be?"

"You're asking if he might be, in fact, Hyperion, simply in a damaged state. And you're asking if he is turning back into the man you knew."

"Yeah. That's what I want to know."

"I cannot tell. I am sorry. I will keep trying. Right now, you have to go and tow that shuttle, and I have to prepare to defend the brig if the Andervarians fail to screen Steve from the Hybrids."

Rohan sighed. "I hear you. Thanks for the information. I'm not sure it helps, but . . ."

"Go." She slid to the side, leaving him a clear path to the airlock.

He nodded, fixed his mask to his face, and walked under the open hatch, *lifting* immediately through it and entering vacuum.

Bright colored lines emerged on his mask, directing him to the shuttle's position at the beacon perimeter.

He *pushed* harder than he normally would, making up for some of the time he'd lost talking to Wei Li.

The shuttle loomed, its exterior covered in a matte-black coating, its name marked in a subtly glossier paint on one side.

"Hail, *Ironic Womb*."

"Hail, Tow Chief Second Class Rohan of Wistful. I believe you are to bring me to dock at this time."

"Yes. I'm attaching you to the central hub. Power down your bootstrap drives."

"Affirmative."

Wistful's voice spoke through his mask. "Shuttle is powered down, Rohan. You may bring it in." He tapped over to their secure channel.

"Roger that, Wistful." He switched back to the open channel. "Approaching now, *Ironic Womb*. Do you have an anchor point?"

Starships were designed to be towed; they all had a structure that could withstand the forces needed to accelerate the ship through space without tearing the hull apart. Shuttles typically did not.

"I have an anchor point, Tow Chief. Exposing it now." Metal plates retracted, revealing a nest of metal struts joining into a knotted sphere.

"I see it."

He grabbed the anchor point and began to push, gradually increasing the force, eyes on the struts to check for any signs of strain or buckling.

"*Ironic Womb*, where is your crew?"

"All assigned personnel are on board, Tow Chief."

"Of course they are. They're not going to board Wistful, are they?"

"I do not believe they intend to, Tow Chief. You'll be able to ask them yourself in about ninety seconds, as they plan to emerge when you've finished docking me."

"That's exactly what I needed to hear." *I am wasting my thickest sarcasm on a non-sentient ship. That head trauma is worse than I thought.*

33

Rrekhagnition

Rohan spent an extra two minutes securing *Ironic Womb* to Wistful's central hub. The docking clamps there, unused during Rohan's tenure on the station, were subtly different from the ones on her limbs, and he needed greater precision to form a seal.

His hand bounced off his diamond mask as he reflexively reached for his forehead to rub away a sudden throb.

"Wistful, shuttle is docked. I think I'm about to be busy for a few minutes. I'll get to the rest of my queue as soon as I can." *If I'm still in one piece.*

"Understood, Rohan." *She can't help me in a fight, not while that shuttle is close enough to be damaged. I am on my own.*

He pushed off from the shuttle and drifted away, exhaling slowly, willing the tension in his neck to subside. It refused, silently.

Three familiar forms emerged from the shuttle, flying graceful arcs around it and toward his position.

Rrekha's commanding tone burst over an open channel. "Hail, Tow Chief Rohan."

He switched them to a secure channel, his comm pinging theirs with automated instructions. *Try to sound meek, Rohan. Subservient. Come on, you can do it.* "Hail, Lance Primary Rrekha of Karse. What's a nice girl like you doing in a space like this?" He couldn't do it.

Rrekha's thick body was in front, swollen with muscle. Flint, a half meter shorter but just as wide, followed close behind. The Gray, as tall as Rrekha but slender to the point of emaciation, hung back, her face oriented on the station.

Rohan's heart fluttered as she stared hard at Wistful's hub, her gaze lined up directly with the brig where the Andervarian rebels were hopefully concealing Steve's aura.

Rrekha answered. "Wistful has assured the safety of our cargo for the immediate future. I would like to continue our discussion from earlier."

He sighed. "Are you sure? We can't just, you know, text? Email? Telegram? I answer all my emails, I swear it. Okay, you caught me, not all. Most."

The Gray hung in space, focused on the station, and drifted closer to Wistful's hull.

Rrekha laughed. "I imagine others find your chatter annoying. I, however, appreciate a man who displays bravado, however unwarranted."

He exhaled again and drifted farther away from the station. The Gray slid closer to Wistful, pressing her hands against the diamond layer covering her hull. "Inane banter is my best feature; everybody tells me that. What did you want to say to me?"

Rrekha's head swiveled, pausing on Flint's stoic presence, then turning farther to find The Gray. "Gray, do you sense anything?"

The Gray's voice was barely more than a whisper. "Something. Or perhaps nothing."

Rrekha's tone grew stern. "Clarify."

"I'm not sure. No, it's nothing." She pushed off the station and flew over to the other Hybrids. Rohan exhaled.

The Gray pointed to him. "He is nervous."

Rrekha smiled. "Is this true, little Hybrid?"

He sighed. *Distract them with the truth.* "Of course I'm nervous. You asked me to keep an eye out for Hyperion. I haven't reported anything. I'm worried you're going to punish me. I'm barely healed from the beating I took last time."

Rrekha chuckled. "I am not an easy person, Rohan, but neither am I needlessly cruel. If you've reported nothing because there is nothing to report, then you have no punishment to face. Unless you prefer one? Perhaps something small?" *Is she flirting with me?*

"No, I'm good. Had enough punishments this week."

The Gray shook her head. "He is hiding something."

Rrekha's smile hardened. "Is this true, little Hybrid? And here I was, being so pleasant. What are you hiding?"

Rohan wanted to rub his head. "I'm hiding lots of things. You'd be amazed. Well, maybe shocked. I have a collection of back issues of *Naughty Girls of Lukhor* that would blow your socks off. If you liked Lukhor girls, and if you were wearing socks."

"Careful, little Hybrid. I enjoy your banter, but my patience has a limit, and you are rapidly approaching it."

He swallowed. "Oh yeah. I'm hiding stuff. I once participated in a martial arts tournament, did you know that? Final Fists of something or other. And it was fixed! Totally rigged. Bet you had no idea."

Rrekha turned to The Gray, who held up her hands in helplessness. "I can see truth and lies, but I cannot read his mind, Lance Primary. He speaks truth, but there is more."

Rohan laughed. "You bet there's more! I'm a very private person. We could float out here all day long going through things I'm hiding. You want another one? I have to fight so hard not to punch this one guy in the face, just a normal guy, no Powers. Because he calls this one woman his wife, even though I know they're divorced."

Rrekha sneered at him. "I care nothing for these details, little Hybrid. Which you know. So, they cannot be the source of your anxiety, can they? Tell me, what are you hiding. Not generally, not from others. I mean *from me.*" She pushed one hand into the other and bent the fingers back. Cracking her knuckles, though the sound didn't travel through vacuum.

He swallowed again. *Should have had more to drink this morning. Maybe I'm still dehydrated from that drinking binge? Was that last night? It was.*

"Can't you narrow it down some? I'm not hiding Hyperion. Isn't that good enough?"

Rrekha shook her head. "Your feelings betray you, Rohan. As I said, if you weren't hiding something of value to me, you wouldn't be nervous. Out with it before I begin a more thorough method of questioning."

He smoothed his hair over the back of his head, pushing it onto his shoulders; it immediately puffed up again.

"Okay, you got me. I *am* hiding something, kind of. Something I was hoping people wouldn't find out."

Flint looked at Toth 3, hanging overhead, bored by the conversation. The Gray's eyes narrowed in concern.

Rrekha smiled. "Tell me. Or choose not to tell me, which is a challenge to my authority."

He sighed. "What would happen then?"

"We would have to fight again. But this time I would be fighting to teach you a stronger lesson."

"Let's avoid that."

The Gray interrupted. "Lance Primary, he isn't as afraid as he should be."

Rrekha dismissed her with a wave. "Tell me, little Hybrid."

"You thought you recognized me. You did. I'm not in Fleet anymore, but I was. You might have heard of me. The Griffin."

Rrekha turned sharply to the other female. The Gray nodded. "True." The Lance Primary swung back on Rohan, darting forward.

"You? You're smaller than I expected."

Flint turned to face her. "I keep telling you . . ."

"Hush." She drew closer, peering into Rohan's mask, her own faceplate almost touching his, a cloud of pink hair billowing out to all sides without gravity to keep it in place. "You do seem familiar. You fought by Hyperion's side."

"I was on the Ringgate for two years. By his side? Maybe in his shadow. He brought me from Earth along with half a dozen other Hybrids."

"Ah, yes. I remember you now. With the strange mask, printed with the beak of a bird."

"An eagle. Yeah, because my codename . . . You don't care."

"About that? No, I do not. Why are you here? Are you . . . undercover? Is this an assignment?" Her expression was difficult to read.

He rotated his head, loosening his neck. "The opposite. I got burned out. Too much fighting. Too many blows to the head." *That one's uncomfortably true.* "I retired. Came here to live a quiet life. My biggest stress most days is deciding where I want to get lunch."

Rrekha turned to The Gray, who nodded. "True."

She turned back to Rohan. "You." She pointed a thick finger at his chest. "Are truly The Griffin."

He shrugged. "Were. Was."

"You know, before the Rebellion, there was talk that you, not Hyperion, might be the one to lead us to victory against the Fathers."

Rohan's eyes widened. "Was there? They should have asked me first. I wanted nothing to do with it."

"The Fathers thought you were a threat. They sent you to Tolone'a to die. Instead, you returned to Drach with a great victory."

"You and I are going to have to agree to disagree about the definition of 'great.' But I guess I survived."

She grinned. "I once said I wanted to meet you! And here you are, already fallen before my fists. Wait. You fought well, but not to my expectations of The Griffin." She turned to The Gray, who was nodding her slender head.

"He was holding back when he fought you."

"Why didn't you so inform me, Gray?"

"He was afraid. I thought he was afraid of you, not of having his identity exposed."

Rrekha looked at Rohan. "You allowed me to beat you. That is something of an insult."

"Huh. Sorry?"

She shook her head. "My feelings are not important. Do you wish to challenge me for authority over the Hybrids in this system? We can fight again."

"Not really. At least not in a fight. Maybe a backgammon tournament. Two out of three."

Rrekha paused. "I cannot fight you for no reason, for you have already submitted to me." *She's a real stickler for the old rules.* "But someone else can challenge you."

Rohan sighed. "Why would they do that? Really, I'm no threat to anybody. I just tow ships, keep my head down. See? I'm not interfering in any of your . . . things. Whatever you're doing. Don't tell me, I don't want to know."

Her smile widened, teeth white and stark against her crimson skin. "Yes, you have already fought me. Whatever the reason, you did not show me your full potential. Unless you issue a challenge of your own will, you shall remain subservient to me."

"Sounds great. Just tell me what to serve and where."

"I wasn't finished. Given your reputation, it is obvious that your rightful place is directly under me."

He swallowed. "I'm flattered, but no thank you. I have a girlfriend. I think. Plus, I don't think I'm your type. You're cute, don't get me wrong, but you can do better."

She snorted. "Not that sort of under. I meant only that you clearly outrank Flint, here."

Flint looked up suddenly, his eyes hard as rock. "What?"

Rrekha shrugged. "What can I do? He is The Griffin."

Rohan muttered. "Was. I keep saying 'was.'"

Flint shook his head. "He was a barely adequate punching bag for you, and you would have me treat him as my superior?"

She held her hands up. "What can I do? It is the way. If you disagree with my assessment, you are free to challenge him yourself."

Here we go.

Flint looked at Rohan. "You want me to challenge him? To prove my status?"

Rrekha shrugged. "Only if you disagree with it, my dear Flint. What say you?" She winked.

He bared his teeth: startlingly white, lined with blue and red veins, like marble. "I see. Very well. Tow Chief Rohan, I challenge you."

Rohan scratched at his jaw where his mask sealed to his skin. "I guess I have no choice, then, do I? Now, let's see if I remember this correctly. If you challenge me, I get to pick the location. Isn't that right?"

Rrekha nodded. "You may claim that privilege. Where do you want to fight?"

Rohan smiled. "I'm going to guess you have gravity-control Powers like your cousin, right?"

"You know The Dwarf?"

"We were friends. Good friends, actually. I wouldn't want you to complain of any disadvantage. Afterward. Why don't we go to the surface?" He pointed up, directly at the center of Toth 3.

Flint's mouth opened, but The Gray interrupted him. "If you go to Toth 3, you will die."

Flint turned to her. "What?"

She nodded. "He is certain. Absolutely certain. If you follow him to the surface, you will never come back."

"How is that possible? As he said, I have the advantage there."

Rrekha looked at Rohan, who felt his smile broadening against his will. He nodded.

"Oh, she's right. Undoubtedly." *The kaiju on Toth 3 will rip him to shreds. I can control my anger, but Flint? Not a chance.* "But the challenge is issued already. No backsies. Sorry, Lance Primary, you're going to need a new subordinate."

She held up a hand. "Wait. Flint is a good friend and a loyal soldier. I do not wish to lose him."

Rohan windmilled his arms, feeling warmth settle into his shoulder joints. "Should have thought of that before starting all this."

Flint was staring at The Gray. "How?"

She shrugged. "I do not know."

Rrekha shook her head. "Rohan, fight him somewhere else. As a favor to me."

Rohan paused and tapped the side of his mask with his fingertips. "I'm flexible. I leave him alive, you start cutting me some slack. Leave me alone, for one thing."

She nodded. "I can try. We have other ways to monitor the happenings on the station."

"Great. And you promise—all of you—on your honor as Hybrids, you won't tell anybody outside this system that The Griffin is alive, or that he's in Toth."

Rrekha nodded. "Agreed."

The Gray nodded as well. "I have no issue with that."

Flint sputtered. "What are you saying? You think this stick figure of a man can defeat me?"

Rrekha turned cold eyes on him. "We will find out soon." She looked back at Rohan. "What location do you choose?"

Rohan fell backward, away from the station. "How about right here?"

Flint growled. "Fine by me."

◆ ··•·· ◆

Compared to other Hybrids, Rohan had never been particularly large. He had never been the strongest, or the fastest, or the most gifted fighter.

The one area where he had always excelled was with the *speed* at which he could muster up his Power.

Rohan growled softly, relaxing his limbs so he looked like a helpless target while poking and prodding at the rage that lurked just behind his burgeoning migraine.

Anger at Lahnegarn for pulling him into his doomed rebellion.

Flares of energy surged and tore at his midsection.

Anger at Rrekha for adhering to a ridiculous code of honor that forced cousins to beat each other's heads in just to establish meaningless dominance.

Twin tendrils arced up and around his lower spine.

Anger at Steve for . . . existing. When he had no right to exist. For being so much of what Rohan was running away from.

Energy wrapped around his backbone like vines around a signpost, twisting and reaching for his skull.

Anger at the Fathers for sending Hyperion to his death.

Bubbles of energy swelled and burst as the lines crossed.

Most of all, anger at himself. For letting Hyperion die in the first place. For genocides on Tolone'a, Zahad, the Ringgate. For leaving Earth and his mother behind.

And above that, anger for surviving when so many others had not.

Energy locked into the base of his skull, sending shuddering pulses of Power out through his limbs. Clearing away the dryness in his mouth, the fatigue in his arms and back, the dull ache in his belly, the scratchiness in his throat, the pounding in his head.

Details came into sharp focus. Flint's hands were relaxed, his path a lazy drift toward Rohan. The Gray's eyes opened wide, her mouth opening to issue a warning. Rrekha's lips parted in an expression right between hunger and joy.

Power reached his nails, the tips of his toes, the ends of his hair.

Rohan grunted and *willed* himself forward.

Driven by the full mantle of his Power, Rohan's speed took Flint by surprise. The shorter Hybrid barely had time to flinch before Rohan's knee impacted his sternum, the lankier man following up with a stiff fingertip strike into Flint's esophagus.

The short Hybrid curled forward and coughed. His hands opened and closed, as if reaching for something, his Power searching for a source of gravity.

It's his reflex. He's trying to increase gravity, slow us both down. Won't work in deep space, buddy.

Rohan turned a somersault, extending his right leg with perfect timing, the tip of his boot coming up just as Flint's chin came into range.

The shorter Hybrid flew away from the impact, tumbling chaotically in space.

Rohan blasted toward him, unrelenting.

The Earthling stopped Flint's spin by powering an elbow down into the shorter man's rising head. Flint's body spasmed, his arms and legs jerking wide like a starfish.

Rohan stayed close, giving no more than a few dozen centimeters of space. He drummed fists into Flint's body, working up and down the shorter man's torso, wrapping around his back, then returning.

Ribs, armpit, liver, kidneys, small of the back, back of the neck, armpit, ribs, solar plexus.

Flint covered up at first, trying to wedge his forearms between himself and Rohan, but the Earthling was circling too quickly.

The Dwarf was never great at fighting without solid ground under his feet. As I suspected, it's a trait common to his people.

Blood stained the inside of Flint's mask when he gave up his defenses. He relaxed, absorbing a trio of punishing strikes to his abdomen, then reached out to grab an arm.

The short Hybrid's hands felt hard as stone as they dug into Rohan's left bicep.

Flint climbed Rohan's limb, pulling himself closer to the taller man, looking to secure some kind of grappling hold on Rohan's body.

Rohan cast a quick glance toward Rrekha. She watched, her face as cold and calm as Flint's flesh.

"I get the impulse. You're getting boxed up: grab a hold and try grappling." Rohan punched Flint's mask with his free hand. "It's not a terrible instinct. It might even make sense if we were evenly matched. And if we were on the ground."

He punched again, snapping Flint's head back. For a follow-up, he drove the first two knuckles of his fist into the shorter man's exposed throat.

"But in zero gravity? When you grab me, you're just giving me leverage. Physics doesn't care if it's you holding my arm or my arm holding you. Either way, it lets me devote all my attention to doing this."

He dug his fist low, scraping it along his own thigh, then up. Powering the hand up with all the strength of his arm, shoulder, and upper back.

Rohan's back arched fully, his own chin flying high into the air as his uppercut smashed into the bottom of Flint's jaw.

The short Hybrid might have spun away, dissipating the energy of the blow, but he was still anchored to Rohan. So all the energy of that savage swing went right into his brainstem and.

Stopped.

Flint's mask tore off and went sailing through space. His body relaxed, consciousness severed, and his grip on Rohan fell away.

Rohan glanced at Rrekha.

The match wasn't over.

Flint hadn't submitted.

He could hold the man in place, grab his neck as the last of his air boiled out of his lungs.

I probably should. Doubting me. Challenging me.

I should teach them a lesson. Make them remember my name. Remember The Griffin. Remind them that they should be afraid of me.

Rohan shook his head, exhaled slowly, willing his anger away. Held his lungs empty for a count of three. Then he shook the lingering pain out of his left arm and grabbed Flint by his uniform collar.

With a burst of speed, he pulled the shorter man along and intercepted the tumbling helmet.

Rohan grabbed it out of the air and smushed it into Flint's face. A moment later, he felt the air supply kick on with a whoosh.

The unconscious Hybrid's belly moved as he took in the fresh air.

Rrekha still hadn't moved.

Rohan pulled the shorter Hybrid to her.

"I assume—" His voice had come out as a growl. He coughed, willed his temper back under control, and started again. "I assume you'll accept his lack of consciousness as a satisfactory end to this challenge."

She nodded, her eyes wide, face solemn but not angry. "That was impressive."

Rohan shrugged. Aches accumulated over the previous week and a half were returning to residence in his bones and joints. "I'm not The Griffin anymore. That doesn't mean he forgot me. Or I him."

She bared her teeth. "You're wasting yourself here. Towing ships."

He shook his head. "I'm perfectly happy on this station. And I'll disagree strongly with anyone who interferes with that happiness."

"I understand. I am not your enemy, Tow Chief Rohan. At least not today."

He nodded. "I hope that's true. For both of our sakes. Mostly yours, though."

He nodded to The Gray, pivoted in place, and flew toward the beacon line.

I have ships to tow.

34

More to Life than Living

The Fleet Hybrids kept to Rrekha's promise, disappearing inside *Ironic Womb* and staying there. Wistful's work took just half an hour, after which she cleared Rohan to tow it back out to the beacons.

Rohan did so, sighing with relief as the ship powered up its bootstrap drives and left for its resting spot near the edge of the system. He continued his shift, towing the usual assortment of ships to and away from Wistful.

Halfway through his shift, Rohan received a message from Tamara. He knew she was sleeping; it must have been sent on delay so he'd get it while working. She asked after him; told him she'd be spending the next day with Rinth but was looking forward to seeing him again after that; hoped he was feeling better.

The note put a sorely needed but short-lived smile on his face.

Ten songs later, *Love Boat* approached the beacon barrier.

"Hail, Tow Chief Rohan."

"Hail, *Love Boat*. Power down your drives; I'll tow you in."

"Permission to speak privately, Tow Chief?"

He sighed. "Of course." She opened a tightbeam channel between them.

"Tow Chief, you don't look so hot. I don't mean to embarrass you, but there's some blood on your uniform."

He looked down. So there was. "Don't worry, *Love Boat*, it's not mine. Are you worried I'll scare your passengers? I promise I'll clean up soon. It's just been a rough couple of weeks."

"Oh no, Tow Chief, I'm sorry, that's not what I meant. I just worry. You know. So hard to find a true gentleman these days, I'd hate to see anything happen to you."

That brought an unexpected smile to his face. *Day started off poorly, but it's looking up.* "I appreciate the thought, but you can relax. I'm fine."

"Yes, I know. But that's not why I wanted to talk."

"Oh?"

"Sugar, do you remember a little while ago I mentioned spotting an Imperial ship out near the edge of the system?"

"I do."

"Well, this is going to sound mighty strange, but there's another one there now. Even farther out, past the fifth wormhole. Right at the edge of Toth's heliosphere."

"Are you talking about the same ship? The cargo ship?"

"Oh, no, love. I wouldn't bring that up again. This is an honest-to-goodness starship. It's sentient."

"What was it doing?"

"Just waiting. If I didn't know better, I'd say she was hiding, Tow Chief. Loitering. Not that I want to cast any aspersions on another ship's intentions."

Rohan exhaled. "She's Imperial, you said?"

"I believe she is, Tow Chief. One of those long-range troop transports that were all the rage, oh, a thousand years ago. Not much in the way of fighting ability."

He scratched his jaw. "Thank you, *Love Boat*. I will look into it. The ship wasn't aggressive toward you at all, was she?"

"Oh goodness no! You're so sweet for asking."

"All right. Thanks again, *Love Boat*. I'll take care of it. Are you ready for your tow?"

"Anytime! Powered down."

He thought while towing the ship to her dock.

Lahnegarn pinged him, requesting a meeting. *Don't you sleep? It's the middle of the day!* Rohan ignored it.

"Wistful?"

"Yes, Tow Chief."

"Are you aware of an Imperial ship lurking on the outskirts of the system? Near wormhole five?"

He took two full breaths before hearing an answer.

"I am now. It is the ship that brought these Hybrids to staff the shuttle. It had permission to bring them here, though I thought it had left again."

"Okay. Just making sure. Thanks, Wistful."

"Thank you, Tow Chief."

Fifteen more songs played before another ping from Lahnegarn. He ignored it.

Steve sent a text, asking if they could meet. Rohan was about to delete it, then sighed and responded, "Tomorrow." *Give me a chance to get rid of this headache before I acquire a new one.*

Twenty-three more songs. Rohan was humming along to the refrain of "Coca Cola" when he got another urgent message from Lahnegarn.

"Oh for . . . Personal."

His artificial intelligence, a non-sentient piece of Wistful that spoke in her voice but wasn't really *her*, answered. "Yes, Rohan?"

"How bad would I feel if Lahnegarn got killed doing something stupid?"

"I do not fully understand the question, Rohan."

"I mean, he's very irritating. I do not like the guy."

"I cannot comment on that, Rohan."

"And, I mean, we can all just agree to agree that Tamara is better off without him. Am I right? She should be with me. Clearly. We're like, star-crossed lovers. Wait. Does that mean we're destined to be together or that we're doomed? I don't remember."

"I am not familiar with that expression, Rohan. Is it Drachna? Or a language I don't know?"

"Right. That's not the point. We're not linguists."

"We are not."

"But he is Rinth's father. Right? That means something. I think. I don't know, my father's a jerk."

"Yes, Rohan."

"He's in over his head with these rebels. He thinks he knows what he's doing, but he doesn't. They're going to kill him. And then Rinth will be sad. Which will make Tamara sad."

"I do not have the computational resources to analyze these interpersonal relationships."

"Exactly. I don't want her to be sad. Especially if it's not the drive-her-into-my-arms kind of sad. Which this wouldn't be. Since she asked me to save this jerk's life."

"You're not even pretending to respond to my statements, Rohan."

He sighed. "You're right, I should meet with him. I'll do it. And I'll save him. Maybe I'll feel better afterward. If I don't, I can just blame you for giving me bad advice."

The AI didn't answer.

"What ship is next?"

<hr />

At the end of his shift, Rohan entered through his private airlock, showered, and put on a clean, blood-splatter-free uniform.

He fiddled with the soulgem, working to perfect Spiral's technique. Stretching his energy out into a band, then curving it into an arc.

Every time he came close to forming a link of a helix, he'd pull a bit too much energy, bringing with it a spike of anger that disrupted his concentration, dissolving the shape into ether.

He lay down on his bed and tried to nap.

Unsuccessfully.

I should sleep. I should also meet Lonnie and try to talk sense into him again. I don't think it will work, but it would be good to be able to honestly tell Tamara that I did everything I could.

An hour later, eyes still wide open, he gave up on sleep and headed over to the rebel-themed diner where he'd met Lahnegarn the first time.

The Dripping Bucket? What kind of a name is that for a diner?

He entered, the crowd's reaction to him muted compared to the first time. The Lukhor was at the same table as before, a tray in front of him. He half-stood, a smile on his green face, nodding at Rohan.

"Good, good, I'm glad you came."

Rohan shrugged and took a seat opposite the Lukhor. "Lahnegarn. You realize there are two thousand restaurants on this station? You don't have to eat here."

"I told you, this is authentic Lukhor cuisine. Can't beat it."

"If you say so. I'll have some of those fried buns, I guess. They have wine? I could use some wine."

"Sure they do. It's breakfast for me, but they don't serve only the nocturnals here." The Lukhor waved his hand and placed an order.

Rohan nodded and tried to relax in his seat. "You want to tell me what was so urgent? Or should we eat first?"

"I do, I do. Food can wait." He looked around, checking the crowd. Nobody seemed to pay them any special attention. He leaned forward, his antennae twitching anxiously. "I saw you had a fight with the Imperial Hybrids. I knew you were on our side, Rohan. You were savage!"

Rohan rubbed his forehead. "That was barely a fight. Why were you watching, anyway? Don't you have, I don't know, a job?"

"I told you, I'm a genius; my job doesn't take all my concentration. Look, I really think you could help us steal that cargo."

"I already told you I'm not interested." He paused as a server delivered his wine and a tray of hot food. "I wasn't fighting all three Hybrids. If I did, you'd be hearing about my funeral right now. That fight was just some stupid Hybrid monkey dance."

"Monkey dance? I don't understand. Who was the monkey? What music was playing?"

"It's a human expression. It just means a fight for dominance, the kind you find in primitive mammals."

"Ah. Well, still, you showed your dominance over the short one, didn't you? And you have way more at stake fighting the Empire than you're willing to admit."

"What's that supposed to mean, Lonnie? It sounds a little bit like a threat, and I hope for both our sakes it isn't one." Rohan rubbed his temples.

"No, no. Of course not. But I know what you're hiding, and what you have to lose when the Empire finds out. Look, I'm not going to tell them! But they will find out, and, well. You know."

"What are you talking about, Lonnie?"

"I know you don't want to discuss it, but I have cameras everywhere. Just remember that I know everything."

Rohan sighed. "Lonnie, I have a question."

"What?"

"If you're such a genius, why does Tamaralinth's father hate you so much? Why didn't he think you were a suitable match for his daughter?"

Lahnegarn's face paled. "Um. You know about that?"

"You're not the only one who knows things, Lonnie." Rohan bit into one of the crunchy buns.

Lahnegarn nodded, his eyes softening. "My father-in-law respects power and money. Yes, I am a genius, but I don't have either of those things."

"Why not?"

"Well, to be honest, I'm kind of a socialist. Using my brain just to make a whole pile of money never appealed to me. I'll work for a living wage, but not more than that."

Rohan pointed a finger at the Lukhor, then pulled it back in. "You know what? I respect that. No shame there."

"Really? You don't think I'm a moron? I could have gone into finance like my parents wanted, made a pile of money in high-frequency trading or managing hedge funds."

"I do still think you're a moron, but not for that. I judge you more on the fighting-the-Empire thing."

The Lukhor finished his sandwich and drained half a glass of tea. "Okay. But the point is, you have your friend to think about, and with the Empire around, you know he isn't safe."

Rohan's stomach dropped. "What friend are you talking about, Lonnie?"

"You know. The big guy. In the brig? The one the Hybrids are after. Nice job hiding him from them, by the way. I don't know how you managed it. I thought for sure the skinny Hybrid was going to sense him." He sipped his tea.

Rohan exhaled slowly. "How are they going to find out, Lonnie?"

Lahnegarn shrugged. "I don't know. I found out, and I'm just one guy with a bunch of cameras. Someone else is going to find out for sure. And maybe they won't let it slip, but the next person will. That guy's a crate of theonite on a timer, and you don't know when it's going to go off, but it will."

Rohan sat back in his chair. "What do you suggest?"

"Help us steal the ship. The Hybrids will get in trouble; they'll get recalled by the Empire for sure. That's assuming we don't have to fight and kill them."

"Killing those three isn't going to be easy."

"No, sure. But if we get the cargo, they get recalled. They won't be able to just hang around here on their own personal mission."

"Then what?"

"Then what, what? I mean, your friend will be safe. At least for a little while, right? But I mean, he won't be safe, not really. Even if we get rid of those Hybrids."

"What do you mean?" *I know what he means. Don't say it, Lonnie.*

"I mean, clearly the il'Drach are afraid of your friend. They're going to keep looking for him, and you can't just hide him forever, can you? Not if he wants to have any kind of life. Trust me, I've been in hiding. It's not fun. And I wasn't running from the whole Empire."

"No. You weren't. What do you suggest?"

"It's not what I'm suggesting, Rohan. It's just what's obviously true. It's either him or the Empire. They can't coexist in peace. Look what happened to him last time. He signed his life away, enlisted in their army, saved the lives of everyone in the sector, if half the things I've heard about the Wedge are true. And what was his reward for all that? They killed him."

Rohan swallowed. "It's not that simple."

"No? Okay. I'm not trying to start an argument with you, Rohan."

"Of course you aren't."

"I'm just saying, I bet there's a place for him in this rebellion. I bet he'd be welcomed. And I bet their chances for succeeding, and for keeping him alive, would go up a lot if they could get their hands on a once-in-a-century warship that's ripe for imprinting."

Rohan blinked. He bit into another bun and chewed without tasting.

"I know you're not a fan of the Empire, Rohan. And I know you're no coward. Maybe you've always felt there was no chance at success. I sympathize. But there's a chance now. You helped create that chance. I think you'd feel bad if you sat on the sidelines while other people did the hard work."

"Hard work."

"Rebelling. Taking on the might of the Empire, head-on. Yeah, the hard work."

Rohan rubbed his forehead, pinched the flesh between his eyebrows. "You think I'm afraid of hard work?"

"I didn't say 'afraid.' Reluctant, maybe? I don't know. Hey, if I'm wrong, show me. Join up. Help us. We could use it! We could use both of you."

Rohan nodded. "I'll consider it. You should consider paying a little more attention to changes in lifestyle that will keep you alive so you are there for your little boy."

"There's more to life than just living. I think you already know that."

Rohan stood. "I'll be in touch."

Lahnegarn nodded. "Cool. I have a shift soon. Have a good night."

Rohan turned and left the diner.

35

Walk in the Park

Tamara had promised that evening, and the following morning, to dedicated mother-son bonding time with Rinth, leaving Rohan to fend for himself.

He considered seeking out Ben Stone or Ang and Ursula, but decided that with his headache and general mood, he was going to be rough company.

Dinner alone would suffice.

I should really learn how to cook.

He got takeout from a Kratic stall just outside the central hub, on the eastern arm, and ate in his apartment with his screens set to show scenic views from beaches, mountaintops, and isolated caves on fifty different worlds.

His head throbbed through his meal. *Have I had brain injuries that lasted this long before? I think I have. Hard to remember, though, because they're brain injuries.*

He picked up from episode five of *Fists of Lukhor*. It was a derivative remake of *Swords of Lukhor*, an acknowledged classic of serialized holocinema, that focused on unarmed combat and relied heavily on fanservice moments with popular starlets and overly enhanced computer-generated fight sequences.

It was rapidly turning into his favorite show. Four episodes were enough to put him to sleep.

He blinked his eyes open. It was still dark; the artificial night imposed by the station.

"Light." The diamond ceiling turned transparent, letting in a flood of sunlight from Toth 3.

He was getting out of the shower when his comm beeped with the tone denoting a call from Wistful. He checked his clock, wondering if he'd somehow misread it and overslept, missing his shift, but it was early.

"Hello?"

"Rohan." *Not Tow Chief Rohan. She wants something.*

"Yes, Wistful?"

"Wei Li suggested I contact you. To ask for . . . a favor." *When was the last time Wistful asked me for a favor? Never?*

"Sure. What is it?"

"I understand that you are reluctant to be involved with Steve's rehabilitation."

"Is that the term we're using?"

"I am not presently concerned with terminology."

"Fair. Sorry, go ahead."

"Steve's temper seems to be restrained. Dr. Simivar, who has been overseeing his care in the brig, has suggested that some time outside might be in his best interests."

"Outside? You mean in space?"

"She means outside the brig. Her suggestion, to quote directly, was that he be allowed to 'take a walk.' She believes we cannot assess the danger of his temperament directly without exposing him to stimuli outside those present in his cell."

Rohan exhaled slowly. "She wants him to deal with more things so we can see if he can manage that without flying off the handle."

"I believe that is an accurate representation of her proposal."

"What does Marion Stone think of this plan?"

"She concurs."

Rohan cracked his neck. Then he ran his fingers through damp hair.

"When are you doing this? No, better question, though I think I know the answer. Why are you telling this to me?"

"Wei Li and I would like you present. In case it becomes necessary to restrain Steve."

Rohan sighed. "Tell me there's more to this plan than me beating him unconscious if he loses his mind."

"There is. Dr. Simivar will be present with an array of soporifics. A group of Ursans have volunteered to provide additional security."

"The Ursans forget that he's a Power. Big as they are, he'd tear through them if he lost control."

"They are willing to accept that risk. Given his fondness for them and ensuing reluctance to cause injury, and their mass and resilience, they should be able to restrain a small outburst on his part."

"The Ursans pile on if he gets annoyed. And I'm there if he's mad enough to hurt the Ursans."

"That is accurate."

Rohan sat on the edge of his bed and let his head hang loosely, his beard tickling his upper chest.

"You said this is a favor."

"Yes. This activity is outside the scope of your contractual obligations as a tow chief."

"Great. Then you can do me a favor in return."

She paused before responding. Rohan imagined microprocessors heating up somewhere deep inside her central hub, fans bursting into life to cool them. "What would you like?"

"Tell me what you think Steve is."

"I do not think that is wise."

He exhaled. "At least tell me if Steve is Hyperion resurrected."

"I do not believe it is possible for a deceased sentient being to return to existence."

That's probably as good an answer as I'll get.

"I'll accept that for now. But I might really need to know, later on. And when I do, you're going to answer me."

"I will."

"All right, then. I'm in. When is this excursion happening?"

"In forty-seven minutes."

Of course it is. Not the end of the day, not tomorrow. Right now.

"I assume you've arranged coverage for my shift?"

"I have."

He sighed. "Where do I go?"

"Please meet the Ursans at the brig entrance at your earliest convenience."

"Do I have time to eat?"

"You do. Forty-six minutes as of now."

"Great. I'll be there."

Forty-two minutes later, Rohan patted his full belly and entered the hall leading to Wistful's brig.

"Brother Rohan!" Five hundred kilograms of fur-covered muscle barreled into the Hybrid, sweeping him off his feet.

"Ang!" Rohan had long given up attempting to moderate the Ursan's greetings.

Ang set Rohan gently on the floor. "We had been for betting on if you would come. Ang said yes, for sure War Chief will be here, but others bet against." He smiled, exposing an impressive display of ivory teeth. "Winnings will fund many days of celebration."

Rohan smiled ruefully. "Glad to help. To be honest, I'm not sure I *should* be here. I think this is a terrible idea."

Wei Li walked up to them. "I agree. I have been reminded that I am not, in fact, in charge of this station."

Ang chuckled, a deep barking sound emerging from his belly. "It is always this way. One is in charge until being reminded that one is not." He glanced at Ursula as he said it, a good-natured smile on his maw.

Wei Li shrugged and looked at Rohan. "You also attempted to dissuade Wistful?"

"Of course."

She sighed. "Free will is an annoying trait. Life would be much simpler if others would merely do as I told them to."

"On behalf of all sentient lifeforms, I apologize to you."

"I accept. Here comes Dr. Simivar."

Ursula greeted the Drexian, a tall woman whose black horns reached close to the Ursan's eye level.

Dr. Simivar walked over to Rohan and Wei Li. A boxy pack was strapped to her back. "Are we ready?"

Rohan shrugged. "Will we ever be?"

She smiled, showing teeth that came to sharp points. "He'll be fine. You'll see. His berserker state is a result of violence and a lack of understanding on his part. I don't think it will happen again."

"That's reassuring, because you're betting all our lives on it."

She tilted her head. "Am I? He seems to think you could stop him if needed."

Rohan sighed. "I could have two weeks ago. Now? I'm not sure."

"Well, we have this." She patted her side where a tool like an electric drill was holstered, connected by a thick white hose to her backpack. "Enough sedatives to knock out half the station."

Rohan snorted. "That will just make it easier for him to kill them all."

"Very funny. Now come on. Let's take our boy for a walk."

Wei Li led the way, followed by Ang and Ursula. Two unscarred, brown-furred Ursans, each matching Ang's two-and-a-half-meter height and five-hundred-kilogram mass, fell into step behind their leaders.

Rohan and Dr. Simivar trailed the formation.

"Where are we actually going?"

She laughed. "We are going for what young dating couples might call 'a walk.' Or perhaps even 'a stroll.' Try to contain your excitement."

He rubbed his forehead. "I've been meaning to ask you, I was hit in the head by a dinosaur, and the headache has lasted for a week. What should I do?"

"Wait it out; you'll heal." She withdrew the device on her hip. "Or do you want me to knock you out? This is probably strong enough to make you forget your headache for at least a few hours."

"Tempting, but they need me conscious for now."

They walked down the hall, past rows of cells with darkened windows. Wei Li tapped something on her tablet, and one of the windows turned clear.

Steve stood in his cell, facing out, hands behind his back, glasses perched on his nose. He nodded to Wei Li, his lips pressed tightly together under a bushy mustache.

She returned the nod and tapped the control panel next to the door. It slid open.

He looked over the assembly, eyes widening slightly as he got to Rohan. He nodded and stepped out into the hallway.

"Hey, guys."

Ang ambled forward and clamped a heavy paw over Steve's shoulder. "This is good, no? We will walk, breathe fresh air. Ha! Fresh air on space station. Is funny!"

Steve smiled and put his hand on Ang's shoulder.

Wei Li turned to address the group. "We're heading out onto the southern arm. We'll turn around when Steve or Dr. Simivar says we turn around. Does anybody have any questions about their role here?" Furry and less-than-furry heads shook in unison. "Let's move."

The Ursans formed a box around Steve, but he stood and waved Rohan over. The Hybrid shrugged and fell in next to him.

"Thanks for coming. I know you're mad at me."

"I'm not—okay, maybe I'm mad at you. It's not just that, though."

"If it helps, I'm pretty mad at myself."

Rohan sighed. Wei Li led them out of the brig, then turned down the wide hallway that opened onto Wistful's southern arm.

"I don't know, Steve. I'm glad you have your glasses on."

Steve touched them, pushing them more firmly on the bridge of his nose. "I'm trying to be more careful."

"You think this walk is being careful?"

"I think my temper isn't going to go away. Which means I need to learn to control it. Which I can't do by myself in a cell. That's what I think, but it's also what Dr. Simivar thinks. And Wei Li."

"I will bow to their expertise."

"How did you learn? To control it? The anger?"

Rohan exhaled. "What makes you think I did? You already forgot what happened on the Ringgate?"

"That wasn't your fault. I dragged you into that situation. If not for me, you probably would have kept your cool. And before that, on Earth. With Dr. Kraken. You weren't out of control, not completely. I stopped you with just a couple of words."

"I suppose. It was just a lot of practice. A lot of breathing. And growing up with it. It's not as strong when you're young. I think I had time that you don't have, learning to live with the rage when it's still small."

Steve nodded. "Wei Li thinks mine is like an adult's."

"Right. And you never got to practice with the weaker prepubescent berserker impulses."

They stepped onto the promenade, sunlight bathing the group through the diamond roof.

Wei Li led them down the center of the promenade, twenty-five meters away from the storefronts on either side, grass tickling their ankles as they walked. The walkways on either side had people on them, but nowhere near the density that would come in another hour or two. Past those walkways rose ten-story buildings packed so close together they formed solid walls.

Steve stretched his arms. "It feels like I've been tied up in there, even though there was actually enough room to stretch out if I wanted to."

Rohan chuckled. "It's psychological. You deal with it when you start spending a lot of time on ships. You—Hyperion taught me how to handle that. When he took me away from Earth."

"I took you away?"

"Yeah. We were needed on the Ringgate."

Steve nodded and inhaled deeply, following Wei Li as she set a brisk pace around benches and flower patches.

Ang stepped closer to Steve. "Is good day for walk, yes? What do you want to be doing, Brother Steve? Breakfast?"

"Let's just walk. Make sure I'm not completely crazy, right? Don't go flying off the handle because I stub my toe on a bench. Or because the sun is too bright."

Ang started humming a marching tune, the other Ursans joining one by one until they formed a subvocal chorus. Wei Li turned to the group, smiling, and caught Rohan's eye.

They continued, passing through block after block, strolling with relatively little discussion until they reached some of the less-populated areas of the arm.

Wei Li looked around. "This has been an extensive walk. Should we return?"

Steve sighed. "Can we go a little longer? I know you all have things to do, but I'd really appreciate it."

Wei Li looked at Dr. Simivar, who shrugged.

"I'm interested in this experiment, so I'm happy to continue. He isn't agitated; there's no particular reason to go back."

Ursula nodded. "We are for being free today. It is our honor to help Brother Steve."

Rohan looked at the big man. "You made a strong impression on them."

Steve looked down, running his hand through his hair. "I kind of lost it at their show, didn't I? It seemed to make sense at the time, but now it's embarrassing."

"Yeah. That's going to happen again."

"What?"

"Looking back on stuff you did and being embarrassed. Part of growing up."

"Right. Right. Like the Ringgate. Maybe embarrassing isn't the right word for that."

"I hope it isn't."

Wei Li held up a hand. "Something's wrong."

Rohan looked at Steve. "Big guy seems okay." Steve shrugged, holding his hands up in innocence.

The security chief shook her head. "Not with Steve. Out there."

She turned to face the buildings on her left, studying the storefronts and passersby. Rohan followed suit but didn't notice anything unusual.

After a moment, she muttered and tilted her head to look up. "By the Seven."

Five stories up, a row of balconies stretched across the entire block.

Rising to the railings on them all were Drexians with crimson skin, flat yellow eyes, black twisting horns, and wide leather wings.

Dr. Simivar whispered from behind them. "That's a lot of death cultists."

36

The Devils You Know

Rohan's head throbbed.

Wei Li turned to Dr. Simivar as the Ursans formed a protective circle around Steve. "What can you tell us about them? Quickly."

"Um . . . well . . ." The physician's eyes were wide, shining pastel yellow against her crimson skin.

"I said quickly."

Dr. Simivar shook her head. "Right. They're stunted males. The cults let them stay together after birth, when they're supposed to be separated."

Rohan grunted as he rubbed his temples. "Less of a family history and more of a 'how do we fight these guys,' Doc."

She nodded. "Right. The wings are a separate organism. An engineered symbiote. They pump the males full of stimulants, make them faster and stronger while greatly shortening their lifespans."

Ang smiled. "So if we are for waiting here long enough, demons will die of old age?"

"Not that short, sorry. They're low-level empaths. Not very smart as individuals, but they connect to each other. It's almost like a hive mind."

The first balcony emptied as six Drexians dove toward the group. As they reached the halfway point short, brutal spikes emerged from their wrists.

Dr. Simivar pointed. "They have those, too. Implanted at birth. They sometimes carry venom, so be careful."

Ang grunted. "Has been long time since we fought, yes, Ursula?" He took off his black leather coat and tore it in half, winding one piece around each of his forearms to armor them.

She growled softly. "Maybe too long." She and the other Ursans copied Ang's actions.

Rohan watched Steve. The big man took off his glasses, folded them, and tucked them away in his pants pocket. He pressed his lips together and turned to the Hybrid.

"I'm a lot stronger now. Not useless like I was the last time we faced these."

I'm not sure whether that makes me feel better or worse.

Wei Li looked at Rohan. "Should I call for backup?"

He shook his head. "You'll just be adding to the body count."

She nodded, reached for her thighs, and drew a pair of telescoping batons. With a flick of her wrists, she extended both and faced out.

The Drexians drew first blood.

They moved in, so fast their features blurred into a streak of red and black and shiny teeth. Ang stepped forward to intercept; he caught most of the spikes on his jacketed forearms, but two scored hits on his meaty shoulder and thigh.

He growled and swatted at the Drexians, too slow to catch them, but the younger Ursans were ready. They pounced, one catching a wing with the tips of his paws, quickly securing a handhold.

The other Ursan leapt on top of the Drexian, weighing it down, and they savaged it with claws and teeth until it stopped twitching.

Ursula leaned in to take quick sniffs of Ang's wounds. "No venom." She looked up and shouted. "More coming!"

Ang's growl built.

Steve clenched and unclenched his fists. "We have to help them."

Rohan nodded, wincing as the movement brought a flash of pain through his head. "Fly over there and grab that gazebo. We can use it as a shield. I'll work on the Drexians."

Steve looked poised to argue, but followed instructions. Wei Li swung her batons in the air, loosening her arms.

Ang absorbed the brunt of the next wave as well, but Rohan stepped forward to help. The Hybrid grabbed one flyer by the throat, wincing as two others sliced across his ribs. His Power surged in response, angry and offended.

He reached over and gripped the Drexian's wings where they met over his shoulder blades. With a grunt, he tore them free from the male's body, then tossed the convulsing creature to the side.

Dr. Simivar called out. "Check those wounds!"

Ursula slid over to Rohan and sniffed him. "Clear!"

Blood formed growing stains on Ang's brown fur. He smiled at Rohan. "I am for missing my gauntlets, Brother Rohan."

Rohan nodded. "I wouldn't mind one of those right now. Heads up."

Steve carried a metal gazebo overhead, dirt and grass dripping from the base where he had torn it loose. He ushered Dr. Simivar under it. "It's better than nothing."

She nodded. "Thanks. I need to help, though."

"Help by staying safe."

The next wave struck.

Rohan flew up to meet the leader, his knee rising to strike the creature full in the face. Bone crunched with the impact, the male's face buckling inward, his nose twisting and turning down, his horns pointing forward as his teeth shattered.

The Drexians flanking him struck at Rohan, spikes lacerating his forearms, penetrating uniform and Power-reinforced flesh.

"Be careful, they're pushing Power into those spikes."

Ang grunted. "Now he is for telling us. Is too late for such speaking, Brother Rohan!" He held up the heavy leathers on his arms, showing the rents and tears that were accumulating.

Ursula bled from a cut along her muzzle. The younger Ursans panted, eyes dark.

Wei Li had clipped one of the Drexians and finished him with a rapid double-strike to the base of his skull. "Another wave is coming. Larger."

Fourteen fresh Drexians dropped into the fray.

Wei Li took Ang's left flank, dancing among the demons. She swung her baton into the air, seemingly without purpose, but each time a Drexian popped up to meet it, as if she had known what their path would be.

Ang absorbed more blows on his arms, lifting a leg that weighed as much as Steve's entire body, stomping down on one of the aliens. The young Ursans smothered one demon apiece.

Rohan flew over them, plunging down into their formation, tearing through the wings of two more males. Ursula finished one off while Rohan twisted the other's neck until it snapped.

Blood leaked from a slash across Wei Li's collarbone.

Ang's other leg had a fresh puncture.

The young Ursans were cut.

A gash across Rohan's forehead leaked blood into his eyes. He blinked rapidly to clear them.

Steve surveyed the group and stepped forward, away from his position protecting Dr. Simivar.

"I'm going to help."

Rohan shook his head. "Guard the doctor. We have this."

"No. They'll die if I don't help, and it will be because of me. And after, I'll still have to fight."

Wei Li coughed. "We have no choice. We can't hold them. They're bringing more."

Rohan looked at the others.

Ang grinned at him, his organic eye just as defiant as the red cybernetic orb on the other side. "We are not for giving up just yet, Brother Rohan."

Wei Li shook her head. "They are very fast, but the real problem is their tactics. Their teamwork. They work well together."

Dr. Simivar banged on the side of the gazebo three times. "I told you, they're semi-empaths. That's how they cooperate. They're dangerous. We need to get out of here."

Wei Li surveyed the open grass all around. "They would chase us down, Doctor. There is no easy escape."

She banged again, twice, then stopped. "I have an idea. I need some time."

Rohan cracked his neck, his Power surging in response. He saw an angry gleam in Steve's eyes.

The next wave of Drexians struck.

Rohan and Steve met them in the air; Ang, Wei Li, and Ursula met them on the ground, with the younger Ursans ready to fill in the gaps.

Steve grimaced, teeth bared, and grabbed the first two Drexians he reached by the horns, clashing their heads together with a tremendous crack, dropping their bodies to the ground.

Each had stabbed him in the flank before falling.

Rohan grabbed another one, spinning the male around to knock aside half a dozen others as he made his way to Steve. More Drexians came toward the big man, recognizing their target, and he had no apparent interest in defending himself.

Wei Li pointed to Ang, who nodded and clasped his hands together in front of his knees. She ran at him, leaping up into his hands, and let him fling her into the air.

She spun as she sailed into the Drexian formation, her batons breaking wings on four separate demons before she fell gracefully to the grass. The Ursans fell on the fallen Drexians.

Steve growled and headed straight for another pair of Drexians, shouting wordlessly as he grabbed one by the neck, driving his other fist into its face. Three fresh stab wounds and one dead Drexian were the reward for his recklessness.

Rohan's Power rose in response to the other man's anger. He exhaled hard, trying to calm himself. "Steve! Back to ground! You can't take them all!"

Steve growled and tore apart another Drexian, taking another pair of cuts across his back. His head turned rapidly from side to side, seeking fresh targets.

Rohan closed on the bigger man, whose eyes showed little signs of recognition.

The Hybrid flew just over Steve's shoulder, ramming his elbow into a Drexian just before the male drove a spoke into the big man's neck. The Drexian crumpled and fell, but two more engaged Rohan midair.

Wei Li shouted. "Rohan! He's losing control! Dr. Simivar, how's that plan of yours coming?"

The Hybrid grabbed one Drexian, spun, and threw it into a second. He dropped closer to Steve, his feet impacting hard on the back and neck of another assassin.

Steve bent his head to the throat of another male, tearing it out with his teeth even as two spikes penetrated his arms, coming completely through the meaty parts of his biceps.

Rohan shouted. "We have to get down to the ground! Listen to me!"

Steve turned and raced for another demon.

Rohan grunted and dropped onto his friend's back, *pushed* down, and drove him toward the grass behind the Ursans.

Steve reached back with his arms, flailing but unable to reach the Hybrid.

Rohan exhaled as they dropped, willing his own Power down, pushing away the rage. The desire to dominate. To crush this man pretending to be a hero. Who was risking all their lives for his own hubris. Who refused to listen. Refused to obey. Who insisted on clumsily pursuing his own path, despite everyone telling him that it was impossible, that he needed help.

The hatred for a man who acted with all the thoughtless confidence that had filled a younger Rohan.

Steve's face hit the dirt, little ripples rising in concentric circles around the strikezone, waves in the grass. The bigger man pushed against the ground, spinning to view Rohan.

Steve's eyes widened as he recognized the man who had taken him down.

"Hyperion! Calm down! You have to fight it!"

Steve swung one heavy fist, then another, clubbing Rohan's head.

Rohan grabbed the bigger man's chest and rode with the blows, pain blossoming in his temples with the accumulated damage to his brain.

"Fight it! Don't make me stop you!"

Steve's mouth worked wordlessly.

Wei Li faced Rohan. "They're coming back. We need help."

"Give me time!" He turned back to Steve. "Calm down!"

Wei Li muttered. "Everybody wants more time. Time is a very expensive commodity at the moment."

Steve struggled, wiggling his hips, slapping at Rohan's shoulders and head. Rohan rode the bigger man, his legs wrapped around Steve's waist, kicking back to knock his feet out when they sought purchase on the ground.

Steve screamed, then slammed his own head back into the dirt. "Let me fight!"

Rohan shook his head and locked eyes with the big man. "If you do, we'll have another Ringgate! Not here, Hyperion! Not here!"

Steve's eyes widened.

Rohan leaned close and shouted. "Not again, Hyperion!" The big man's struggles slowed.

Wei Li pointed at Ang. "I have a plan! You four, project as much feeling as you can. Anger, calm, whatever you've got." Ursans did not have Powers per se, but their auras were potent, as Steve had discovered during their play a week before.

Ang nodded. "Anger, we are having plenty. You think angering these Drexians will be for making easier fight?"

"No. I think the noise will disrupt their communications."

Dr. Simivar shouted. "Yes! Do it! You can break apart their shared mental structure! Fill the air with feelings! Just give me a little more time, I'm almost done with this." She was working on her backpack, adjusting something in the soporific container.

Blood dripped off Rohan and onto Steve's chest.

"Breathe out! No, slowly. Slowly. Stop fighting me, Hyperion. Breathe out. Good. Now hold it. Hold it."

Steve stared into Rohan's eyes and did as he was told.

Drexians swooped in, aiming for Rohan and Steve.

The Ursans roared; the edges of the world shaded pink, tainted by a blast of pure, unadulterated anger.

Steve's head whipped from side to side as his lips pulled back from his teeth.

Rohan shuddered. "Breathe! Exhale! I'm right here with you!"

Wei Li leapt in, picking Drexians off with her batons. The Ursans followed, massive paws tearing at wings and flesh, blood spurting. Dr. Simivar stood from her small shelter, pack returned to shoulders, hands fumbling with the drill at her hip.

The Drexians, perhaps confused by the noise of the Ursans' anger, didn't turn to cover the threats. They walked and flew and fell toward Steve, ignoring their wounded and their fallen.

Rohan released Steve's chest and grabbed him by the sides of his face, forcing the big man to look at him. "I'm here! I believe in you, Hyperion. You can do this! Hold it back!"

Spikes dug into Rohan's back.

Ursans swatted the Drexians away from him, tearing out their throats. More came in.

Steve looked into Rohan's eyes; he balled his hands into fists, pressed the back of his head into the grass. His breath came in quick pants.

Rohan shook his head ever so slightly. "Slower. Slower. Forget them. Trust our friends to take care of them. Just breathe."

A spike passed between the bones in Rohan's left forearm. Something crunched as Wei Li delivered a blow to the creature's head.

Rohan held tight to Steve's face. "Forget them. Just you and me buddy, all right? Just you and me. See? Ignore everything else. Breathe out. Slow. Slow. That's it."

Something went into his lower back, slicing through muscle and barely missing his spine. Someone growled and pulled it free. Rohan felt blood pulse out of the hole in little spouts.

The Drexians continued, falling in on Rohan, ignoring their flanks, all thoughts of strategy and tactics wiped away, leaving only their urgent need to eliminate their target.

Steve panted again.

"No, forget all that. See? Everything's fine. Just breathe. Slower. You've got it, man. You've got it."

Another flash of pain in his right temple. Rohan's vision clouded on that side; he reached up to clear his eye.

His hand went farther than it should have gone. *That's not good.*

Dr. Simivar shouted. "Get back! Get back! Run!"

Rohan stared at Steve with his left eye. "Forget her, Hyperion. This is what heroes do. They breathe, and they slow down. Okay? This is what heroes do. What you do."

A powerful hissing sounded behind Rohan's ear. The air filled with a peculiar smell, sour and sweet at the same time.

Dr. Simivar shouted again. "You need to stay clear of the gas, but they'll be fine! I think. Get back, no. Stay back."

Drexians thumped to the ground. More flew in, eager to make contact with the Hybrid.

As they entered the cloud of gas, they fell, senseless.

Rohan stared at Steve. "Good job, buddy. Good job. Just exhale."

Steve's lips softened into a half smile. His eyes closed.

Rohan nodded. "Good man. That's the way." He turned his head, trying to see what he could out of his single eye.

He knelt over Steve. The ground around them was piled two meters deep with Drexians, half of whom twitched and moaned, locked in some strange assassin nightmare.

Wei Li and the Ursans stood five meters away, flanking Dr. Simivar. The doctor was frantically working some mechanism in her equipment, slowing the gas coming out to a trickle.

Ang stepped forward, as if to help Rohan, and Dr. Simivar shouted. "Don't do that! It's still concentrated enough to kill you. Step back. Farther."

Wei Li was on her tablet. "Wistful is adjusting vents and airflows here. The air will clear soon."

Dr. Simivar nodded. "Get medical units over as fast as you can. We might lose civilians." She pointed to the sides of the promenade. "Good thing everybody cleared out when the fighting started."

Ang stepped away and fell to one knee, his other hand reaching for the ground to support him. Ursula stumbled to his side. Both were covered in blood.

Ang locked eyes with Rohan. "You are for owing me new jacket, Brother Rohan. This was for being my favorite."

Darkness fell over the Hybrid.

37

Status Updates

R ohan blinked open his eyes.

His *eye*.

He saw light, but not much else. He was prone, naked, and nestled between soft sheets. Could be his own bed. The air smelled of sweat and disinfectant. His mouth was dry and foul.

He reached his hands up and gingerly probed his face. Heavy bandages obscured the right side. The left was crusty, and a quick rub cleared it.

He blinked again, relaxing a bit as the familiar contours of his room came into focus. Toth 3 directly above him, visible through the diamond plate ceiling. The door to the bathroom, half-open as he usually left it. His dining table, Steve sitting in one chair, one leg folded over the other. The sadly underutilized kitchen. Bare walls.

Wait.

Rohan put his hand against the bed to push himself upright; a stabbing pain made him think better of the idea. He switched hands and sat up.

"Steve?"

Steve smiled and stood, crossing the room toward Rohan. He wore his prisoner's uniform, a pale and loose-fitting jumpsuit woven out of some kind of space linen. He held a water bottle, straw embedded in its lid, in his hand.

Heh. Space linen. Linen, but in space. I need to remember that.

Steve reached for him. "Easy there, chum. You were hurt pretty badly the other day. Doctor said you'd want water when you got up."

Rohan took the bottle. He sucked at the straw, taking the liquid too fast, and coughed. Steve waited while he recovered and drank more.

"What time is it?"

Steve pushed his glasses up on his nose. "It's early. About four in the morning."

"What day?"

"We fought the Drexians yesterday morning. You've been out less than twenty-four hours, chum."

Rohan grunted. "How are the Ursans? Wei Li?"

"They're fine, superficial injuries only. We're the only ones who were poisoned and hurt more seriously." He pointed to Rohan's right eye as he said it.

Rohan touched the bandage gently, shivering slightly as he felt the indentation in his face.

Steve nodded. "Doc says it might grow back, with you being a Hybrid and all. She said something about regen tanks and eyes that I didn't follow."

"I'm glad she looked into it. A regen tank is good for a lot of things, but not eyes. They heal too fast, so they don't quite come back . . . right. You have to dig them out and start . . . you know what? I don't want to have this conversation."

Steve smiled. "I don't blame you. That was pretty gruesome. Just this gaping red hole right there in your face—"

"Can we, like, not talk about that? I just said that. Didn't I just say that?"

"Right, you did. Sorry."

Rohan took in the room. There were empty food containers scattered on the table. "You were waiting all night?"

"No, actually. Just for the last half hour or so."

"How did you even get in here?"

Steve shrugged. "Door just opened. I figured you set it up that way."

Did I? Can't even remember.

"Shouldn't you be in the brig, though? What did I miss?"

Steve smiled. "Wistful said she can restrain me anywhere inside the central hub, so I'm free to roam it on my own. It's nice being out of my cell. I even get to talk to people."

Rohan adjusted pillows around his back. "Who are you talking to?"

"You know. Ben and Marion Stone. I visited Ang and Ursula in the med bay. I even had some of your friends come for a chat."

"My friends? I have other friends?" *He couldn't mean Tamara, could he?*

"Of course you do, chum. You're a hero. It was strange, though. They didn't give me their names. Just came to talk."

"Oh boy. Can you describe them?"

"One was a green man with these cute little antennae. The other was a thin woman with feathers. Feathers! Space sure is weird."

The rebel contact. And Lonnie. Probably.

"I'm not sure I would have called them friends. Maybe acquaintances. People I've met. What did they want to talk about?"

"Oh, this and that." Steve sat back down at the table and picked up a half-eaten sandwich. "They were quite nice, really. The woman especially. I think she likes me."

"Really? She doesn't seem like the type to like anybody."

"Oh yeah. She was actually bowing and everything. I figured, you know, alien culture, it's weird, but what can you do? She kept calling me something. Vishar-baya. It must be a term of endearment."

Rohan nodded. *I know what that means. I don't know why she'd call him that . . . unless I do. Oh crap.* "Must be. I'm not sure."

Steve took an enormous bite of his sandwich, chewing it rapidly. "How do you feel? You took several doses of Drexian venom. Doc said it would have killed anyone other than a Hybrid."

Rohan cracked his neck and raised his arms overhead. "I feel like I need another week of sleep. Like I got run over by a battleship."

"You want some food? I have another sandwich. Wasn't sure your stomach would be up to it."

Rohan paused. "Yeah, that sounds good."

Steve brought it over. He stood over Rohan. "Yesterday was almost a catastrophe, wasn't it?"

Rohan took the food and nodded. "Almost."

"What would have happened if you hadn't been able to talk me down?"

Rohan sighed. "I don't know exactly. You're a lot stronger than you were on Earth. I think I could have stopped you the hard way, if I had to. The question is, how much damage would that have done to Wistful?"

"Your friends had an interesting point."

"My friends? Green guy and bird girl? What about?"

"They said that my problems all come from the Empire. The il'Drach. It's true, isn't it? The Empire killed me the first time. They sent the Drexians. Without the Empire, I wouldn't have needed help yesterday."

Rohan swallowed. "That's one way of looking at it."

"What's another way, chum? I don't see any alternatives."

Rohan nodded. "You could blame the il'Sein for creating us with these tempers. Our whole species was a bio-metaphysical-engineering accident. You could blame the old Hyperion for getting tangled up with the Empire to begin with. There's plenty of blame to go around. The question is, what are you going to do about it?"

"I'd like to show those il'Sein a little bit of old-fashioned Earth face-punching." He banged his right fist into his left palm.

Rohan shrugged. "Good luck finding any. Also, the ones who did this are probably long dead. We're talking about fifty-thousand-year-old stuff." He bit into his food.

"Maybe I could take a swing at some il'Drach instead."

The Hybrid swallowed. "Is that what this is about? You want revenge on the Empire?"

Steve sighed. "Not just revenge. I feel like they need . . . something has to happen. They need to be taken down a peg."

"And you plan on doing this yourself? How, exactly?"

Steve leaned forward, his eyes wide and eager. "That's the thing! Green boy and bird woman have some interesting ideas! Plans, even! And they want my help. They want to make me part of something useful."

"Let me guess. No, don't, just tell me."

"I didn't get all the details. Something about negotiations with Rejuvenation being finished, and stealing a ship. I didn't get the middle part, but stealing a really tough ship sounds like a great idea."

"Repentant. Don't do it, Steve."

Steve's face straightened. "Why not, Rohan? Why shouldn't I go after the Empire? They're not pulling any punches coming after me."

Rohan ran a hand through his hair. It came away a bit greasy; too much time spent lying in his own sweat and not enough showering.

"That's the problem, right there. You think they aren't pulling punches, sending Drexians after you, but you're wrong. You just don't understand what they'll do if they start taking you seriously."

"What do you mean?"

"Right now, they're sending assassins after you. Yeah, that's not very nice. But when the il'Drach get serious, they sterilize *planets*. They'll commit genocide—slaughter entire species—to make sure single people don't survive. Fifty Drexians? That's a love tap from the il'Drach."

Steven smoothed his mustache with his fingers. Rohan shivered; that was something Hyperion had done so often that when his friends wanted to mimic him, all they had to do was touch their upper lips.

"You don't think I should help them? The rebels?"

"I don't. It will backfire on you, Steve. Things will get bad."

"How do you know?"

"Because I was the one they used to send in with situations like that. I was the one who made things bad, Steve. I retired, but they have more like me waiting in the wings."

Steve stared at his sandwich for a while, turning it to the side, then back, studying its contours.

"You taught me who I am, Rohan. I was . . . struggling, back on Earth. You brought me out of that."

"I guess. I don't know."

"I do know. You did. And you showed me more, on the Ringgate. Maybe you showed me things I didn't want to know, but it was stuff I needed to know. And yesterday, you saved me. Saved my life, maybe. Saved me from myself, too."

"I did my best."

"I know. You lost an eye for me."

"Not so much lost. It should grow back. More like misplaced."

Steve smiled. "You know what I mean, chum. What I'm saying is, I owe you."

Rohan sighed. "It's more than that, Steve."

"What?"

Rohan exhaled and gathered his thoughts. "You don't have to trust *me*. You don't have to take my word for anything. Trust Hyperion."

The big man's eyes widened. "What do you mean?"

"He—you—didn't fight the Empire. He was the strongest Hybrid they'd seen in centuries, and instead of rebelling, he negotiated treaties to leave Earth alone and spent his life, literally, serving them."

"Which got him killed."

"Yes. Bad ending. But why did he do it? Because he knew the consequences of doing otherwise. If he hadn't served them, maybe they would have wiped Earth clean. Or maybe they would have failed on the Ringgate, and the sector would have been overrun by Wedge. I'm telling you, rebellion sounds great, but it's more complicated than that."

Steve nodded. "Trust myself. That sounds good, buddy. Really good."

"Trust—that's not exactly what I said." Rohan rubbed his head. His headache, not surprisingly, had not gone away. "Whatever."

Steve stood, a wide smile on his face. "Thank you, Rohan. I appreciate your support. I'll do the right thing."

"That's great. Or is it?"

Steve's back was already to the Hybrid. He waved over his shoulder as he left the room.

Rohan groaned and leaned back on the bed.

Should I try to confront Lonnie? Talk him out of this?

Won't help.

Talk to Wei Li about stopping the rebels?

Wistful might want them stopped. But she likes the idea of them sticking their fingers in the eye of the Empire. The il'Drach can always bring another ship for Repentant.

He called Ben Stone.

"Rohan! How are you? Never mind, I can see your face, I already know the answer."

"It's worse than it looks."

"Really?"

"No. Look, I just wanted to check. Did you guys make any progress figuring out what Steve is?"

"Steve? Oh, right. Well . . . to be honest, no. I will say that he's acting more and more like the Hyperion we knew. Not the same, but closer."

"Right. Okay. Thanks. I'll talk to you later."

"Sure. Get some rest, Rohan. I heard you got knocked around pretty badly."

"Just another day at the office, Ben. Thanks."

He checked the time: close to the end of the overnight shifts. He messaged Tamara, asking her to have dinner/breakfast with him.

He called Wistful.

"Yes, Tow Chief? How are your injuries?"

"I feel pretty bad, actually."

"The Drexian toxins presented a systemic strain to your body. Dr. Simivar suggested you would feel physically incapacitated for several days. Especially considering your preexisting head injury. Do you wish for me to send her in to check on you?"

He scratched his beard. "Not unless you need me for something strenuous. I hear the negotiations are done? Repentant is getting what he asked for?"

"Yes, Rohan. Tomorrow, before the ports open."

"Do you have me on the schedule for the day? Doing any towing?"

"Dr. Simivar instructed me to remove you from the duty schedule, Rohan. Is that not appropriate?"

"No, that's good. Thanks. I'm not sure I'd be much use today. I feel pretty bad. And I'll need time to adjust to flying around with just one eye."

"I understand."

"Thanks, Wistful."

"You are welcome, Rohan. I hope you recover quickly."

He smiled and ended the call.

Tamara responded, offering to eat with him, but it would have to be quick.

I'll be quick. No, I mean, no, I won't be . . . I'd rather not be?

He checked the time again.

That leaves me with exactly one day to take a lovely woman on a date, find a way to stop these rebels from trying to steal a baby warship out from under the noses of a set of Hybrids, and convince a half-wit Power not to anger the nastiest, most powerful political entity the galaxy has ever known.

Good thing I'm badly hurt or this would all seem too easy.

38

True Believers

S howering was an adventure in itself; the bandages were hydrophobic, but every movement tugged at freshly healing wounds and scar tissue. As he washed, he discovered a half dozen cuts and punctures that he couldn't remember getting.

He dried himself and sat on the edge of his bed for a full ten minutes, waiting for the strength to return to unsteady legs.

He stood in his closet regarding the meager selection of uniforms remaining. His lifestyle was hard on clothes. "Personal. Order more uniforms. Three."

A voice answered from his mask. "Acknowledged, Rohan."

He dressed in a lightweight suit, amber and orange with white accents, and brushed his hair.

It was too early for his date.

He left the apartment, stepping in the careful way of someone who isn't sure their legs will support them, gaining confidence as he passed through the hallways that led to the medical bay.

The Ursans were on beds lining one wall of a larger room, curtains affording a minimum of privacy.

Rohan walked by the first two, smiling as he saw that the curtains had been drawn back from the last two beds.

Ursula's voice was soft. "Game is over now, Ang. I have captured majority of territory."

"What? No, not so soon. Is not possible. Let me count."

Rohan closed on the pair. They had dragged their beds close together, a table between them holding a board and game pieces. At a glance, it reminded Rohan of Go.

Ang's mouth moved as he pointed at the squares with a single claw. Ursula saw Rohan's approach and smiled.

Ang shook his massive head. "Bah, woman. You are for winning again. Every time! Cannot you let your war chief win, even once in while?"

"What kind of war chief cannot defeat a mere ship captain in game of strategy?"

"It is only game! This is not being good for morale."

She tilted her head, pointing her nose at the Hybrid. "We are for having visitor, Ang."

The bigger Ursan turned to Rohan and grinned.

"Brother Rohan! I see you have come for advice on living with only one eye. Come, sit. Brother Ang will instruct."

Rohan smiled at them. "Can I get a cybernetic eye like yours? I'm sure Rinth would want me to have one."

The Ursans traded a look. Ursula nodded. "We can make one for you, Brother Rohan. It would be an honor."

He held a hand up. "Whoa! I'm kidding, really. The eye should grow back. It will take a while, is all. Take a while and itch like crazy."

Ang's black lips pulled back from his teeth. "That is good for hearing, Brother Rohan."

Rohan looked them over. Covered in bandages with three intravenous lines on each, they looked relaxed.

"The doctors must have you on some pretty good drugs."

Ursula nodded. "Not so much, I think. Why?"

"You seem happy."

Ang laughed softly, stifling the noise as he glanced toward the other two beds, still behind closed curtains. "We were for telling you from start, Brother. We Ursans like war. Yesterday was most fun for me in long time."

The Hybrid's knees quivered. He sat on the bed next to Ursula. "That's good, I guess. Maybe we could wait a while before we do it again, though."

Ursula nodded. "Some good things are better for special occasions, yes? Too much fun, too often, is for becoming dull."

He smiled.

Ang patted Rohan's knee. "You had much fun yesterday. Today, rest."

Rohan scratched his beard. "I don't think I can. I have to stop some people from starting a war they can't win. A war that might be fought in this system."

Ursula patted his back. "War is best fought far from home."

The Hybrid nodded. "With any luck, it won't come to that."

Ursula looked at Ang. "Speaking to luck, are we for playing again?"

Ang sighed. "Yes, again."

Rohan stood. "I'm glad to see you two are okay."

Ang waved him off. "Go, see to your woman."

"How did you know I was going to see a woman?"

Ursula laughed and tapped her nose. "No secrets with Ursans."

<hr>

Tamara asked to meet Rohan at the restaurant instead of him picking her up. *Not ready to chance me running into Lonnie, I suppose.*

He arrived first, easing into a chair from which he could watch the front door. He stretched one leg, then the other, and tried to determine which position aggravated his injuries least. He sipped at a glass of water, eye widening when she came through the door.

She had changed into a blue sari and wore just a little makeup: dark around her eyes, red on her lips. His headache eased as she caught his eye, smiled, and walked to the table.

Her smile dissipated as she got a better look at him.

"Oh, you poor thing! Rohan, what happened?"

"You'll excuse me for not getting up to pull out your chair. I'm afraid I'll tear something open, and nothing annoys the servers here more than leaking blood on their tablecloths."

She stepped around the table and leaned down to kiss him softly. She reached up and touched his cheek, her fingers grazing the edge of the bandage over his missing eye.

He sighed. "If getting injured is what it takes to get you to kiss me, I'm going to have to start picking more fights I can't win."

She smiled and sat across from him. "You may kiss me even without injuries, Rohan. In fact, if you are too hurt to stand from your chair, you might find yourself unpleasantly inconvenienced. Later."

He grinned. "Good thing I heal fast."

"Yes. What happened? This wasn't something to do with Lahnegarn, was it?" Her voice held a serious note.

He thought for a moment. "No, nothing to do with him. Separate issue. I have a . . . friend that has some enemies."

"And you made certain to place yourself between that friend and those enemies."

"I can't seem to help it! To be fair, it usually works out better for me."

"It usually does. I am glad to see you alive, though I am sorry for your lack of depth perception. You were always so fond of binocular vision." Her lips curled up in a smile, her eyes on the menu.

"I am. Ha. I know what you're talking about."

"Do you, now?"

"But don't fret too much. The eye will grow back. This isn't even the first time."

"No?"

"It's a story! Not a good story. I'll tell you someday if you want."

"We have time." She studied the menu.

He sighed. "I like the sound of that." He watched her picking items. As her smile faded, her eyes took on a hard setting.

She looked up at him, and he recognized how forced her smile was. "What did you order?"

"I got the noodles."

She reached over and put her hand over his. "Add the meat. Double. You know you need the protein. For healing."

He smiled and tapped the tablet. "Yes, ma'am."

Tamara's wine came; Rohan had tea. He sipped the steaming liquid and watched her face.

"Your forehead is crinkled. What's wrong?"

She sighed. "Are you mocking my age, Rohan? If you so value smooth skin, perhaps you should stick to younger women."

He shook his head. "That's not what I meant. You look worried."

She tried to smile. "Rinth is worried about his father, and I am worried about Rinth."

"I get that. I'm worried about Lonnie, too. I'm worried that Lonnie's friends are going to start a war, and that Wistful will end up being ground zero."

Her cheeks paled to a lime green. "Tell me you are joking again."

He rubbed his forehead. "I wish I were. Like you said, he's a true believer, our Lonnie. He has a cause. People like that are dangerous."

"To whom?"

"To everybody, that's the problem. Themselves, the people around them."

She sipped her wine. "I take it you weren't able to talk him out of this course of action."

"I'm trying."

"Rohan, I realize you enjoy pretending to be less than intelligent, but I know you choose your words carefully when you speak. 'Trying' is a term you use when you want to say you are not succeeding."

"That's accurate. But I'm not done yet, okay? I'm still working on some things. I'm doing my best, I promise."

She shook her head. "I do not doubt that, Rohan. I did not mean to imply any lack of effort on your part."

He drank the tea, letting the heat seep into his chest. He had a chill, something his Hybrid physiology didn't usually allow. *Must be a side effect of being poisoned.*

"I could just grab him up, stick him in a locked room somewhere. I have no shortage of places to put him. Do you want me to do that?"

She pointed a finger at him. "You are tempting me, Rohan of Earth. The problem is, you would have to release him eventually, and he would be furious. I do not like what that would do to Rinth. Or Lahnegarn. He would be likely to attempt something truly foolish to prove his mettle afterward."

Rohan slumped back into his chair. "It wouldn't help anyway. If his plan works, he's going to have an in with the rebels. They'll be looking for him, either to rescue the guy or to make sure he isn't off somewhere betraying him."

"If his plan works."

Rohan shrugged. "That's what I think. I'm not sure my judgment is too clear at the moment, given my general state, but yeah. If it works."

Tamara looked hard at his face, her antennae twitching. "Rohan, we never went dancing."

"I know. We broke up, remember? We only dated for like a week and a half."

"I'm not berating you, I meant, we should go. Dancing. As you suggested."

"I can barely walk and you want to go dancing?"

"You have my permission to recover first. But once you have, you are to take me dancing. As you suggested to me, one and a half years ago." Her smile reached further up her cheeks, twisting the corners of her eyes.

He smiled back. "Is that the way it is? You're giving me orders now? You're just *telling* me what to do? I don't have any say in this?"

She paused. "Do you not want to take me dancing?"

He laughed. "Oh, that hurts. Yes, I do. Not today."

"Then why are you arguing?"

"I feel like this is a dangerous precedent we're setting."

"Is it? What other things are you worried I will order you to do in the future?"

"Well, I'm not sure."

She smiled again. "I think I know what concerns you, and let me just say, if I order you to do those things, you will do them, and you will enjoy it."

He laughed again, harder, pressing his elbow to his ribs to contain the pressure. "You're killing me here. Okay, you win, order me around all you want. You can tell all your friends you have your own pet Hybrid on call."

"Not pet. Perhaps devoted admirer."

"I'll accept that."

39

Prelude to War

Dinner/breakfast ended in the least satisfying way possible: Tamara fielded an urgent message from Lahnegarn demanding they meet to discuss something.

She sighed, apologized, promised it would not become a habit, and stayed long enough to finish dessert and another glass of wine.

Rohan smiled, nodded, and felt mild irritation coupled with a small sense of relief. He was tired and, for the first time in Tamara's presence, was looking forward to going to bed alone to get some rest.

He watched her leave, paid the bill, and made his slow way back to his apartment.

The Hybrid collapsed onto his bed and closed his eye.

Sleep was elusive.

His thoughts bubbled to the surface, then sank back down, dragged by a quicksand of distraction and fatigue.

He was close to grasping the relationship between Steve and Hyperion. How could he protect Steve and fulfill his promise to Masamune?

How could he stop the rebels without getting Lonnie killed, starting a war, or overly angering Wistful?

What was going to happen with Tamara if Lonnie stayed in the picture? Not an urgent question, but it came back with annoying regularity.

What was he supposed to do with Spiral's gift? Perhaps the question was, what did Spiral think he could do with it?

While the baby warship was in stasis, did it dream?

If a joke isn't funny, is it still a joke?

He woke with a start, a dream about Ares evaporating in his memory.

I haven't thought about Ares in a long time.

His skin smelled sour. He ordered food, showered, and put in a request for his cleaning staff to change his sheets.

The food came. Nothing tasted right, but he ate anyway, then dressed, queued up "Hauli Hauli" on his comm, and started walking.

Ten minutes later, he sat in the big conference room, leaned far back into the leather cushions, set his mask down on the circular table, and set his location to public.

I wish I was at Pop's right now. Eating eggs. Drinking coffee. By the grass, with crowds of people.

If only it weren't so hard to maintain privacy with those people around.

He held Spiral's soulgem in his fingers and worked on stretching a band of his energy out, then curving it back on itself.

Wei Li walked in and took a seat near him. Her face was calm, her vertically-slit pupils focused directly on him. The arc of energy popped into nothingness.

"How are your injuries?"

He touched the bandage over his eye. "It's starting to itch. That's the worst part."

"For most people, the worst part of losing an eye is either the partial blindness or the permanent disfigurement. If itching is your primary complaint, you are lucky."

He shrugged. "I'll thank my dad. Not really, of course, because I try to talk to him as little as possible."

"All joking aside, and I realize how significant a demand that is for you, what is your condition?"

"Why? Worried as a friend or do you think I'm going to be called into action soon?"

"Honestly, both."

He pushed his hips back in the chair, straightening. "I feel about as bad as I can feel without thinking I'm going to die."

She nodded. "You have mobility and can communicate."

"My head isn't right. Food doesn't taste good. I'm pretty weak."

"Then, why are you here and not in your apartment, resting?"

He smiled. "I can't seem to relax. And even though I'm not the empath in this room, I am pretty confident you're here for the same reason."

She drummed her fingers on the table. "I have concerns about the transfer scheduled for tomorrow."

"That makes it unanimous."

She studied him. "I understand *my* concerns. What are yours?"

"I think a group of rebels are going to try to steal that ship before it makes it to Repentant. I think that will upset the Empire and potentially start some kind of war."

"I see."

"I'm also worried about Steve."

"You believe he remains a threat?"

"Well, he almost lost it out on the promenade the other day. We were being attacked, which is something of an excuse, and you can take some heart from the 'almost' part. But I don't think the Empire is going to stop coming after him, and he's not going to want to stay in a cell for the rest of his life."

A deeper voice answered from the entrance. "He's not."

Rohan looked up. "Ben and Marion. Have a seat. Tell me you brought donuts."

Ben smiled, but his eyes were worried. Marion's were more than that. Haunted. They walked down the main aisle and sat across from Wei Li.

Ben nodded to the security chief and turned to Rohan. "None today. I can whip up a fresh batch tomorrow. Actually, that sounds good. I could use some donut therapy."

"What brings you guys here? Looking for me, or . . ."

Ben shook his head. "We were visiting Steve." He looked at his wife, who seemed close to tears.

Rohan sighed. "Is everything okay?"

Marion shook her head. "It's just hard. He looks and acts more like Hyperion every day. I know he's not, but seeing it is . . . difficult."

Ben patted her hand. "He's like a ghost, haunting us. I thought maybe having some version of him back to talk to would be good. Instead . . ."

Rohan sighed. "We need booze. Or coffee. Or food."

His comm pinged. Wistful's voice projected from his mask. "*Ironic Womb* is in motion, Rohan."

He grunted. "That's weird. Oh, right. I set the comm to alert me if the shuttle moved. I forgot about it."

Wei Li looked at him. "I was not expecting it to do anything before morning. A full twelve hours from now."

He shrugged. "No idea. Doesn't seem likely they'd abandon things now, does it? Right on the verge of completing the deal with Repentant?" He tapped on the comms. "*Void's Shadow*, come in."

"Yes, Captain?"

"If you're not busy, could you do me a favor and scout out *Ironic Womb*? She's moving, and we're not sure why."

"Sure thing, Captain. I see her heading insystem. Right for Wistful."

Wei Li shook her head. "That is not anticipated."

Wistful's hologram popped up inside the empty area at the center of the table. "*Ironic Womb* is requesting emergency servicing. It claims to be experiencing some minor errors in its life support systems."

Ben looked at them. "It's possible, right? Nothing much to do about it but let them dock and see what happens."

Wistful answered him. "I have already granted permission. I will have her towed in by shuttle, Rohan. You are to continue to rest."

He saluted the hologram, which winked out.

Rohan looked at Marion. "You know, you don't have to see him if you don't want to. Just, like, stay away."

"I'm still trying to figure out what he is. I can't just stay away. We all need an answer to that."

"I think I know what he is. Or let's say, I have a really strong idea."

Ben turned to him. "Care to share that idea, son?"

"Not so much. I mean, not yet. Let me work out some details, okay? I'll let you know in a couple more days."

Ben frowned. "That's all you're going to say?"

370 of JCM BERNE

"Some ideas are dangerous."

Wei Li glared at him. "Where did you hear that?"

He rubbed his head. "Is that a secret? That would be ironic. If the idea that some ideas are dangerous were itself a dangerous idea."

"It is not a secret so much as an unusual proposition. Never mind."

Ben stood. "I'm going to order some food. You all look as hungry as I feel." He took out his own tablet, one small enough to fit in a pocket, and suggested restaurants until the group agreed on one.

Rohan reached down and found a release for the back of his chair, reclining it halfway to flat. He rubbed his forehead, wishing his headache would go away.

The order was placed.

Wei Li and Marion compared notes, scheduling a time for a game of Drachna tiles. They sent the calendar entry to Ursula.

Food arrived.

The others seemed to enjoy, but Rohan could barely taste anything.

He had almost pieced together the mystery of Steve's identity. There were ramifications, if he was right, but he couldn't figure them all out.

His comm pinged him again: an automated alert telling him that *Ironic Womb* had approached the beacon line.

Void's Shadow called.

"Captain?"

"What's up?"

"The shuttle is stopping, but the three Hybrids left it behind."

Rohan sat up straighter. "What? Are you sure?"

"Don't be silly, Captain. You know I wouldn't make a mistake about something like that. Silly captain."

"No, of course not, sorry—"

Wei Li stood and half-yelled at the spot where the hologram had been. "Did the Hybrids have your permission to exit the shuttle? Wistful?"

The image snapped back into place. "No, they did not. Do not."

Wei Li turned to Rohan. "You fought them. What assets do we have that can engage those Hybrids successfully?"

Rohan let out a dry laugh. "Successfully? You mean security assets? Wei Li, the totality of your forces wouldn't even slow those guys down."

"What are our options?"

He coughed. "I could slow them down. Shape I'm in, I might hurt one of them, at best. But slow them down for what purpose? It's not like reinforcements are coming."

Ben cleared his throat. Wei Li turned to him.

"What are you thinking, Ben? Steve?"

Ben looked at Marion, who shook her head. He turned back to Wei Li. "That's the obvious answer. Or it would be, if he were Hyperion."

Rohan shook his head. "Steve's not strong enough. A day and a half ago, he lost his temper, and I was able to hold him down. He'd need to be much, much stronger than that to stand a chance against Flint, let alone Rrekha. She's on a different level. If I were healthy and we were working together? Still no chance. Unless Wistful herself pitches in."

Wei Li faced the hologram. No response came.

"I do not believe Wistful is inclined to engage directly at this time."

Marion cleared her throat. "She was willing six months ago. When the Empire attacked."

Wei Li grimaced. "She was not acting freely, remember? And she was attacked. These Hybrids have so far avoided that."

Void's Shadow spoke through Rohan's helmet. "Um, guys? You didn't ask where the Hybrids were going."

Rohan sighed. "Where are they going?"

"You know that nice cruise ship, *Love Boat*? That's always taking people around, checking out the wormholes? The one that's supposed to be super luxurious?"

Rohan's gut tightened. "Yes."

"Well, she's near the beacon line, I guess waiting for a tow or something. And the Hybrids just surrounded her. Also, and I'm not sure this is connected, the ship that was lurking out at the edge of the system is moving this way."

The hologram reappeared. Wistful's voice emerged from the room's audio system.

"Wei Li. Rohan. I am being addressed directly by the Hybrids. I would like to patch the transmission through here in case either of you are able to advise me on this situation."

Wei Li locked eyes with the Hybrid; two to one. "Go ahead."

The wall behind Rohan fired up, turning smoke-gray for a few seconds before bursting with a grainy image, magnified to fill the full five meters from floor to ceiling.

Rrekha wore a mask similar to Rohan's, a clear faceplate covering her red skin, a cloud of pink hair exploding outward in all directions. Her face took up almost the entire wall, looming large over the group, as if they could all fit together into her mouth to be eaten and swallowed.

The audio gave out a burst of static, then began conveying Rrekha's words.

"I repeat, message for Wistful and crew."

Wistful's voice responded.

"This is the independent space station Wistful. You may proceed."

Rrekha smiled. Several of her teeth had been blackened, making her incisors stand out prominently. "This is Lance Primary Rrekha of Karse. You are holding the impostor and heretic claiming to be Hyperion on your station."

Rohan coughed. "What do you mean 'heretic'?"

Rrekha turned her head, mouthing something off camera, and turned back. She opened her mouth and growled a word.

Only Rohan, speaker of the Fire Speech, understood.

It was a Karsan word, from an old language. It meant something like an incarnation, a perfect representation of some human attribute. The highest possible rank; the alpha among alphas. A title Karsans who desired to rule their planet would aspire to, would claim for themselves, would slaughter thousands to uphold.

Something akin to a superman.

Rohan laughed, then snatched a hand to his mouth to stifle it.

She continued. "Hyperion was this. The perfect warrior, the strongest Hybrid. I can't say what other cultures worship, your immaterial gods, but he was everything Karsans pray for. Pray to. That was Hyperion. He was the love of my life, my soul itself.

"Any claiming his identity are not simply charlatans; they commit heresy."

Rohan nodded. "All right, let's play your game, Rrekha. What do you want?"

"We want the impostor. Put a mask on him and send him out an airlock. We'll take him."

"Take him where?"

"We have a ship. Don't worry, you'll never see him again. For the honor of Karse, for the honor of all Hybrids, he has to die."

The people in the conference room traded worried glances.

Ben spoke. "What if he's not an impostor? What if he *is* Hyperion?"

She laughed, the kind of mocking, wide-mouthed laughter that people use when they're mimicking villains from cheap holodramas.

"If he were really Hyperion, he would come out and face us in battle, and he would prevail. It is that simple. The fact that he's hiding in there like a coward is all the proof I could ever ask for."

Rohan rubbed his forehead. "Maybe you're the real cowards. You want him? Why don't you come in here and take him?"

Her eyes blazed. "We know better than to violate Wistful's personal space. She is a warship at heart. All know and respect Wistful. Nor are we interested in direct conflict."

Ben continued. "Then, why would the impostor come out to you? What's your game, Rrekha?"

She grinned, each tooth half the height of a human on the giant screen. "He comes out to face judgment for his crimes or we start tearing bits off of this adorable ship here. And if he continues to delay, we will find another ship. And so on. I've spent weeks in this system; there is an unending supply of them coming and going."

Wei Li's eyebrow-scales bunched up. Marion's skin turned an unhealthy pale.

Rohan pressed his palms to his temples, closed his eye, and tried to think.

Void's Shadow's voice came over Rohan's mask. "Captain, a shuttle is heading for *Ironic Womb*. Probably to provide the service it asked for. The Imperial ship is also closing." Rohan tapped a confirmation on the screen and lowered the volume on his mask.

Ben shook his head and spoke toward the screen. "The Empire has a treaty with Wistful, Lance Primary. You can't just come in here and terrorize ships in her territory."

Rrekha shrugged. "I certainly can. In fact, I'm doing exactly that. If you're trying to insinuate that the Fathers will be angry about it, you're probably right." She leaned closer to the camera, her teeth filling the image. "If you think that's going to stop me, you're very definitely wrong."

Rohan waved a hand, a signal to cut their audio transmission. He looked up at Ben. "She was truly, desperately in love with Hyperion. You could say she worshipped him." He giggled, quickly stifling the sound. "It's a Karsan thing. You combine a kind of almost filial devotion they have toward anyone of higher rank with romantic love that's been very twisted by a warrior culture and this is what you get. She's mortally offended by Steve's very existence."

Ben nodded. "What do we do?"

Rohan shrugged. "We can't fight them. We could put out a call for Imperial ships. They might come and help, but they might not. And even if they do, there's no saving *Love Boat*. Those three would probably tear through half a dozen ships before we could lift a finger to stop them. I don't know what we *can* do."

A voice spoke from the door. "I do. I'll go to them. It's what heroes do. What Hyperion would do."

They all turned to watch Steve walk up the aisle, his eyes serious.

40

Punish Him

Steve looked around the room. Ben nodded back gravely. Marion wouldn't meet his eyes. Wei Li gazed back coolly. He took off his glasses and handed them to Rohan.

"I won't be needing those."

"Steve, this isn't a good idea. They're going to kill you. It's not a trick."

Steve shrugged his shoulders. "I've been listening at the door. I don't think there's any other choice, is there? I can't just let those people die. I'll go and fight them."

"You'll lose."

"What if I cut loose? The way I did on the Ringgate?"

"You'll lose, just a few seconds later. Whatever extra boost you think your rage can give you, Rrekha's is bigger, and she's experienced using it. You're not."

"Then, I guess she'll kill me. It's okay, I died years ago. I just got a short reprieve. It was fun."

Rohan shook his head. "Give me a minute. I'll figure a way out of this."

Steve walked over and wrapped his arms around Rohan. "It's okay, buddy. I know you can't. I'm okay with this, really. It's fine. It makes sense, actually. I'm a danger to everybody, aren't I? At least this way I'll be out of the way. Safe. And my death will mean something."

"Satisfying Rrekha's insane sense of pride is not 'something,' Steve."

Ben stood and hugged the big man. "I think it is. I think it is something pretty great. I'm sorry it's come to this, but I think what you're doing is brave. Heroic."

Steve looked at the hologram. "Do you have a mask I could take? I have a trip to go on."

A compartment opened along one wall. Steve walked over and took out a mask. "Nice."

Marion looked around. "Are we really going through with this? Who's to say she'll even keep her word if she gets Steve?"

Rohan sighed. "She will. She's very, um, honor bound."

Steve held the mask out to Rohan. "Can you show me how to use this?"

"Yeah. I don't like this, Steve."

The big man laughed. "I like it even less! But I can't go on with more lives on my conscience."

Rohan showed him how to put the mask on and activate its air supply. "Wistful will project lines onto the inside of the clear part to show you where to fly. Space can be disorienting."

"Thanks, chum." Steve reached his arms out and hugged Rohan. "Thank you for trying."

"I promised Masamune I'd keep you safe."

"We can't always control what happens, Rohan. You did your best."

Did I?

He escorted the big man to the airlock; watched it cycle open; exhaled as Steve's huge feet disappeared through the hatch.

Rohan headed back to the conference room.

The others stood around the table, faces dull.

"Is the line still open?"

Wei Li looked at him. "What?"

He slapped the table. "The line. To Rrekha. Is it still open?"

Marion tapped at her tablet. "Yes. You can talk to her."

Rohan cracked his neck, cleared his throat, and inhaled.

"Rrekha."

"It is too late to talk me out of this, little man. The heretic is already on his way here. You can't save him."

Rohan poured as much spite into his voice as he could muster. "I don't want to talk you out of it. The fact is, the whole 'oh look at me, I'm Hyperion, greatest hero in history' thing was annoying the crap out of me. I've been completely crap-less for days."

"What do you want? Do you wish to partake in his execution?"

"I do." The Stones looked at him quizzically. "But more than that, I want you to do more than just kill him. I want him punished."

Rrekha's eyes narrowed. "What do you mean?"

He gripped the back of his chair to steady himself. "For what he's done, death isn't enough. I want him to suffer."

"You want us to torture him?"

"Physical pain isn't enough. You see, he really thinks he's Hyperion. Go ahead, have The Gray look him over. She'll confirm."

"So?"

"It's because he doesn't understand what he's saying. He's never met Hyperion. He doesn't really know what he's pretending to be. How far short he falls. He's walking around claiming to be a great warrior when he doesn't have the first idea what being a great warrior means."

Her eyes narrowed further. "You want me to torture him by . . . what?"

"Tell him. Tell him about Hyperion. The stories. Come on, you fought by his side for years. Explain to this impostor just how great Hyperion was. To break his mind, his will. Break his soul. Then kill him. But not before."

"I did not know you were cruel, Griffin."

"I'm usually not. But I make exceptions. Guess this is one of them."

She turned her head from side to side, making eye contact with people off camera, then faced it again. "I like your idea, Griffin. I will make it so."

"Great, just give me a minute to get out there so I can enjoy the show."

"I do not believe we require your presence for this, Griffin. Take care. I hope we can meet again under better circumstances."

"Wait, Rrekha—" The channel closed.

He sighed and turned away from the screen. The others were staring at him.

He held up a hand and spoke into his helmet. "*Void's Shadow*. Are you still there?"

"I'm here, Captain."

"Have the Hybrids spotted you?"

"Of course not, Captain! They'll never find me."

"Good. Please monitor them. I think Rrekha will take Steve on that Imperial ship and go somewhere. I want to be able to follow."

"Yes, Captain."

Ben put a hand on his arm. "Do you know what you're doing, Rohan?"

Rohan scratched at the bandage around his missing eye. "I have an inkling. A suspicion. Maybe even a hypothesis. But do I *know*? Probably not. In my defense, nobody had a better plan."

Wei Li looked at him. "You *do* have a plan. I must admit, I do not understand it."

He fingered the soulgem around his neck. "I'll explain it if we survive."

◆◆◆

His stomach churned as he made his way to the airlock. He stood in the tube, waiting as the air was pumped out, then as the hatch cycled open.

He looked up at open space, Toth 3 directly overhead. His hands shook slightly.

I've done all I can already. Do I need to be there? To watch what happens? Can't I just leave him to meet his own fate?

The shaking increased.

I guess I can't.

He flew out into space.

"*Void's Shadow*, where can I meet you?"

"Fly out to the beacon line, Captain. I'll pick you up."

"Where are the Hybrids?"

"They're heading for that ship that was out on the edge of the system. It's close."

"What about the cargo shuttle?"

"Let me check. It just took off. It's going straight for Repentant's wormhole."

"Okay. Wait. What? Are you sure?"

"I'm sure, Captain."

He grunted and switched channels to one that would catch the main conference room. "Can anybody tell me why the Imperial cargo shuttle, the one with a once-in-a-generation baby warship on board, is doing high g right now on its way to Repentant?"

No answer for two long breaths, then Wei Li spoke. "We cannot."

"Oh good. Is this an issue for anybody?"

Another pause. Wei Li continued. "Wistful would be satisfied if that ship makes it to Repentant. The rebels, presumably, would not be."

"Any sign of them pursuing the ship?"

"None."

"Well, okay then." *Guess Lonnie's plan isn't going to work.* "Did anybody check on *Love Boat*?"

"She is safe, as are all passengers. The Hybrids never even boarded."

"Small victory. Okay, I'll be in touch." He closed the connection.

A wall of darkness suddenly blocked his way. A hatch opened, and he entered his ship.

"Captain, you don't look so great! Vitals aren't good either. Do you need the regen tank?"

He sighed. "Most of the damage I still have won't respond to the regen tank. It's not great with poison. I'll be okay, I think." *I've been saying that a lot.* "Can you follow the Hybrids?"

"Of course. I'm not sure what to do when they pass through a rift."

"Can you follow? Make a rift of your own?"

"That's hard, Captain. And the other ship might sense my rift. If I knew where they were going, even approximately, I could narrow down the possibilities. Then we could wait, so they aren't paying attention on the other side when I come through."

He nodded and eased himself into the piloting couch. *Where will Rrekha take him?*

"They've boarded the ship. Captain, the wormhole is opening. One of the five static ones."

"Which one? Wait, are the Hybrids going to it?"

"No, Captain, the Imperial ship is going in a different direction. Wormhole number two, the one that goes to Repentant, is opening. The cargo shuttle is heading for it. You don't want me to follow, do you?"

"No. That's not my problem. You stay on the Imperial ship."

"Yes, sir."

His eyes drifted shut.

She woke him some time later.

"Captain, she's going to form a rift right here."

He scratched his face. "Can you track the rift?"

"I don't know, Captain."

He pressed his palm into his good eye.

"What if they're headed to the Ringgate? Does that make sense?"

"Hold."

He waited while she performed calculations.

"That's possible, Captain. If you're right, I can trace their route."

"Can you get us there without being noticed?"

"I can. We'll be behind by half an hour, but I can do it."

He nodded. "Make it so."

One moment they faced the twin stars of Orechalc Prime, the next a hole opened in space, and through it Rohan saw the familiar contours of the Ringgate.

"Great job, *Void's Shadow*."

"Easy peasy. What now?"

"Can you find that ship?"

"Right! Checking." A pause. "Found her."

"And?"

"She's approaching the Ringgate. She's going to land."

Rohan sighed. "They won't stop an active Fleet ship from landing. Pink thirty-two, right?"

"How did you know, Captain?"

"I know how Rrekha thinks. Can you bring me in?"

"I can't hide on the surface."

"Just drop me off at the atmosphere's edge, okay? Please. Then, I don't know. Maybe hang about. If I survive, I'll want a lift back home."

"Are you traveling down into shadow again, Captain?"

"Not this time. She's taking him to a place where the Wedge broke through to this plane of reality. It's not in shadow."

"I hope you survive, Captain."

"Me too. Now bring me in. I need to be there for this next part."

"Yes, Captain. Good luck."

The ship flew toward the Ringgate, passing the smooth outside, then turning over the sun-facing, inhabited side.

Pink 32 was a wasteland.

The ground had been torn to shreds, everything larger than a patch of moss shattered and destroyed. On a world without tectonic activity of any kind, it looked like lava fields, craggy and uneven, sheltering nothing more than bone fragments and stagnant water.

Against the uniformity of the devastated landscape, Rrekha and the others stood out.

Rohan flew closer, head pounding. Steve was on a flat patch of ground, unmoving.

The Gray tapped her leader's shoulder, then pointed to Rohan's approach.

"Griffin." She stepped over to Steve and kicked him in the ribs. His body rolled into a boulder, chips of stone flying away from the impact.

Rohan drifted to a stop about ten meters from her. "Did you kill him?"

She laughed. "Hardly. We brought him here to take your advice."

"Oh goody."

"Why are you here?"

"I told you, I wanted to see it for myself."

She shook her head. "I told you not to come. We're going to have to kill you once we're done."

He walked to a meter-high outcropping of stone and sat heavily. "Maybe you'll change your mind. Or maybe I'll surprise you. Or maybe I just don't care anymore."

The Gray tilted her head as she looked him over. "He is soul-weary, Rrekha."

She nodded. "So be it." She pointed to Flint. "Wake him."

Rohan rubbed the soulgem between thumb and forefinger. *I should have given it to someone, just in case I get killed here.* He *reached* inside and grabbed a line of energy to bend, something to keep himself occupied.

Flint knelt by Steve's body, nudging it with his hand. The big man flopped over to his back with closed eyes and open mouth.

The short Hybrid sighed and stood. "Be right back." He flew to the ship.

The Gray walked to Rohan. "What are you doing?"

"This? Just a technique I'm trying to figure out. You start by making solid objects with your ki. Chakra. Spirit. Whatever you call it."

"Why? You'll be dead in a few hours."

He shrugged. "What should I do instead, just sit here?"

She pointed to his chest, at a space where the energy was being manipulated. "You won't be able to keep that going once the rage comes on you. That's no technique for a Hybrid."

He smiled at her. "Then, it doesn't matter if I practice, does it?"

Flint returned with a small tube. He opened it under Steve's nose; the big man sat up, gasping.

"What?" His face was bruised and battered, one eye almost entirely red with broken blood vessels. He looked at Rohan. "Why are you here?"

Rohan shrugged. "I couldn't let you just die alone, chum. That's not what heroes do."

Rrekha glared at him. "Silence. You may watch, but any chatter and we'll kill you first."

He raised his hands. "Sorry."

She turned back to Steve. "You pretend to be Hyperion."

He coughed. "I am Hyperion."

Her eyes blazed. "Your friend suggested that you do not truly understand your own lie. You have never met him, spoken to him, touched him. You speak from ignorance."

"So you're going to let me go?"

"No. We are going to educate you, then kill you. You will learn the depths of your mistake before you die."

Steve sat up, his head bobbing up and down. "Actually, I'd like that. Not the dying, but the learning. I'd like to hear about the man you knew. The old me."

41

Tales of Hyperion

R rekha turned to The Gray. "You first."

The Gray nodded her slender, hairless skull and sat on the stone in front of Steve.

She cleared her throat, as if giving a performance.

For fifteen minutes, she told the story of The Swarm.

A race of semi-intelligent, two-meter-tall locustlike insects had stripped seven worlds completely bare of life, killing eighteen billion sentient beings in the process.

Their queen, a Power capable of creating spatial rifts, moved The Swarm from planet to planet, driven by an instinctual desire to feed.

Twenty-two Hybrids had been sent to stop them; all had become food for the queen.

Hyperion and The Gray were sent in alone.

For seven days, they fought their way through millions of the giant bugs. Seven days without sleep, without rest, wading through ichor so deep they nearly drowned.

On the eighth day, Hyperion fought the queen, a fifty-meter-long winged locust with Powers sufficient to slay any dozen other Hybrids at once.

He became truly angry when she bit off his arm.

The Gray saw him swallowed, entering her throat. She lost all hope, knelt in blood and fragmented chitin and waited to die.

Three minutes later, Hyperion burst out through the queen's head, ending the power of The Swarm. They abandoned the planet, leaving the mutant bugs to starve.

The Gray looked at Steve. "This is what Hyperion meant. Power unequaled. Bravery unequaled. Savagery unequaled. To see you steal his face and his name disgusts me."

Steve didn't flinch as she spat on his forehead. He stared at her with wide eyes.

He isn't coughing anymore.

Rohan sat to the side and continued channeling metaphysical energies. Draw them out into a flat shape, like an unsharpened blade. Curl the end, bringing it back toward the start, as if forming a wheel, but bending it up ever so slightly as it went. The beginning of a spiral. Or a helix.

Rrekha turned to Flint. "Tell him."

Flint nodded and took The Gray's place in front of Steve.

Even standing, he was almost eye-to-eye with the seated Earthling.

For twenty minutes, he explained how Hyperion saved the planet Gigarath.

Flint's people had settled the planet, lured by rich mineral deposits and undeterred by its high gravity or geologic instability.

After a thousand years, that instability reared its ugly head. The surface became unlivable, wracked by earthquakes even his people's unmatched expertise in plate tectonics and geo-engineering couldn't predict.

Volcanoes made the atmosphere difficult to navigate, and millions of people were doomed.

The Empire sent in a dozen Hybrids to assist with the evacuation, but a shortage of ships capable of escaping the gravity well and handling the caustic atmosphere meant the effort was little more than a gesture.

The Hybrids complained that they were ineffectual. Most abandoned the planet.

Hyperion saw their ships take off, set his feet, and shook his head. He gathered the best scientists the planet had to offer in one room, locked the door, and emerged three days later with a plan.

He flew up to the edge of the atmosphere.

He summoned a knot of Power that glowed like a second sun to Flint's Third Eye.

Then he dropped.

Hyperion punched a hole through the tectonic plate, releasing a burst of magma large enough to alleviate the pressure and end the earthquakes. A supervolcano rose in its place, devastating the area for kilometers around but sparing the rest of the planet's surface.

He rearranged a planet's crust. With his fists.

Flint's people continued to live on that world in safety.

The short Hybrid leaned over and stared into Steve's eyes. "We thought he died under there. But two days later, he crawled out, burned and torn. He smiled. That is what Hyperion was.

"The strongest of us all. The most selfless."

He stood and walked away.

The Gray watched Rohan's energy manipulations. He twisted his energy around, the tips almost meeting, then passing each other. Sweat beaded on his forehead. He exhaled softly, willing his heart rate to slow.

Rrekha walked over to Steve. He pushed himself up against the rock pillar, straightened his back, then clenched and relaxed his hands.

She spoke for twenty minutes.

She told the tale of Hyperion first joining her team. She'd challenged him for dominance, as was appropriate, and he defeated her and her lieutenants in minutes. They couldn't put a mark on his face.

It was the time of a Great Surge. Wedge had fought their way out of shadow all over the Ringgate, emerging in dozens of places. Every available Hybrid was sent to one hotspot or another to drive them back.

The worst of the fighting was at Black 17. The Imperial forces converged there to prevent the Wedge from escaping.

But the true threat came at Pink 32. The Wedge coming through were more intelligent. They waited just inside shadow and gathered enormous numbers, then stormed their way around the Ringgate and formed the beginning of a portal so they could spill out to other worlds.

All available forces were tied up elsewhere. Hyperion and Rrekha were sent to Pink 32 alone.

They fought and scouted for two days. The situation was hopeless; the Wedge were too many, too large, and too well organized.

Hyperion kissed her and sent her away. As she left, she saw him fully surrender to his Power. Summon every last iota of rage and anger that his gift contained.

She returned ten days later. That section of the Ringgate had been just as devastated as any planet devoured by The Swarm. The seas ran red; the ground crunched with bones; the air stank of decaying meat for two thousand kilometers.

She found Hyperion sleeping on a stack of Greater Wedge: monsters two hundred meters long, piled four high.

His face was peaceful. She kissed him awake.

She looked into Steve's face. "This is what he was. The most powerful of us all. The most feared. The most loved. My Hyperion. I will tear his face from your skull."

Steve nodded slowly. The color had returned to his face.

Rrekha pulled back a hand.

Rohan called out. "Wait. Let me."

She turned to him. "What?"

"I was his friend. I have my own story to tell."

"No tricks."

He held up his hands. "What could I do, even if I wanted to? Let me tell the Hybrid story."

She nodded and ceded her position.

Rohan walked over, limping slightly, and cracked his neck. He maintained his ki spiral, noting that The Gray watched him do it.

He looked into Steve's face.

"Hyperion was with me. I don't even remember where we were. Between missions? It doesn't matter.

"Nine Hybrids gathered. Three sets of three. All lance primaries. They wanted to rebel against the Empire. They fought each other, to see who would lead the Rebellion.

"Then they came to Hyperion and asked him to do it.

"Instead, he fought them all at once. No tricks, no special tactics. He just went at them, by foot and by fist, and pummeled all nine into submission.

"I can still see him, standing over their bodies, glaring at them. He crouched down, and I thought he was going to kill them all. I even thought about trying to stop him.

"Instead, one by one, he caressed their foreheads.

"He told them he cared about them. That he loved them. That we were all cousins.

"But the Empire could not be fought. That it was our duty to serve it.

"He was the strongest. The most savage. But the most loving."

Steve's eyes shone.

Rrekha coughed. "Is that all? Anyone else wish to speak?"

Steve stood. "I'll talk now."

◆·•·◆

The Gray's head jerked as she faced the big man.

"That's not possible."

Steve smiled.

Hyperion smiled.

"Thank you all so much. You've honored me today. No more talk of killing me, though, okay?"

Rrekha growled and stepped in, swinging her right fist in a looping overhand punch that had the force to level a mountain.

He reached up and caught it in his left palm, the smack of impact knocking down piles of stone for twenty meters around.

Hyperion growled, his lips tightening. "I said no more of that." He lashed a right hand into her belly, doubling her over.

Flint was at his back, landing one, then another blow to Hyperion's kidneys.

The big man turned his head, then whipped one leg up behind him in a hooking motion, catching the shorter man by the temple and sending him sailing into a boulder.

"No more."

The Gray moved in, her hands flashing in deceptive sequences, her body shifting a half step to one side or another with each strike.

Hyperion took a step back, then set his heels into the stone and leaned forward.

She struck his sternum, his upper chest, his thigh.

He returned fire, thudding a palm into her chest, then slapping her cheek, sending her twisting away through the air.

Rrekha growled as she wrapped her arms around his waist.

Hyperion took a step, then a second, dragging the woman with him. He grabbed at her hands and pushed them away, giving himself enough space to spin and face her.

He pushed down on her shoulders, slamming her into the ground.

Flint's fist cracked across his jaw.

Rohan stumbled back as the short Hybrid sent a pulse of energy through the stone beneath their feet.

Hyperion snarled as he *lifted* up into the air, then shot like a bullet from a rifle into the body of the shorter Hybrid.

Flint went down in a tangle of limbs. Hyperion stayed on top, his knees grasping Flint's sides, and rained down a series of punches that left Flint's head loose on his neck, tongue hanging out of his lax mouth.

Rrekha charged again.

Hyperion rose to meet her.

"I said enough, my love. Enough."

He took her punch full on the face; returned it with one of his own.

She went down.

The Gray closed.

Hyperion waved a hand at her face, causing her to flinch, then kicked her left calf.

Her right calf.

Flicked his left leg toward her knee, but raised it and clocked her on the temple instead.

The Gray went down, eyes rolling back in her head.

Rrekha stood, blood streaming from her red nose, pink hair in disarray. She charged.

Hyperion bent his knees and waited.

They traded punches again.

Again, Rrekha went down.

She stood and charged.

Hyperion caught her head in his hands, pulling his hips and belly back to avoid her desperate punches. As she cocked her fists to start again, he lifted his knee into her face, stunning her.

Her hands dropped, shoulders limp, upright only because he still held her face.

He pulled her close to him and kissed one cheek, then another. Then her lips.

"That's enough. It's me. I'm back. No more fighting."

She coughed, a bubble of blood forming at the corner of her mouth, and relaxed.

He lowered her to the ground, careful to ease his hand out from underneath her head without dropping it.

Rohan stood at the edge of the clearing.

Hyperion walked over to him. "Hey, chum."

Rohan swallowed. "Steve."

Hyperion smiled. "I have to tell you, I thought I was a goner for sure! Then they started talking and, hoo boy, I got a charge from that."

Rohan coughed. "I thought you might."

The good-natured smile fell away from his face. "Why did you come here, Griffin? They weren't after you."

Rohan scratched his beard. "I thought I could help."

"Help how? Did you know this would happen?" He waved his arm, taking in the fallen Hybrids.

"I had a pretty good idea. I wouldn't say I was sure, but . . . yeah."

"You had to be here for it to work?"

"Not exactly. I thought I could help distract The Gray. If she'd figured out what was going on early enough, they might have been able to stop you. So, I came here and worked on Spiral's technique."

Hyperion nodded. "What am I, then? Am I really Hyperion?"

Rohan studied his face for a moment. "I don't think so."

Rohan expected the big man to argue, but he didn't. "That bird girl. The rebel. She called me something. Vishar something? You understood it. I'm sure of it."

The Hybrid nodded. "Vishar-baya. It's hard to translate. Supraphysical instantiation. Unmediated being-in-itself from for-itself. Those are terrible. Idea made matter. Word made flesh."

"Word made flesh. Like a god. I'm a god?"

Rohan shrugged. "Small *g*, maybe. Look, as much as Poseidon is a god, you are one too. Except the idea of Poseidon is divine, and the idea of Hyperion is just a man. So maybe demigod."

Hyperion nodded. "A demigod."

"That's as close as you're going to get in English. I can't tell you how it works. But you're stitched together from the *idea* of Hyperion. People's thoughts, their wishes, their dreams. Maybe their prayers.

"On Earth, you were made up of the images made by people who knew you as a kids' cartoon. When you met me and the Stones, you started gathering up aspects of the real Hyperion. Which was possible because we *knew* the real Hyperion.

"Here, you got all the thoughts and impressions from more Hybrids who knew you. Who fought by your side, who loved and admired you.

"And not only that, there's more, just sort of hanging in the air."

"What?"

"The final thoughts of the million Wedge Hyperion slaughtered here on this shattered plain. Their images of the man who battled them. That's a powerful set of ideas. All pulled into . . . you. Whatever you are."

"I like this. I feel good. Strong."

"I bet you do."

Hyperion looked up sharply. "That story you told. About me fighting those Hybrids. Refusing to fight the Empire. Was that true?"

"Every word."

"Didn't work out so great for the real Hyperion, did it?"

"I guess not."

They stood together, listening to wind whistle through the bare rock formations all around, Rohan swaying slightly on weak legs.

The Hybrid broke the silence. "You ready to go? I'll call *Void's Shadow* for a pickup."

"Go?"

"Yeah, back to Wistful. Why? Did you want to stop somewhere else?"

Hyperion smoothed his mustache. "I was thinking."

"Don't do that, it's not your strong suit." As soon as the words came out, Rohan could feel them falling flat.

"Don't make fun of me, Griffin. It's mean."

Rohan sighed. "Okay. Sorry."

"As I was saying. I was thinking. On Earth, in the beginning, I was sort of simpleminded. Nice, but a bit goofy. Silly."

Rohan stared at him. "Maybe."

Hyperion nodded and held up his hand, ticking off fingers. "Then I added your memories of me. Wove them into me. And I got smarter. Stronger. Angrier."

"Yeah. You almost punched General Ryan in the face."

"I met the Stones. My head cleared up. I felt more like, I don't know. A grownup."

"They knew you growing up. Makes sense."

"And you made me angrier."

"I'm a Hybrid. I know what that anger is."

Hyperion waved his hand over the fallen Imperial Hybrids. "They're Hybrids too. But their memories didn't make me a monster. They made me strong."

"It's not that simple."

"Isn't it? Isn't it exactly that simple? I could go back with you to Wistful. Live in a cell. Live in fear: afraid of another Drexian attack, afraid of how I'll react to it.

"Or I could stay with these guys. Not here in this spot. Travel around. They have a ship. Maybe meet up with the rebels. I have bird girl's contact information.

"Maybe it's time I showed the Empire that they can't mess with Hyperion and get away with it."

Rohan rubbed his forehead, right between his eyebrows. "Steve, that's not a good idea. They'll come after you again. They'll be serious this time."

"So will I. I don't have to become the Hyperion from your story, Griffin. I can be different. I can be a Hyperion who survives. Instead of being scared of the Empire, I can make them scared of me."

"You're giving the Wedge image of you too much influence, Steve. It's not good. Not healthy."

"You want me to be nice, Rohan. I get it. I really do. But nice didn't work out for me the first time.

"I think it's time to try something new."

"You think those three will just accept you? Go along with this plan of yours? They were ready to kill you an hour ago."

"An hour ago, they didn't know who I was. They do now. We'll be good. Besides, by their own rules I think I'm their leader now."

Rohan's head throbbed. "I can't think. This isn't a good idea, Steve."

"Call me Hyperion." His eyes opened wider, and he snapped his fingers. "Come with us, Rohan. Fight the Empire. I know you have no love for it. I know you want revenge. Justice. For what they did, what they made you do."

"I'm retired. I just want to tow ships and fall asleep in someone's arms. No fighting the Empire for me."

Hyperion shook his head sadly. "That's okay. You've done a lot for me. Tried to do a lot. You can get on your ship and go. Just don't let me find you standing in my way."

Rohan swallowed. "What?"

"You heard me."

"That's how it is now?"

Hyperion bent to The Gray and arranged her unconscious form into a more comfortable position. "You'll always have a place at my side. But if I have to choose between going back to that cell and being like this, with Rrekha . . . you have my answer.

"Unless you want to fight me? Force me to go with you?" He caressed Flint's brow, patting the little man on the chest.

Rohan watched him for a moment, exhaling slowly. "No. I don't want to fight you, Hyperion." He rose into the air. "If it matters, I really hope I'm wrong. I hope your way has a happy ending. And you should know that if you change your mind, you always know where to find me."

Hyperion nodded. "I don't think I will. Change. Anymore."

Rohan turned and flew toward the edge of the atmosphere and *Void's Shadow*.

42

The Answer

*V*oid's *Shadow* woke Rohan with the gentle sound of running water as they approached Wistful.

His eye itched terribly, but otherwise his body seemed to be bouncing back from the Drexian poisons. And the stabbings. And the concussions.

She dropped him off near the beacon line. He flew to Wistful, came in through his airlock, showered, and changed.

He took a slow walk to Tamara's house, knocked on the door.

Rinth answered. "Hey, Rohan. You look awful."

"You mean the clothes or my face?"

The boy scrunched up his nose before answering. "I think both! What happened to your eye? Is it gone? Are you going to get a fake one like that Ursan? Will it glow? What color will it be? You should get a purple one to match your uniform."

"It's just a flesh wound; I don't think I'm in the market for a prosthetic eye. I'll let you know. Is your mom around?"

"Oh, yeah. Let me get her."

The boy disappeared into the apartment.

Tamara came out after, wearing her uniform jumpsuit. Her hair was tied up in a bun.

"Rohan! I wasn't expecting you." Her lips pulled up in a restrained smile.

He nodded. "Can we talk for a couple of minutes? It won't take long."

Her smile settled. She looked at Rinth. "Can you watch the pot? If it starts to boil over, lower the flame, okay?"

He nodded. "Sure, Mom. I'll help, but I don't want to miss cartoons so you can do kissie stuff."

"Not kissie stuff. We won't be long."

"Okay."

She led Rohan to a back room; closed the door behind him.

He walked to a chair, lifted a pile of folded laundry off the seat, set it on the bed, and sat.

She sat on the edge of the bed. "You look better than before."

He smiled. "Hybrid blood. I heal fast."

"I'm glad."

He nodded and scratched his beard. Looked around the room. "Nice place. Cute paintings."

She shrugged. "Thank you. It is home. Humble, but mine."

"Yeah. So, listen. I was doing some thinking. About everything that happened."

Her expression hardened. "I see."

"I wasn't going to, not at first. I mean, everything worked out, right?" He held his hand out and began ticking his fingers with each sentence. "Hyperion is safe. Weird and scary, but safe. The Ursans are okay. So are the Stones. Wei Li is fine. Wistful isn't in danger."

He looked at her, closed his hand, and resumed counting. "Lonnie's plan failed. The rebels didn't steal the warship. They're not going to give him the time of day, so he is safe.

"I understood most of it, but try as I might, I could not understand how the Hybrids knew Steve was here. You know, the critical piece of information that led them to bring the shuttle in, abandon it, and run off half a day before the transfer was supposed to happen. Half a day before the rebels were prepared to steal the ship.

"Even stranger, how was it that as soon as they left the shuttle, someone immediately flew over to it from Wistful, did something, and sent it on a course through the wormhole?

"It's enough to make me feel bad for those rebels. If not for the Hybrids finding out Steve was here at exactly the wrong time and the shuttle being reprogrammed the minute it arrived here, Lonnie's plan might have still worked. Weird, isn't it?"

Tamara lifted her chin, her lips set and hard. Her skin paled slightly. "I am sorry, Rohan."

He sighed. "It *was* you."

"Lahnegarn told me about Hyperion. And about his plan to steal the baby. I knew if the Hybrids came for Hyperion, they would leave the shuttle. I flew out under the guise of doing maintenance, overrode the controls, and sent it to Repentant."

"So Lonnie's plan would fail."

She shrugged. "So my son would be spared the pain of attending his father's funeral."

Rohan sighed. "I'm pretty sure that course of action put me at risk."

She shook her head ever so slightly. "It might have. I am sorry. I thought they would take Hyperion and go. I didn't think you would be hurt."

"But you didn't know. Or at least, you were willing to take that chance."

"You are so strong, Rohan. The rest of us are . . . not."

He nodded. "I guess. What about Hyperion, though? You sacrificed the guy so your husband could stay safe. You're okay with doing that?"

"Hyperion nearly got my lover killed. I don't owe him my loyalty."

"He's my friend."

"Is he? Then, I am sorry. I never got that impression. But all I did was choose the time of the confrontation. Lahnegarn knew who he was, and so did the rebels. The Hybrids were offering money for information about Hyperion. Sooner or later, someone would have taken them up on it. My actions cost him a day, or two, of freedom. Not more."

Rohan sighed and ran his fingers through his hair. He was tired.

"I'm going to have to think about this. You could have asked me. We could have worked something out."

"I understand. If it's any consolation, this plan of action was not my first choice. I tried everything I could think of. Including asking you for help."

"So, it's my fault?"

"No. That's not what I meant, Rohan. At all."

"Okay. Just so we're clear."

They sat in silence. Rohan counted five long breaths.

"I should go. You enjoy your dinner."

"You can stay. There's enough for three."

"No, that's okay. I need some time. You two have fun."

He stood, opened the door, and left the apartment.

———————

Thirty minutes later, he was in Wistful's big conference room, the door closed and security-locked behind him.

He sat and stared at the empty space where the hologram would appear. Cleared his throat.

The hologram phased into view. "Tow Chief Second Class Rohan."

"Wistful. I have questions."

"I have warned you about questions."

"You warned me about answers. Never said anything about questions."

"Go ahead."

He stretched his arms out. "Easy one first. We saw the cargo shuttle head for the wormhole. Did Repentant get his baby?"

"He did. He considers the transaction a success."

"Huh. The rebels are definitely going to be unhappy."

"That is not my concern."

"No. Of course not. Until we find out he's using the warship to fight the il'Drach. Or hunt down the il'Sein, wherever they are. More problems for another day."

"Yes. I have a question of my own."

"Go ahead, Wistful."

"I see you have returned without Steve. Is he dead?"

"Steve is fine. He won't be coming back, but he's fine."

"I see."

He rubbed his forehead. "In related news, I figured out what Steve is."

"Ah. I recommend carefully considering the ramifications of that understanding."

"Yeah, I'm trying. But there are a couple of pieces I'm missing. A few gaps in what I grok."

She didn't answer.

"These . . . beings. Gods? Thoughts made flesh. They don't happen everywhere. Just on a few worlds."

"That is correct."

"Why? How? Is it . . . it doesn't just happen, does it? Something does it. Someone. Like a catalyst."

"Lyst calls them godfathers. Then she laughs. I do not understand the joke."

"Ha. But that ability must be extremely rare. And Earth has one. Who is it? No, I bet they keep themselves secret. In hiding. Why come out now and create Hyperion? We haven't had a new god in thousands of years. Unless all those Elvis sightings mean more than I thought they did."

"I do not know the specifics of the situation on Earth."

"Maybe our godfather got scared. Giant sharks running around." He tapped the table. "The il'Drach have a bug up their butts when it comes to gods. Probably because some are nearly as powerful as Hybrids."

"Yes. Perhaps more than that."

"How do they stop gods? Kill the godfathers? They're hard to find, but I bet that's happened. Or wipe out the population entirely, and I know that's been done. They wouldn't have wanted to destroy Earth, because Earthlings breed such good Hybrids. But wait . . . what if people worship something formless? That doesn't even have a shape? Those ideas couldn't be turned into flesh, could they?"

"I do not believe they could."

"Is that where the Hebraic religions came from? Get people to stop worshipping idols, things with shapes, and switch to something more abstract? The il'Drach planted that idea to stop the formation of new gods?"

"I already said, I am not familiar with the specific situation on Earth."

"Hold on, my brain is starting to work, and I'm not enjoying it." His stomach churned. "A god formed from the thoughts and prayers of a billion people would be, I don't know, bigger, than one formed from millions, right? And if a trillion people worshipped something, and that became a god . . ."

"You see the scope of the concern. The il'Drach are rightfully afraid that any being of too great Power poses a danger of waking the Old Ones and unleashing a cataclysm."

"Wow. Okay. That's a lot of explaining you just did."

"I have moments."

"That's why the Empire can't allow any big religions. Too dangerous." He ran his fingers through his hair. "Wait. Hyperion. There are a thousand worlds where people basically worship him. Providing energy that Steve can draw upon."

"Yes."

"Rudra save me." He leaned forward at the hips, pressing his belly into his thighs. "I think I'm going to throw up."

"Is this a residual effect of the Drexian poisons, Rohan?"

He grunted. "No. It's an effect of me realizing that I might have just made a huge mistake."

"I know. I was making a joke."

He braced his arm against the table and panted. "I put the whole sector at risk. Should I have let him die? Is that what I was supposed to do?"

"I shall assume that was a rhetorical question."

"Yeah. I guess it was." His stomach settled slowly. "I tried to help a friend. He was finally acting like a hero and I didn't want that to be the last thing he did.

"I think I just made a move that's going to have very big repercussions. It feels all too much like my old life."

"I am sorry, Rohan. I am aware that you wanted to distance yourself from that existence."

"Not your fault. To be honest, I don't even know whose fault it is." He reached up to scratch his eye and caught himself before making contact.

"Nevertheless, I am sorry."

He pulled the soulgem out from under his collar and held it up to the light. *Pushed* a tiny bit of energy into it and looked at the helix it formed.

I really wish I could make this thing work. Or at least understand what 'working' means.

"What am I supposed to do now, Wistful? Just . . . go about my days? Work my next shift? Eat donuts?"

"You are free to choose to do whatever you wish. As am I. It is quite unsettling."

"That doesn't make me feel much better."

"I shall break with habit and offer you advice, Rohan."

"Go for it."

"If the galaxy were not in danger, what would you want to do tomorrow?"

"Probably work my shift, then eat some donuts."

"Is there anything you can do instead, tomorrow, to save the galaxy?"

"Nope."

"Then, let me put you on the duty roster. You can contact Dr. Stone and ask him to prepare donuts. I suspect he will be amenable."

"Just . . . do it like that?"

"Just like that, Rohan."

"You're pretty smart for a hunk of silicon."

"You are quite charming for a bacteria-infested mass of putrefying meat."

"I'll see you tomorrow, Wistful."

"Have a good night, Rohan."

Epilogue

Two weeks later, Rohan eased himself into a leather chair across from Masamune's desk, in a fortress located one layer of reality anti-shadow from Earth.

Masamune poured tea for them both, wrinkled hands deftly manipulating a ceramic pot. "ar'Tahul. You here for an artificial eye?"

Rohan shook his head. "It should grow back."

"Must be nice."

Rohan scratched his beard. "I'm here about the cape."

Masamune sighed. "Ah. You want to claim it?"

"I want you to tell me a story. Fill in some blanks."

The il'Sein rubbed his fingers along his jaw. "I thought he was probably a god. But I wasn't sure. I hoped I was wrong. If he turned out to be Hyperion, I wanted you to keep him safe. I wanted to give him the cape. I owe him that much. We all do."

"Where did you go while I babysat god-Hyperion?"

"Lyst and I were trying to find the godfather. He—it—is dangerous."

"Did you?"

Masamune shrugged. "It hid its tracks too well. We lost our chance. It could be centuries before we get another."

Rohan sipped his tea. "So, we're even now? My debt is cleared?"

Masamune grinned. "You don't owe me anything. However, you may call on me anytime, because of your rank."

Rohan nodded. "Good to know. Another thing to keep in mind: Hyperion's going to be a problem. Potentially, a catastrophic one. He wants to fight the Empire."

"Gods are always trouble. That's why I'm glad we have you, ar'Tahul."
Rohan searched the man's face for a hint of sarcasm. Of mockery.
There wasn't any.

I wish, even for a minute, that I had even half as much confidence in myself as other people seem to have in me.

The End

The Hybrid Helix continues in Turn Five, *Eyes of Empire*

What's Next

The adventures of Rohan and company will continue in the next turn of the Hybrid Helix, Return of The Griffin.

If you enjoyed this book, please review it on Amazon and/or Goodreads and tell your friends about it! They'll enjoy it, and you'll seem cool and smart to have done so.

Please also go to jcmberne.com and sign up for the Book Berne-ing newsletter, read JCM's blog, and find other amusing things. Follow JCM on the social media platform of your choice! Links at his website.

The Hybrid Helix:
Arc One: Platinum
Wistful Ascending
Return of The Griffin
Blood Reunion
Shadow of Hyperion
Eyes of Empire
Arc Two:
Suppression of Powers

Also by JCM Berne:
Partial Function